Wolf Coven
Blood Moon

Second Edition

C.X. Cheng

Wolf Coven: Blood Moon
C.X. Cheng
Published by C.X. Cheng at Amazon

Copyright 2013 C.X. Cheng

Discover other titles by **C.X. Cheng** at Amazon.com

Electronic Book ISBN: **978-0-9920597-4-3**
Print Version ISBN: **978-0-9920597-3-6**

Dedicated to,

All my friends who have always encouraged me to write my ideas into a story to share with people.

To the creators of shows and movies which have inspired me to create my own work.

To the many authors whose work I have researched to inspire me.

Special thanks to Anne Rice for her many interviews and advice videos on her page which always helped me get back to writing.

C.X.Cheng

Wolf Coven: Blood Moon

Wolf Coven: Blood Moon

<u>**The Cosmic Eye**</u>

The three outer eyes represent the three worlds: the Divine World, the Supernatural World and the Mortal World. In the center of the three eyes is one final fourth eye which watches over the other three, called the Eye of Sanctuary.

Designed by

Darryl Hopkins

http://www.Facebook.com/pages/Darryl-Hopkins/188318338696

And

http://www.Facebook.com/BODOHdesign

SPECIAL THANKS

Sebastian Bubrick

Donovan Cerminara

Kevin Freedman

Lucas James

Sebastian Kwapich

Cole Lolacher

Danny Loubert

Skye Lowry

Simon Martel

Kevin Miller

Ryan Moss

Peter Ritossa

Thank you to my Beta Readers

Dianne Thomas

Amy Matthis

And especial thanks to my editor:

Caroline Ng

PROLOGUE

Sern paced back and forth within the waiting chamber in one of the hundreds of Aurastar's Synodium central construct. It was typical for the Intendants and Superintendents to make him wait, but considering his circumstances he understood why they were making him wait. A decision of this scale should never be taken lightly.

He couldn't help but continued to pace in circles, then back and forth again from one glowing crystalline wall to the next, relentlessly pondering the possible circumstances and their consequences in his mind, over and over. Anyone, if facing a potential promotion of this magnitude would be just as nervous as he was. It wasn't typical for the cool-stern Sern to face this type of anxiety. It was during moments like these where he certainly felt the more human side of him take dominance over the Essence-level control that he would normally have.

The doorway melted open through the crystalline wall. Immediately snapping to attention, Sern put his arms down by his sides and stood straight, and with as much as a calm demeanor as he could as he stood standing in the doorway with one of the Principle Secretaries.

"Deputy Intendant Sern?" The Principle Secretary called from the entrance, announcing him to those who were waiting for him inside the council chamber.

"Yes?" Sern replied firmly, for a brief moment enjoying the echo that his voice caused in the cavernous chamber that he was going to enter.

"Please come with me" the Principle Secretary requested. As he stepped into the chamber, Sern couldn't help but scanned the enormous amphitheatre that he was entering, which was just one of the many dozens of others in the Synodium. At a semi-circular table that faced him in the concave direction were seven individuals, seated and awaiting his arrival. At the center was Archon Alena.

Alena had the reputation of being one of the most respected of all officials of the Sanctuary Organization. And despite being an older woman and physically short, her composure and presence were formidable. Alena was a no-nonsense but yet appreciative and caring individual, whom Sern and many had seen as a true epitome of what should be expected of a Sanctuary Official.

As he approached, the Principle Secretary took his position at the edge of the table, and seemed to stand motionless as Sern took center stage.

"Deputy Intendant Sern," Alena stood up. Though she was short, her presence alone was enough to warrant immediate attention from everyone there. "Through the review of this council, we have noted your interest in becoming a full Intendant. However, there are many questions we have to ask that were not on the application." Her familiarity with what she had said and the flow of the words heavily suggested that she had done this many times before.

"Then I shall answer all to the best of my ability," Sern responded, with a slight hint of confidence in his voice. A slight smirk of approval appeared on Alena's face.

"Very well," Alena sat back down as the official to the far left side of the desk stood up. He was an unfamiliar face, but the rank indicators on his robe showed that he was a Director, a rather high rank and bureaucratic, probably less fieldwork.

"Thank you Archon Alena," he thanked his superior, noting her other title as Archon, he then turned towards Sern. "Deputy Intendant," he started. Sern turned his respectful attention to the one who was addressing him. "Your knowledge of the Supernaturals on Earth is quite formidable; in fact, you were even bold enough to edit and correct some of our information. However, despite the accuracy of your knowledge, you have yet to actually examine them in the field, correct?"

"Yes sir, that is true."

"Then how did you acquire the information?"

"Through the use of eye witness testimony from those who come here to Aurastar."

"Ah, eye witness testimony. But you are aware of the potential inaccuracies that can be gathered from testimonies? Even human science considered testimony to be the lowest form of evidence."

"Indeed, sir, that is true. However, the credentials of those being interviewed come from direct supernatural beings themselves. The potential for inconsistencies is there; however, as you can tell from the sourcing of the knowledge, I interviewed a considerable number of these beings before making these corrections, and these were minor corrections."

Satisfied with his answer, the official sat back down. Alena then turned to the opposite side of the table and gestured for the next person to speak. This official, a regal-looking blond-haired woman, perhaps in her early 40s, stood up. Unlike the previous individual, Sern knew who this was. She was Superintendent Lya.

"Sern, the proposed position that we have in mind for you will involve a great deal of direct one-on-one interaction with Supernaturals; in fact, you will be living among them. You will also potentially be needed, to interact with the human public on a day-to-day basis. Refresh us on the purposes and the main duties of the Sanctuary Organization, our mission statement if you will."

"Our mission is to maintain the shroud of secrecy between the Supernatural World, and the Human World, to allow humans to live without fear of the supernatural, and to prevent knowledge of the supernatural to leak into the human presence."

"And you know that this, is our utmost and primary goal," she reminded him.

"Without question, Superintendent."

"Then allow me to give you a hypothetical situation," she started to walk towards Sern, more along a pondering pace. "A Type-2 Lycanthrope pack, or Packwalkers, descends upon a settlement of humans. The pack consists of enough wolves to bite, and turn the entire troop of humans. The humans don't know what happened to them, survive and turn into Lycanthropes amongst their families who live in dense human cities. What are your duty and response?"

"Three fold. First and foremost is to identify the pack and attempt to prevent them from attacking the humans, if not by persuasion, then by immediate force relocation." Sern began. His mind was working quite according to a brutal sense of logic and protocol. He knew well that human safety was the priority. "Secondly, if they attack the humans, then the humans attacked as well as the wolf attackers must be subdued and mentally persuaded, by force if needed, to forget the situation. And thirdly and finally, if the attack succeeded despite my efforts, which is hardly possible, but if so, immediate forced relocation of everyone involved and immediate declaration of death of those involved, to the humans."

"Mental persuasion, or manipulation, is a very drastic measure. Sern, are you sure it is warranted?" Superintendent Lya asked him. It was clear that she was almost tempting him to give a more serious response.

"Without question, Superintendent," Sern answered without hesitation. "The blocking of memories is paramount to maintaining secrecy."

"What if they have children who survived?"

"Then the children's memories will be blocked and left to the human authorities."

"And what of the freshly turned humans who are going to become lycanthropes?" Superintendent Lya continued.

"They will be kept at the nearest Sanctuary Coven House, safe and rehabilitated. Every Coven House has the members required for these training sessions."

"And if they choose not to?"

"No choice can be given. The future of human safety cannot be sacrificed for the heartache of a few. If they refuse, they will be mentally persuaded to accept, or we can relocate them to a house where they can be trained."

"But what if they insist and attempt, and perhaps even succeed in escaping?"

"Protocol dictates the final measures. Recapture or execution," Sern stated coldly. Superintendent Lya wasn't surprised that he would give this answer; it was the only one that he could give. Being Intendant wasn't a duty that one could take lightly; it was a serious and deadly matter.

"An Intendant is required to be the judge, jury and executioner in a case like that," Archon Alena spoke. "No leniency can be permitted because the risk of public safety must be avoided."

"I understand," Sern answered.

"One more question please, Sern," Alena stood up and walked towards him. In front of them all, rose a projection of the Cosmic Eye. "Can you please tell me what this is, and what it symbolizes?" Alena headed back to her desk as Sern walked up to the hovering three pronged symbol.

"This is the Cosmic Eye,," Sern pointed to the shape which they were all familiar. "It is the symbol of the Sanctuary Organization and its purpose. The three eyes which surround the central point represent the three realms or worlds, the Mortal World, the Supernatural World or sometimes referred to as magical or the arcane, and the final, at the top, the Divine World or the realm of the gods."

"What is the significance of the eye in the middle?" Alena asked.

"It represents the Sanctuary Organization and the motives of the Va'Nai," Sern answered. "The three spires that come out from it block the others from seeing each other; the Eye of Sanctuary in the center also blocks the others from interfering with each other."

"Which fittingly describes our purpose, correct?"

"Yes."

"Then I guess it's a final conclusion that we will release now, unless anyone else has any questions," Alena looked around to see a consensus amongst the others. "Your application has been approved. Congratulations, Intendant Sern," Alena addressed him, with his new title. The group clapped generously as they stood up. The table melted back into the floor. As they gathered around him in the center of the room, a sudden brilliant flash of light appeared, which left the presence of a vast vortex of white swirling energy.

It was a graceful entity, one of the Va'Nai, the caretakers and leaders of the Sanctuary Organization. Appearing in its natural form, the Va'Nai looked like how science fiction portrayed a black hole, as a swirling vortex, but instead of black and dark purple swirls, this being was composed of bright white and yellow light, and the energy radiated outwards, not inwards. Through his mind, Sern could hear the voice of the Va'Nai speaking to him.

"Your dedication and service has not been without notice. Your commitment to the protection of humanity will not go unpaid," It spoke, as an echoing almost digital and divine voice through to his mind directly. From the core heart of the Va'Nai, a smaller version of itself, a small swirling vortex of energy emerged, and floated slowly and gracefully towards Sern. The glowing ball of light left a hazy trail of energy as it went towards Sern, and then slowly phased itself into his chest.

It felt like a comforting warmth that started to expand, upwards through his arms and neck, downwards through his stomach and then legs, infusing every cell of his body with a force of power, a power greater than anything else he had felt during previous infusions. His eyes naturally closed to maintain this concentration of power as the Essence of the Va'Nai started to modify him from the inside out. His eyes then flashed open, beaming out a brilliant aura of light from them, as the silence was interrupted by his gasp for air.

This was not his first Infusion, but with his promotion to the rank of Intendant, Sern was gifted with another Essence of the Va'Nai, which would double his abilities easily. He stumbled at first, thankfully with one of the Directors at his side he didn't fall over. The Infusion always left everyone slightly light-headed, but now with the addition of yet another Essence, he felt even more clear-minded and level-headed. He looked up to see the Va'Nai still hovering there. He bowed respectfully as it slowly vanished, leaving nothing but a faint glow of where it was, that slowly also vaporized.

"Your appointment will be to Wolf Coven House. You will be replacing Intendant Hasaan, who will now return here to Aurastar. There, you will find mainly Sanguinarians and Lycanthropes active," Alena instructed him. She reached out her hand. Sern accepted the handshake graciously. "And I have every confidence that you will make us proud, Sern." She smiled.

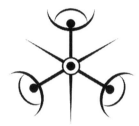

Chapter 1

"I still don't know why you have to leave," Gavin protested as he stood there, seeing Hasaan finish packing his things which fit neatly into a single suitcase. As an Intendant, the need for clothing or luggage wasn't something that was required, or even of interest to him. There were only a few mementos and trinkets from their time together that he was going to bring back with him.

"You know this day would eventually come. I've been recalled back to Aurastar for re-assignment," Hasaan replied without much concern. "You know it's a part of our duties. We are at the will of the Sanctuary Organization and when they see fit that our skills are better suited elsewhere, they will recall us anytime." He patted his friend on the shoulder. "Besides, I'm not the first Intendant that you've had," he reminded Gavin of Intendant Zera and a few others that had come in the past.

"Yeah, but they were never much fun to be around," Gavin crossed his arms across his chest. "And you never had to execute anyone." He pulled out that memory, reminding Hasaan of his cooperative history with Wolf Coven members.

"I was lucky," Hasaan exited the office, not even bothering to look back. "Execution is the most unsavoury but one of the required actions that any Intendant has to perform in field duty. Believe me when I say it's an action that we only take under the most dire of circumstances. You know we much prefer memory blocking and suggestions rather than killing."

The two of them entered the hallway, which led to the central atrium of Wolf Coven House. The ultra modern rooms with their steel and leather furniture contrasted greatly to the almost Edwardian-styled furnishings of classical hotels of the nineteenth century. It was a true contrast that the original owners of the house, High Order Vampires, had used their wealth to decorate. Without doubt, it was a stunning building that Hasaan did have some regrets on when it came to leaving.

"I'm sure that my replacement, Sern, is more than capable. I've made requests to Aurastar, that my replacement respect the more understanding administration that I had put in," Hasaan assured Gavin. The tall Vampire was imposing in his own right, but was a gentle soul. It wasn't usual that Hasaan saw him moping around like this, but understandable. Humans, and their supernatural offshoots still felt emotions like the rest of them, especially with one Intendant leaving, and another replacing him, and no one knew who and what Sern was going to be like. "Just remember, the guy spent most of his time in the archives of Aurastar, so he may be a bit more bureaucratic than I am."

"So we're getting a paper pusher as our new replacement?"

"From what I understand, they promoted him and he also applied for it so I'm sure he knows what he's getting into."

"The fact that you call him a bureaucrat doesn't really inspire much confidence," Gavin groaned.

"Gavin," Hasaan looked deeply at the Vampire, "look, I made sure to remind my superiors that the success of Wolf Coven House and the Coven Houses is to let field operatives give more freedom to those people whom they are protecting. It's not in their interest to interfere with a successful institution like this."

"Well I just hope he will respect us the way you did."

"I'm sure that he will."

Gathered in the Atrium were all thirty members of Wolf Coven House. They all looked upwards as Hasaan and Gavin descended down the main staircase that wrapped around the central fountain where the portal to the Hub, then Aurastar was hidden. He could see all of them, the Wolves and Vampires together, one of the most successful cooperative stories that the Sanctuary Organization was proud of. Hasaan felt all the eyes focusing on him as he came down the stairs.

They naturally opened a pathway for him to approach the fountain. As he did, the water slowly stopped and re-appearing from its invisible status was the portal, which was a swirling image of his destination, which was more of a wormhole than a portal. As he looked into the projected image, he could see the approach of another Intendant, ready to take his place. He stood there waiting for a moment, as did everyone else, for the Intendant to arrive first. Not many noticed, but at the base of the atrium, the floor design was that of the Cosmic Eye.

Chapter 2

Sern stepped through the wormhole, and into the Atrium of Wolf Coven House. As he did, suddenly he felt the presence of thirty individuals. Instantly he could sense what most of them were. Directly in front of him, standing only a few feet away was the one who he was to replace, Intendant Hasaan. They had never met, but Sern could instantly recognize his portrait from the reports. Behind him stood a Sanguinarian, of a rather imposing size and build. Around him were an assortment of other Lycanthropes and Sanguinarians, though none around him were human or otherwise, only limited to the two major Supernatural offshoots of humans.

Everyone else noticed Sern's appearance in contrast to Hasaan's. Sern was clearly East Asian, possibly Chinese or Japanese or Korean in heritage, as opposed to Hasaan's Middle Eastern look. Sern's black hair was short but neat in a rather modern and professional style. His eyes were dark brown and he carried himself with a great deal of dignity and professionalism.

"Intendant Hasaan," Sern greeted with a hand reached out with a head nod.

"Intendant Sern," Hasaan reciprocated as he accepted the handshake. Sern activated a small holographic projection from his hand and began to read a short speech.

"With the orders of the Sanctuary Organization, I request executive control over the Administration of Wolf Coven House, its members and facilities," Sern formally stated. It was a line that he never had difficulty remembering since it was a part of his application process.

"And by the orders of the Sanctuary Organization, I relinquish executive and administrative control to you, Intendant Sern," Hasaan stated.

"I understand that it is a human custom, to give a speech before one departs," Sern announced to everyone present, "so I now give Intendant Hasaan that opportunity." He stepped out of the way to give Hasaan the center of attention.

"Ten years ago when I first arrived as Intendant, I didn't know what to expect. My limited experience with Vampires and Werewolves was something that I felt really hampered my success rate in bringing you under Sanctuary Protection. Over the years, many who trained, have left Wolf Coven House for other Coven Houses, and there's only two of you who are here from that time, Gavin and Dominic. I am sure that over the course of many years, you've had ample time to hear of my first rate failures but also of my successes," Hasaan wasn't getting emotional by his words but many of those who watched and listened were. There were a few sniffles and even a few tears in the crowd. "My proudest and most morbid sounding achievement is that I never had to perform a final sanction on anyone. I believe that everyone had the potential to succeed and thanks to your efforts, you succeeded. Wolf Coven House has grown a great deal, and my colleague here will continue our legacy of success, in protecting you and humans from danger. I will miss you all, but I will miss you the most, Scarecrow," Hasaan smiled. There were quite a few chuckles to the Wizard of Oz reference that Hasaan had put in. Sern was impressed with his bonds with those present. Immediately, Sern felt that he had quite a challenge ahead of him, not in protecting them, but matching the legacy that Hasaan had created which was greatly successful.

With the last of his words, the people started to crowd in for hugs and handshakes and final words. Sern stepped aside, giving them as much time as they needed to do so. A series of long heart felt discussions took place between Hasaan and the others, but eventually as they finished, Hasaan approached the portal, before turning around to give one final bow to his colleagues of the past decade. Then he stepped through and only seconds later, the wormhole vanished.

The thirty Wolf Coven Members turned to face Sern who was standing patiently letting them say their final goodbyes to their friend Hasaan. It seemed now, that they wanted him to give a few opening words for the start of his tenure.

"Intendant Hasaan's departure was not a recall of disgrace," Sern them. "It was a recall of success. The Sanctuary Organization noticed Hasaan's successes here and they wished for him to replicate it elsewhere. I was chosen not to change his methods, but to continue them," Sern started to pace, something he had naturally always taken to. Instead of standing high and mighty, lecturing his now new followers, he preferred to speak as though he was talking to each of them individually, something that Hasaan had noted in his reports, that Humans would be more receptive towards. "As I said, I cannot replace Hasaan and I have no intention of doing so. But I am also new at this position, so I will need you to teach me as well. I have his reports, but nothing can beat actually working with those who knew his success," Sern realized that what he was saying almost sounded like a funeral eulogy more than an introduction speech. "For the next few days, I suggest everyone relax and take some time to adjust to leadership differences. But before that begins, I will need to speak with Gavin, Trey and Dominic in, I guess, what is now my office. Thank you." They slowly started to disperse, while Dominic, and Gavin, two Vampires and Trey, a towering tall werewolf, who was in human guise, stood there remaining. "Please, gentleman, come with me."

Once all four of them had entered Sern's new office, the doors closed automatically at Sern's command. Hasaan's desk which functioned like a high-tech computer responded to Sern's presence by slowly lighting up its light green surface.

With a single wave of his hand above the crystalline layer, it showed the roster and names of everyone present at Wolf Coven House, as well as overlays of the reports that Hasaan had sent to the Sanctuary Organization in the past few weeks before his replacement.

"Gavin, physical age thirty, true age ninety eight years old," Sern stated bluntly as though reading it from a list. He turned to the stalwart almost soldier-looking vampire. "Dominic, physical age thirty-three, true age, sixty." He turned to the towering werewolf. "and Trey, physical age twenty-three, true age, same thing. Thank you for meeting me so soon. I realize that this trade off took place rather fast and short notice," Sern assured the others, as he pulled up a few chairs for them, gesturing for them to sit down around the desk. Sern took his position behind the desk. "As I said before, I'm only here to administrate, and help continue what Hasaan did. I don't have any intention of changing things."

"How come you didn't ask my brother to join us?" Trey asked, referring to Trenton who was in the atrium earlier with the rest of them.

"I figured that you would tell him the contents of this meeting anyways. I just wanted to talk to the three of you. The information, no doubt, would spread amongst everyone else. This is not a secret meeting."

"It was a rather fast move," Dominic uttered with a hint of contempt in his voice as he folded his arms across his chest.

"I understand your frustration, Dominic," Sern apologized. "but the Sanctuary Organization has some urgent plans that required Hasaan. I am not at liberty to give any information, but suffice to say, the Coven and Cloister Houses have to be maintained with newer, less experienced officials."

"What can we do to help?" Trey asked. Sern smiled when he heard the towering giant of a man speak and offer assistance. The smile caught them off guard for a moment. "Did I say something funny?" he asked back.

"No. It's just, I've read all of Hasaan's reports. He always mentioned that Trey was always the first to volunteer and lend a hand. He called you a gentle giant." The revelation of this news brought a smile to Trey's face. The others weren't that surprised either, with confirming glances going from one to the other. For a few silent moments, Sern scanned over the three individuals in his presence. The awkward silence didn't escape their attention.

"What are you looking at?" asked Dominic, who hadn't flinched with his stone cold gaze.

"Comparing your physical sizes," Sern answered. "Trey is a Lycanthrope, but he's also six feet and seven inches tall. His physical mass is almost 300 imperial pounds. Now, normally in human terms, that would make him the strongest of all three of you."

"Yes but he's a Wolf, and we're not," Dominic interjected.

"Yes, and your Sanguinarian physiology has actually a far denser muscle mass than even they do, and a controllable metabolism, and adrenaline, which means you both, though smaller in size, though Gavin not by much, are still stronger and faster than him even faster, considering your shorter size and lower center of gravity."

"Well, not that much lower," Gavin looked over to his side where Trey was standing. Gavin was only a few inches shorter than Trey, but he was well aware that he was stronger and faster, and this was more likely due to his supernatural abilities than just physics. He playfully stood on his tiptoes for a moment, just to see how much taller he could get for that brief moment. Trey gave him an awkward glance.

"Well I am aware that Sanguinarians and Lycanthropes have different strengths and weaknesses, and it's good that you all can work together nicely here without conflicts," Sern thought briefly, then corrected his words, "serious conflicts that would hinder performance."

"So what is your game plan then?" Dominic leaned back in his seat.

"Well according to Hasaan's reports, during mid-October of the year, sightings of Lycanthropes is greatly higher, and spikes almost exactly on Halloween. Sanguinarians, keep a steady appearance." Sern read off some of the holographic display of charts.

"Could you stop calling us that?" Dominic asked with a slight rubbing of his temples. Sern's notably aloof speech patterns were starting to get annoying.

"Sorry?" Sern asked, for a clarification.

"Sanguinarians and Lycanthropes," Dominic grunted. "Just call us vampires and wolves." His insistence struck Sern as odd. For someone like Sern, using the classical terms like Sanguinarian and Lycanthrope was something completely natural to him. Even Hasaan had written his reports using those terms.

"Why?" Sern asked, in honesty with true inquiry in his voice. Gavin looked like he was going to give an answer, but then even he had to process Sern's one word question for a moment before he turned to Dominic, letting the one made the request do the explaining.

"We just don't call ourselves Sanguinarians, and the Wolves don't call themselves Lycanthropes. We just use the simple basic terms," Dominic rubbed the bridge of his nose in irritation more of the situation and Sern than actual physical discomfort.

"Alright, according to Hasaan's report, which I note, he used the classical terms, he stated that as the nights grow longer in the late fall to winter, the number of nocturnal intrusions increases dramatically. In fact that is where you usually get your freshly turned wolves and bitten vampire victims, correct?" Sern continued almost without any notice of the slight segway they had taken on the basis of vocabulary.

"And you want to stop them at all costs?" Dominic presumed, attempting to finish Sern's statements. But instead of a confirmation from the Intendant, they were greeted with silence.

"No," Sern answered bluntly. "Only, if it puts at risk, the secrecy between the supernatural and the human world," he clarified, "and I must be extremely clear on that. Every Intendant, and every member of the Sanctuary, has to follow that specific mission statement, because it's our very main purpose for being here," Sern sat down and leaned forward, as though he had something very sincere and heartfelt to say. "The purpose of the Sanctuary Organization, I am sure you are aware, is not population control. It's to maintain secrecy," he restated, this time even more clear. "Who you transform, or whatever happens, is not under the control of the Intendants, but those who are doing the transforming. If you want to make more Sanguinar....Vampires, or Wolves, that is entirely your decision on how many you want to make. As long as you can keep them under control, teach them, train them, and maintain of course, secrecy. I'm just here to make sure things don't get out of control, just like how Hasaan did. Extreme measures are only taken if that secrecy is threatened. And I think that's the third time I've stated that in the past few minutes," Sern took a deep gaze at each of them. Little did they know, he was sensing their thoughts and memories, a handy Intendant ability.

"Dude, check out his eyes!" Trey nudged Dominic. Sern's eyes had started to glow, all visual features like the light that was emerging blinded irises and pupils. The light was almost blinding for a moment.

"He's scanning our minds, recent memories," Gavin answered as he started to play Angry Birds on his phone, not needing to look up to notice the bright light.

"Why?"

"To make sure that we understood what he was saying," Gavin muttered without much interest. He was more focused on killing those green piggies.

"And I'm glad to say that you do understand," Sern's eyes stopped glowing as he stood up. "Your cooperation during my tenure is greatly appreciated," Sern returned to his desk.

"So what should we do for the next two days?" Gavin asked as he slid his phone back into his pocket.

"Relax a bit, I won't be sending out any assignments yet until some actually come in," Sern started to flip through various other reports and data streams that were being displayed on the display above his desk, many of which were in pictograms that were illegible to the other three in the room. An awkward silence came about the room. Gavin, Trey and Dominic weren't sure if Sern actually was finished with them for a moment. Sern was still flipping through various displays when the three of them walked up to the desk.

"Um, Sern?" Trey tapped the desk to get his attention. Sern looked up at the three of them, slightly puzzled. "Can we?" Trey pointed to the door.

"Excuse me?" Sern asked, curious as to what they were referring to, and then suddenly the thought popped into his mind. "Oh yes. Yes, I am finished, you can go if you like," Sern then immediately turned back to the pictograms that were still cycling past his eyes with blazing speed.

Dominic flashed a look of bewilderment at Gavin as the three of them walked out the door. Gavin gently closed it, not wanting to break Sern's concentration. Standing there right outside the door, the three of them gazed at each other. The ranges of expression came from a smile to disapproval, especially from Dominic. Gavin was rather passive, but this may have been likely due to the fact that he had encountered new Intendants before.

"So, what do you think?" Trey asked the other two as he shuffled his hands into his jean pockets.

"He's weird," Dominic answered as he started to walk away, as though his verdict was the only one that really mattered. Gavin sensed there was justification to this.

"He's new," Gavin stated, to an extent coming to Sern's defence. "I remember when Hasaan first came. He wasn't any better." There was a certain hint of acceptance in his voice; that was definitely something that Dominic hadn't expected.

"So he'll melt in time?" Dominic probed further into Gavin's statement.

"Yeah. It takes time for everyone to warm up to anyone. Just be grateful he's not one of those super-enforcer Intendants we've heard of," Gavin patted Dominic on the back, helping him appreciate the fact that it was much better for Sern to be quirky than strict.

"How bad could those be?" Trey asked as they continued towards the kitchen, through the maze of hallways of Wolf Coven House. He heard Gavin take in a deep sigh of air, something that usually wasn't a good thing before explaining a situation like this.

"Well you know how powerful Intendants are, right?" Gavin asked the young, yet massive, werewolf.

"Not really. I've never seen Hasaan get in a fight."

"Ah. I see," Gavin ended.

"What's he like?" Trey asked.

"Well, it's hard to describe," Gavin started to ponder through his past memories. There were very few occasions where Hasaan had to take a firm hand in situations. "

"Well was there one where he actually had to defend himself?" Trey sounded like a curious puppy.

"There was one, off the top of my head."

"Come on, let's hear it!" Trey pestered, like he was a child wanting his Christmas gift early. Quite the sight considering he was six feet and seven inches tall and over 300 pounds of solid muscles.

"I'm going to go for a run," Dominic made his quick exit down another hallway that led to one of the side entrances to Wolf Coven House.

16

"Maybe in private. Hasaan had very sensitive hearing, and probably Sern does as well," Gavin whispered into Trey's ears.

"Yes I do," Sern's voice called from the doorway that they had left well back down the hallway. This impressed and surprised them to quite a high standard. Gavin simply gestured to Trey to follow him. The two of them went up the grand staircase around the fountain where they had gathered earlier.

Chapter 3

Like all the residential apartments in Wolf Coven House, the rooms were ultra-modern, polished hardwood and tiled floors, steel and black leather furniture, and a generous supply of mirrors that made them look even larger. Gavin's was very clean, and furnished with the appropriately themed black, steel and white furniture. Trey always loved how Gavin decorated; it was extremely classy and very dignified. Gavin closed the double doors, and even locked them out of a slight sense of paranoia as they sat down in his sitting room.

There was an unusually large painting on the end wall, which stretched to the enormous windows that showed a stunning view of the natural beautiful forests and scenery around the house. The painting was a pure black canvas with a single white circle, slightly off center. It resembled the flag of Japan, but the strangely placed center dot was definitely one of these examples of what some called "modern" art. Trey just stood there for a few moments staring at it.

"It was a gift from Hasaan when he was trying to explore the art of painting," Trey looked carefully at the brushstrokes, which were perfectly aligned and perfectly straight, and the circle was again perfectly formed. Gavin went over to the fridge.

Gavin looked like he belonged in such a professional looking environment. Immediately after opening the fridge, Trey caught the iron-like scent of blood. It wasn't a scent that he was very used to. But since he was in Gavin's home, it was considered proper manners to say nothing about it.

"Sorry about the smell," Gavin apologized as he reached in and grabbed a blood bag from the cool interior. He poured the contents into a large mug, like one of those used for outrageously large coffees at those trendy hipster cafes. He slipped it into the microwave only for a few seconds, which was long enough to make the blood warm enough.

Gavin had always been considerate when around people who were not used to his choice of diet. For him, conforming was just like that old motto, "When in Rome …". It was just a simple courtesy that made for polite atmosphere. That was one aspect of Gavin that made people respect him more. The fact that he was able to level a house or pickup and throw a car and yet maintain the dignity of a kind person, had earned him a great deal of respect from others.

"Would you like something to drink?" Gavin offered as the microwave beeped. He grabbed the mug and eagerly took a sip of the warm red fluid. For a brief moment, Trey noticed an expression of satisfaction on his face. Gavin noticed Trey watching him for a moment. It certainly wasn't the first time that someone had observed him drinking blood.

"No thanks, I'm alright," Trey replies as he sat down on one of the extremely comfortable looking leather couches. The couch that faced out towards the beautiful view of the outside attracted his attention in particular.

Gavin took a seat across from him, and continued to sip from the cup. The smell of the blood was something that, though he could appreciate as a Wolf and it was one of the few rare ways for him to get a fresh meal especially in the wild, it wasn't something that he would make as a priority to smell.

"So you were saying, about Sern and Hasaan's fighting techniques," Trey continued the conversation. Gavin placed his mug onto the coffee table between the two couches.

"Well it's difficult to explain everything about these folks. Now you've only been here for a year, so you haven't had the chance to see an Intendant use his abilities." Gavin leaned back in his seat. "First thing that you should know about the Intendants is that they are not completely human," Gavin started to explain.

"So what are they?" Trey asked curiously, like a child wanting to hear more of a story.

"The body that you see, Hasaan and Sern are human, but there is a type of entity inside them that gives them access to special powers. You've already seen Sern's ability to read our minds. Well, add to that telekinesis, and the fact that he has some protective shield around him, that pretty much makes him unkillable."

"In what way? Like Superman?" Trey continued, bewildered at what he was learning about their old Intendant, and even new one.

"Somewhat. He explained to me, that their powers are defensive, meant to keep them safe and self-sufficient. They don't need food or water, or sleep. He can even shoot out beams of energy like a Dragonball character. It's pretty insane." Gavin took another gulp from his blood. He swirled the liquid around in the mug. He particularly enjoyed this blend of blood, and thanks to the heating, it was almost indistinguishable from the taste and temperature of blood from the vein.

"Wow," Trey's eyes widened. It wasn't quite the expression that Gavin had expected. Trey wasn't afraid or bewildered but it was almost like he was hearing that he had discovered his boss was some type of superhero. "That's awesome!" He smiled with giddiness.

"Well, Hasaan preferred to keep his abilities low key, and I would guess that Sern is the same way. If news leaked out to other Wolf Clans, or Vampire Orders, Witch Covens, not under the control of Sanctuary, that our Intendants are virtually invincible and have the power to change and persuade minds, not to mention take on entire armies solo, yeah, it seems secrecy, or at least humility, is the wiser course of action," Gavin reassured Trey.

"Well we could ask him to show us," Trey suggested as he gave Gavin a coy look. He wanted to see Sern's powers in a demonstration, but wasn't quite sure how he was going to bring it about.

"I don't know how he would respond to that," Gavin finished off the last of the blood, licking a little bit off of his lips, and then smiling with a slight sense of satisfaction. He breathed in a deep sigh.

"What if we surprise him?" Trey suggested.

"You mean like an ambush?" Gavin coughed, a bit surprised by the suggestion that Trey had just given without realizing the full consequences of the action that he had just proposed.

"Considering that Sern can hear your heartbeat from a hallway away, that would prove rather difficult, not to mention the fact that if you do surprise him, he may respond by accidentally vaporizing you."

"Yeah that wouldn't be very good," Trey folded his arms across his chest in frustration. "or maybe the best way, is just to ask him?" He asked Gavin, wondering what his opinion on the matter would be.

"That could be possible. Again I don't know Sern any more than you do, and he's been here for less than an hour. His response could be anything. But maybe the most direct way is the best way," Gavin advised.

"I may do that instead," Trey got off the couch and stretched. He gazed out at the view through Gavin's window for a moment," Anyways, I have a few wolves to meet up with while we've got some free time," Trey let himself out. Gavin sat quietly for a while, as he just cherished some quiet time to just sit with his feet up without a care in the world. That was one of the big advantages of living in a Coven House - the living expenses were non-existent.

Gavin watched as he saw a winged being, soaring and gliding through the woods. By the wingspan of those enormous dragon-bat like wings, it was only Dominic who could go that fast above the canopy and still keep close enough so he wouldn't be seen that easily from a higher altitude. Thanks to excellent High Order vision, Gavin had no problem picking him out, even in the sunlight of the mid-evening. It was always something he liked, just standing on his balcony, looking out at the beautiful natural scenery around Wolf Coven House; the cooling breeze of the evening air was always something welcome.

Then his moment of serenity was temporarily interrupted by the howling of another wolf pack that are likely going out for a run, competing with Dominic as they always do. Despite their ferocious speed on all fours, they were no match for a being who could fly and would not be limited by terrain.

The following few days went without incident. Sern was frequently talking to most the members of Wolf Coven House, wanting to get to know them. He knew that he was already aware of many of their abilities and skills from the reports, but it was more along the lines of their personalities that he was going to have to familiarize himself. All of them had a good working relationship with Hasaan, so for Sern, it was important that he, too, maintain those good working relationships. Of course there were still the requirement of meeting with Dominic, Trey and Gavin for their own individual conversations and simple interviewing processes. Dominic actually had refused an interview, saying that if he had anything worth saying to Sern, he would notify him in due course.

Trey was busy doing his pull-ups in the gymnasium. The entire room was quite generously well stocked with workout equipment, some of which were far more than what a human would need. He wasn't only pulling up the 300 pounds of his own physical mass, but attached to his belt were another 90 pounds of weights, in the form of two enormous plates, each 45 pounds.

Sern entered the room to find that there was only Trey who was there. He was quite impressed by the construction and building itself. He had heard that a sorceress, at the request of the Wolf Coven owner and then agreed to by the Sanctuary Organization, had put in safeguards and enchantments onto the building itself that would help its inhabitants protect themselves should anything dire happen.

Trey landed gently on the ground, and then undid the enormous leather belt that weighed him down. Even as an Intendant gifted with abilities far above human strength, he was impressed with the prowess of Trey, who was easily far larger and taller and stronger than any average human. Even other Supernaturals would think twice before challenging Trey, even if he was just a human, let alone a Prime Wolf.

"Hey!" Trey reached out with a glove-covered hand to shake Sern's with a friendly welcome.

"Greetings," Sern smiled as he accepted the handshake, and for a moment was almost tugged in a bit by Trey's strength but only for a moment.

"Come for a workout?" Trey smiled, through a series of a few gasps as he took a few deep gulps from his workout bottle. Seeing Sern wearing his long Intendant suit, which resembled a suit jacket but went all the way down to his knees. The beige canvas colour had almost veins of silver light that beamed through it, but only at right angles, like a pulse. Hasaan also wore something very similar when he was around.

"No, I just came to talk," Sern casually sat down on one of the workout benches that were in front of a vast long line of dumbbells. He seemed rather proper and looked completely out of place to be in a gym. "You are Trey, correct? Physical age 23, true age 23, Trenton's younger brother?" Sern asked in a very mechanical way.

"All right," Trey gave a puzzled look at the introduction Sern gave him, "What's up?"

"Well, I was wondering how your pack was," Sern asked curiously. Suddenly he realized his question gave Trey a rather confused look.

"Pack?"

"Oh yes," Sern almost face-palmed himself. "Forgive me, you're a Prime aren't you?" he asked again.

"Yeah, Primes don't have packs," Trey reiterated to Sern.

"I apologize. I've been meeting so many people with so many different types of classifications that it's difficult to recall exactly who is what and who can do what," Sern clarified. He felt somewhat foolish, considering he could remember vast quantities of information but this little tidbit of information completely escaped him. "though it has not been unheard of to lead a pack of lesser wolves."

"I've heard of situations like that, but why would you join a pack that you could never ascend to Alpha status?" Trey asked.

"Some don't seek leadership, just protection. You may find, that many wolves, even of lesser breeds, do see you as something like a leader even though you don't want leadership."

"I guess I can respect that. I kind of envied Vamps. They have it easy, no need to worry about packs or alphas," Trey wiped the sweat from his forehead with a towel which sat off to the side of his bench.

"Yes but their diet is their greatest test of strength," Sern replied. "From what I read up on them, even the High Orders have a tough time."

"Yeah, bloodlust. Once every hundred days!"

"You've seen the Bloodlust?" Sern asked, curious now to get Trey's perspective on what he had witnessed.

"Oh yeah. Wasn't a pretty sight."

"Who was it?"

"Gavin," Trey recalled.

"Oh my," Sern relented for a moment.

"Yeah, the strongest of all of them."

"What happened?"

"Well it was during the full moon, about six months ago. So by pure luck, we were hit with seven werewolves who were all going moon crazy, and a High Order Vampire, the strongest of them all, who was going through his bloodlust all within the same 24 hours." The sheer description of the scenario did not sound like it had an optimistic outcome, but Sern sat, continuing to listen attentively. "Gavin had helped seal them into the isolation chambers downstairs because only he and Dominic were the only ones who were strong enough to do it without getting hurt. A few others did help but they weren't strong enough for rabid wolves. Since myself, Coltrane and Trenton were Primes, we had more control, so we helped seal Gavin up as well. But we didn't realize how strong and how berserk he went," Trey squeezed his towel for a moment then looked at the attentive expression on Sern's face that was clearly listening to every word he was saying before he rubbed his eyes, then continued. "Well, we never learned before that High Orders were actually half-demon half humans, and were actually undead."

"That's correct. High Order Vampires are the only Vampires who actually retain a pulse and heartbeat," Sern confirmed.

"You're going to have to tell me more about how that works later," Trey finished off the water in his bottle. "Well anyways, Gavin started to change, his demon wings came out, and his actual face and body started to change as well. Turns out he wasn't fed enough before his bloodlust to control himself so he wasn't just blood lusting, he was hungry and blood lusting at the same time. Normally they eat plenty before that happens to keep themselves under control, but since the full moon was happening, he had been too busy keeping the wolves under control."

"So with his hunger and now going out of control, he reverted?"

"Yeah, and boy did he," Trey's eyes widened for a moment. Sern recognized this as a sign that Trey only had more to tell.

"Continue, please,"

"Well, he basically turned into his half-demon form, and shattered the bullet-proof, reinforced glass, as well as the titanium bars."

"Where was Hasaan during this?" Sern inquired. "The presence of an Intendant would have helped in something like this."

"He was on evaluation from Aurastar, so he wasn't around."

"So how did you manage the situation?"

"Well, luckily the wolves who were under the influence of the moon were still sane enough to see the beast in the cage next to them as a greater threat than the rest of us, and luckily Dominic was there. Dominic had to come up with enough anger and aggression on himself to temporarily stall Gavin. Luckily, in vaults we kept some chains, and thanks to those we managed to subdue Gavin."

"I would have guessed that the chains would have been your first course of action."

"Well, I don't think they want to use them first right away, because there could be other options."

"So you subdued him and then chained him up?"

"Yeah."

"How did he take it?"

"Gavin has a big heart. He felt so guilty about what he had done; we didn't see him for almost a week. He locked himself up, and went under intense meditation with Hasaan when he returned."

"Unfortunately I don't know you all that well, but it gives a very useful perspective to learn these things about you all. I hope to learn more as time goes by," Sern gets up from the workout bench.

"Wait, you're leaving?" Trey got up, with a hint of protest in his voice.

"Well, unless you have anything else to discuss?" Sern offered while Trey stood there for a moment. Trey thought carefully for a moment while he still had Sern's attention. For a few days now he's been wanting to ask the big questions. His brother, Gavin and others at the house had told him about Intendant abilities. He never had the opportunity to get answers out of Hasaan, but this may be a chance. Sern could tell that Trey had something on his mind. Though he could initiate a mindlink at any moment to find out, the human concept of mental privacy was also something he had to consider.

"Yeah, there is," Trey started. "It's about what you and Hasaan are."

"We're Intendants," Sern answered bluntly without realizing the deeper nuances of what Trey was getting at.

"Yeah but 'what' are you?" Trey emphasized the key word in his reply. Through an intensive look, almost yearning for an answer, it seemed even the somewhat awkward Sern knew what he was referring to.

"You want to know what we are capable of, and where we come from?" Sern asked, clarifying the question he was asked.

"Yes. I mean you look human, but humans don't do what you can do. Humans don't travel through wormholes and portals, and humans don't have the ability to link minds." Trey listed off.

"I could be a very special human," Sern suggested for a moment. "There are humans who have telepathic abilities, and humans who know magic and can use the arcane forces."

"True, but if that were the case, you would have told us and we would have known."

"How so?" Sern inquired, somewhat knowing the answer but wanting Trey to reveal it to him. Trey simply pointed to his nose. "Ah, our scent," Sern smiled, for a moment underestimating the power of the Prime Wolf's noses.

"You don't smell human. I've met magic users before. And though they're special, they still have that human scent; you don't have any scent at all."

"I'll take that as a compliment. As I understand it, in human culture, to possess a strong odor could be seen as a potentially negative aspect," Sern lectured in a rather impersonal and academic tone, which, to many who have met him recently, was something he reverted to rather frequently.

"And let's not even start with how you talk," Trey chuckled.

"Is my speech pattern something unusual to you?" Sern inquired again.

"Well you sound like an Alien, like some man from outer space," Trey laughed as he flung his towel over his shoulder, and crossed his arms across his massive chest. For a moment, Sern looked speechless, but not moving a bit. Trey's smile suddenly melted away for a moment as that key word "alien" sank into his head. It was that word that seemed to strike a chord with Sern's expression. Then Trey keyed in on the situation as he stepped up closer to Sern. "You're an alien?" He whispered into Sern's ear.

"No," Sern answered with instant bluntness. "I am not an alien, not exactly," Sern stepped towards the doors of the gymnasium for a moment. With a mere glance, the doors slammed shut, and locked themselves. Then the doors above at the second level also automatically closed and locked. There were loud bangs echoing throughout the chamber for a moment. Trey grew frightened, and instinctively defensive, after realizing that he and Sern were locked into the room together. His natural fangs and sharp wolf teeth emerged. Sern raised his hand gently in the gesture of calming Trey. "Don't worry, I did that, for security reasons."

"Security?" Trey growled through his mouthful of fangs.

"Yes," Sern answered as he stepped up again to Trey. His face was more serious now, and Trey instantly got a feeling he should pay special attention to what he was going to say. "What I am going to tell you, I will have to make sure you can never reveal to anyone," Sern instructed the werewolf. Trey stood there for a moment listening intensely. "In order to guarantee secrecy, I must create a mental block in your mind, with a control that you will never, and cannot ever, reveal what I will tell you, not to anyone verbally, mentally, through writing or any other form of communication, be it subconscious or conscious," Sern commanded, his voice echoing through his mind.

"So you'll tell me?" Trey clarified as his fangs merged back as normal teeth.

"Yes, but after I tell you, your mind will file the information away, and you will never be able to tell or reveal it to anyone else unless I give direct permission," Sern gently tapped Trey's forehead with his right finger.

"You can do that?"

"I just did," Sern pointed to Trey's head.

"Alright, let's hear it," Trey sat back down on the bench and waited for Sern to tell him.

"The body that you see in front you, it's as human as you were at one time," Sern began as he started to pace slowly around, "but it is also inhabited by two non-corporeal beings."

"You're possessed?" Trey wondered, trying to get what Sern was saying through his mind.

"Not exactly. We are all sharing the same form and a merging of minds and consciousness. Essentially all three of us,are one being, Sern, who you see right here."

"So what are these spirits?"

"They're not spirits, they're Essences," Sern could tell that Trey didn't quite understand what he was meaning without further detail. "You've heard us reference the Va'Nai before?"

"Yeah, they're your bosses, right?"

"They're much more than that. The Va'Nai are a race of powerful, cosmic beings. They're not even from our dimension, but they created the Sanctuary Organization to protect Supernaturals. When they entered this universe from their own, they found that when they reproduced, their offspring could not grow."

"So they're stuck as babies here?"

"Yes, in a manner of speaking, they are babies, if that term helps you. The Va'Nai young, called Essences, can grow mentally, but they can't grow anymore in our universe. So to protect them, they need a physical form to shelter them."

"And that's where you come in."

"There are many ranks of people who have Essences implanted inside them. Intendants like me are just one of many ranks. When we reach a certain rank, we become infused with one Essence; we raise another rank, we receive another, which doubles our abilities. This process is called Infusion."

"Is it painful?" Trey wondered, still curious as a puppy about what Sern was telling him.

"No, not at all. Anything but. The Infusion of an Essence opens our minds to the cosmic awareness of the universe itself. That is probably why we may seem so alien; we see everything so differently after we are infused. The Essences, though they don't physically age, are aware of their power and abilities. To protect themselves as well as their hosts, they share their power and abilities with us, which is how we can do things like travel through portals, perform things like the mindlinks, telekinesis, even matter conversion and materialization."

"Materialization?" Trey seemed to have a problem with big words.

"The ability to seemingly create objects out of thin air. Some would even call this 'reality warping'," Sern reached out with his left hand. Trey watched as the air and space around his hand rippled, and then in Sern's open palm start to form a fist-size sphere of glass. It shone as though it was perfectly sculpted in the light. Trey stared at this procedure for a few moments as the rippling effect ceased, and in Sern's hand was a perfect glass ball. Sern gently tossed it to Trey who caught it in his massive hands.

"This is real?" he asked as he examined the crystal orb.

"Yes."

"But how?"

"I compressed the oxygen molecules in the air above my hand. Then by modifying its molecular structure, thanks to the Essence's abilities, we turned the oxygen into glass. And because they were compressed into a solid state, it took the form of the orb," Sern explained in a rather bland fashion. Trey was still in amazement examining the orb, as he looked up with a question clearly at the tip of his tongue.

"Can you make money?" Trey smiled. That also brought a rather quick giggle from Sern.

"I do believe it is possible. It's all just molecules to us," Sern took the glass orb back from Trey. "though it would hardly seem to be an appropriate use of our abilities, considering our responsibilities." The orb casually vanished from sight, as it was re-converted into air.

"So what else can you do?"

"Many things. It all depends on the circumstances," Sern released the doors mentally and they slowly opened again. "You know what you need to know for now," Sern turned around to look straight at Trey, his eyes once again, like the mindlink, were glowing brilliantly. "You will see no need to share this information with anyone else," his voice echoed into Trey's mind.

"Wait!" Trey protested. Sern stopped his advance towards Trey for a brief moment. "I heard you can do energy projection, like, as a weapon."

"Yes. It is our primary method of defence."

"Can you show me?"

"Very well," Sern again, telekinetically shut the doors and then locked them once again. He stepped into one of the larger gym rooms and stood in the center of the room as Trey followed him. "Try to hit me," he instructed the werewolf.

"You sure?" Trey asked.

"With all your might, Wolf!" Sern commanded

Trey crouched down as though he was starting to prowl, his eyes, blazed yellow with that glare that every werewolf would possess when preparing to attack. His claws emerged from his nails, and his fangs re-emerged. The fur started to sprout from his neck, and down the line of his back. He wasn't going to go into full form, but enough to strengthen himself significantly to what he thought would be enough to get through Sern's defence. He bellowed loudly with a bone-shattering roar, and then swiped immediately at Sern with his right claw. Instead of hitting Sern's body, he hit what felt like a solid bubble, what seemed like glass, a few inches from Sern's body. He swiped again with his left claw, again hit the same barrier between them. This time with the power of his superhuman fists, he repeatedly pounded on the shield, but Sern stood there, completely unscathed.

Sern's eyes started to glow brightly, like he was going to initiate a mindlink. Trey's massive werewolf form kept pounding on the barrier without any luck. With a powerful flash of energy, Sern emitted a wave of light at Trey, knocking him not to the ground, but back at the entrance of the room, slamming the enormous werewolf at the wall, almost winding him and losing enough focus that he reverted back to his human form. As Sern slowly walked towards Trey, the vein-like designs on his robe were glowing as furiously as his eyes. Sern slowly brought out his hand, which was also glowing brightly towards Trey, pointing the palm right at him. But before he did anything, he pointed it at one of the large punching bags in the main gym area, and from his hand, a stream of light shot out and hit the black punching bag with so much concussive force, that it snapped right off its chains, smashed through the windows and flew out into the garden.

Trey only watched, with his jaw wide open in a stunned expression as Sern stopped glowing. He ran to the hole in the windows to see the punching bag only just now landed at the end of the gardens. Luckily no one else saw it. As fast as it flew out, the punching bag suddenly started to float upwards, levitated by some unseen power. Trey turned around to notice that it was Sern who was directing it, as it flew right back in, through the massive shattered window, and then almost like it was a video being played in reverse, all the damage was repaired by itself. This took no less than a few moments to happen, barely enough time for him to wrap his mind around what had just occurred.

"Satisfied?" Sern asked.

"Yes," Trey hypnotically agreed, as Sern left the Gym, leaving Trey in a slight trance.

<u>Chapter 4</u>

Jett slowly opened the door to Paxton's room. He had taken the liberty to invite himself in. The slight crack of daylight flooded into the bedroom as his special someone was still under the covers. Then again the time on the clock did say it was 7:30am and on a Saturday morning, not exactly morning time. Jett was eager and excited, already his hair was perfectly combed and his jeans and sweater were perfectly colour-coordinated.

"Oh, Paxers!" He whispered into the ear of his special someone. No reply. But Jett knew Paxton was already awake. Slowly climbing onto the bed and nibbling on Paxton's right ear. "Oh Paxton!" He taunted again, this time rewarded him with a grunt. Jett gave up and laid down on the bed too, but not without wrapping his right arm around Paxton for a big morning hug.

"You had to wake me up this early?" Paxton groaned as he still kept his eyes closed. Jett's natural playfulness demanded attention as Jett nuzzled up to Paxton's neck and gave him a series of gentle kisses along his neckline.

"Alright." Paxton surrendered as he rolled over to be greeted by the refreshing minty kiss from his boyfriend, which lasted a good thirty seconds. Along with the typical groaning, moaning and hand wandering, Jett was quick to cut it short.

"Ok, out of bed." Jett teased as he grabbed onto Paxton's hands, mockingly trying to pull him up.

"Fine, fine, fine." Paxton snarled as he slipped out from under the covers in nothing but his tight pair of boxer briefs.

"Ok, you got to shower. I'll take care of everything else." Jett leaped off the bed and quickly ripped open the blinds, pouring sunlight into the bedroom, just enough to generously give him a good look at an escaping Paxton who retreated into the washroom to shower and clean up.

Jett heard the rushing water of the shower, and hurried around the room, making the bed, throwing the pillows back into place, straightening up every single crease of the blanket to make it seem perfect. He spotted Paxton's bags already lined up along the closet, and grabbed them, almost tripping as he darted out the front door, and threw them into the trunk of his hatchback. Then he made another round, getting Paxton's other larger bag and also threw that into the trunk. He knew exactly how Paxton packed his bags. Then he quickly and carefully grabbed a styrofoam box.

As Jett walked back to the house, he saw Paxton slipping on a pair of jeans, though he was still shirtless. Jett quietly stood there at the door watching him search for a shirt in his closet.

"Breakfast?" He called as he held the box in his hands like a waiter holding a tray. Paxton slipped on a stretchy but tight black t-shirt, something that made no effort to hide his physique.

"What is it?" Paxton asked curiously as he slipped on his runners. He already knew that Jett had pretty much stuffed everything into the car.

"Sushi," Jett smiled. He knew it was Paxton's favorite food.

"How did you get sushi at 7:00am?" Paxton asked as he smiled back at his boyfriend. He certainly did appreciate the gesture.

"I have my sources," Jett winked. Paxton wrapped his muscular arms around Jett's shoulders.

"You do know how to treat me right, don't you?" He smiled as their noses touched.

"Well, this is a bit of a special occasion. My boyfriend is taking me up to spend the week with the duo stars of Eternal Knights, Gavin Varsen and Cazian Saint!" Jett giggled. "I think sushi is the least I could do."

"Alright," Paxton mockingly snatched the box from Jett. "You drive then," Jett dangled the car keys from his fingers.

"Already got them."

A few hours later, the Yaris was steadily going up the Sea-To-Sky highway past the beautiful ocean-coast view of the forested islands. The warm late summer air was still around, and the sun was brilliantly bright with no clouds to block the perfectly blue sky of the Pacific coast. Just relaxing, leaning back with his sunglasses over his eyes, Paxton enjoyed the gentle rocking of the car as Jett continued on their way. They reached an outcrop of roads that took them off the highway, which descended to the lower roads along the waters. It wasn't a difficult drive for them, just long but with lots of beautiful scenery.

As for Jett, he was still giddy from the fact that he was going to meet two stars from his favorite show, not to mention he was going to spend a week with them. With his hunky boyfriend and two of television's hottest celebrities, it was going to be a lovely week. However, since he was also with familiar company, it may seem that intimacy was not necessarily in the cards.

"How did you get to know Gavin?" Jett asked as they kept going down the seaside road.

"Well, I told you before. It was pure luck stumbling on an audition like that, and then getting the part, then literally filming for two weeks with them."

"How did you hear about the audition?" Jett asked, being ever so curious.

"Pure luck. They weren't even holding them anymore and were ready to close up. They were renting a studio in the University for a covert casting call. I happen to have been in the area when one of the producers noticed me. They asked me to read a few lines so I did, and the next thing I realized, I was in the movie set making nine-hundred dollars a day for two weeks."

"Sweet deal!" Jett cheered.

"Yeah, but things like that don't happen so often. But when they do, it can be very worthwhile."

"Any chance you may get another gig like that?" Jett asked as the GPS indicator on the screen showed that they were nearing their destination. He slowed for a more comfortable and scenic speed.

"It's all up to the makers of the show," Paxton replied as he stretched his arms over his head. The long drive had always made him tense up, considering that a small hatchback wasn't exactly made for roomy comfort. But then, again it had always suited his basic needs.

Jett steered the car down a nicely paved road that curved towards a very modernist looking building. It was like one of those ultra modern cube-like houses. It seemed like more of a retreat than an actual home that a person would live in for the majority of the year. But it wasn't surprising since actors would only need a place of temporary residence while filming. A pair of large trees provided the perfect amount of shade and cover that helped cool the place down on hot summer days, and the location of the house right next to a bay that led to the ocean while still being isolated enough for privacy seemed perfect for a weekend and holiday.

There was no car in the driveway but they could see someone on the outer balcony, one of many balconies actually. Instantly they could recognize who it was. Standing a tall six feet and four inches tall and that perfectly combed black hair, the famed figure of Gavin Varsen was outlined by what almost seemed to be a perfect halo of light that shone in from the sun. The shimmering reflections and sparkles of sunlight that reflected off the bay back towards him.

Jett sped down and parked the car outside the house on the roadside, not wanting to take up any driveway space while they were guests. They climbed out and while stretching, didn't notice Gavin had leaped off the balcony. They turned around to see Gavin walking towards them wearing, a white dress shirt which he only buttoned up halfway, and a pair of jeans and white leather sandals. Jett wasn't aware that he was staring.

"Gavin Varsen is walking towards us," he gritted through his teeth at Paxton. His face was full of bewilderment and clearly he was star-struck.

"Boys!" Gavin greeted with his arms open.

"Hey, Gavin!" Paxton greeted back as he was welcomed by the expanse of Gavin's chest and arms in a friendly hug.

"Oh my god, Gavin Varsen is hugging my boyfriend." Jett thought to himself, his mind naturally wondering what it would be like to be embraced by that Hollywood hunk. He had wanted to meet Gavin for ages, as he was his favorite celebrity. He always asked Paxton if he was jealous of his huge crush on this celebrity but Paxton never minded. But now that Gavin was here standing in person, there may be some potential problems. For the moment, Jett didn't care because Gavin Varsen was standing right now, in front of him.

"And Gavin, this is my boyfriend Jett." Paxton introduced. The towering Gavin walked up to the almost giddy Jett and offered his hand. Jett eagerly grasped Gavin's large hand and shook it.

"I love your show!" Jett squeaked losing momentary control over his voice. That sure made Gavin laugh as he wrapped his arms around Jett's body and also gave him a hug. Paxton smirked as he shook his head in mocking disapproval as Jett signaled a thumbs up to him.

"He never misses it." Paxton groaned. "Ever. Not once."

"Well, that's good! We need loyal fans to keep the show going," Gavin squeezed Jett, teasing him by almost squeezing his face between his pectoral muscles. Gavin could certainly hear Jett's heart rate soar for a moment, almost felt his heart pumping against his skin. He didn't want to seem like a home wrecker so he released Jett.

Paxton started unloading their car. Gavin helped carry some of the bags with them as they went to the house.

"This is where you usually live?" Paxton asked as he continued to examine the beautiful home's modern exterior.

"Yeah. Cazian and I stay here when in town. It's a nice place, and lets us have some privacy. Here, let me give you a tour." Gavin opened the door and let them inside. The house's twin steel front doors opened to an entrance room where another pair of doors in front led to a corridor to which there were a few other doorways. "Those are the guest rooms," he instructed. To the side was a stairway that turned and went upwards along the side of the walls to a second level. Further back was a large kitchen, and beyond, a dining room. From the left of the entrance was another room, and this one looked like it was a sitting and entertainment room.

The house was almost a "T" shape with the rooms for sleeping along the middle. Gavin carried the bags into the first room on the left side of the central hallway. Inside was a lovely king-size bed, a large wardrobe and dresser, and a doorway that led to a walk-in closet as well as an en suite bathroom. They certainly didn't spare any luxuries. Then again, Paxton guessed that with the paycheques that Gavin pulled in from Eternal Knights, it would be generous.

"Here you are," Gavin gently placed the bags on the floor next to the large bed. "Inside the washroom are towels and soap and other stuff you need," he guided. "The windows and walls are reinforced glass and concrete, so it's quite well-insulated, not to mention safe and protective."

"Why would you need this level of protection?" Paxton asked.

"You know fans," Gavin teased Jett with a friendly hand on his shoulder. "they may get rabid and try to break my door down."

"Well, you invited me in, now I can enter whenever I like," Jett smirked. "I always wondered why it was like that with vampires. Why can they only come in when invited?" he asked curiously.

"They're very polite," Gavin smirked as Paxton started to unpack some of their stuff in the bathroom.

"So, is Cazian going to be back soon?" Paxton asked from the bathroom.

"Yeah, he's going to be here later tonight. There's a get together and bonfire party later tonight. "

"Who is going to be there?" Paxton asked, curious as to who would show up.

"Just a handful of friends, no more that five or so. You'll recognize them from filming," Gavin replied as he went to the kitchen. "By the way, everything in the fridge is open game. Help yourselves to anything, and I mean that literally," he called in from the very large and professional-looking kitchen with a large island in the middle and steel matching appliances that were all nicely spaced and, oddly, looked quite new as though they were rarely, if ever, used.

Jett and Paxton also walked in, quite amazed by the almost spellbinding, sparkling clean kitchen. Gavin gestured to them to take seats behind the island. He had taken out a trio of bottles from the fridge, filled with a watery red, slightly pinkish coloured fluid. The two of them got a glimpse of the inside of the fridge. Sure enough, the inside seemed to be quite well-stocked, with an assortment of drinks and fluids in brightly coloured bottles. From what they got a view of, there was food in there too.

Gavin popped the caps to the bottles and handed one to each of them.

"Cheers!" Gavin smiled as they all simultaneously took a sip. He could tell that they were quite impressed by what they had just tasted.

"Nice, tastes like strawberries and peach," Jett remarked with satisfaction on his face.

"And a bit of orange!" Paxton added. "Nice, though not very strong," Paxton referred to the rather lack of any alcoholic punch that the drink had.

"That's because it's a juice, not a 'drink' type of drink." Gavin smiled as he took another sip.

"Ah," Jett smirked.

"If you want to spike it, I got stuff for that too," Gavin opened up a white cupboard next to the large steel fridge. As he did, a massive collection of various types of liquors, rum, gins, and a vast assortment of other alcoholic substances were inside. Paxton and Jett were aware that being a star of a successful TV show, Gavin had a very generous paycheque every week. The odd thing about this collection was that its perfection in stock meant that it was rarely touched.

"I don't see any opened bottles," Paxton remarked as he looked at the more than generous brews in front of him.

"I don't drink...wine." Gavin smirked as he took another sip from the bottle. The Dracula reference didn't escape the two of them, as he couldn't help but giggle under the well-placed laughter.

"You know, I have to admit," Jett leaned over and put his arm around Paxton. "one of the things most convincing about your character as a good guy is how un-vampire he is."

"The wings and fangs don't match your image?" Gavin couldn't help but be amused by his statement. Oh, the things that his guests don't know about him.

"Wings are a new thing; that's definitely the coolest part." Jett gushed. "They look so crazy and real. It's like they're part- demon."

"Well that's one of many people's favorite parts," Gavin turned to what looked like a large pantry at the edge of the kitchen. Lo and behold, the inside wasn't just shelves of canned and dried foods, but also another pair of larger fridges, perhaps one was a freezer. Again, Paxton couldn't help but notice that all the cans, bags and everything were perfectly stocked, not a single can or bag missing. They were perfectly lined up as though organized by an obsessive compulsive. It wasn't even lunchtime yet, and for some reason, it seemed like Gavin was preparing for a big meal cook up.

"You're already preparing for dinner?" Paxton asked from the kitchen. Then he noticed that the two large fridges had locks on them, as well as security keypads.

"Oh, no. Cazian's bringing that in later. I don't really have a hang of cooking for myself. When you live 15 hour days with catering, you learn to just trust whoever brings you a plate," Gavin laughed as he came back out of the pantry, as though he was just checking the stockpiles of stuff.

"Your organization skills are pretty good!" Jett commented, admiring the fact that everything was spotless, and had its place. There wasn't anything in the kitchen that was even remotely disorganized, everything was perfectly placed and lined up.

"Well I do like to keep things organized. You don't lose things if you know where everything is."

"So what now?" Jett asked.

"How about a swim?" Gavin, Jett and Paxton simply looked at each other, rather surprised at Gavin's suggestion for multiple reasons.

"Well, we didn't bring swim suits."

"Who said anything about swim suits?" Gavin grinned as he unbuttoned his white dress shirt, and then slipped it right off. A look of near shock and bewilderment came across Paxton's face, but a more eager and giddy smirk appeared on Jett's face. Clearly one was stunned but the other was more eager than surprised. Gavin couldn't help but grin at their mixed expressions as he neatly folded the shirt and casually put it over the backs of one of the barstools at the kitchen island. "I was kidding!" He stressed, almost like he was pleading with them for a moment. "I got extras upstairs. I bought them one size smaller than me so they should fit you guys.

Chapter 5

Jett lay there on the warm wooden plank surface of the small pier, enjoying the hot sun and warmth of the heat on him. Paxton was inside the water, doing a few laps around, the thumping of the water occasionally stirring a bit of notice from Jett, but nonetheless leaving his boyfriend still oblivious to the activity in the water. Paxton and Gavin were both in the water, occasionally talking, but Jett had better things to do than to be interrupted with conversation. The mere idea that there was activity elsewhere didn't seem to phase him at the slightest. Here he was, at the private home of one of his favorite celebrities, enjoying a sun tanning session on the private dock of a TV star. It was something that he hadn't even realized was happening.

Through the heavily shaded sunglasses, he would occasionally stare up at the crystal clear blue skies, seeing the occasional bird in the heavens above passing by, but never anything artificial, not a single car horn, not a single helicopter or airplane.

"GAH! What the hell??!" Jett screamed as a tidal wave of cold freezing water splashed all over him. The sound of the water was interrupted only by the squealing giggles of Paxton who was still eager in the water trying hard to restrain himself as the ripples of the waves showed, without a doubt, that he was the origin of this cold wake-up call. "Oh, that's it!" Jett threw off his shades and plunged into the water, chasing after his boyfriend.

Gavin couldn't help but admire the playfulness that this couple had with each other. At first, Paxton seemed a bit tired, having endured a few hours of driving as a passenger up the coast, but now he was much wider awake.

"Are you guys hungry?" Gavin asked as he pulled himself up out of the water at the pier. For a brief moment, the two in the water couldn't help but admire the view. Hours with personal trainers and nutritionists, and a mobile gym that went with them from location to location seemed to have clearly paid off for Gavin.

"Yeah, I'll help," Paxton yelled from the lake as he tried to get to the pier, but Jett caught up to him.

"Oh no, you don't!" Jett wrapped his arms around Paxton keeping him in the water.

"I think you both should enjoy yourselves," Gavin laughed as he slipped his feet into a pair of flip flops.

He watched for a moment as the two kept their mock struggle going for a few moments but then relaxed. Quickly, Gavin hurried back into the house by the kitchen entrance, making sure that the two were still enjoying themselves. He slipped into the pantry and quickly went over to the inner fridges that were kept there. Touching the keypad, a set of squares illuminated, but instead of what one would expect for the numbers 1-9 to be placed in order, they randomly appeared to increase security. Punching in his six digits quickly, it unlocked the fridge doors. He quickly reached in and grabbed one of the many well-stocked blood bottles, unscrewed the cap and started to gulp it down. It was a refreshing feeling, his entire body felt invigorated. He didn't really have a massive appetite, but he figured he wouldn't get another free chance to feed for a bit with guests around.

Quickly turning around to make sure that they two of them were still in the water, he screwed the cap back on and shut the fridge door, re-securing it safely behind the lock.

"Sneaking a snack," a familiar voice came from behind him. Gavin turned around to see the dashing appearance of Cazian, his co-star and roommate. He leaned his back against the pantry door entryway, his pair of silver sunglasses, and gold reflective lenses resting on his nose, and his trademark hairstyle, with its blond stripe always perfectly combed as always.

"While our guests are pre-occupied, yeah," Gavin licked the blood off his lips.

"You may want to retract those before you go back out." Cazian pointed to his own teeth, notifying Gavin that instinctively his fangs were extended as he went back to the kitchen. Gavin quickly shrank them back to normal size as he stepped back into the kitchen, and closed the pantry door behind him. On the table were three large platters of sushi, freshly made and with lots of varieties. "I wasn't sure what to bring so I brought a bit of everything," He slipped the sunglasses onto his head, and then started to roll up the sleeves to his black silk dress shirt. Luckily the clothes were quite cooling despite their colour in the sunshine.

"I remember they love sushi. So this should be plenty enough, considering we won't be eating much," Gavin examined the fine display of the exotic foods in front of them, the wide assortment of colours and types, some of which were more rare to get than others. He always did appreciate the exotic East Asian cuisines even though he never had to eat them himself, but the sheer variety was so much more interesting and appealing than meat and potatoes.

"So, this should be an interesting week," Cazian remarked as he looked out the window to see Paxton and Jett climbing out of the water and drying themselves off. He was quite impressed by what he saw. "He's been working out, I see," Cazian grinned, for a brief moment licking his fangs.

"Count on you to notice that," Gavin smirked as he took out a number of cheese blocks from the kitchen fridge, under the wide assortment of liquor. He placed over a dozen of them on a large tray, and a nice white porcelain square plate, with a cheese knife and an assortment of various crackers. Adding to that, a few bottles of the assorted strange juices that they liked earlier to complement the various foods he was stacking onto the platter.

"What's the name of his boyfriend?" Cazian kept watching as he folded his arms across his chest, still viewing them from the kitchen windows.

"Jett," Gavin answered as he took a step back to admire his excellent organization skills on the platter. In just those few moments, he was able to slice up all the various cheeses, more than twelve different types, all neatly and place them on the plate, with the various cracker variations and snack meats there as well.

"A week of pretending to be human should be fun," Cazian smirked. "Always with the masquerade."

"Well, I doubt they'll stay for that long. I just told them we would have a week to spare," Gavin replied from the kitchen island where he was doing the set-up. He slipped the three platters of sushi into the enormous kitchen fridge, to keep the food fresh while he laid the tray on the kitchen table.

"I'm going to greet our guests," Cazian slipped the sunglasses back over his eyes, making himself look even more mysterious and seductive in the process. That type of look was what gave him his huge fan following. Cazian, though the co-star, had a rabid fan base that rivaled Gavin's easily. Though he was introduced later in the series, the two of them sure made quite the duo on screen, and Cazian made sure to milk it for what it was worth, making him just as marketable as the main star.

Jett and Paxton headed up the pathway back to the house, to see a stern but handsome looking man standing on the balcony watching them approach. He wore a black silk dress shirt, and had a stunning pair of silver and gold sunglasses over his eyes. The blond stripe in his hair made his identity less of a secret.

"Cazian!" Paxton yelled from the pier as he and Jett walked up. Cazian descended down the stairway to greet Paxton in person. Paxton held hands with Jett as they walked, and he could instantly feel Jett's grip getting tighter as they walked.

"Hey, Pax!" Cazian shook his hand, and then did the same to Jett, who obviously was quite happy to meet him. Cazian couldn't help but be flattered when he could instantly see Jett's pupils dilate, and his heart rate speed up, telltale signs that he knew meant that Jett was instantly drawn to him. It came in handy when dealing with humans. Cazian didn't really need vampiric abilities to tell that Jett was gushing. "I heard the producers are planning to bring your character back for a few more runs!"

"Really?" Paxton asked, clearly excited at the news. "Wait, how sure are you?" he inquired skeptically at the news.

"Well, the character name came up a few times in the writing sessions," Cazian lifted up his shades, revealing his almost ice-blue eyes.

"Wow!" Jett was almost ensnared by the instant view of Cazian's magnificent blue eyes. "I thought those were contact lenses that you wore," he exclaimed, still unable to take his eyes off Cazian's icy blues. Cazian couldn't help but blush a bit at the flattery he was getting. Detecting their attraction to him didn't hurt his ego one bit.

"Nope, they're real as you can tell," Cazian quickly flashed Jett a wink; that alone made Jett's heartbeat quicken. He could almost hear him whimpering, even though it was just for a second. "We've got food inside if you're interested," Cazian invited.

Day turned to night rather quickly as they filled their time with activities. When Gavin took out his high definition camera for a makeshift photo shoot, they had a creative time with posing and doing some natural looking shots just spontaneously in the house and around by the pier.

Gavin had a plan for Paxton, and that was to use the photo shoot to make shots that could promote the return of Paxton's character's. It was always a method that stars used to promote their friends, especially if they were actors. One of the pictures that they made was of Gavin in vampire makeup, biting Paxton. Since Paxton played a vampire hunter on the show, it could be a huge potential plot twist to have him return as a victim. Later, five other friends of Gavin's showed up, and with them came even more alcohol and snacks. Preferring to take this into a unique location, the group of them moved the get-together into the forests upwards from the house.

The bonfire was roaring, and the music from the portable iPod dock was blaring, something like the customary party music found in trendy clubs, as the few handful of the guests were dancing. One even brought with him glow sticks, something that interestingly did make the situation seem a bit more surreal and over-exaggerated. For Paxton and Jett, it was just comforting, while leaning against a tree, sitting on a thick blanket, to nuzzle up to each other and enjoy the view of the fire. Of course not everyone was very interested in moving around, Cazian was sitting close by quietly also, observing the fire. The five guests, of whom their names Paxton and Jett couldn't even remember, were just going about their own way.

It was as though there were two parties happening at the same time, but perfectly acceptable since it was more for relaxation than anything else. It wasn't like there was anything else to do besides sitting and relaxing while everyone was having fun. Paxton was leaning against the tree, with Jett curled up against him.

The two of them were a few meters away, chatting with beers in their hands, and three seemed a bit overly excited, and were still dancing to the thump of the music, waving their hands in the air, with the customary 90s tradition of glow sticks still being very much enforced by some of them.

"Wow," Paxton whispered to Jett. Jett looked upwards at Paxton, without saying much, but wanting him to clarify his expression. "Some people will never grow up. I see." He smirked, referring to the glow stick-toting alcoholics nearby.

"Nope," Jett complied as he slowly sat up, stretching his back. Cuddling was fine, but for them it was never going to be enough, sitting outside on a blanket compared to Paxton's fireplace back at home. Still dozing off for a moment, they didn't even realize the crowd had already departed. It was just the four of them, sitting around the fire once again. Paxton gently started to rub Jett's back; no doubt he was a bit sore from the awkward position he was in, from leaning against a tree and his boyfriend. "Ah, thanks." He groaned as Paxton worked his spine like a xylophone.

Then without any warning, Gavin leaped to his feet, like he had almost caught fire, but then stood completely still. His eyes, slowly scanning around them, every single crackle of the fire, every leaf that they stepped on, snap of a twig, breeze on the branches, he was keenly keeping track of in his mind. Cazian, only a split second later, also took up a defensive posture, apparently alert of what was going on.

Paxton at first thought it was the presence of the departing partiers that had caught their attention, but nothing quite like this. Through a single look that Gavin gave Cazian, they two of them almost took up opposite sides of the fire, as though they were scouting something with their eyes. Puzzled by their strange reactions, Paxton and Jett got up off the ground, stretching their legs.

"Stay still," Gavin whispered to them, he was still almost on the prowl around them. They were almost certain that he was looking for something, an anomaly, a fluctuation of movement, anything. "There are wolves nearby," Gavin whispered, even softer, this time with his eyes locking onto Cazian, indicating the words were meant for him. Paxton and Jett couldn't hear his whisper, but Cazian could hear it perfectly fine. A slight nod indicated Cazian got the instruction and started to sharpen his search, slowly and steadily keeping an eye out. It was clear though, that if there was something watching, then the bonfire still lit was not going to help them hide at all. "Everyone, get back to the car!" Gavin whispered to Paxton and Jett again, this time, his voice sounded dead serious.

"Could it be one of our guys?" Cazian whispered back to Gavin quietly.

"No, they wouldn't be out this far from the house." Gavin answered as he kept his eyes open.

"What's going on?" Jett asked, bewildered at what the two were doing as they packed everything up, quickly folding up the blanket and stuffing it back into his backpack. There wasn't anything else around, since Gavin and Cazian were simply alright with sitting on the raw ground without any worries earlier.

"Follow me," Gavin commanded, yet with a tone still soft and quiet, as though he didn't want anyone else to hear. He started to hurry away, with Jett and Paxton following him. Cazian was behind them, almost as if they were escorting them back to the car. However the cars were quite a fair distance away since they had found a remote location that sat at a small plateau opening in the trees of the forests north of Gavin's home. They kept following the barely visible pathway that was now only lit by the moonlight leading down many winding pathways. Jett and Paxton were almost gasping a few times trying to keep their balance going down these pathways, but Gavin and Cazian didn't seem to have any problem at all, as though they were able to see in the dark.

Dodging tree branches, Paxton kept his hand held onto Jett's as he led him through, while still following Gavin who was always just a few steps ahead of them. Paxton, while looking back, suddenly collided with a huge hulking mass in front of him. For a moment, he didn't know what he hit, and pulled Jett with him, until that hulking mass itself was revealed to be Gavin who suddenly stopped. Behind them, was Cazian, whose eyes somehow seemed almost to shine, like an animal's, in the darkness? For a brief moment, Jett dismissed it as just natural lighting effect due to Cazian's unusually bluish grey eyes. But then, it was very clear what made them all stop.

In front of Gavin, though still a fair distance away, almost thirty feet away, was the dark shaded outline of someone blocking their path. Gavin didn't make any attempt to get any closer; he stood there protectively between the other three of them, and whoever it was who was blocking them. Paxton peered around Gavin to get a look. It wasn't one figure, but two. He could barely make out any features at all, except that they had unusual looking hands, almost like long fingers, and they eyes were definitely visible, like shiny yellow.

"This is some kind of show you guys are putting on?" Paxton whispered to Gavin. He was almost entertained rather than frightened at what he was seeing. "Getting some stunt guys to ambush us?" He turned, facing Cazian.

"Those aren't stuntmen," Gavin looked to his left, and right, only to notice that those two weren't the only ones around them. The cars were still a fair distance away, and he didn't know if he could protect his two human guests and make it back to the cars fast enough.

Cazian got up closer, but still kept Paxton and Jett between him and Gavin. He turned around only to see that again, roughly thirty feet away from him, were others surrounding them.

"I see eight, but I can hear twelve," Cazian grunted to Gavin, with almost a snarl in his voice. He wasn't happy to be stalked. Normally this wouldn't be an issue, but with two humans here, he couldn't react in a way that was natural for him and Gavin.

"Same, twelve," Gavin, reached back and grabbed Paxton, and pulled him in front of him, and locked his gaze right into Paxton's bewildered eyes which now stared right into a pair of solid red irises. "When I give the word, you will run straight to the car, which is down the pathway straight ahead, as fast as you can," Gavin commanded with a firm whispered tone. Paxton, unable to do anything else but process and accept the information that Gavin had just relayed to him, was almost in a trance-like state, now awaiting another order.

"You too," Cazian turned Jett around, and repeated the same instructions. "You're going to run as fast as you can, on Gavin's word, right as fast as you can to the cars," he repeated. His eyes were now also red, and gazed deep into Jett's mind. Jett had no option but to agree, and suddenly stood ready to make his mad sprint.

"GO!" Gavin commanded, as the two of them started first, but Gavin sped right past them in a dash of speed faster than anything they had seen before, tackling the two beings in front of them first, with Cazian following them from behind, making sure that no one got close. As Jett and Paxton kept their pace, which was fast even by what they were used to, the others started following, not running but on all fours, like they were animals!

One of them was getting close; but with a swift kick, Cazian knocked it away just enough to give them a distance advantage. The stalker yelped a high pitch squeal like that of a dog when injured as it smashed into a tree, only to be overtaken by two more that came from behind! Jett and Paxton kept going, leaping over fallen logs, then dodging more tree branches, as another pair of these creatures came up closer. Paxton didn't bother to look, only keeping his pace, and quickly mentally calculating the steps he was taking and dodging whatever was in his path, while desperately trying not to trip. Jett also maintained his close distance to Paxton; but as they kept going, Gavin and Cazian seemed to disappear.

They heard a scream behind them, as it was clearly Gavin's voice, but then a few more snarls. They were the snarls and growls of wolves! For a quick moment to catch their breath, Paxton and Jett were heaving, almost out of breath from the adrenaline-fuelled sprint they had just taken. Around where they were standing seemed to be void of any of these creatures. They heard the roars and commotion continuing, and while getting a check on each other, Paxton grabbed Jett's hand and started to run yet again.

Jett was still out of breath, and was struggling to keep up. Unaware of what was happening behind him, Paxton kept running; with Jett's hand linked to his own, now they could only hear the sound of their heartbeats and the treading of their feet.

Out of nowhere, one of the creatures leaped out from the shrubbery that they had been passing, and with a massive swipe of its hand claws, slashed right into Jett's left side! Jett collapsed to the ground in pain for a moment, as the creature, which wore human clothes and still looked human but with bestial facial and hand features, roared at Paxton! Jett, stunned, didn't even realize what had taken him down, but was slightly disoriented from collapsing to the ground, as Paxton looked around for anything to use as a weapon, and instantly grabbed a rock the size of his head. Not even straining for a moment, he threw it as fast as he could at the beast, but it leaped out of the way, only to use that same momentum and try to charge at him while Jett struggled to his feet, not even feeling the wound to his side.

This were-beast leaped towards him for what looked like few moments, before the enormous size of a familiar being came between them. Paxton tried to call out but he was still so out of breath that nothing came out but a wheeze, and then an instinctive gasp for air. It was Gavin again. His shirt was ripped by what looked like claw marks as well, only visible because the shirt was white. Paxton tried to get to Jett, but another pair of the creatures leaped into the same opening, followed quickly by Cazian, who tried to throw them off Jett witch his bare hands.

Gavin and Cazian's sheer physical strength were of a power never seen by Paxton before as they punched these creatures, and then with swift movements, kicked or threw them away. Then Paxton soon found that he was being picked up and dragged away, not by these creatures but by Gavin himself, who dashed through the forest with blazing speed, as he soon blacked out. The last image that he could see was Cazian fending off the creatures from Jett who was running and following them.

Chapter 6

Paxton gasped as he sprang up from the bed. He looked around the room to familiarize himself with his surroundings. He saw his bags sitting at the base of the bed.

"Where's Jett?" he yelled out, apparently at no one, but he sensed that there were people outside. Immediately, panic struck him right in the heart as he turned to get out of bed, but then a sharp pain in his side. He looked down to see three huge scabs on his left side, from the base of his ribs, roughly five inches long, in a trio like claws. "Where is Jett?" he yelled out again.

Quickly the door opened and Gavin came back in, but another person followed him. This person was dressed unusually. He wore a canvas-colour suit, but the jacket was rather long, down to about his knees, with almost silver glowing veins throughout, that pulsated as if they were alive, surging through various angular designs all over him.

"Where is Jett?" Paxton pleaded, tears were starting to form in his eyes. Before he realized, he had collapsed back onto the bed. Gavin looked back, to see Sern's eyes were glowing once again.

"What did you do?" Gavin demanded from Sern, shocked by the fast response

"There was no way you were going to be able to put him under control. He was hysterical so I put him back to sleep." Sern stated without emotion in his voice. Gavin slowly sat down next to the freshly asleep Paxton and tucked him back in.

"Those were Bloodbane Wolves," Gavin sighed, "which means, he will turn into one of them in the next 24 hours, and so will Jett if we don't find him."

"Which means you have limited time for your options." Sern started to walk towards the door.

"What options?" Gavin demanding a clarification into Sern's wording. As with many of Sern's words, they often had more than one meaning and suggestions. Sern turned around, not to say a word but only to give him an assertive gaze. "You mean to turn him?"

"As stated when I arrived, the control of your numbers and bloodlines, is entirely up to you." Sern reminded him. "If you don't want him to become a Bloodbane, your blood can counter it, but then of course he will become one of you instead." Sern exited the room. Gavin sat there for a few moments, looking back at Paxton who was fully asleep in his bed. Gavin didn't know what he was going to do. It has been years since he turned anyone, and Cazian was his most recent childe.

For Gavin, the option now was either to make him a vampire or a werewolf, but either way he would never be human again. For Sern, the choice was going to be easy, entirely logical; choose the one that would do the least harm. Bloodbanes were ruthless hunters, and always sought to increase their numbers. Paxton would likely be ensnared into their bloodlust, but sadly many Bloodbanes would also be slaughtered by hunters. It would also be likely that a newborn like Paxton would inevitably become a victim of a werewolf hunter raid or become a monster.

On the other hand, as a High Order, like him and Cazian, he would only need to control a bloodlust attack that would happen every one hundred days. Bloodlusts, while dangerous in comparison to the far more frequent bloodthirsty nature of the Bloodbanes, would not be a good thing for him to go under. Even under the Sanctuary Organization's protection, Paxton's struggle as a Bloodbane would be an experience filled with internal pain and torture.

And then there was the additional issue of Jett, if he would be found. Gavin was fairly confident that Jett was alive. Bloodbanes didn't kill outright because it was better to secure larger numbers than to loose a freshly-turned wolf. Bloodbane infection would only require a full day before the change was irreversible, and they had to find Jett as soon as possible. Thankfully upon returning to his home, Gavin had taken some measures.

"Have you heard from Trey or Coltrane yet?" Cazian asked as he waited calmly in the kitchen, with Sern sitting and also waiting.

"Not as of yet." Sern answered.

"Can't you detect where these Bloodbanes are?" Cazian was visibly frustrated despite his calm exterior. The last thing he wanted was a friend of his to lose his lover, especially in this manner.

"Unfortunately, I can't. I don't have any ability to track over a distance like this," Sern stated in his typical matter-of-fact type of way. He was also concerned, but oddly there was little that he could do in this situation besides helping everyone keep calm. As an Intendant, his jurisdiction in this case was rather limited because the transformation from human to either wolf or vampire was something that was he couldn't prevent. "The Wolves have far more powerful senses of smell and they will be able to track and find him better than we can."

Gavin came out of the room, quietly closing the door behind him. He looked worried, as expected. Sern suspected that he hadn't done anything yet since he was only in there for a few minutes, hardly enough time to fulfill the need of a full turning. The task of actually creating a new fledgling for Gavin wasn't a difficult task in itself but it was the responsibility of what happened afterwards that was going to be more difficult. It was the equivalent of creating a new life, a powerful life that could be a potential danger for anything else around it. They weren't called "High Orders" without a reason.

Sern didn't want to push the issue with Gavin. He knew that Gavin would make the eventual decision in time, but needed a period of calmness to come to that conclusion on his own. Sern went to the fridge in the back of the pantry where the blood was kept. Unlike the others, he simply waved his hand past the security lock which unlocked by itself. He grabbed one of the packages of blood which hung neatly and organized in the fridge, and went back into the kitchen where he took a large mug and poured the red liquid into it. Without the need for any microwave, Sern simply commanded the blood cells and molecules to move faster, heating the particles up to slightly below body temperature.

"Have something to drink." Sern asked as he brought the large mug over. Gavin didn't seem to pay attention for a moment, until he realized Sern was standing next to him, as he stood there staring out the window towards where their wolves had gone, to find Jett.

"Hmm?" he groaned for a moment as he snapped back to the present. "Oh, thanks." Gavin took the mug into his hand and took a sip. Somehow, Sern had heated the blood perfectly to mimic the temperature close enough as though it was fresh from the vein. "I haven't transformed anyone since Cazian." Gavin turned around, still seemingly speaking to himself out loud rather than to anyone in particular.

"I'm sure you will do what is right," Sern assured him. "I have trust in your ability to make a sound judgment."

"You make it sound like I'm dealing with some type of bureaucratic decision," Gavin snuffed at Sern's way of describing his situation.

"I apologize for sounding impersonal; but unfortunately from my point of view, the decision is simple and bureaucratic. Perhaps in time I will develop a stronger sense of empathy for your situation."

"Yeah, let's hope," Gavin took another sip of the warm blood as Sern stepped onto the patio.

Gavin spent the next few hours sitting next to Paxton, waiting for him to wake up. He had already decided what Sern had predicted. He was going to transform Paxton; but before doing that, he had the arduous task of introducing the entire world of the supernatural to him. It was never an easy task for anyone to do. To tell them that they were living in a world full of deception and that human kind were not the only intelligent life out there was always a difficult thing to tell people. For them especially, this was going to be extremely awkward considering their participation in Eternal Knights.

Paxton's eyes opened. Gavin was there by his side. As expected, Paxton was still asking for Jett, desperately trying to find out what happened to his boyfriend. Gavin could still see that the bite mark on Paxton's left shoulder and side were still scabbed, meaning that the wolf effect had not yet taken over him, and there was still time to offer him something else. In his mind though, Gavin did have one fear that he didn't address at first, and that would be the possibility that Paxton may decide to reject his offer and keep transforming into a Bloodbane Wolf. There was only one guarantee at this moment, and that was that he would only have a day left to be human.

Paxton at first thought that everything Gavin was saying was some sort of a joke. The very fact they both worked on a TV show based on the very things that he was telling him about sure suggested that this was some elaborate prank, and that Jett was probably hiding in another room waiting to see the expression on his face. But as every sentence, every word of explanation came out of Gavin's mouth, the picture of his future grew more and more grim and bizarre. The idea of vampires being real, and werewolves, sorcerer, witches, zombies, mummies, gargoyles and even dragons being real was something that he had been taught from a young age, nothing more than fantasies. Little did he know, that not only were they real, but for years he had known a few of them, and they were deliberately hiding their identities from him.

Despite the recent pop culture references, wolves and vampires didn't seem to be enemies. In fact, as soon as Gavin explained things, there were wolves helping them find Jett while Paxton was attempting to process the information that Gavin was now unloading into his mind. Surprisingly, one of the aspects of a potential life as a vampire that gave Paxton thoughts to consider was that he wouldn't actually have to avoid his old life. He could go home, live in the same house, and even see the same people as long as his secret was kept from them. He could continue with his part time acting as well. It was possible that his career as an actor could even be more successful with his additional abilities that would come with his transformation. Gavin hinted, at the fact that some of the latest stars in Hollywood may have used many forms of trickery, besides good agents, to get their gigs.

"So how do we do this then?" Paxton asked, sounding somewhat hopeless as he sat there in his boxer briefs, staring at the floor, with Gavin sitting next to him. He seemed to resign himself to the preference of drinking blood rather than becoming an animal.

"You drink my blood, then I drain you until you're basically dead," Gavin explained in just one sentence. For a few moments, Paxton couldn't quite get over the fact that it was so easily summarized into such a blunt explanation.

"Don't beat around the bush, do you?" Paxton sneered.

"Once I'm done drinking your blood, you'll be weakened enough that you will fall asleep. When you wake up, you won't be human anymore," Gavin continued, still lacking any poetic expression that would remotely make the situation worth cherishing. He knew that in other circumstances, this would be a case where they would be less tense; but with Jett still out there, and Paxton choosing what he was going to do out of very few options, there was nothing to smile about. Gavin also stared down at his hands. There was a very awkward silence in the room, with enough tension to cut through with a chainsaw.

Gavin turned around and picked up an empty glass that, at one time, had held water that they had brought in for Paxton. Bringing it over, he slowly handed it to Paxton. He looked up at the towering vampire in front of him. Gavin's fingers now had some fairly long and sharp nails, almost resembling claws. They were sharp as well, and looked somewhat bestial; they certainly were not human nails anymore. Paxton wanted to look up to meet Gavin's gaze eye to eye, but somehow something in his mind told him that Gavin's face wasn't going to look the same again. Summoning a moment's courage mixed with spontaneity, he looked up to see a pair of deep yellow eyes looking back at him.

"What's with the eye colours? In the forest, your eyes were red, now they're yellow?" Paxton asked with a powerful sense of demanding in his tone.

"Red is rage; yellow is when we feed. Blue, is when we are afraid, or in sadness. Silver is when we're trying to manipulate your thoughts or read your mind." Gavin noted as he brought one of the super-sharp nails to his right wrist and pierced the skin. Immediately, a few drops fell right into the glass that Paxton was holding in his hand. He deepened the cut even more, and the droplets turned into a small stream that slowly started to fill the glass. The glass was half empty, or half full, depending on how Paxton was going to view it.

Gavin thought to himself, how awkward the next procedure of transformation was going to be. Despite the rather romanticized versions of biting one's neck were in literature or the movies and TV shows, it was always going to be physically awkward. Considering that one would have to lean into their victim and practically push themselves against someone, and then bite in, then add to that, the additional awkwardness of the actual biting. Because there was always the chance that the fangs wouldn't be able to break through the skin right away, then there would have to be repeated tries to get the job done with as much speed as possible.

"This is going to be strange," Gavin confessed. The ideas of having to physically lean downward and bite someone's boyfriend's neck were always something that would make any situation awkward.

"That's an understatement," Paxton agreed as he brought the glass of warm blood to his lips. It was an unpleasant sensation. The blood was still warm.

"Think more of it as drinking warm soup," Gavin suggested as he kept watch on the gagging and drinking that Paxton was desperately trying to do. Realistically there wasn't more than half a glass full, and it was more than just the fact that it was a warm salty liquid, it was the fact that it was freshly bled blood from his friend's wrist and he was sitting right next to him. Paxton fought every single natural urge to gag and spit out the stuff that was still invading his mouth, but he had to take it all down. He knew that for sure afterwards he was going to feel incredibly sick from what he was doing right now. Just to make things worse, he opened his eyes just for a moment to see Gavin staring right at him as he was drinking the stuff, almost as though he was completely unaware of the discomfort that Paxton was going through.

"Could you stop that... GAH!" Paxton gasped and he nearly vomited the blood he had just swallowed.

"What?" Gavin asked, shocked at the reaction that Paxton gave him. Paxton was trying to speak, but it was clear that the blood was still obviously distracting him from making any meaningful conversation. He was trying to put words together, but the sheer overwhelming taste of the blood was enough to give anyone a serious shock.

"Staring!" Paxton coughed as he then struggled to maintain control. He knew he would have to drink the stuff, and knew that sooner or later, in the near future, it wouldn't be an issue anymore.

"Oh sorry!" Gavin apologized as he got of the bed, and started to almost aimlessly wander around the room, looking around and fiddling with anything, anything to get his mind off Paxton, and to make him more comfortable. It was always going to be something that could potentially be disruptive, but Gavin tried to be discreet.

Paxton gulped down the last of the blood, and swallowed. He almost dropped the glass before he put it next to him on the bedside table. The residue of the blood was still in the glass, and was starting to coagulate and clot at the edges. Despite this, Paxton oddly felt alright. He sat up from his slouching position, and almost in a temporary feeling of bashfulness, grabbed his black shirt that was draped over the opposite end of the bed. Considering how long he was sitting there shirtless, it seemed strange that suddenly he would feel so self conscious about his state of dress, or lack thereof.

"So... what's next?" Paxton groaned. "Oh god..." he almost gagged.

"You ok?" Gavin asked, without realizing how dumb his statement was. Paxton only rolled his eyes at him as he got his bearings back. He clearly knew what was good to happen next, but it seemed like the natural thing to say to ask the obvious questions. Gavin sat back next to him. He knew what Gavin was going to say, in fact the whole situation was running around his head dozens of times while he was trying to keep his mind off the blood that he was drinking. "Dinner time for me," Gavin smirked. And despite the seemingly odd timed remark, it did reward him with a slight smile on Paxton's perfectly handsome face. Gavin knew that Paxton would make a remarkably successful vampire, with his good looks and natural appeal that now would only be amplified as he would become something beyond human. He would have little trouble getting someone to donate blood to him. "This is going to hurt," Gavin admitted. "It has more to do with the fact that two sharp knives will be puncturing your raw neck more than anything else."

"Just do it quickly, and as fast as possible, please," Paxton requested. The idea of someone nibbling on his neck was a turn on, but feeding on him was a completely different thing. For most people, they never even have to think of something like this happening to them, and certainly not in this context.

Gavin didn't bother beating around the bush with the oddities of the moment, the quiet awkwardness that no doubt running through their minds. Without hesitation he grabbed Paxton by the shoulders and with little effort he planted Paxton on his back over his lap like he was a child. Paxton was rather shocked at this pull but before he realized what was going on, Gavin bent down and sank his fangs right into his neck. As expected, two sharp points stabbed right into his neck. It wasn't quite as painful as he expected, though it certainly wasn't comfortable. It felt like two sharp stinging sensations in his neck as expected. Suddenly the pain of the moment completely vanished as he could actually feel Gavin feeding from him.

He didn't know why, but a sudden wave of safety and protection pulsed through him, as though Gavin was not taking blood but giving him something, something far more powerful and potent. He could answer that easily; Gavin had taken a significant amount of blood already. He could feel himself getting weaker. He lay there across Gavin's lap now, very much weaker. Gavin held his head up not only for Paxton's comfort but also easier access to his neck. As Gavin continued, Paxton was realizing his fate.

"This is it," Paxton thought to himself as he could feel his life starting to drain in remarkable peace. He could feel his own pulse slowing, each beat taking its time before the next. His arms, his legs all were now weakened to the point where he knew there was no way that he could regain his strength. "Jett, I'm going to find you when I awaken!" he promised himself, as darkness overcame him, as he died in Gavin's arms.

Chapter 7

Gavin sat in the living room, staring out at the sunset. It had been almost half a day since he gave his blood to Paxton. He knew the procedure and the process that was happening to Paxton's body that he was going through a very peaceful and quiet transformation. The change from human to High Order was unusually peaceful, one that took place between life and death. Other vampire Orders would often have transformation processes that were extremely painful and filled with the screaming of shrieking pain and agony, but for their own, High Order Vampires would be calm. The body would drift into death as though it was calmly sitting one raft between the realm of the living and the dead.

For them it was a very unique transformation since High Orders were not considered undead like other orders. They maintained a beating heart and their bodies weren't cold like others. Also, words and spells that would normally affect the undead had no effect on them. Their original history, which had become legend, grooms them that their progenitors were at one time undead, but we're so noble and honorable that their creator rewarded them with new life and more powerful abilities. Out of jealousy, the other orders had cursed them to never become superior in numbers, which meant that there could never be any High Order Vampire females.

Gavin would have to explain all this to Paxton when he woke up. Sern had known that the art of transformation was extremely intense for both the sire and the childe, and so he refrained from speaking to him. Cazian was keeping an eye out around the house for the wolves, if they did return with any news of Jett. He was confident that they would find Jett since there were few who could avoid the noses of Prime werewolves.

Sitting quietly while thinking, Gavin couldn't help but think back to his last childe. In fact that childe was pacing around the house right now. He had transformed Cazian a little over ten years ago, and Cazian was quite a well-adjusted and adapted High Order. It was during one of those many sessions in acting class, where Gavin walked into a room full of fresh-faced young students who were all convinced that they were going to be the latest star in Hollywood. Of course since they were up in Canada, this made it particularly intriguing, though not as likely. But that said, Gavin saw and instantly was fixed on the handsome chiseled face, naturally dark brown hair that almost looked black, not unlike his own. But unlike his natural thick swept hair this guy's was stylishly spiked, his eyes were surprisingly gentle. And despite his body which was obviously physically strong from many hours at the gym, he did seem to have a demeanor that was much more softer than his at first, harsh exterior seemed to show.

It wasn't long before they struck up a conversation, then a friendship that developed into a relationship between them. But one thing that Gavin had not realized was that despite their being actors, he didn't apply an actor's level of observation to their relationship. Cazian was always sharp-eyed and always seemed to notice things, and patterns in people's behavior. Gavin didn't realize that Cazian was this scrutinizing in what he saw, so much so that he was even observing his boyfriend.

Since Gavin lived far outside the city, it was not easy for Cazian to find out where he lived. He had always stayed at Cazian's apartment in town when he was there and when he came to visit, so eventually Cazian would want to know where he lived. It took just a quick glance at Gavin's driver's license to learn the address and a GPS lock on Gavin's phone. It was not anything that was entirely out of the ordinary for Cazian, until he arrived at the current home where Gavin lived, and through one of the windows, he spotted Gavin drinking blood, and not just drinking it from a glass, but from someone's neck. To him, at first he felt betrayed, because at first Gavin was getting intimate with someone else; until then it clicked back to him, that it was that Gavin was drinking blood, and from someone's neck.

Of course no one would believe him if he said anything, and he certainly, for a few moments, didn't believe it himself. There were no such things as vampires in the real world, let alone his boyfriend. If that were true, it could only be the plot in some sappy teenage vampire novel. But when the guy who he was feeding on got up and left, and they were carrying a conversation as though it was a real event, Cazian got scared. Since most humans wouldn't quite know how they would react in that situation, the situations are always different when they have their first encounter with the paranormal.

Gavin remembered seeing Cazian walking almost aimlessly away from his house, which was when he sped out of his door to get him, and bring him back. It took a great deal of mind manipulation to get him to calm down. It was then that he had to consult with Hasaan on what to do, but the Intendant, as usual, had the simplest and most effective solutions to offer: sire or erase his mind. Gavin had to go through a similar mind confession right now, doing the same thing to Paxton; but in this case, the circumstances were extremely different. Siring him would not be something like what happened to Cazian; it would be the difference between transforming into an uncontrollable monster, or a controllable monster. Gavin and Paxton both agreed the latter would be the best.

Sern approached Gavin who was now still sitting quietly on the couch, still staring out, but still his mind wandering back to his past. He couldn't really help himself; it was just the natural thing to do, considering the circumstances. Sern placed a tall stainless steel thermos on the coffee table in front of him. Gavin looked down at it with an odd expression of curiosity at the Intendant. His face was looking for an explanation.

"Within the next one hundred and twenty seconds, Paxton will awaken. In there, is freshly drawn donor blood, straight form the veins." The Intendant smiled at him. It was an unusual, and extremely unnatural looking smile, in which the mouth and lips moved but his eyes were still extremely deadpan.

"Experimenting with expressions?" Gavin inquired with one eyebrow raised.

"Unsuccessful, I take it?" Sern asked back.

"I find it amazing that you haven't been that used to our customs and rituals, considering you're an Intendant and you've had encounters with normal people before."

"There hasn't been a need for rampant emotional expressions," Sern sat down. This was also a rather unusual event. Sern rarely had any need to sit. "Perhaps it's time I balanced my host's emotional side with my Essence level intellect," he suggested to himself, "but nonetheless, your childe will awake very soon, and I highly recommend you attend to his needs."

"Yeah," Gavin said almost dismissively, and got up to grab the thermos off the table.

"Otherwise I will have to kill him," Sern stated, again without emotion. Gavin turned back to see the same blank expression on his face. He took a few moments to scan Sern's expression, ever so curious to find out what he meant by what was happening. "How's that for humor?" Sern grinned, as he reached for one of the many magazines to flip through.

Gavin slowly turned the doorknob. The room was still completely dark despite it now nearing darkness outside, and oddly how appropriate that he would now be awaking at sunset. The room was virtually silent, but he could already hear the steady breathing. Paxton was now reanimated and his breath was slow but perfectly rhythmic. He was lying there under the covers, but still wearing that black t-shirt when Gavin drained him. He had made sure to make Paxton as comfortable as possible as he lay there. For a few hours, he was literally dead.

Gavin remembered hearing his heartbeat slow to the point where he no longer had one; in fact, he had to make sure. Luckily with his own blood in Paxton's body, it was just a few hours before he would be resurrected to be one of them. Gavin moved silently towards the bed. He knew what he could do to instantly awaken a newborn, and he was also aware he had to be a bit careful.

Slowly he unscrewed the top cap to the thermos, instantly releasing the scent of iron and blood into the air. Gavin kept an eye on Paxton who, for the moment, was still asleep. But then his eyes flashed open, yellow with hunger. A single sniff of the air revealed the scent of blood, and he was now caught into it. Paxton leaped right at Gavin, like a hungry beast, craving his first taste for blood. Gavin saw the reaction coming and stopped him with his hand, grasped onto Paxton's shoulder, and with a firm hand, quite literally pushed him back down onto the bed. He locked his gaze onto Paxton's now vampiric yellow eyes, hungry for blood. He slowly handed the thermos to Paxton, whose eyes were still fixated on him. The young fledgling snatched the thermos into his hand and started to down the contents without so much as a second thought.

Unlike the Paxton of a few hours ago, this one was hungry and eager to consume. It was usually the case with newborns; they were always hungry and needed to be satisfied quickly. Gavin also knew that they were never in the right frame of mind when they were first transformed and awakened. He watched as Paxton's normally chiseled perfect face was now slightly covered with some of the blood he was slurping down. As he downed the last drop, Paxton looked down almost disappointingly at the now empty thermos, then upwards.

There was blood smeared over his mouth. He was almost panting, due to the fact that he had consumed so much so quickly. Those yellow hungry eyes faded back to his normal blue.

"How do you feel?" Gavin asked as he put his arm around his new childe, holding him close.

"I'm still hungry," Paxton looked up.

"Gotten used to the taste?" Gavin recalled a few hours ago, Paxton couldn't even drink a small cupful of his blood, but then again he was also human a few hours ago.

"Its incredible," Paxton stared back at Gavin. "I can't really explain it; it's just perfect." He stammered, trying to sift through and organizing the massive bombardment of thoughts that were in his mind. He couldn't put it to words; it was this tidal wave of new emotions, feelings, and sensations. He got off the bed and started to look around the room. Despite it being mainly still very dark, he could see everything perfectly fine.

His eyes focused on everything, the mirror at the end of the room, the glass that earlier had contained Gavin's blood, the same blood that had now resurrected him. Then his mind immediately flashed back to the wound that was supposed to be on the left side of his chest. His hands first reached under his shirt for the scab wounds, but they were no longer there. Not a single blemish, not a single flaw was there, his fingers ran along his skin, but there was not a single mark that he could find.

Not wanting to trust his sense of touch, he darted over to the mirror and immediately threw off his t-shirt and looked in the mirror, trying to find where the wolf had scratched him. He also then just recalled, it also bit him on the shoulder, and not a single mark was found on his skin. In fact, after searching his upper body for any marks from the wolf attack, he couldn't help but also now saw his own face looking back at him. Despite the slight smear of blood that had dripped from the side of his lips, he looked to see someone now new starring back at him.

Paxton was always handsome to everyone who saw him. He had the most perfect smile that made anyone blush, but now, somehow there was this unusual haze around him, a type of natural aura. Gavin got up and walked up behind him. He knew what Paxton was feeling and seeing, he had gone through the same thing himself; and every time someone was sired, he also would feel the same thing going through his own mind.

"Feel something?" Gavin asked his childe.

"I see something," Paxton whispered back. It was like he was trying not to disturb his reflection, as though he was looking into a foreign face.

"You have this natural sexual allure," Gavin said, in a fast attempt to educate his childe.

"You mean I sparkle?" Paxton looked back with a growth of panic on his face. "Oh god, please don't tell me I sparkle!" his voice now was almost churning with terror.

"No you don't sparkle," Gavin laughed. The expression of pure fear that was on Paxton's face was absolutely priceless. He wished for a moment that he had a camera to get a picture of that. To a point he couldn't blame Paxton, since there was one particular franchise that had pictured Vampires as sparkly love-torn eternal teenagers, but thankfully that wasn't Eternal Knights. "But you may find that people will be looking at you more."

"That's a good thing," Paxton smiled as he started to get closer to his reflection. Gavin watched as he opened his mouth, starting to examine his teeth.

"Looking for your fangs?" Gavin asked him.

"Yeah," Paxton slurred, finding it odd that he couldn't see them. His canines were just as normal as they were before.

"Focus your mind on the place where your teeth are." Gavin advised. Paxton looked and concentrate on his fangs, and right there in front of him they lengthened and sharpened almost instinctively at his mental concentration. It only took a brief mental thought to do it. "You're going to need those checked out later."

"What do you mean?" Paxton asked through his new fangs, but suddenly almost jabbed his lips with the sharp fangs. "Damn, how do you talk with these things?" he was careful to pronounce his words carefully around the fangs.

"You'll get used to them." Gavin showed him his own. It was a look that Paxton had thought, at first, were the result of makeup, since he had seen Gavin with fangs on.

"Wait, so all those times we worked before, wasn't makeup at all? Your teeth were real?" He asked, thinking back to the many times on set where Gavin and Cazian were surrounded by makeup ladies, polishing his looks.

"Yeah," Gavin retracted his fangs again. "You have to realize, that Eternal Knights is as much as it is a fiction behind the camera as it is in front of the camera. We have to pretend we're humans and actors even when the cameras aren't rolling. When we make appearances in public, we still have to act," Gavin reminded Paxton.

"Luckily I don't have to face that," Paxton mentally commanded his fangs to return to normal, and sure enough to his amazement and astonishment, this time they did exactly what he commanded without any problems.

"Not bad," Gavin patted him on the back as he handed back to Paxton his shirt and then a pair of grey workout sweats pant.

"Thanks," Paxton slipped on the clothes.

"Let's get you some more blood."

As Gavin opened the door, he found Cazian there, as though he was also reaching for the doorknob. The look on his face was an expression of relief. He had no idea why Cazian was standing there, but he could tell that there was something urgent.

"They found him, he's alright!" Cazian shoved his phone back into his pocket as he fixed his eyes on the newborn vampire who was coming out of the room with Gavin.

"He's alright?" Paxton gasped, his face lit up with joy as well as an obvious sign of relief.

"Yeah, they're coming back already; he should be back in a few minutes." Cazian reported.

For Paxton this was a moment long time coming. He had to be virtually sedated twice because of the hysteria that he was feeling. Though for a few moments after he awoke as a vampire, he felt oddly completely oblivious to the fact that his boyfriend was missing. Though he had some confidence that they would find him, he wasn't entirely too sure, even despite the fact that there were now real werewolves and vampires around him, let alone that he would eventually become one himself. It was one of those odd moments where he knew that if he was going to be able to concentrate on anything else, it would be a virtual impossibility.

"Here, I'll get you a drink," Gavin hurried to the kitchen to fetch more blood from the fridge. It was very fortunate that they kept a well-stocked supply. Paxton's stomach growled for a moment, letting loose that tingling vibration from his gut that seemed to attract everyone's attention into him for a brief moment, just enough to assure them that yes indeed, this new fledgling was hungry. As he also turned to the kitchen, he found someone else standing there, someone he didn't recognize.

He wore a canvas colour, almost beige suit. It was quite loose and looked almost more like a robe than a suit that went down to almost knee level. It had some strange geometric designs on it that were silver and almost looked illuminated. The lines went up, down sideways in a series of right angles. Paxton couldn't tell what ethnicity he was, or what cultural background he was, but it seemed to be possibly half Asian and half Caucasian. He certainly had similar black hair to himself, but his face seemed almost artificial, in that he didn't seem to have any true form of expression. Despite this, the fellow calmly approached Paxton and reached out his hand for a handshake.

"Greetings," He welcomed. His voice had a tinge of enthusiasm in it. His tone sounded like he was testing a new phrase he had just learned. It was awkward to say the least.

"Hi," Paxton welcomed the handshake back. "Sorry, you are?" he inquired.

"My name is Sern." he introduced himself with a slight almost oddly timed smile.

"Paxton," Paxton replied, almost like he had to repeat himself to make it clear to the guy.

"Yes I know," Sern shook the hand firmly before letting go.

"Do you work with Cazian and Gavin?" Paxton asked the fellow who now pulled out one of the kitchen chairs for Paxton to sit. "Thanks." He replied as he sat down.

"Yes, I am one of the Intendants." Sern introduced in a monotone.

"Well I've never seen you on the set before," Paxton commented.

"Sern doesn't work on the set." Cazian came up, and started to get a few towels from one of the cupboards in the hallway. He had to prepare for Jett's return. He had no idea what kind of state he would be in; likely he would have to be cleaned off first before they let him rest. For beings like Vampires, cleanliness was always still something to maintain. He disappeared back into the guest room with a stack of black towels in his arms.

"There's more that I believe Gavin should explain to you," Sern described with his simple tone, "but suffice to say, you are now a part of a far larger and different world."

Gavin, through the entire discussion, was waiting for the microwave to heat up a rather large beer mug of the blood. It was about three cups full, more than the thermos. Though it was storage blood, and not entirely fresh, with the warming to body temperature it would be more than adequate. He wasn't going to be picky on the blood types, but he knew that a variety was usually the best way to go. For him, he had never even cared about what type of blood he was drinking, though usually he preferred human. That was another entire discussion that he would have to explain and teach Paxton. It was always these things, about getting used to a new lifestyle that he had to explain, and somehow made him seem more paternal than normal. Though now Cazian could also share in some of this, but even Gavin wasn't too sure how Cazian would react into being conscripted as a new parent.

"Here!" Gavin placed the enormous beer mug, made out of glass, onto the table in front of Paxton. He stared at the blood, its perfect colour and scent was almost calling to him. The metallic smell, which at one time would have easily made any human nervous, now didn't bother him one bit; in fact, he savoured the aroma. Sern wasn't reacting one way or another, but Paxton seemed almost to resist its taste just to experience the rare opportunity to see blood, unspoiled, in front of him before he grasped it with both hands and brought it to his lips.

This time his drinking was far less ravenous and bestial. It was civilized as he took gulp after gulp. Gavin looked almost proudly at him as he slowly but steadily downed all of the blood with a steady pace. When he was done, he gently placed the glass beer mug back onto the table. Gavin casually handed him a paper napkin, then pointed to the top of his own lips, indicating to Paxton that he had a blood moustache on his face. Slightly embarrassed, Paxton quickly wiped it off. He certainly felt different, as though his body was completely energized and restored. For a few moments, he was actually able to feel enhanced sensations on his skin, more so than before. It was slightly distracting that almost every bit of skin. He looked around to notice that everyone was somewhat staring at him silently. Sern in particular, was looking rather intensely at him. Cazian, though had his eyes on Paxton, was only giving him a glance while he was also tapping his phone against his hand, waiting for additional news.

"I think you're the first fledgling young childe they had met." Gavin whispered to Paxton, in reference to Sern's rather inquisitive nature.

"Yeah, but its kind of creepy," Paxton whispered back. Immediately Sern halted his visual inspection of Paxton, reacting to what he had just said.

"I apologize. I did not mean to cause offence," The Intendant stated rather formally. "You are the first, of the High Order Childes that I have met," Sern started to inspect Paxton again, paying attention to his eyes in particular. It was as though he was examining sinew sort of biological experiment taking in the view of his eyes and how they seemed to change. The instant that they tasted blood, their eyes would naturally change yellow. This was really the only way to reveal their true abilities and nature to people. Slowly, even without realizing it, Paxton's eyes had reverted to their normal blue. "Your eyes are quite fascinating. Though I am sure that over the course of time, Gavin will familiarize you with your newfound abilities."

Gavin knew that he was going to be the guardian and teacher who would be responsible for teaching Paxton what it was to be what he had now become. It was something that Gavin had gone through before with Cazian and other Childes so nothing entirely new for him was going to be expected. However, there was one notable difference in the situations. Assuming, of course, that Jett was going to be turned into a werewolf, even modern fictions and stories haven't covered the possibilities that a werewolf and a vampire would be boyfriends. It was a strange situation, to say the least.

There was an unusual benefit to this situation, and that was that Paxton was now a High Order Sanguinarian, meaning he would be completely immune to all werewolf bites. To make it even safer for him, he would be stronger and faster than them in a few weeks, and with a werewolf boyfriend who was going to be fighting his urge to transform rather frequently, having a vampire boyfriend may not be such a bad thing.

In the corner of his eye, Gavin spotted three figures coming down the road towards the house. Thanks to the design of their home, he could see out of smaller windows without the outsiders being necessarily able to see inside. Two of them were rather tall and powerfully imposing, and the third was a shorter fellow. Already Gavin could smell the scent of blood on him; what he could smell was instantly recognizable, not of human but animal, likely deer. The game-like scent was one that even humans could recognize, especially if they ever ate meat from wildlife. The slight musk and pungent scent of deer blood, was something that was rare for even vampires to drink from, but all it takes is just one sniff to recognize it.

Like Gavin, Paxton also caught the scent of blood, over his finished drink; it was strange and distinctive. Naturally sniffing the air and looking around, Paxton wondered where that scent was coming from. Then out of the corner of his own eye, he caught sight of the three people walking towards the house. He could instantly recognize the face and form of the shorter one! It was Jett! Paxton sprung up from his seat and raced for the door, faster than any movement that he realized was possible, zooming past Sern and Cazian like a speeding car, leaving almost just a blur behind him. He grasped the metallic handle and pulled. The door was ripped right off its metal steel hinges, scattering crumbs of drywall and wood everywhere. Paxton looked bewildered, not realizing that already in that short time, his strength had already grown enormously. The door was still well weighted in his hand, but as he put it down, he looked back to see Gavin and Cazian with smirks on their faces.

"Sorry," he apologized, suddenly losing all attention for a moment at the stunned revelation of his now superhuman level of strength. Suddenly he felt a wave of guilt at his destruction of someone else's property.

"Don't worry about it," Gavin took the door aside, then gestured out of the door at the three who were now coming up the porch. Tears almost filled Paxton's eyes as he ran down and picked up Jett in a hug. He dashed past the other two wolves who were escorting Jett. He squeezed so hard for a moment that he almost crushed his boyfriend who gasped for air. There were no words exchanged and there didn't have to be any. Paxton didn't let go and neither did Jett as they stayed in their embrace. Gavin could see tears streaming down Paxton's newborn face, same with Jett who hugged him back. At least now, they were reunited. But now came the tougher tasks.

Trey approached Gavin through the quiet hug that Paxton was giving to Jett. He ushered him a bit farther away for some slight privacy.

"I'm going to be heading back to town. I think it's best if I keep a watch on the local wolf hangouts, just to make sure everything is alright."

"Do whatever you can. I'm sure Sern will be fine with that."

"And I'm trusting that Coltrane and Trenton will be fine training this new wolf, right?"

"They should be fine, yes."

"If I have any news I'll let you guys know." Trey shook Gavin's hand as he got back into his car, and drove off into the distance, disappearing from sight.

Chapter 8

Sern viewed the holographic projection of various data documents in front of his eyes. The glowing green display, with various text forms that he had conveniently translated into North American English were flowing steadily as his eyes moved from paragraph to paragraph. Thanks to a very reliable connection to Aurastar and the Transport Hub's information networks, which would make the human Internet seem like smoke signals, Sern was able to access vast amounts of data from their central archives; and so far, after reading through a few dozen novels by various writers, it was a fascinating portrayal of the supernatural.

Apparently each writer had his or her own interpretation of the supernatural. The fascinating part was that there was always something unique that each writer gave to their creatures, and yet no one got them right. There was one writer who was quite accurate, a quiet one in Vancouver, but there was little else that was found on his identity. Apparently the use of alternative names, better known as "pen names" was frequently common amongst writers. The most interesting thing that was present was the vast majority of large scale exposure of the Supernatural, was actually sponsored, and created by the Supernaturals themselves.

Eternal Knights was a prime example of this global system of reverse psychology. Sern had to admire the effectiveness it had, in not only numbing humans to the concept of the supernatural but also in bringing in enormous amounts of income and money, that helped them supply their many Coven Houses, and Cloisters that protected the Supernatural. It was an ingenious system of open deception that they used. In some cases they were outright lampooning themselves right in front of a human audience, and other times it was more serious but still open deception.

Sern had to admire the cunning plan, to take the money from the very people they were fooling, to portray themselves as over the top. Oddly in some cases, other Supernaturals even fell for it themselves. Sern saw the financial records for just the Eternal Knights franchise since it was handled by much of the Sanctuary Organization as well as influential Supernaturals. By using those financial resources that they had acquired over centuries to fund this enterprise, then to turn the benefits back into larger investments, Supernaturals had considerably financial clout.

Without a doubt they were also familiar with the fact that they had to maintain secrecy and desensitizing the public to their existence was the best way to accomplish this. It was probably the smartest method that they could use for multiple purposes. On the one hand, take money from the humans, second, making them believe that the supernatural world was nothing more than a figment of human imagination and creation. All in all there seemed to be few other methods around that would make the benefits high and the risk low.

To Sern, the arrival of two new Supernaturals within his first few days was already something that he had not fully expected. He did trust that Gavin, Trenton, Cazian and the others would be able to handle the situation without any problems. The records that Hasaan had left were more than accurate in portraying the Wolf Coven Members as reliable teachers in these cases. Sern had confidence but he also knew, that nothing spoke better than first hand encounters.

One of the many holographs that he was inspecting was the frequency in which Wolf Packs would be seen. Normally, the Prime Wolves would have little trouble finding them or even detecting their scent as they moved through the areas. Many werewolves preferred to transform during full moons, deep in the forests, even those who didn't live with them at Wolf Coven House. They knew that Wolf Coven members and Wolf Coven land was safe to change, so this was where they would often stay during full moons, but this attack was not like the other ones.

Sern did mind searches on Gavin, Cazian and the identities of the wolves was not known. However, it was clear, based on their attack, physical appearances, scent and abilities were clearly Bloodbanes. The identity wasn't difficult to come by. Bloodbanes were known for their aggression and their tendency to attack, however usually they would try to attack vampires since vampire blood gave them enhanced strength, and was an addictive drug to them, but normally they would never be foolish enough to attack a High Order, let alone two of them. Something about this entire situation did seem extremely suspicious. Sern was not one to let something this obviously sinister go unchecked. To him, if something didn't make sense, it's worth investigating

"He's a werewolf." Paxton sighed as he closed the door to the bedroom behind him. Jett was exhausted. Cleaning off the blood on his hands and face was something that, for him, was an odd feeling. He wanted to lick it off, since the scent of blood was still alluring. But for him it was an odd feeling, it was like even though you were on a full stomach, you still enjoyed the scent of your favorite food cooking nearby. Though he liked the scent, he wasn't interested in having anymore. He had enough. Gavin came up and put his arm around Paxton, comforting him with the feeling of a huge arm around him.

"Yes. I can't transform him with my blood like how I did with you. He already shifted once into a wolf, I can't override that transformation," Gavin admitted with a sense of apology in his voice.

"Is there anything that I can do?" Paxton asked, desperately seeking some way to help his boyfriend.

"You already know. Turning into what he is, will vastly increase his aggression. He's basically an animal now, but luckily for him, and somehow fatefully he won't hurt you. He'll need you." Gavin assured Paxton. "And on top of that, we're here too."

"Wait, what about our lives? His job, family, my job and friends, our mortgages, taxes?" Paxton started to panic again, but this, in Gavin's eyes, was a worthwhile reason. One thing that books and movies never covered, was the fact that if one had been transformed into a supernatural creature, what would happen to their human lives? This wasn't found in other sappy teenage vampire love stories except to live through high school forever.

"Well, when it comes to something like that, there are usually two options. New life or old life. New life will require more work, which Sern will take care of."

"Why is a new life tougher?"

"With your old life, you will go back to your place after this week-long holiday is over, and proceed with everything as though nothing has changed," Gavin started, however, he followed with strong hesitation. "But, if you do that, you will have to be always on your guard, always watching your moves. And since you can be revealed, by the taste of blood, and even your hormones, you may risk exposure, and that would lead to serious trouble and damage control."

"Is that what you chose?"

"Yeah. I live a relatively normal life. I have two homes, this one and another one at Wolf Coven House, where others like me and the wolves live. But when in public making those appearances, I have to be extremely careful. Luckily I never slipped up."

"And a new life?" Paxton leaned against the wall, looking up to Gavin who stood next to him.

"That is usually the easiest. I don't know the exact details because it's always done by the Intendants who are in charge. But suffice to say, all your records, your very existence, everyone's memories of you, are wiped. They literally go through your memory, go through every thought that you have ever had, which usually takes a long time, and then reference those, and erase you from everyone else who is not a supernatural being."

"What about family?" Paxton asked, this time, for a moment, considering the future he would have, losing everyone he had known. It was as though he had died, but things like, never ever seeing his friends, family, and relatives again was something that he never considered.

"As from what the Intendants tell me, everyone has their memories blocked and modified. I don't know how they do it, but it just ends up being done. The most important thing is you can never reveal yourself to them deliberately. You may run into them, but they won't recognize you." Paxton sighed as he leaned on the door, then almost collapsed to the ground. He cupped his face in his hands as he sighed deeply.

"You alright?"

"Alright?" Paxton murmured. He groaned yet again, this time visibly frustrated, but again under the circumstances, Gavin could sympathize. "In the past few days, I was attacked with rabid werewolves, learned that vampires and werewolves were both real, then being turned into a vampire myself, found out that my boyfriend had just been turned into a werewolf, and now I have to make the choice of hiding my new nature from everyone or deciding to erase myself from all their memories, losing all friends, family and relatives forever?!?" Paxton's volume was getting louder. "How do you fucking expect me to be?" He threw his hands off his face and leaped to his feet. Gavin knew that there was little that he could do to respond at the moment. He knew that Paxton was justified in every bit of frustration that he felt.

Normally for someone who was bitten and transformed, that alone would be enough to warrant this type of internal frustration.

Gavin could only sympathize with what was going through Paxton's mind. Even for him, when he was transformed, he didn't have to go through this much distress. But for Paxton, it was also the addition of his boyfriend being transformed, and now the prospect that they would not ever be able to return to their normal lives, and potentially lose contact with their families, friends and everyone else they have ever met. It was a position that no one would want to be in, and Gavin knew that he had his duty, as a Sire, to help Paxton.

"You don't need to make any decision right now," Gavin assured him. He placed his hand gently on Paxton's shoulder, then hugged him. It was all that Paxton needed for the time being to keep himself calm. Cazian came around the corner, after fixing the door that Paxton had ripped off the hinges earlier. He patted Paxton on the back gently. He could instantly tell what was going on. The sheer mental stress that Paxton was going through, luckily for Cazian, he had never had to go through before.

"We're brothers now," Cazian assured Paxton. "You don't have to go through this alone."

"He still has a week until the full moon. When that happens, you will have to be there for him, and even until then it will be tough," Gavin warned, not wanting to bring the issue up so soon, but he knew it had to be said sooner rather than later.

"I thought he only transformed during a full moon," Paxton wondered as Gavin released him from the hug. He stepped over to where the large leather couches were and sat down. He needed to sit down even though his legs weren't tired. It was just so he could process the information going through his head.

"He was bitten by a Bloodbane type of werewolf. They're slightly different. They're a very aggressive race of wolves," said a familiar voice that came down from the upstairs. It was the six-foot-seven frame of Trenton followed by Coltrane, another equally imposing man, descending down the stairs.

"Not like you?" Paxton was slightly confused. Trenton sat down at the couches, joining Cazian and Gavin.

"No. We're Primes. We don't have anything like packs." Trenton explained. "Wolves, like Vampires, aren't just two basic species; there are lots of sub-species, divisions between them. There are some werewolves who actually turn into an actual wolf. Then there are some who remain mostly human, but can morph partially into wolf-like humans."

"And then there's the enormous man-wolves." Gavin pointed at Coltrane and Trenton, indicating that they were the ones whom he was referring to.

"Well we can do more than that," Trenton smirked with a friendly nudge from Coltrane. Paxton noticed that Coltrane, despite being introduced earlier, was a person of few words. Unlike Trenton who was surprisingly quite gentle despite being physically imposing, Coltrane was shorter, though still taller than the average man, and much rougher in appearance. He also looked older than Trenton, possibly up to ten years older. He certainly had quite the eyes. He had his own imposing appearance that gave others a good warning that he wasn't one to be messed with. Coltrane seemed like the type of guy who, if you messed with him, with a single glare, he could freeze your blood.

For a brief moment, it seemed like Trenton was going to continue explaining, but then there was an awkward silence that filled the room. It was almost like he didn't realize that he was expected to continue explaining the situation.

"Well?" Paxton interrupted, breaking the silence that was filling the air. It gave Trenton a little surprise for a moment until he realized he was expected to mention the additional forms they could take.

"Man-wolf," Coltrane stated, with a sense of pride in his voice. "Some wolves can turn into true wolves; others take on wolf-like qualities but remain mostly human. Then there are those who can take on the best of both. We can do all of them, but it takes a certain amount of training."

"And what about the aggression that takes over? And what about the full moon?" Paxton asked, not only for himself but also for Jett, who, if anything was going to happen to him, he would have to control that animalistic rage that Paxton guessed would come, with being part animal.

"Our rage is easily controlled. We don't really feel it, but you have to remember, Jett is not a Prime Wolf, he's a Bloodbane, meaning that for him, rage will always be an issue. And I think that Gavin told you earlier, the fact that you're a High Order will actually help you keep him under control. You're immune to the wolf bite, and you're stronger than he is now. If anything, he's lucky to have you," Trenton said, with comfort in his voice. Despite the fact that his sheer size could make him a force to be reckoned with, Trenton's physical size and imposing strength was diffused by the fact that he seemed to be a gentle giant. "And as for the full moon, we're not affected by the moon at all, except when we want to create another Prime Wolf."

"You do it during the full moon?"

"It's only possible on the full moon. If a Prime Wolf bites you on any other day, you won't be turned. But if it happens on a full moon, a human would be turned into a Prime Wolf."

"Crazy, all this stuff," Paxton thought to himself. "How much does he already know?"

"On the way back, we explained most of it to him, his situation and that you were also changed. When we found him, he was already feral."

"Feral?" The term confused Paxton for a moment. As he realized, what they were implying was that Jett had already gone through his first transformation.

"Yes," Trenton nudged Coltrane. "Show him," he asked the other wolf.

"Wait, I thought you two and Jett were different types of wolves." Paxton asked, perplexed at what they were about to show him. Wolf Primes? Bloodbanes? So many different types, and what they could and could not do.

Coltrane stood up, and took off the leather jacket he was wearing, casually dropping it onto the couch. Underneath was a tight white t-shirt that did quite little to cover up his physique, which was that of a very powerful, fit man. He closed his eyes for a brief moment, like he was mentally concentrating on something. Paxton watched in amazement, as Coltrane seemed to be able to change his own eye colour at will. They were fading into a bestial form of yellow, though not like how his own looked. His were a solid, almost organic colour, but Coltrane's were something very different, yellow but speckled with lines of black. They were certainly wolf eyes. It gave Paxton a slight shock to see them at first, until he realized that this was more of a demonstration than anything else.

His hands were the next thing that he demonstrated to Paxton. He brought them down close to Paxton so he could get a good view of them. The fingernails were thickening, darkening as they started to lengthen and sharpen. Paxton watched intently as the claws started to form, and even the fingers slightly lengthen to accommodate them. The hair on Coltrane's arms were also thickening, growing out more, as though their purpose was to deflect the slashing of tree branches and debris as they sprinted through the forests. Paxton looked up from the claws to the face that was now staring down at him. Coltrane's fangs were emerging. Paxton watched, as not only the top canines but the bottom ones also extended. Unlike his own vampire fangs, which were sharp but still had the regular thickness of a normal tooth, Coltrane's were noticeably thicker.

Coltrane's thick slick black hair stayed the same, but seemed to grow down along the sides of his face, much like the fur on a wolf's face. Thankfully he didn't look like the wolf man from those black and white movies. His face was now far more bestial, some ridges, from between his eyes, slightly down to the top of his nose. Combined with the claws, and eyes, and fur, Coltrane truly did look like quite the half-human half-beast that they were describing earlier. For Paxton, it wasn't a matter of words that helped the image, it was actually seeing him standing there, fangs ready, claws ready that gave him the realization of what his boyfriend was going to turn into.

Seeing Jett standing there in front of him, Paxton couldn't help but be worried about what he was seeing. He he was also constantly reminded of the fact that he was actually stronger than all werewolves, which did give him a strange sense of comfort. But it was something that he wouldn't have expected if he hadn't been told on what the extent of his own abilities were.

"Grrr," Cazian teased Coltrane, who shot him a dirty look. Coltrane faced him and gave out a powerful, bestial roar, his mouth and fangs glistened as though he was going to attack. Paxton almost leaped back out of his seat when he did that. Coltrane's back was crouched over like he was ready to leap and attack Cazian. But Cazian didn't flinch at all. Instead, he turned, from casually leaning up against one of the walls. He had his arms folded across his chest, as though he didn't have a care in the world, almost mockingly ignoring Coltrane's posture, which was clearly aggressive.

Cazian brought down his arms, and then out of his back, he sprouted two enormous dragon-bat like wings! Paxton couldn't believe his eyes as the two wings unfurled themselves and spread outwards, displaying their enormous wingspan, right there in Gavin's living room. He stared at Cazian as he showed off an ability that he had seen, but like many abilities prior, he swore it was just a result of special effects. He walked over to Cazian, still staring at the two wings that came out of his back, somehow magically, just going through his clothes without ripping them. Somehow out of the back of his shirt, two openings appeared for his wings to emerge. Looking closer, Paxton could tell that those holes were pre-made into the shirt, and had reinforced schemes to avoid them from ripping any further.

Paxton was anything but scared, in fact he was rather fascinated by what he saw. He couldn't help but watch as Cazian expanded his wings closed them for his benefit.

"That's so cool," he gasped. Without intention, he reached out and touched the wings. They were large, like they were made out of leather, but the skin was thick, yet soft to the touch, firm, yet also from what he saw, they could take quite a beating if they needed to.

"That was one feature I was hoping to surprise you with," Gavin grunted at Cazian, who had effectively spoiled his surprise. Paxton, unknowingly, was ignoring the fact that Cazian's own eyes had morphed to a deadly red; his own vampiric fangs ready and out of his own hands were sharp talon-like nails. Almost by accident he looked upwards, to see the vampiric face glaring down at him, though with a certain playfulness that was a trademark of Cazian's personality.

Paxton almost fell backwards when he saw Cazian's face, and now with the addition of his wings, and claws, it was something more ferocious than playful to his image. He was aware of what he was seeing, the vampiric form that was always featured on the Eternal Knights posters that were on bus stops and billboards that were always featured around town. All this time, he had sworn that these looks were the result of special effects. Even when he was on the film set, he would always see them surrounded by makeup ladies, special effects people who were gluing small prosthetics to their faces.

"I swore that when I was filming the show with you that these were fake," Paxton realized, after thinking back to his experience on the TV show's set.

"Well yes, and no," Cazian smirked as he slowly retracted the wings back into his back. When he did, Paxton got right back up to him and watched as Cazian's wings simply vanished, almost magically back into Cazian's back, not leaving a single bump or indication that they even existed there before! The openings in the back of his shirt were still there, like they were made for his condition, but the wings, nothing.

"Take off your shirt!" Paxton demanded, like a child wanting to find the solution to a magic trick that he had just seen. Cazian couldn't help but smirk at the sexually suggestive words that came from Paxton's mouth. Even he had not realized what he had just said, with the fact that his boyfriend was asleep in the other room just off the side of the hallway from where they were sitting. "I never knew that you were into group things, Paxton," Cazian grinned at him. Even Gavin and the wolves were slightly amused at this.

"No, I just wanted to see..." Paxton started to explain before he even caught on to what Cazian was implying. "Oh, shut up, you know what I mean!" he nudged Cazian. "I want to see where your wings went!" he almost demanded. Cazian's expression changed to a form of submission, as he slowly unbuttoned his white silk dress shirt. Almost like he was performing a mock strip tease that certainly did help in lightening the mood he dropped the shirt right to the ground with that typical seductive tease that Cazian was known for both in front and behind the camera. Paxton then immediately put his hand on Cazian's back, the natural chill of his touch giving Cazian a slight surprise.

Aside from normal human looking flesh, there was no sign at all of the wings. Paxton, though perplexed was able to accept this as some form of supernatural power that he had at first not heard of, but in this situation, he was going to just accept it without question, something that normally he wouldn't do. "Gavin, when do I get my wings?" Paxton demanded from his sire. It seemed that this ability was one that he was already quite eager to get.

"It's not an easy task but I'll explain that all later. It has to do with a mental awakening. It's not an easy task to achieve for yourself. Not everyone goes through it the same way," Gavin explained with some disappointment. He could tell that in part, it was the hyper-sensitivity of Paxton's emotional state that was making him excited one moment, then sad the other, a trait that was not uncommon amongst fledgling newborn vampires. He knew that he had to maintain some level of training with Paxton. Emotional mood swings was one of the most unnoticeable symptoms of a new form, unnoticeable from the perspective of the fledgling, but not for a Sire It was natural that he have some form of emotional link to his creation.

Paxton turned to Coltrane who was still in his werewolf form.

"So this form that you're in right now, is that what Jett will look like?" he asked Trenton. The tall werewolf nodded in compliance.

"Yes. This is the form. We can take the same form but we, as Primes, have different ones as well. We can turn into the man-wolves, which are basically while walking on two feet; we become the half human half animal creatures, full wolf-form faces and heads, claws and feet but on two hind legs; or we can drop to all fours, and fully take on a true wolf form, albeit a much larger creature than those in the wild," he explained before pointing back to Coltrane. "But that is what Jett will look like, and unlike Coltrane, he's probably going to be a lot meaner."

"Can I do anything to help him calm down?" Paxton urged, hoping for a cooperative answer from Gavin and the others. Gavin looked over to Cazian, who was slipping his shirt back on. Cazian simply pointed to his own eyes, indicating something to Gavin.

"Well, there's the power of mental suggestion. You can try to calm him down with your gaze."

"Is that another superpower that I have?" Paxton asked his sire.

"Yes," Gavin admitted with some reluctance. His emotional state was something that Paxton did not expect at the moment.

"What's wrong?" his childe asked him.

"For the time being, you have to be aware that you are going to have to learn to control all of these new abilities you have. You're not human anymore ,and you have to learn how to deal with these effects," Gavin warned. He knew that he was going to have quite a time to train Paxton how to control his abilities, his strength, his various mental abilities, everything. It took Cazian some time to learn his abilities as well. And after going through this with seven different childes, Paxton being his eighth, Gavin already knew the techniques. With other Orders of vampires, it was much easier considering their lesser abilities mainly involved strength, and blood; but High Orders, with the myriad number of powers that they had at their disposal, was a bit complicated. Of course the last power, which was flying, was the skill that only Dominic had mastered since that was more of a matter of aerodynamics than it was about supernatural control, mental stability, or bloodlust.

Without doubt, Gavin was sure that Paxton would be willing to go through this training, in part due to the fact that he was also going to be responsible for maintaining safety for Jett. Paxton had the unusual position of protecting his boyfriend with his vast array of new potentially superhuman powers.

Paxton sat in the bedroom, watching over Jett who lay in bed. Of course he was exhausted and unlike Paxton, he was able to put himself into bed. Paxton remembered Trenton and Coltrane had told Paxton, that they found Jett devouring the body of a deer that no doubt he had killed himself. He was feral at the time, having temporarily lost his sense of control. Luckily, the two Wolf Primes had little problem tracking him down despite his newly enhanced speed. They tracked and cornered him. Trenton and Coltrane did find it odd, that he wasn't with any of the other wolves.

The instinctive need to hunt and kill prey was something that all wolves naturally had. Being bitten by a Bloodbane and turning into one of them, then being abandoned without anyone helping or training Jett to keep in touch with his humanity, he was effectively a wild animal. It didn't take much to bring him back, though an effective karate chop to the back of the head from Coltrane knocked him out. When he came to, they gave him the speech on what he was. Like Paxton, Jett had difficulty accepting what he became, until he looked down to see the corpse of a dead deer, killed by his own claws, and flesh ripped apart by his own fangs. His clothes were covered in blood, and there were bits of the deer's fur and flesh dug into his claws, from how he killed the creature.

Thankfully he was in more of a daze and was exhausted enough to fall right to sleep after Paxton cleaned him up. A good thing too, considering it would have been difficult to get him to fall asleep if he was enraged. But it was still enough mental discontent for the time being for him to stir around. It had already been a good five hours since he was put in at sundown. Now it was already late evening, and Paxton could tell that he was going to be awake soon. Watching him sleep was something he never really did before. He knew that he had to maintain a distance, in case he had some form of night terrors.

After a while, even Paxton was starting to doze off for a bit. He didn't want to rest on the bed, in case he would wake up Jett from his sleep. Resting his head up against the wall, Paxton had to take a temporary mental time out. It had been a long few days and enough had happened already. For the moment, what mattered now was that he was safe, Jett was safe, and they were protected from the outside world. Everything else for the time being could wait until Jett woke up. Paxton dozed off; his eyes slowly drooped shut from sheer exhaustion of the day's worries. It was enough to make anyone tire himself out.

Jett's eyes sprang open, yellow and speckled. Without moving, he could instantly detect a familiar scent. It was a primal scent, something he was instantly drawn to. He gave the air a few more subtle sniffs before he turned his head. In the corner of the room, sat Paxton, quietly sleeping, with his head lay back against the wall. Jett's claws started to form at the edge of his hands, the razor sharp claws, growing out of his nails, his fangs starting to grow sharper as he rolled over off his back. Every movement he made was silent, as his claws moved him quietly closer to the edge of the bed, every single move, smooth and silent. His vision focused on Paxton, quietly sleeping there, and completely unaware of who was watching him, unaware and vulnerable.

Prowling like the beast that he was, he watched for a few moments, almost crouched down on the bed. Jett was now almost as still as a statue, like a wolf in the wild, stalking his prey, but this time it was something more. The familiar scent of Jett didn't trigger his stomach, but another primal urge, just as vital as the need to eat. Jett quietly crawled off the bed onto the ground, as stealthy and silent as ever as he prowled towards Paxton, who was still unaware of what was going on. The naturalistic primal call of his instincts had taken over as he neared Paxton; there was only one thing on his mind. Without even a word, he sprang to his feet, and grabbed Paxton by the shoulders with his claws, but careful enough not to rip or hurt him. His enhanced werewolf strength kicked in, as did his adrenaline, as even without a single sound, he threw Paxton onto the bed. Paxton was momentarily stunned when Jett grabbed him; but now, in his bewilderment at his position, lying there on the bed, and seeing a primal, feral half-shifted Jett standing over him, Paxton had a feeling that he knew what was going to happen.

Chapter 9

Outside Jett and Paxton's room, the sounds of the inside ruckus were somewhat audible, to Trenton who was sitting, watching television. Cazian and Coltrane had returned, and said that Sern was going to go back to Wolf Coven House. A text message from Coltrane indicated that Sern wanted to have them housed at Wolf Coven House for everyone's safety, including theirs. Gavin was in the kitchen, preparing some of the sushi that they had bought, for Jett. Jett was still on a human diet, and so likely he would be hungry after such a long ordeal. As for Trenton, he instantly detected the subtle noises coming from the bedroom. Certainly it was rough but not violent.

Without turning down the volume of the television, Trenton turned his eyes over to Gavin who didn't seem to notice anything from the kitchen. He crept quietly up to the door and placed his ear against it. Carefully filtering out the noise from the television, he concentrated carefully on the sounds inside. A lot of grunting, panting, and heaving of breath, some almost primal growls, but certainly nothing that he could tell that was disagreeable. Trenton realized what was going on inside! If he opened the door, he would not only see what was happening, but also smell it. Though he would never dare interrupt such an intimate moment, Trenton did want to make sure that his sense of hearing wasn't fooling him, but he was pretty sure he knew what was going on inside.

Slowly, crouching down to the bottom of the door, where the slight opening between the hardwood floor and the doorway met, the scent of the intimate actions within the room was slowly filtering out. A High Order couldn't detect anything, but Trenton's nose was far more sensitive. And sure enough, that scent of sweat, and other smells confirmed it right away.

Gavin looked over from the kitchen to see Trenton crouched down at the base of the door, with his face stuck in the corner between the bottom of the door and the hardwood floor. Wondering what he was doing, Gavin walked up to Trenton with one eyebrow raised.

"Something going on inside?" Gavin inquired. He had a feeling that it had something to do with his wolf senses but wasn't entirely too sure.

"No, well yes, but..." Trenton tried to explain, but was caught trying to censor what he was going to say before he said it. It was clear from the expression on his face that Trenton clearly knew it was a deeply personal situation that they really shouldn't interrupt.

"Are they...?" Gavin asked, the last word was missing but it was well implied what it was. Then a loud groan, then another series of heavy gasps, and more noises of a very sexual nature were being emitted from the room. Even Gavin was absolutely sure what was going on.

"Yes, they are." Trenton smirked. Sometimes there really was no need for any words to be spoken; a single expression can say as much as a thousand words.

"Do you think they were doing it doggy style?" Gavin laughed, unable to resist the temptation to make that type of remark, which only rewarded him with a sarcastic smirk from Trenton.

"They are what?" Sern asked as he came through the front door, only hearing the end of the conversation. His sudden appearance gave them a slight shock of surprise that they weren't expecting. They had known that Sern would be returning after doing some checking at Wolf Coven House, probably was preparing some quarters for them there too before they would all return to the house.

"Nothing." Gavin and Trenton said, at the same time. Their instant denial didn't go unnoticed; but from what Sern knew, it was probably best not to push the issue. However that said, their remarks were quite odd.

"I have made accommodations at Wolf Coven House already. We have an abundance of surplus apartments there and they can move into a secure location."

"We haven't asked them about that yet actually." Gavin replied. "I'm not even sure Jett is awake yet."

"Well it is imperative that they be relocated quickly. When they wake up, please have them brought to Wolf Coven House." Sern walked over to the kitchen. Trenton turned to Gavin.

"We have to get these boys ready soon." Gavin instructed Trenton.

"Sern," Trenton followed the Intendant to the kitchen, "we will handle things here." he suggested to the Intendant.

"Very well," Sern answered, "we have all the accommodations ready." Sern headed out of the front door again.

"You know, if all you had were these instructions, you could have just texted them to us," Gavin suggested to Sern while holding his smart phone in his hand, showing it to the Intendant.

"I enjoy the walks," Sern replied as he again headed out the front door. The vampire turned towards the werewolf, "So when do we stop them?"

"You may not need to." Trenton replied, still with his ear to the door. "I think they just finished up." Trenton smirked.

"Don't tell me how you know that," Gavin went back to the kitchen. "Just tell them to clean up, and get something to eat, and get the luggage packed up again, because we're going to move to Wolf Coven House as soon as possible."

The car drove up the winding pathway, which diverted from the main mountain highway. There was little that was needed to be said inside the car. Paxton and Jett seemed to be happy to be together, and they sure expressed it while in the bedroom. Though Gavin and Trenton didn't say anything, it was implied enough when they came out, hair messed up and clothes wrinkled. Jett got to see Paxton drink blood for the first time, and see his eyes turn that vampiric shade of yellow when he did. Much to the surprise of Gavin, he wasn't remotely spooked, in fact he was more fascinated by it than he had expected.

After he had his share of food to eat, Jett and Paxton were informed that they would need to move to Wolf Coven House. Their relocation would be necessary to safeguard everyone, especially for Jett since he could go into a blood rage any minute. It was a good thing that Paxton was nearby to provide some physical as well as emotional support. Gavin was particularly careful not to rock the boat, as was Trenton, since they knew there was a chance that they could do real damage to their fragile mental minds, especially in the case of Jett.

There was one side effect of his unification with Paxton though. In both Jett and Paxton, their senses were quite a bit more enhanced, and considering their romp in the bedroom, they were still in the midst of their afterglow, though it was more potent for Jett. He sat there in the back of the car, nuzzled up against Paxton, nuzzling with a grin on his face. He didn't seem remotely frightened or scared, or even nervous about the situation. Paxton was just happy to have his boyfriend back with him; they enjoyed the gentle rocking of the car as Gavin drove them down to what they had just learned, was called Wolf Coven House.

The scenic Sea to Sky highway was the pathway that many tourists would take from the big city, up to the ski resort town of Whistler, a world famous ski location. But few people knew, that it also led to one of the main safe havens for Supernatural beings. Of course it was one of the many offshoot roads that was taken, and only those who were already aware of its location could find it. Gavin, of course, already knew his way to get there since he had been living there for a long tim; there were some obvious ways to miss the turn.

Wolf Coven House was shrouded in a thick fog and mist that never seemed to disappear. It only appeared if you got close to it at ground level. The thick trees and forests were effective in covering, and the fog was a magical enchantment put onto the area to deliberately hide it. The fog could not be penetrated by non-Supernaturals or those who were not given permission to reach Wolf Coven House. Humans who accidentally found their way onto the road would simply be led back out by the same road. They would not know how they entered, just that they would exit out the same way they entered. This was one of the most effective yet simple ways to keep Wolf Coven House a secret from the general public. It had yet to fail them for security.

The car drove through the fog layer and was still on the same type of road though, for a few seconds, they couldn't see past a few feet outside. Then the fog vanished around them, and Jett looked behind them out the back window to see that the fog layer had vanished again as though it wasn't there. Apparently it only appeared if they got close to it and vanished once they were at a far enough distance.

Paxton was looking out the windows again. Through the canopy above them, there was the hint of the fading orange light of the twilight hours of the evening. It was quite a remarkable sight as the road started to wind in a large round curve. Through some of the tree lines, they could see the shimmering evening sunlight reflected on a large body of water, giving that warm glow of the late summers to the view. Before they knew it, the car started to creep up to the vast estate. The central tower of the house, as well as the towers on its two wings, were prominent from a distance. As they got closer, its triangular peaked roofs were more prominent amongst the treetops.

At first what looked like the silhouette of the house became the dark red brickwork of a chateau-styled mansion. What was deceptively called a house was more of a huge hotel to their eyes as they approached the front gates. Curved with that typical archway of iron and two gargoyles at the pillars at the side of the gate, the iron fences opened automatically for them as the car approached. Gavin didn't even need to slow down that much for the car to clear the gates and then passed, before they automatically closed again. There was no guard station at the gate so Paxton and Jett only assumed that it was some automated sensor that would let approaching cars inside, but considering the things that they had learned in the past few hours about the supernatural, anything was possible.

Moments later, the car slowed down and parked next to a few dozen other cars, ranging from practical sedans, to luxury cars, and even a few sports vehicles. Of course no assembly of vehicles was complete without the presence of a handful of motorcycles. There were the speedy sporty bikes and the more biker gang types. Paxton and Jett were never that familiar with car types or motorcycles, so they only judged them on a most vague and basic understanding.

The car slowed, then came to a steady halt. Gavin turned off the ignition and locked the emergency brake in place as he slipped out of the car. Trenton and the others followed. Taking a breath of that cool crisp evening air, Jett gazed at where they were now staying. The House was massive. The two large wings expanded around them, like two giant brickwork arms that enclosed them within a great central courtyard, complete with a central fountain in the middle of the circular path. Though simple, the fountain was dignified and gave a strong aura of professionalism and old-fashioned class to the entire view.

Without a doubt the rooftops did make this manor seem like the old classical chateau styled-hotels of the golden era of the railways. Perhaps this was one of those hotels but now in newer hands, Jett thought. He and Paxton remember learning about these chateau-styled hotels in history, how glamorous they were back in the age of rail. Jett thought to himself, if this was really one of those old-fashioned hotels, then this was kept in remarkable condition. Everything looked well-kept, even the landscaping and gardens.

Though he couldn't see the lake or bay behind the house, Paxton did get a good view of it from the road earlier. Likely the house was sitting right on the edge of one of the lakes, or at least near an access point. Perhaps it would be possible to go swimming here in the water, though it may be quite cold. Surprisingly to him, the bags and luggage seemed much lighter than before. but then it also dawned on him that the supernatural enhanced strength was probably what made him lift them as though they were empty bags. Gavin and Trenton led them to the large twin oak doors that were at the top of the porch way, which featured five smoothly carved stone steps.

Beside the five steps were two small pillars of red bricks, capped with lanterns that illuminated the entrance in a rather elegant way, not unlike the overall design of the mansion from the outside. Gavin didn't seem to need to unlock the doors as he simply pushed them open. Trenton opened the other door, and they got their first glimpse of the inside.

It was like a grand lobby to a hotel. The floor was made out of white marble with richly decorated rugs that lay out the lobby. It was clear that this, at one time, might have been a hotel since there were two large counters at both sides of the lobby, no doubt for where people would have checked in, and at the far end of the enormous lobby was a pair of staircases that curved and wound up to meet a central point where then they joined and rose to another floor. Beneath the stairway was another hallway that probably led to another section of the hotel.

"Welcome!" a voice boomed from the top of the staircase. It was Sern, who was now slowly descending down the marble white steps. His own dignified presence seemed to work perfectly well for this environment. "I'm glad that you've decided to join us here," he greeted as he eagerly shook Paxton and Jett's hands

"Quite the set-up you have here!" Jett admired as he couldn't help but keep looking around. "It's like you guys live in a luxury 5-star hotel!"

"Well, this building has much history. But one great benefit is that there is a very large abundance of space, and for the time being, for your stay I have arranged an apartment for you both." Sern gestured with his hand for them to follow him up the stairs. Gavin and Trenton followed them as they were led up, and then down the main corridor towards the main wing.

The building was clearly designed as a hotel. Atop the first twin stairway was another flight of stairs that continued upwards and also formed a lovely balcony and atrium over the lobby. It was down this hallway that there were large doors down a corridor leading also to an assortment of rooms.

It seemed that space was set-up here to give guests a true sense of accommodation, that they were not being shoved into hovel-sized rooms. Paxton wondered if the place was renovated specifically to give more space since they were now hosting a much smaller number of people. It seemed possible, but between every door was a generous amount of space, and then also large windows on the wall sides. So it went window, door, window and door and so on down the hallway where there was another large pair of windows that, during the day, must have flooded in generous amounts of lights.

Sern led them past a number of doorways and windows until he reached one that seemed to be the last one before a t-intersection at the end of the hallway that branched into left and right. It seemed to be an inner corner suite. Sern stepped aside to let Paxton and Jett in first.

They stepped into quite the contradiction of a space. What the hallway was classical hotel, very baroque and old fashioned, with the rugs and marble floors, but this suite was like those seen in those architecture magazines, ultra modern. The floors were white tiled; the tables and furniture were made of steel and black leather or ceramics.

Paxton wondered why they had such vastly different types of designs. Surely something like the rest of the hotel would have been sufficient for everything else, but he certainly didn't object to this.

Jett didn't have anything to say. His expression was enough.

"I see you like your accommodation," Sern assumed, as Gavin and Trenton also went in, dropping off the rest of their luggage. He went to the fridge and opened it to show them the contents. It was a large one, divided in two sections: one stocked with blood bags, the other with an assortment of typical human food, from a jug of milk, a block of butter, bread, and a wide assortment of fruits and vegetables. "I did some research to accommodate your needs," Sern announced, with some pride in his voice.

"Thanks," Jett said, as he took a look at the food stocks. He grabbed an apple from the fridge, and ran it under the chrome tap above the sink.

"The bedroom is over here," Gavin guided them to a doorway that led past the kitchen area and down the side of what was a sitting room that stood a few steps down from where they were standing. The windows were massive and gave a nice view of the forests around the house. At least it would bring in some sun before it was fully set. Though through the moonlight, they could imagine that they would see still a lovely view from these windows.

"Feel free to explore the house. We have swimming pools, a gym, and lovely gardens, as well as many people eager to meet you. At least I would think so," Sern explained without realizing for a moment that there would be a chance that the newcomers may not necessarily be interested in a vacation. It was one of those bizarre situations that called for a certain strange balance between hospitality and privacy. The subtle nuances were best left to those who had more experience in dealing with this type of situation. That said, it was likely that due to the situation in which Intendants were appointed, they learned as they went. In his reports, Hasaan went through the exact same thing and was considered distant and almost robotic when he was first appointed to Wolf Coven House. That said, now Sern faced the same learning curve.

"If you need anything, my room is just down the hallway, or you can call me," Gavin pulled out his phone to double check if he had the phone numbers ready. Sure enough he had already put in Paxton's number on his speed dial.

"Things should be alright," Paxton assured his sire. He still had to get accustomed to hearing that word, even in his mind, Sire. It was a term that he had heard of while reading Wolf Coven scripts and preparing for his role back in the days, but never did he think he would have to use a term like that in casual thought.

"Blood supplies are in the fridge as you know, clean towels in the closets," Gavin felt like he was giving a quick tour of the necessary amenities to tourists. In some ways he was, but like Sern's thinking, this was necessary. They both watched quietly as Jett wandered into the bedroom, and then collapsed onto the bed.

"Can we chat outside for a minute?" Paxton whispered to Gavin.

"Sure," Gavin answered as they quietly left the room. Trenton stayed inside to watch over Jett. Paxton and Gavin stepped out of the front door, then quietly shut it behind them.

"How often will he transform?" Paxton asked his sire. There was that word again in his mind, repeating itself without any hesitation. It seemed always to strike an odd sounding note in his mind, as though it was out of tune.

"He's a Bloodbane wolf, not Prime Wolf like Trenton. He's going to have a very difficult time with his shifting. It comes and it goes during their first few weeks without any warning," Gavin comforted Paxton by putting his hand on Paxton's shoulder. Paxton avoided eye contact since his own nervousness about the situation was leaking through his normally much more composed exterior. "He may have to relieve his stress by simply running. It's the typical thing that they do in order to vent, either that or ..." Gavin trailed off the end of the sentence. His eyes locked onto Paxton's who suddenly looked right back at him, wondering if he was going to finish the sentence.

"Or what?" Paxton asked. But then Gavin simply raised his eyebrows, suggesting to Paxton that the answer was already there in his head. Paxton wondered for a moment what Gavin's expression was implying, and then it suddenly dawned on him. "Oh....OH!" Paxton recalled the first time he had seen Jett shift in front of him, he had been more interested in one thing, and that was done in the context of a bedroom. Alright, it was pretty damned obvious what Gavin was referring to.

"Ya, the shift for them, can drastically increase their sex drive, but it's not always the case," Gavin explained. "Thankfully you're stronger than him, but you may not be as fast right now." Around the corner came another familiar face, tall, chiseled and stunningly handsome with that typical Hollywood hunk type of look. "Hey, Caz." Gavin greeted.

"Hey," Cazian gently gave Paxton a comforting hug. It never quite occurred to Paxton how well-built Cazian was, especially under the very typically loose dress shirts he liked to wear. He had something in his hand that he handed to Gavin. Paxton got a good look at it. It was like a wristband with an adjustable strap. There was a small black metallic circle at one end of it that looked like one of those balance bracelets that people wore. This one, on the other hand, had a blinking red light in the center of the black metal circle, probably indicating that it was on or something like that.

"What's that for?" Paxton asked, he had a slight feeling he knew what it was going to be meant for.

"It's a tracking bracelet, or anklet, depending where you want to put it." Gavin answered.

"In case your boyfriend goes a little too rabid and you lose track of him, we can track him with that," Cazian elaborated.

"Like a tagged animal?" Paxton coughed out, slightly resentful of the idea that his boyfriend was being treated more like a prisoner than a guest.

"It's also in case you need to find him as well," Gavin responded, naturally expecting this type of reaction. It wasn't everyday that a tracking device was a welcome accessory to one's fashion collection. "Do you have your phone on you?" He asked.

"Yeah," Paxton pulled out his smart phone. It was one of those large, giant ones, with the enormous screen that was as large as some entire phones. He keyed in the security sequence of numbers to unlock it.

"I'm going to download the app."

"There's an Android App for the tracking device?" Paxton was somewhat jolted back to reality by this revelation.

"And for the iOS and Windows phones," Caz smiled.

"What about Blackberry?"

"Pfft, no one uses those anymore," Gavin snubbed as he proceeded to click through a few pages on the Google Play menus then the small progress bar finished up quickly, indicating the download was completed. He handed the phone back to Paxton. The icon, which was the shape of a red heart, as in the love heart, was on his main screen. Paxton touched the icon on the screen and activated the application. The screen switched to the map view of their area, puzzling since it wouldn't be typically secure for Wolf Coven House to have its presence known on Google Maps.

"How can this detect us? I thought you would have some kind of method to remove our presence from everyone's knowledge?" Paxton asked.

"The app is shrouded, meaning that its information is protected and can't be accessed by non-Supernaturals."

"But it's on the Google Play store!" Paxton laughed at the explanation that Gavin was giving him. That sequence of words that he used to justify the situation was simply ludicrous, thought Paxton, now a vampire. Then the irony of the moment just hit him.

"With magic, people can make books disappear and words vanish, why not computer code?"

"You know, I'm just going to nod my head and say yes."

"Alright," Gavin smiled as he pointed back to the phone screen. "Simple directions, really, every ten seconds, GPS locators will lock onto that tracking signal," he pointed to the red blinking dot on the screen. "And the center crosshairs is where you are. So all you have to do is follow that to find him."

"And what if he takes it off?"

"Then it will also tell you that," Gavin showed him the back of the tag, pointing what was simply bland metal plating, but clearly he was implying that there was something far more to it. "It's a built in heat sensor, meaning if he takes it off, his body heat won't touch it, so it will also notify you of that too."

"Convenient."

"Very convenient. We have never had an incident of anyone going missing, thanks to these. And also the benefit that even if someone did try to take it off, we had a few Wolf Primes who could track them down the old fashion way, with their noses."

"That's very convenient," Paxton was handed the tag. It was very much like one of those straps people wore while exercising to monitor heart rates.

The door then suddenly opened. Jett stepped out, wearing track pants and a loose tank top. His arms were exposed and he didn't seem to notice or care about the cool air in the hallway. It looked like he was in the mood for some exercise.

"Where are you going?" Paxton asked as Trenton followed him out of the doorway. It was quite a revelation on how giant Trenton was when Jett stood in front of him. Trenton towered over him by almost a good foot.

"I'm going for a run." Jett admitted.

"Well, before you do, can you put this on?" Paxton handed him the tracking band. Jett looked at it, puzzled for a moment, then noticed Paxton avoiding eye contact.

"What's this?" Jett accepted the band but was naturally inquisitive to its function and nature.

"In case you go feral, or get lost." Paxton looked at Jett. Oddly Jett didn't seem to be remotely concerned about it.

"Alright," Jett undid the strap and put it on his wrist, like no other care in the world.

"Actually, could you put it around your ankle?" Gavin asked. Paxton wondered why, but it was likely due to the fact that it would be harder for him to lose that way.

"Oh, sure." Jett bent down and secured it around his right ankle without hesitation.

"You're not upset about it? That I want to keep track of you?" Paxton asked, almost disappointed that he didn't get any rejection.

"No," Jett smiled at him. "When I was lost in the forest, not knowing what I was and where I was, I was so scared. I'm glad I have this, so you can all find me," he reached his arms around Paxton's shoulders and pulled him in for hug.

The three who were watching almost let out an "ahh" at the sign of that, with the somewhat mushy sappy words that were coming out of Jett. It was clear that these two were perfectly made for each other. Jett almost playfully shook his right leg, trying to feel the tracker.

"Can't feel a thing." He gave Jett a peck on the cheek.

"I'll look after him," Trenton assured Paxton. "He won't get far from me."

The two wolves walked around the corner and disappeared down the hallway. Oddly leaving Cazian, Paxton and Gavin there in an unusual moment of calmness and quiet serenity.

"You don't have to worry about him." Gavin assured his young sire. "Trenton will treat him fine. Now lets start to get you trained up"

"I'm not worried about Trenton, I hope my boyfriend doesn't turn into a monster."

"He won't," Gavin smiled at him as he put his arm around Paxton, leading him down the hall. "He has you." The words of warmth and comfort from Gavin certainly hit Paxton well. It seemed a bit sappy but it did dawn on Paxton, since he was stronger than Jett and later maybe even faster, he would be the key to helping him keep control of himself."

<u>Chapter 10</u>

Sern watched from the top balcony of his office, which offered a spectacular view of the perfectly groomed gardens, and pools that reflected brilliantly in the moonlight, two individuals approaching the center of the gardens where there were open seats. The two approached them with a casual stroll. Though the distance was significant, Sern could hear every word they were saying, but he didn't really care too much about what they were saying. He heard the sounds of their voices, but not the words they were saying. He was more in a state of mental contemplation. He ran through the various situations that had happened recently in his mind.

The most serious of all was the fact that there was a serious wolf attack on civilians. The presence of Bloodbanes was something of great concern to him, but so far he had not yet heard any word about their current locations after the attack. Since Trenton and the other Wolf Primes were not known to lose their tracking of targets, the disappearance of this Bloodbane pack was something that he certainly had to think of as a very serious matter. Bloodbanes were dangerous, and the fact that they now had one under their roof was worth monitoring. He knew already that Jett willingly wore a tracking band on him, but it was the circumstances of the attack that were suspicious.

Sern couldn't figure out any particular reason why they were interested in anyone at Wolf Coven. Hasaan's reports had previous indicated that though Bloodbanes were welcome to use Wolf Coven Lands to roam, like all Supernaturals, they were never seen before. They preferred their own agendas and isolation away from the other wolf breeds. Though they enjoyed the addictive nature and supernatural gifts, albeit temporary gifts that vampiric blood could offer them, they had other ways of acquiring it rather than attacking Wolf Coven Members, especially if they were under the protection of an Intendant. Still the thoughts did make him rather wary about what he would encounter in the near future.

As his thoughts flowed through his mind, Sern couldn't help but be distracted by what he saw in the forests beyond the garden. Already Trenton and Jett were long gone but he could sense a presence coming to the house.

Sern's own physical senses sharpened immediately as he detected this presence coming towards him from the edge of the forest. Without a doubt he had a good feeling he knew what was heading his way. As with many of Hasaan's detailed reports he had read about this occurrence before, it seemed to him it was only a matter of time before he would encounter this entity.

Without sparing a moment, Sern leaped right off the balcony of his third floor office. His descend slowed down as he was just about to hit the ground, enough for him to gracefully land with dignity and the proper etiquette of an Intendant of the Va'Nai. Slowly he proceeded down between the isles of the flowers, the silent night around him interrupted only by the calming steady stream of water flowing down from the fountains. He could now sense that the presence was on the very edge of the garden, right inside the trees, not entering, but it was still invisible to his eyes. Sern guessed that he could probably adjust his vision to see the entity, but instead, chose to deliberately remain ignorant of its physical form as he approached it.

As Sern reached the end of the garden, he stood on the farthest edge, nearest to the fountain, keeping a formidable amount of clear empty grass between him and the tree line. He stood there for a clear few moments, not moving. It was his way of making sure the entity knew that he could sense him, but was not going to move to intercept it. The entity was there, watching him. They both knew that they detected each other but Sern, out of respect, did not step forward.

Slowly, Sern raised both hands and arms upwards, palms facing upward in the welcoming gesture of the Native Peoples of the region. He knew that this entity was definitely related to the First Nations people. As he performed this gesture of welcome, he could sense the entity breach the tree line, and slowly step forward. Sern noticed that though the creature was walking towards him, the grass didn't bend. Sern slowly adjusted his vision, letting his eyes glow ever so slightly, just barely enough to make out the outline of the enormous form of the creature.

It was a Spiritwolf, a legendary creature of the Native cultures of this region. Its outline became clearer, as its glowing white and grey fur revealed itself and its shining golden eyes gazed right into Sern's own. The creature was truly magnificent, even to the wonders that Sern had seen in Aurastar, this creature, its fur was flowing as though every hair was alive, leaving behind a glowing mist of haze and light around it. Its sheer size dwarfed Sern himself. Even a Wolf Prime, in full beast form, was only half the size of this guardian spirit.

"You've come to meet Hasaan's replacement?" Sern asked the being. It didn't speak a reply. It didn't even seem to need to communicate one telepathically, but instantly Sern could tell that it agreed with what he was saying. Its enormous size certainly left even him in awe of its presence. It sat down, resting its back and legs like how a dog would sit. It casually looked around, sniffing the air. No doubt it had easily picked up the scent of the new wolf, Jett. The enormous beast lifted up one of its paws towards Sern. Sern could tell that it was inviting him to touch its paw. Sern did, placing his hand against the vast giant black leathery bottoms of its paw. It was as though it was initiating some form of communication.

Cazian, Paxton and Gavin headed towards the garden from the gym area of Wolf Coven House, while passing one of the large windows, they could see the outside, and what was going on. Paxton's eyes widened as he almost lost track of where he was walking when he saw. Sern was standing in front of this enormous, giant glowing wolf! He struggled to put together words to describe or ask what he was seeing, his mind almost failing to process anything as he just dropped his jaw at the sight of this stunningly regal creature.

"It's the Spiritwolf." Cazian whispered. "One of the Spirit Guardians of this land."

"That's insane!" Paxton gasped! He was still barely able to say anything else but those two words. "Can we get closer?" Paxton turned to Gavin, who could easily read the excitement on Paxton's face.

"I think so," Gavin turned down another corridor with them. Paxton quickened his pace to keep up.

Sern had already started a light mindlink with the Spiritwolf. It was here to evaluate him, just as much as Sern was evaluating it. It had let his hand go, and was now slowly walking next to Sern towards the house, but not to necessarily enter it. Somehow, the Spiritwolf had sensed that someone was in the house and wanted to see it. It was not going to let that natural curiosity be dissuaded. Sern didn't seem to notice at first, but three people started to walk up the garden towards them easily recognized as Paxton, Cazian and Gavin.

Gavin and Cazian kept a farther distance, not out of fear but respect, and a certain sense of reverence for this creature. Paxton was more curious, almost like a child approaching a big dog. But with Sern standing next to it, and the enormous Spiritwolf showing absolutely no hostility at all, Paxton could only assume that he was going to be safe. But that said, Paxton's steps were slow and careful. He wasn't sure of his abilities but he knew that this creature, even with him being a vampire, could do harm if it wanted to. Its size alone was enough to make someone think twice.

"Paxton, meet the Spiritwolf. It's curious about me, since I'm the new Intendant so it came to pay a visit." Sern introduced the enormous creature. "Guardian, this is Paxton, one of our newest High Orders. His boyfriend is also a Wolf-Kin." The enormous wolf almost seemed to be listening and understanding what Sern was saying. Every word that Sern said, the Guardian was looking right into his eyes, and then as Sern was finished, it naturally turned its head towards Paxton.

Paxton was still a good ten feet away. Sern gestured for him to come closer. Shyly, Paxton approached the enormous creature. Its eyes were gold and glowed with the brilliant sparkle of amber gemstones. The enormous creature towered over Paxton, as its kind eyes looked at him. Its head descended down. It took a few subtle sniffs of Paxton's hair, and face. Then a deep and long inhale, almost like it was reading Paxton through scent, something Paxton had read before in books, those canines had this ability. Then, much to Paxton's surprise, his face was met with a big warm wet tongue! The sheer force of the Spiritwolf's lick was almost enough to tip him over, as he struggled for a brief moment to regain his balance. Paxton busted out laughing, as the Spiritwolf licked him again. The enormous beast looked down towards Paxton and for a moment, Paxton swore that he felt a sudden enormous wave of support and understanding from the Spiritwolf.

Paxton reached up and ran his hand through the thick but incredibly soft, almost cloud-like white fur. Every strand was as soft as a feather. The warmth of the Spirit Wolf's body was felt even through the thick though light coat of perfectly white fur that shimmered with its own light. Paxton was in awe of the mighty creature as it stood there gently gazing at him. Its eyes were remarkably gentle, the two eyes looking like a pair of golden spheres gently looking at him.

Sern and the others could sense the same thing. It was as though the Guardian had read his entire situation just off his scent, but it was more than that. The Guardian could sense everything including the internal turmoil that Paxton was feeling. With that sudden wave of understanding, Paxton couldn't help but release a few tears. The Guardian instantly recognized these droplets and bent down, and lightly nudged Paxton with the side of its face, a powerful sign of affection.

"The Guardian says, that you have nothing to worry about. It says that things will be very difficult and even painful at first, but in time things will most definitely get better," Sern said, almost as though he was translating the Guardian's intentions.

"Tell him, thanks." Paxton sniffed as the Guardian spirit raised its head again. Slowly, it turned and started to walk away.

"He already understood you," Sern said as they all watched the Spirit walk majestically away, leaving behind it a trail of glowing white mist. Each step, as graceful as the last, its movements impacted nothing around it, not a single twig or grass blade was disturbed as it approached the forest, then as the trail of mist started to vanish, the enormous guardian spirit too, started to fade invisibly away, but maintaining its movement back to the forest.

Without a doubt, it was a circumstance that they were facing that seemed to be strange at first. The idea that there was going to be a massive Spiritwolf that came out of the forest for the purpose of greeting them, and then mysteriously vanish back into the forest, was something that was certainly not normal. Then again for Paxton, normal would hardly be the word he would ever use to describe anything that was happening around him right now. For the time being, he just had to accept what was going on as just a natural part of the supernatural world around them.

Jett was already staring to run even faster through the forest, catching up to a much faster Trenton. It was the first time he had run on four legs, using all his limbs like an animal, galloping front then back then front, using as much as his arms to push him as his legs did to kick him through the speed, faster than any human could. Using four limbs instead of two defiantly had its speed advantages, as well as making him able to speed up and catch anything.

At his current speed, it wasn't hard to understand why and how he was able to catch a deer, even in the middle of the forest, which was something that he never thought he would do. Before this transformation fiasco, he was never one for hunting. Even the idea of holding a gun, or rifle disgusted him.

Trenton slowed down a bit to see if the young wolfling behind him was able to catch up. Sure enough, through the forest he could smell and see the younger one following him, almost just as fast. They were both partially transformed, or in Jett's case, fully transformed. His wolf-form was still mainly humanoid, his eyes, and his teeth, and claws were canine but his face still maintained the human facial form. He did have some ridges over his cheekbones and his nose bridge but aside from that, with heightened slightly sharpened and pointed ears he was very human. Trenton could easily have transformed into his full prime form, but he wanted to keep the look more familiar with Jett. Considering that Jett could easily be alienated in his mental state, it was best to keep the sense of a pack familiar to him.

Jett caught up and stood up, panting heavily from his running, his breath causing a powerful series of puffs of mist through the cold night air. He looked quite formidable, with his yellow eyes and fangs fully emerged, and constantly on the lookout for the slightest movement around him. Trenton could tell that his eyes were constantly darting from side to side, watching what was going on around him. Naturally his vision was just as effective under the moonlight. It was only a few days from the full moon, and Trenton knew that things would become even more difficult under that situation.

"So why don't you have a pack of your own?" Jett asked as his hot misty breath pumping in and out of his mouth and lungs.

"Primes don't have packs. We don't' need them." Trenton sniffed the air, also looking around to where they were standing.

"Why not?" Jett asked like a curious puppy.

"We've never felt the need. I guess you can sort of say that Coltrane, Trey and myself are in a pack but we don't have a leader, we just live and work together."

"So Bloodbanes and the other wolves have packs? What's the role of a leader" Jett continued to ask. Trenton found it a bit unusual that he was so talkative, but if their positions were reversed and it was Trenton's first full night as a wolf, he also would probably be just as curious.

"Packwalkers and Bloodbanes both run in packs. The Alpha is the wolf who has the most control, the most strength." Trenton answered as he started walking again, instead of running, just to ease up on his breath and also to let Jett slow down a bit.

"So how would I, become an alpha if I had a pack?"

"You would probably have to kill your alpha and take his place." Trenton answered with little reluctance in his voice. The explanation hit Jett rather bluntly as he stopped for a moment to think about what Trenton said. But then he was distracted by something else as they walked on and a breeze of cool air caught them. Paxton noticed that Jett was standing there, almost letting the breeze flow right over and through his entire body. "What is it?" he asked the young wolf.

"It's incredible." Jett answered with a wispy voice. His eyes were closed, but his feral face was still very much in its Bloodbane wolf form. "I can feel the wind, the air on every hair, every line of fur." He stopped for a moment then inhaled deeply. "It's amazing, I can smell everything!" his eyes then opened again, those speckled gold eyes locked onto Trenton. "Even you, I can smell your scent."

"That's why we're out here, to give your abilities a test run." Trenton quickened his pace into a quick jog. The entire exercise was meant more to get Jett used to his abilities in speed and maneuverability than it was to actually train him to hunt. Taking tiny steps was necessary to get used to the fundamentals of his new form before he got used to anything else, but there were some senses that were naturally more accustomed for him.

One thing that he didn't even notice, was the fact he still had his runners on. He didn't even think for a moment, if his feet had claws on them, like how his hands did. It was a strange thought to have. Maybe his toes did have sharp claws on them, in which case they were probably going to rip through his socks and even his shoes. It was probably something he didn't care to think of that much, since that would only mean he would have to look for new shoes. It was just a fleeting thought for the time that made him wonder about the practicality of transforming, what damage it would do to him, from an economic standpoint, having to always replace his socks and shoes.

For those few moments where he caught up to Trenton, he didn't even bother to look at Trenton himself. It was pretty amazing that a creature of his sheer size was able to be even faster than him. Towering over him when he stood up, Trenton has eyes which were a key sign of his power. They were gold and black like his, but the intensity and potential for sheer beast-like power were unmistakable. If Trenton wanted to be an Alpha, he easily could have become one, Jett thought to himself. His own claws, almost like Jett's, were like slightly longer fingers, but with that dark brown, sharp claw-nail that came out of the tip, almost over his regular human nail, and his own face, just as bestial as his own. Jett had only taken one look at himself as a wolf, in the mirror, and that was with Paxton. It was a slightly odd moment where they both actually compared fangs, Paxton's vampire fangs to Jett's own wolf-fangs. Of course the more dangerous pair was in its application.

"It's weird," Jett ran his tongue over his fangs. He hadn't even really noticed them before. "talking with these."

"You'll get used to it." Trenton assured him.

"You said that Bloodbanes, are addicted to the effects of vampire blood," Jett asked sounding slightly worried.

"Yeah, that's what separates them from Packwalkers."

"You think, if I lost control, I could bite through a vampire's skin with these?" Jett asked again, his natural instincts kicking in after a brief thought about drinking vampire blood flew into his mind.

"I wouldn't try it here," Trenton warned.

"I saw Paxton's fangs," Jett spoke up again. "I have to admit, he looks good with them."

"Yeah, High Orders can do that to you, charm you even when they look dangerous," Trenton's mind would wander back to moments where High Orders, in particular Cazian, would use their vampiric appeal even on other Supernaturals. "Cazian is infamous for that." Without warning, Trenton sprinted off again, looking back to see if Jett was following as he sprinted and clawed through the forest. Instantly without need to say anything, Jett followed, as fast as he could, each limb and leg working to keep up to the enormous wolf form in front of him. It was something he needed, a run, to get his mind more focused and off of the pain that he may have to endure later.

Three Days Later

The isolation cell was rather Spartan and oddly high-tech looking for something underneath such as a classical looking house. Jett couldn't help but admire the oddly warm cement floors, the reinforced concrete walls, and the high overhanging lights, protected by steel and glass. The doorway was even more impressive, made out of protective glass, and with a layer of steel rods between them to make sure nothing got through. It was a good few inches thick as Jett tapped it, seeing how it barely vibrated. The bars between the layers of glass were just to make sure things were extra safe.

"So this is it?" Jett asked as he stepped into the room and craned his head upwards to look around. He could feel the heat coming up from the ground, something to make sure that anything inside was at least still warm.

"It's what we use, even us," Cazian remarked as he tapped the glass himself. "reinforced to the point where not even a grenade could punch through these babies," He gave the reinforced glass front wall a light punch.

"Looks like a Squash court." Paxton commented. "But you said this place was supposed to be a hotel right?"

"Yep. So we converted them. And with a few tonnes of reinforced concrete, steel cages and reinforced glass, a squash court can make an effective cell, if anything or anyone gets a little out of control."

"Like for the full moons?" Jett admitted. He knew that this was meant for him, and that he was going to be in there while things had to happen. Sadly this was one part of the books and television shows that he felt was true, reverting into a beast.

"Yeah, but the good thing is that we will be right on the other side of the glass," Paxton put his arm around Jett, comforting him, "all of us." Paxton pointed to Cazian, and implying the same for Trenton, and Gavin.

"I'm just not really easy with the idea of being locked up in a cage." Jett retorted, clearly very uncomfortable with the idea.

"Could I go in there with him?" Paxton asked the High Order, who was not amused by his request.

"No!" Cazian ordered back. "His strength grows on a full moon, and yeah you're stronger than him now, but you're a newborn, if you go in there with him, he'll rip you apart." The idea of Paxton wanting to be in the cell with Jett during this volatile time, to Cazian, was an admirable, but highly foolish choice to make.

"What about you or Gavin?" Paxton pleaded. "I just don't want him to be in there alone." He was full of anxiety about what Jett was going to face in that cage. It wasn't something that he was expecting himself to deal with completely, but with the help of the others' presence, it was going to be a lot easier.

"It's possible, but I'll have to ask him." Cazian offered. He could understand why Paxton wanted to safeguard Jett, especially under these circumstances. A lunar event like a full moon will undoubtedly affect them. Even the touch of the moonlight against their skin will drive them nearly insane. Bloodbanes especially were famously known for the difficulties that they suffered during these events, and locking them up really was the best thing that they could do for them.

"We're all going to be here." Paxton assured Jett, who looked pretty much accepting of his situation. It wasn't something that he was looking forwards to but he knew that it was inevitable, something he could never avoid, so he might as well approach it with an open mind. He always had that pragmatic and practical side to his personality.

"What about Sern? Maybe he could help?" Jett asked.

"Possibly, but he's meeting with Gavin right now," Cazian told them as he casually started to examine the doors and locks again just to make double sure they were secure. In the chamber, there were sixteen other cells like this, more than large enough to accommodate someone for a short time.

Sern once again was in a state of meditation in his office. It was something that he did in order to clear his mind and sort thoughts in order. For him it was natural to do this fairly occasionally, in order to maintain mental discipline over what he had to contend with, as well as to process the information. Going through his mind most obviously was the state of the members of Wolf Coven, in particular the presence of a Bloodbane wolf. However, that thought was immediately countered by the presence of three Wolf Primes, also present to keep him under control.

The central desk started to illuminate. The natural comforting light-green glow of the polished crystalline top of the desk shone brightly, interrupting his mind's calmness. Sern opened his eyes to see the digital rendering, holographic representation of Superintendent Lya created in front of him. He hadn't expected to hear from them so soon after his appointment. It was more likely to him that he would have encountered the presence of Intendant Hasaan to check up on his former wards before anyone else at the Sanctuary Organization decided to stop by for a holographic visit.

"Intendant. I'm afraid I have to interrupt your service at Wolf Coven House for an urgent mission." She commanded with the same trademark bluntness that was the trademark of all Sanctuary officials, Sern included. The lack of proper people skills seemed to be something that they were all accustomed to.

"For what purpose?" Sern asked, not out of defiance but curiosity and Lya knew this. It was a natural response.

"Secure your area first," The Superintendent requested. With command from his own mind, the doors and windows in the room all shut and locked themselves, and the curtains slid shut with the power of an unseen force. It wasn't entirely required since Sern could sense the presence of someone coming down the hallway even if the doors were locked, but this way he didn't have to concentrate on maintaining that sense of security.

"It's done," Sern replied, now anticipating a detailed explanation for the unusual and sudden request for his presence.

"As you know, our diplomatic representatives have been conducting negotiations with a race called the Ahri."

"I do know the rudimentary aspects of the diplomatic missions, but I was not privy to more information."

"The Ahri are a race of exceptionally powerful magic users, specifically in the art of portals. They can create transport portals easily and we need their assistance. They are willing to assist but they want a treaty of alliance."

"And what does that have to do with Wolf Coven House."

"They want to establish a small presence on Earth. We have selected Wolf Coven House as an appropriate location, at least the lands west from the house itself but still within the protective area."

"Why Wolf Coven House?" Sern inquired.

"Wolf Coven House has a very low incident rate, and is geographically isolated, plus your area has a very large sphere of control. We took into consideration all of the Coven Houses and Wolf Coven was the best option for us."

"I still don't know why I would have to leave."

"The Ahri themselves are asking us to help secure a colony world. They request our assistance, and they also want to meet you since you will be, in part, functioning as our liaison to them when their attaché arrives on Earth after our assistance."

"So it's a trade off, at least for the time being. I'm to meet with their appointed representative, and then bring them back to Earth?"

"Yes."

"I thought the treaty of alliance proposed was about the Va'Nai providing methods for them to travel through space."

"It is, but that comes later. Portals are what they use now, but they want the ability to travel through the stars themselves, not hop from planet to planet. But their ability to create portals and manipulate the elements is just too useful for us to decline, so their term for a tiny group of Ahri to come to Earth was seen as an acceptable amendment to the overall proposal."

"It does sound reasonable."

"And we are sending a force of 15,000 Enforcers and Protectors to secure the colony world currently under siege."

"It's an entire world?" Sern was shocked at the revelation that not only would the Ahri have to defend an entire planet, but that the Sanctuary under the Va'Nai would be sending such a large detachment to assist them

"Yes, and we have little time to discuss this, Sern. I'm afraid you've been immediately recalled. You are to head to your portal, to the Transport Hub immediately." Lya ordered firmly.

"But what of the situation here? Who will be given authority to administrate in my absence?"

"I understand that Gavin Varsen is the most likely candidate. You have been authorized to infuse him with an Essence Echo. You're not going to be required at the front lines here, just to meet with the Ahri delegation. Give him access to the Essence Echo for a period of two weeks. It will be more than sufficient."

"Very well," Sern accepted. He wasn't reluctant to obey these orders. The Superintendent was correct in stating that Wolf Coven House was safe and isolated. It was likely one of the safest of the Coven Houses, and if they were to host a delegation of Ahri, Wolf Coven House would be the best place to do it.

"We expect you soon," Superintendent Lya commanded one last time. Her image vanished from the console as quickly as it had appeared.

Sern reached into the desk and pulled out one of the human communication devices; apparently they called them "Smart phones".

Entering in a simple sequence of words in North American English, he requested Gavin's presence.

"You asked to see me?" Gavin peered into Sern's office. The Intendant was consulting with his holographic display image of various texts, of some strange language that he had not previously seen. Sern had explained that the Sanctuary Language relied on many forms of pictograms and symbols that probably relied more on context and ideas more than sounds, not unlike Chinese.

"Yes," Sern welcomed his guest. "Please do come in." He said as he continued to view the rotating texts. It was like they were displayed on a central pillar, and was read downwards from the top, and rotating left to right. Gavin approached the holographic pillar in the room.

"More reports coming in from HQ?" he asked, inquiring as to the nature of his meeting.

"Yes. And I'm forced to do something that I didn't think I would need to, for some time," Sern reported, as he deactivated the holographic image. Gavin looked concerned for a moment. "I am leaving Wolf Coven House." The revelation of these simple blunt words hit Gavin rather quickly. It was something definitely unexpected. To him it was a strange occurrence to have a new Intendant assigned so quickly.

"That was rather fast, you've been here for a little over two weeks."

"I'm not leaving permanently. I just have to depart for a diplomatic mission for a short while, shouldn't be more than a few days, maybe a week." Sern corrected. The words were enough to give Gavin a sense of calm and assurance.

"Ok, that makes more sense," Gavin signed with relief.

"Are you concerned with my departure?" The Intendant asked, wondering about his response.

"Well, it's just, you can do so much more stuff that I can't." Gavin started, hinting at the fact that Sern's abilities alone were enough to make him a powerful force to be reckoned with. "And without your powers, and the incoming full moon, I don't know if I could handle things as well as you."

"That won't be a problem." Sern reassured him. "I have been instructed, to make you a deputy Intendant while I am gone. The Sanctuary Organization has authorized me to infuse you with temporary abilities in order to make you able to handle the situation here, without fault."

"You can do that?"

"Yes."

"When?"

"Right now." Sern stated without hesitation as he approached Gavin with his hand reached out.

"Wait, now?" Gavin asked as he backed up for a moment.

"Yes. Immediately." the Intendant repeated.

"You know I've never done this before." Gavin said nervously as he was still extremely wary about what he was going to go under.

"I am aware of that; please step forward," Sern instructed directly. With that command, Gavin stepped forward towards Sern who held out his hand. There was a moment of anxious waiting before Sern brought his hand towards Gavin's chest. He didn't reach any further; a slow but steady and bright stream of light emitted from his palm. It was almost like a strobe light, flickering and flashing. The beam shot right into Gavin's chest, as he felt a powerful surge of heat and power hit him. As the beam continued to spread its glow throughout Gavin's body, he felt energized, as if he was being rejuvenated, every cell coursing with raw, unnatural power! It was like he had fed on the blood of a god, every single fibre of his being was being empowered.

Gavin gasped, as the infusion continued to fill him with this unknown force, of which he had never felt before. Sern continued to stand there, hand out and emitting the light towards him, bathing him in the sheer raw power that he was now bestowing on Gavin.

There was a brief moment of what seemed like an eternity of this infusion. Gavin's eyes, which had slammed shut during the entire infusion, suddenly opened, glowing with a brilliant white light. Sern's also were glowing with a brighter light.

"I understand," Gavin stated calmly. It was as though for every single moment, every thought was clear, every question was answered, every single wonder satisfied, and everything he understood was crystal clear. Even his voice was different; it was calm, and calculating, almost with a faded hint of a slight digital quality. He looked at his own hands, there was a faint glow coming from his entire body. He didn't need Sern to explain what was happening to him. The cosmic force which came from Sern was taking its time to be absorbed into his full physical form. He could feel a comfort around him, as though there were a thousand eyes all watching him, not out of fear or paranoia, but rather out of support, like these eyes were his own eyes, that were going to see everything around him. "I'll inform the others of your departure," Gavin stated, in the same, relatively emotionless tone that Sern often had when giving instructions.

Sern approached Gavin with what looked like a scarf, but it was made out of the same materials that composed Sern's clothing. He placed it onto Gavin's shoulders. Slowly, the cloth started to grow, and lengthen, growing to encompass all of Gavin's upper body into what looked like a tunic, then lowered downward towards the ground, forming a pair of pants around Gavin's own jeans. Gavin didn't need to be told what this was. It was crystalline weave, a cloth made out of the same materials that composed the Va'Nai construction materials in Aurastar and the Transport Hub, a biological and mineral-based material that responded to the needs of its wearer, growing and lengthening, thinning and thickening depending on the wearer's needs. The only recognizable difference between Sern's clothes and Gavin's was that the glowing veins in Sern's robe were silver. Gavin's pants and tunic were bronze. At his neck near his new Manchurian styled collar, was a small version of the Cosmic Eye.

"I must depart immediately, the Archons in Aurastar have summoned me." Sern exited the room and headed towards the atrium immediately.

It was quite stunning that over the course of just a few minutes, such a vast and dramatic change happening was enough to fully orientate him to the situation. It was strange, as though all the instructions and questions that he would have had were immediately answered almost like Sern's own mind had been copied and pasted into his own. To him there was also this bizarre sensation, that there was a second entity within him, like a comforting presence that was protecting him. It was all clear to him now. Everything, the purpose of the Intendants and Protectors, Everything seemed to now make perfect sense.

"You know what to do while I am gone?" Sern asked just to make sure. Within an acceptable margin of error he was sure that there was nothing much that he needed to worry about. Gavin's implantation with some of his memories, as well as a formidable selection of his powers would make him more than capable of handling any given situation, of course within reason. For Sern, his duties called him towards the diplomatic corp. that awaited his arrival in Aurastar.

"Yes, I am sure," Gavin replied following him to the atrium, confident in the limits and capabilities of his own abilities. It was still temporarily a bit overwhelming, being implanted not just with portions of Sern's knowledge but also the vastness of the new powers that he had at his disposal.

"Very well," Sern entered the central atrium. Sern gave Gavin a handshake, then without a word, stepped through the portal.

Since the portal was a time and space warp, it was as though he was literally walking through into another room. It was probably one of the most remarkable ways to travel as it instantaneously transported anyone from one side to the other.

Gavin raised his hand to the portal, and with mental command, started to close it, and re-hide it under the surface of the water. For a moment, the thought of him not requiring any training or instructions on how to operate this method of transportation struck him as odd. It was as though he instinctively just knew how it worked after Sern gave him some memories. It was a mind-boggling experience, but had he not thought twice about it, he just instantly knew what to do as though it was second nature to him.

"Sern went somewhere?" a voice asked, from behind him.

"Yes. He's temporarily departed back to Aurastar for a diplomatic mission," Gavin turned to Dominic who just entered the room.

"You look different," Dominic commented, not just referring to the change of attire that Gavin was now wearing.

"Sern has granted me temporary access to a limited range of his memories and powers, should anything get dire here." Gavin replied as without the need of a direct mental command, his eyes began to flash with the same brilliant light, that Sern's did, during a mental link.

"So you're the big boss here now then?" Dominic was slightly impressed by the situation. Normally under Hasaan, they wouldn't have a replacement but just would have to handle things as is. Sern on the other hand, somehow saw the need that there should be someone with at least some Intendant level abilities to take his place, should he depart.

"Only for the time being. I expect that when Sern returns, my abilities will be removed."

"You know, you're also starting to sound like him too" Dominic crossed his arms. Gavin was surprised to hear this but since he now had a part of Sern in his head, Dominic was only stating the obvious.

Chapter 11

Aurastar, the home of the Va'Nai, was a construct of thousands of satellite cities, which orbited around a central large city, which all together, floated within the confines of their own nebula. Taking a portal from Wolf Coven House to the Transport Hub then to Aurastar literally transported one, hundreds of light years away from Earth, to a part of the outer Orion-Cygnus region. The vast glowing and majestic crystalline structures, each unique, seemed to sing with a comforting hum as their white and light green luminosity glows warmed and calmed those who saw them. Even for Sern, someone who had been here for many many years, the sight was always one to behold.

At the center of Aurastar's outer core of city-structures each on their own platforms, was the vast towering spire of the central Synodium. The Synodium is a vast dome-like structure, several dozen miles in diameter, and a central tower spire, which in itself was easily the largest artificial structure known to exist. It alone stretched beyond his eyes, far into the high skies of their nebula, perhaps dozens if not a hundred kilometres straight upward. Decorating the central spire were thousands upon thousands of windows and viewing ports enclosing the vast chambers, offices and meditation rooms for those who served the Va'Nai.

At the top was the realm of the Va'Nai themselves, located in a pinnacle that resembled the form of earth flowers, such as the platforms of lotus leaves that almost warranted a sense of religious worship.

If one were to approach Aurastar from the entrance to the nebula, they would see something resembling a vast ringed planet, only to find that those rings were composed of crystalline compounds used by the Va'Nai to build their cities, which made up the spherical cluster of inner structures. They all orbited around the central Synodium, in a vast spherical formation which resembled a planet from a distance, but as one got closer and closer, it is actually a vast network of assembled cities and fortresses, all linked by transportation beams that carried people from place to place at mind-numbing speeds. Without a doubt, it was one of the most impressive assemblies of technology and engineering that anyone could ever see, far beyond even the imagination of human beings.

Sern's approach to the Synodium did not go unnoticed as he was escorted by a pair of Guardian Constructs, literally walking golems of crystal, made of the same materials as the Va'Nai buildings. Their vast forms were easily twice as tall as the average human males. Being made out of the crystals that the Va'Nai used, these Guardian Constructs were virtually indestructible by human means. Possessing unquestionable loyalty to their Intendant and superiors, they made good soldiers, should the time of war come upon the Va'Nai.

The platform steadily sped towards the Synodium, as above, below, and beside, were also hundreds of others, heading back and forth from one section of the building to the other. Within the vast ether of the space around them were tens of thousands of other floating buildings, from entire clusters of cities linked to each other, to the solitary towers and buildings alone on their own platforms, seemingly rotating in an endless parade around the vast Synodium.

From what Sern could tell, there was a significant amount of activities taking place, a far higher than average transport of people going back and forth from the Synodium, platforms zipping past each other at varying speeds. This was clearly more than just a simple diplomatic situation. As Sern's platform came closer to ground level, he could now see what was going on.

There was an entire force of Protectors and Enforcers, military ranks of the Sanctuary Organization, lined up in formation. From his best estimate, there must have been five hundred of them, all standing at attention. This first five hundred was probably the first wave. Sanctuary and the Va'Nai could field millions of soldiers, but they have never had to for a single operation before; but in this case, even an assembly of just this few hundred was significant. There hadn't been any need for a gathering like this in centuries. Sern's platform reached the edge where it slowed down, and with the guardian escorts, he marched towards the central lower chambers.

Before he even entered the chamber, another Intendant came up to him. A shorter fellow, but no less formidable, was Intendant Gareth. He had a great deal of urgency in his eyes as he quickened his pace to intercept Sern.

"Sern, come with me immediately, please. We are required at once," he commanded in a firm tone filled with urgency. Sern didn't question but followed him immediately, as the ground they stood on slowly lifted up. It formed a hexagon-shaped crystalline platform, which glided over the ground, towards another group of Protectors and Enforcers, this time, numbering in thousands. It turned out that the first groups of a few hundred were already marching to join this larger group in the middle of the Synodium chamber, where a selection of Superintendents and even Archons and Avatars were gathered. This was clearly not the case for them to wait; instead, it was probably a situation that they had to take command to an extent.

The environment around them was completely silent with discipline and dedication. No one questioned; no one spoke. There was only a unanimous mutual consented silence as the Avatars and Archons began to summon a portal, this one, massive in scale compared to the ones that was at Wolf Coven House. The portal that Sern took to reach here was one of only two that were about the same size as a human being. This was required to be large enough to transport hundreds of troops through it. Without a doubt, this was going to be quite the task; but knowing the sheer power of their force of will and skill, it wouldn't be too difficult. Before the thought had cleared Sern's mind, from above the chamber, descended a trio of the Va'Nai themselves.

Their arrival caught everyone's immediate attention, as they began to form a line that would enter the portal. Their military formation was perfect as was their armour. Their natural crystalline-woven cloth had thickened and hardened into powerful thick armour, almost plated to the touch, but light enough that they would never hinder their movements. Their skills depended on their weapons and most were used to using melee forms of combat weapons, hand to hand. They ranged from the simple sword and staff, to the more elaborate weapons like the dual blades and many different types of exotic weaponry from different cultures. Sern spotted even the beautiful and deadly Ara, a whip-like blade that could slice heads off, and enormous war hammers. Every protector and enforcer was dressed in the Armour of their culture, but all with the colours of the Va'Nai and the Sanctuary Organization.

The three Va'Nai began to glow, with a light even more vibrant than what they normally emitted, focusing it on the wormhole in the center of the room which was being stabilized by the other Archons and Avatars. Soon the three of them took over the control of the portal, and it enlarged smoothly and silently. Within the vast bubble of warped space, they could see their destination, a Sanctuary Outpost on another world.

Sern and Gareth slowed down and joined another group of Intendants near the portal entrance.

"This is an expeditionary force, summoned to join and assist the Ahri." Gareth told Sern. He kept his eye on the troops as they prepared to enter.

"I wasn't aware that our current diplomatic status justified military intervention." Sern questioned.

"It doesn't, but one of their worlds, has to be secured to solidify relations with the Ahri. It's only a small force, but enough to help the Ahri. They have offered us the assistance of their portal summonses, if we offer them assistance as well as the potential for one of our city ships."

"That is a significant bargain for them Ahri."

"As it is for us. You are to join in the expeditionary force with us, to assist the Ahri."

"This seems very short notice. I had just recently assumed Intendantship of Wolf Coven House on Earth, and it seems an extremely inconvenient time for me to do so."

"I do apologize, Sern," the short woman form of Archon Alena came up to Sern. She could tell he was reluctant to join them. "Your joining this is important because our hands are currently limited in what we can do. Because Wolf Coven House is in a non-hostile area of the Sanctuary's influence, we figured it would be possible to leave a deputy in charge, which no doubt, you would have done."

"Yes, I appointed Gavin as Deputy-Intendant in my absence, but I did not know why I was summoned," Sern reported back to Alena.

"As Gareth explained, the original negotiations with the Ahri were to assist them in the formation and construction of a vessel capable of leaving orbit. Their arcane powers are extremely impressive but they lack the fundamental knowledge of building such a craft, so we are going to assist as a part of our alliance. However, the Ahri are formally requesting our help. We can't let a diplomatic advantage like this slip by."

"I understand," Sern acknowledged. He really didn't need to be convinced. It was his duty as an Intendant to obey the commands of his superiors, but nonetheless, such a rapid change of orders so quickly was extremely unusual. However, also in his research and records of the Ahri from the central archives, he could sense that this diminutive race of magic users and their versatility in the magical arts would prove extremely useful to the Sanctuary Organization, and that an alliance would be of great benefit to both.

The three Va'Nai enlarged the wormhole enough to accommodate them as Archon Alena herself led the first of them in. Sern followed alongside the other Intendants, twenty-five in all, followed by a well-armed army of their own. They were also joined by Crystalline Constructs, numbering in many hundreds themselves following between the square block formations of the Enforcers and Protectors. To the thunderous synchronized thump of their marching, they walked forwards in perfect formation.

Exiting the portal, they were bombarded by not enemy weapon fire, but instead, the lush vast green plains of the Sarutan fields, which surrounded one of the Ahri cities. Their world was not unlike that of Earth, but from what Sern could see, as this was his first visit, they were within the confines of a Sanctuary Outpost. The same crystalline walls and spires, sat outside the viewing distance of the Ahri City, but with the faint outline of an enormous tree in the far distance. It must have been a good thirty or so kilometers in human measurement to the city.

"They permitted us to build this outpost in order to help with diplomatic relations," Alena told Sern as they came thorough, and then moved aside to allow the troops to follow. A single tall tower, and a selection of walls that formed a star formation around it, almost like the classical European styled star fortresses of the 18th and 19th centuries, dominated the Outpost.

From what Sern could tell, the fortified walls of the outpost were not Va'Nai works but old stone foundations of earthen and stone-built walls, likely from a much earlier era. It seemed possible that this might have been an Ahri outpost many centuries ago, but due to the minimal threat this close to their capital, they abandoned it. When the Sanctuary made contact, this spot was given to them to use as an outpost and embassy.

Another Sanctuary Official who wore an elaborate sash with the gold and silver markings of a diplomatic officer, quickly met them. An entourage of very small little beings joined him. They resembled almost cherubic versions of human children. Their large heads and small bodies, in comparison to humans, certainly did make them seem almost like little children.

Sern recognized them as the Ahri from the records in the Sanctuary Organization's archives. Unusual for any race, the Ahri also seemed to not age past adulthood, and remained quite youthful looking even into their fifth century of life. The Ahri wore elaborate clothing, not unlike the fashion of a very formal ritualistic style, mixed in rich embroidery with elaborate robes and headpieces. The leader seemed to wear an almost tri-corn looking hat with an elaborate red feather atop, with a red suit-like robe. Each of the others also wore similar looking clothing that matched an elegant but egalitarian style. They all carried staves that looked like they were woven out of branches and thick sticks. Atop each of their staff was a large pearl about the size of an orange.

"Archon Alena," the Diplomatic Officer bowed with respect. The little being also bowed, following the human custom that no doubt they were taught. "May I present, his Excellency, Ambassador Kito of the Ahri." Alena and the entire delegation also bowed, almost simultaneously, respectfully towards the little beings.

"On behalf of the Great Enlightened, we welcome and are thankful for your assistance," the little being graciously replied. "These Flame Autarchs erupted from the ground around our settlements and attacked our cities! Thankfully, we managed to evacuate and escape through portals, but they are heading right for our colonial capital city! There is no time, but to boost up our defence! The Great Enlightened is willing to accept the Alliance, but we have little time to waste!" Kito responded, urgency in his voice. The other little Ahri around him also nodded with approval.

"Why have they decided to come directly towards the capital?" Alena asked as the troops started heading out of the outpost, heading towards the vast tree in the distance.

"We do not know! Their force rained from the sky but did not attack us directly, probably knowing that we have many battle wizards within our capital," Kito replied as he and the other Ahri tapped their staves against the ground. From the earth itself, formed disks of earth soon thinned and hardened into something resembling metal. The earth itself and the rocks had compressed themselves into hovering platforms for them to stand on. Sern only assumed this was a method of transport to enable them to walk just as fast as the humans. The troops had started to jog, to increase their speed towards the city.

Chapter 12

"How are you feeling?" Paxton whispered into Jett's ears. Jett's eyes were already wide open. He had come back from that last run, almost like an animal.

"Better," Jett answered without moving. He just lay there in the bed under the covers with Paxton. Paxton could tell that Jett was saying what he wanted to hear.

"Everyday, the full moon gets closer, and for you there's no way you can get better."

"Full moon," Jett sighed. The two words alone had a massive number of meanings for him. "My first one." The typical Hollywood portrayals of an animal locked in a cage, painfully, bones cracking, skin stretching, roars and screams of the transformation occupied his mind. In particular, that graphic transformation scene in "An American Werewolf in London" was one that always stuck out. Jett had never had any interest in the supernatural. He didn't even get that interested after he started dating Paxton, who was on a Vampire TV show.

"When you go into that cell, I'll be right outside," Paxton assured him. "I won't leave your side." His gaze matched with Jett's, in a look that displayed all the loyalty he needed to hear. "Though to be honest, I'm more worried about that Dentist that we have to see this afternoon," he reminded Jett.

"Damn, I forgot about that," Jett sat up and rubbed his face, restoring some blood flow from hours of staring at the ceiling blankly. The funny idea of a dental check-up was something that Cazian had told him and Paxton about earlier when they were examining the isolation cells. "He mentioned that the experience would be more memorable due to the doctor being a Zombie."

"Epic," Jett smirked sarcastically. "As long as none of his fingers break off during the check-up, I'm fine." The comment brought a very grotesque image into Paxton's mind, something that only Jett's sarcasm could bring out. But he did relish the experience of seeing Jett smirk. It was as close to a smile as he had gotten all morning.

"Alright, time for breakfast." Paxton gently tapped Jett's face with a pillow.

After cleaning, showering and getting dressed, the two of them proceeded into one of the large ballrooms that doubled as a dining room. It was strange having breakfast in there, since it was a very massive room, with a single long table in it. Along the sidewalls were other tables, used to display the assortment of sausages, bacon, eggs, pancakes, waffles, toast and an assortment of drinks, one of which was blood red, which made them both curious.

Immediately when entering the room, they could see quite a few people sitting at the table, conversing about various topics. There was Cazian, Coltrane and Trenton who they recognized, but another eight, whom they have not met. It was unlikely that even after introduced, that they wouldn't remember their names all that fast.

"Boys!" Cazian greeted with a yell from the far end of the table. "Help yourselves to some breakfast!" he offered. The two of them nodded and went over to the breakfast buffet table.

"Who cooks all this stuff?" Jett whispered in inquiry to Paxton.

"No idea, but I'm guessing they have someone for that." Paxton could instantly tell what the red fluid was. He took one of the large glasses, and poured himself a healthy amount. The scent was instantly recognizable to him.

"Blood...." Jett commented. "Human," the second word pretty much affirmed that he would have no interest in it. The only blood that Bloodbanes were interested in, was not human but vampire. Trenton had explained to him that, that was the reason for their name, that they were a bane on the Blood Kin.

"Yup, tastes fresh." Paxton remarked after taking a sip of it.

"That's because it is," Cazian came up and gave him a friendly hand on the shoulder. He didn't want to pat him, for fear of spilling the blood. They both looked over to see Jett piling on the eggs, bacon, sausages on his second plate, the first one was already stacked with the meat, which included eggs and ham.

"Is that normal?" Paxton whispered to Cazian.

"What?" Cazian asked as he too, filled up his glass.

"His appetite. I've never seen him eat that much." Jett had placed the two plates down on the table, and went back for a third one.

Cazian guided Paxton to the table where they sat across from where Jett had put down his two plates. They just sat with their glasses of blood as Jett had already started to gulp down the food. He looked at the fork and knife in his hands and then just casually dropped them, going right at the food with his hands.

Like a hungry animal, he gulped down mouthfuls of the bacon, sausages, and ham, all in a few minutes, chomping it down, not caring at all about the fact that most people were looking at him. Cazian didn't look that surprised, but Paxton couldn't take off his eyes with a bizarre reaction in his face.

"Bloodbanes are renowned for getting hungry during full moon, it's also how they maintain all that strength." Cazian explained to Paxton as Jett continued to gulp down more food. His hands, covered with a mixture of egg yolk and grease, just kept grabbing the stuff. It was as though he really was becoming an animal, lips smacking and licking his fingers at every gulp and bite of whatever he could get his hands on.

"He's going to get sick!" Paxton stepped up, wanting to calm Jett down.

"Don't worry, this is normal for him," Trenton called over to Paxton. "He's naturally storing enough energy for his transformation tonight."

"And he's going to need all that food for his wild transformation." Trenton nibbled on a piece of bacon as he sat down beside Paxton.

"And who are the others?" he asked, looking around.

"Well those are Alexander and Gregory, two other vamps but of a more classical order. They call themselves Regals, but we call them Dracs or Drakes," Cazian pointed to, two very handsome young men who sat at the end of the table seemingly having their own conversation. They were very well-dressed, wearing what would look like Victorian style clothes, elegant, to say the least.

"Why?"

"After Dracula. Bram Stoker based his character on their Order. Turning into a bat, mist, a wolf, all that stuff, they can do."

"Wow!" Paxton wrapped his mind around the thought of turning himself into a bat. "Wait," he interrupted himself. "Do they have wings?" He inquired, curiously.

"Heh, nope," Cazian remarked. Trenton could only smirk at Paxton's sudden change of expression from respect to disillusion.

"And them?" Paxton pointed to another four guys, who all sat together. They looked very normal, just your average guys in their twenties and thirties, seemingly nothing that special about them.

"Wolves too. Packwalkers," Trenton whispered to Paxton, keeping their discussion rather more discreet.

"What's the difference?"

"Well Bloodbanes used to be Packwalkers. The only real difference is that Bloodbanes use any method to get stronger, and they found out that Vampire blood is an effective steroid, and a strong mental stimulant. So basically Packwalkers are clean Bloodbanes. And they have packs, with Alphas as their leaders, like real wolves."

"So tonight they're going to go moon-crazy too?"

"Yeah. That's why they're here."

"How much did they eat?" Paxton mentioned, pointing to the cleared off fourth plate that Jett had now just finished, and was wiping off his hands and face with a set of wet towels that Cazian had gotten him. Without a doubt, he was obviously full, but not full enough to avoid moving.

"They don't need to eat that much since despite the full moon, they can remain controllable; but somehow for Bloodbanes, they started to go more and more mad and crazy during the full moon. We don't know why, maybe a side effect from the blood consumption."

"And where has Sern been? Or Gavin?" Paxton asked, wondering where the whereabouts of thetwo primary guardians who they have relied on for support.

"Sern is on some mission. So Gavin's in charge and he's been in Sern's office for hours now."

"Well, I hope he can help Jett tonight."

"After the dentist!" Cazian smiled at Paxton. "You and your boyfriend have to get your teeth checked out."

"Yeah, what is it with that? Why do I need a dental check?"

"To make sure your fangs are good, him too," Cazian pointed at Jett who suddenly realized he's being pointed at by Cazian.

"My what?" Jett inquired, not hearing most of their conversations.

"Teeth checked, by the Zombie dentist," Cazian pointed to his own elongated fangs.

"Then I'm going to go brush!" Jett hopped up to his feet, then almost tilting over from his very full stomach. Paxton raced over to his side, holding him up with relative ease.

"We'll get cleaned up." Paxton told Cazian.

"Don't take too long!" Cazian called as they headed out of the dining area. "The Dentist is going to arrive soon for your check-ups."

"As long as he doesn't lose one of his fingers during the check-ups, I'm fine."

It was already midday before they arrived at the med-room. It was highly unusual to Paxton and Jett, that they would even have a place like this since there was no medical staff around. There was no Wolf Coven Doctors or nurses, and there didn't seem to be any need for any medical staff since everyone had the ability to rapidly heal wounds.

The room was almost like that from one of those mid 90s horror movies. It was definitely a spooky room, the white tiled floors, the twenty cots along the sides of the walls, with a center area, with desks and a few movable racks of medical supplies, bandages, and distilled water. It was still dark, and despite their new ability to easily see in the dark, it didn't look right. Paxton saw a light switch on the wall next to where they were still standing and flicked it on.

Instantly the lights flickered on. The silence of the room was interrupted by an eerie electrical hum, which was only interrupted by the tapping of their own footsteps. The room was still very eerie. There were doors all along the side of the far end, which were painted a very sterile white colour.

"Glad to see you are here, on time," a strange, and croaky voice came from behind them. Cazian stood there, next to a slouching figure. He was wearing a medical tunic that ran down his body to his knees. His face obscured by a medical mask. With a slouching posture, he looked almost a two feet shorter than Cazian. His hair was matted, and looked very unkept. His eyes were probably the most disturbing. Featuring cloudy cataracts, it was amazing that he could see at all as he limped into the room. "I take it that one of these two, is my examination specimen?" He beamed a glare over to Paxton.

"I am, he's not," Paxton pointed to Jett.

"Very well." The partially decomposing undead man grinned through his mask, while rubbing his hands sadistically.

"Good show, doc," Cazian smirked, revealing the fact that his natural persona wasn't in fact as sinister.

"Sorry, I couldn't resist," his deep throaty, almost croaking voice calmed to a much more normal monotone. It was a fascinating contradiction to the fact that he did, in fact, look like a zombie mad scientist. At least the zombie part was accurate. To his credit he did play the part rather well.

"Weren't you on the show too?" Jett asked, recalling the presence of a zombie doctor in one of the episodes.

"Yes. It was a guest star role," the zombie doctor laughed almost mockingly. "I still get fan mail because of it," he pointed towards one of the metal doors at the end of the room. "You, vampire, come with me." He limped over to the doorway.

"Me?" Paxton pointed to himself.

"Yes...." he pulled the side latch as the door hissed open, almost like it was powered by hydraulics; the mental bolted doors didn't inspire much confidence. It was like they were the true forms of isolation chambers that were used in the house.

"You know, these places look more like prison cells," Jett commented to Cazian.

"That's because they were, at one time," Cazian replied, "before we modified the squash courts below, these were what we used."

"Lovely. And creepy."

"And unpleasant. They were definitely not fond of these cells. But they were tough. No one could get through these reinforced metal doors," Cazian banged one of them with his fist, the loud clanging of the echoes were quite resonant.

The room that the Doctor revealed was quite clean despite the clearly old appearance of the larger hospital ward outside. The doors were spotless and the clean dentist chair in the middle of the room was clearly modern, with the full range of x-ray and rinse basins for whatever came out. It was unusual that they would be doing this with a single doctor, and no dental assistant.

"Have a seat please," the Doctor instructed Paxton, as he slipped on another pair of rubber gloves, over the ones that he was already wearing. There seemed to be an ample supply of them on the long shelves around the room. Aside from a sterile sink and a pre-set collection of dental equipment, the room was considerably well-stocked, as though there was already the need for equipment. It was probably more accurate that someone had stocked up the room for this little appointment.

Paxton hopped onto the leather reclining seat as the doctor placed the typical dental bib over his head. The cool chill of the metal chain gave him a slight shock at first, as it did when he was human. The electric sounds of the chair's reclining motion sure brought back memories of those cavities that everyone had to have fixed, and that awkward pose and the feeling of the blood rushing to your head.

"And now extend those fangs, please," the doctor had reached for the sickle-shaped hook, better known as the periodontal probe. Paxton extended his fangs down, which was very awkward in this position. The doctor gave his new fangs a few taps, then reached in with the mouth mirror to get a look at the teeth from the back. He placed a plastic block into Paxton's mouth to prevent his jaw from closing down, and gave him a deeper look. It was very awkward. "Retract them, please," the doctor instructed again, his voice now more clangy than before, almost as though he was straining his voice. He put on a pair of goggles over his eyes, probably something to enhance his vision since he had cataracts. Paxton did what he was told and pulled his fangs back in. "And we're all done." The doctor pulled out the plastic block, then started raising the chair.

"Typical healthy vampire fangs, nothing to worry about," The doctor assured.

"That was relatively pointless," Jett muttered to Cazian, who were both watching from the side of the room.

"Not really," the Doctor took off his goggles. "You would be quite amazed how many vampires have improper fangs. This usually comes from having bad teeth as a human. So there are problems with feeding or just plain aesthetics.

"How would you fix that? Don't we heal fast?"

"Not with a true silver scalpel," the doctor flashed a small blade. It did shine unusually brightly. "Anyways, you're all done. I just needed to make sure that you were ready for natural biting."

."True silver?" Jett asked Cazian.

"Yeah, the only metal that can really hurt us. It can cut through our skin like how normal blades cut through human skin."

"So you won't heal?"

"We'll heal but it will take longer, like how a normal wound is for a human. As oppose to other weapons, which we instantly heal. Bullets don't kill us either despite the presence of a heartbeat."

"What about a bullet made out of true silver?" Jett asked.

"Our hearts are only beating really just out of reaction, it's not required. They pump because that's just what they do, but it's not required. We don't even really need to breathe or need air, we just breathe out of habit."

"What can kill us, by the way?" Jett asked now referring to himself and wolves in general.

"Werewolves?" Cazian asked for a moment with Jett replying with a nod. "Pretty much anything like a sliced off head, or fire, but realistically, anything that can consistently stop your heart from beating."

"Lovely," Jett grumbled to some disappointment. "Nice to know these things. And that my boyfriend can outlast me easily."

"Think of him as a great bodyguard," Cazian nudged Jett with a smile.

"Or an unkillable beast if I piss him off."

"Well that's a risk that we all have to take eventually." Cazian shrugged as Paxton got off the dentist chair.

"Wasn't that little dental trip a little hyped up?" Paxton asked his brother-sire.

"I did notice, that you both didn't seem to care much that this was your first encounter with a true Undead." Cazian pointed to the dental doctor who was putting away the utensils. The Zombie doctor seemed to be leaving the pieces of dental equipment in places that were ready for cleaning, as though there would be someone to handle all of that work.

"Doctor Mazek," He bowed almost mockingly with that seeming faux elegance. His own face was still obscured by the dental mask that he wore over half his face.

"Why are you still wearing that?" Jett asked him, pointing to his own face to indicate the dental mask.

"If you thought bad breathe was horrible enough for the living, you can imagine how foul it would be, from the undead." The doctor grinned, followed by a very sinister sounding laugh and cackle.

"Fascinating," Paxton groaned, just realizing that he was within proximity to that doctor. "So you're a zombie?" he asked, crossing his arms across his chest.

"One prefers the term, Intelligent Undead."

"Which would suggest the existence of the Unintelligent Undead?" Paxton quirked.

"Indeed. For those who have a dietary interest in the cerebral cortex would qualify certainly as unintelligent," the doctor turned towards the two vampires and werewolf in the room, as he held his hands behind his back, slouching prowling forwards like an old man.

"Cerebral … what's it?" Jett turned to Cazian.

"Brains," the taller vampire replied.

"So, undead eh? Lots of types I guess?" Jett turned towards the doctor again.

"Yes but I have no time to give you an entire history lesson on the existence of the undead," the doctor continued to prowl out of the hospital room. He didn't really seem to be in a rush despite what he was saying. "I anticipate that his house has a library full of interesting tomes and books and collections of various writings that, I am sure, will educate you in such matters," the doctor answered as he turned around the corner out of view.

"So he came, tapped my teeth twice, and that counts as a dental check-up?" Paxton asked Cazian.

"It's all you need," Cazian answered. Paxton had to contemplate the thought for a moment. It did seem rather weird but now that it was done, he didn't have much else to worry."

Chapter 13

Gavin didn't spare any of his time when he gained access to the vast book collection that Hasaan and Sern possessed. Within the office, there were vast shelves of books reaching up two floors, of which Gavin didn't mind reading through. With his new abilities, Gavin could scan through a three hundred page book in a few minutes. Whether he would remember this after his abilities died off would be another question.

His concentration was briefly interrupted by the sight of Cazian peering through the doorway. He didn't recall opening the door, so it must have been Cazian who opened it.

"Well, you certainly look different," Cazian remarked as he came in, viewing the holographic image that was hovering in front of Gavin on the desk.

"Indeed," Gavin dimmed the image slightly but still kept it visible, "it was nothing confidential."

"So. This is what you would look like if you were an Intendant?" Cazian examined his sire. He definitely still looked like Gavin, though how he carried himself was certainly not the same. He was more proper, standing with perfect posture. He was almost Sern-like in how he behaved, from the hand gestures he used to control the holographic image.

"I am an Intendant, at least a Deputy-Intendant for the time being. My abilities and status will only last for two weeks, or until Sern returns. If it requires an extension, someone from the Sanctuary Organization will extend my tenure," Gavin spoke. He was extremely formal in how he spoke, just like Sern. But there were some slight inflections that he felt, that were definitely Gavin's speech patterns.

"Wow, you even talk like him now," Cazian had realized now, that Gavin was already not quite the same person that he was before. A part of Sern was in him, and a part of him was going to be in Sern when he returned. Only in a situation like this would he be able to experience something like this. "Tonight is the full moon event. It's going to be sundown soon," Cazian reminded Gavin.

"Yes, it's best that we get them to their isolation cells soon." Gavin agreed as he turned off the console.

"What were you reading?" Cazian wondered as to the contents of the images that Gavin was going through.

"Historical archives of our race and other curiosities. Sern and Hasaan acquired quite the collection of knowledge," Gavin commented as he walked around the desk towards Cazian.

"What does it feel like?" Cazian asked as he sat down in one of the leather chairs. Gavin sat down on one beside him. It had never even occurred to him, to think about the transformation of his mind since the infusion.

"It's very unusual," Gavin started as he began to think carefully through the thoughts of his experience, comparing them to his prior mental state before the infusion. "It is as though now I have two minds, two personalities that merged with each other. I still remember everything that I was before, but with the added knowledge that Sern's mind gave me."

"So you know everything he knows?" Cazian asked, pondering the complexities of Gavin's situation.

"No, it is not like he copied aspects of his own mind and pasted it into my brain; it's more like, he has given me some of his experiences as well as knowledge, from his point of view. So I do know how he would react and respond to certain situations."

"That's....weird," Cazian admitted. The idea of mind transfers and thought reading was something he was never really comfortable with, let alone the full implanting of memories into someone else's mind. "I never liked anything like mind readers. I think that our minds are our own," Cazian stated firmly.

"I can sympathize."

"So you're not really Gavin anymore; you're kind of Gavin with some Sern?" Cazian wanted to clarify.

"It is very difficult to explain. I do feel that a portion of his mind is right here, in my head," Gavin pointed to the left temple of his head. "The presence of his mind or some aspects of it, helps me concentrate, and understand what he has to go through. He gave me some of his strengths and abilities too."

"Like those force field powers and blasting people with energy bolts?"

"I can do those, yes, but I see hardly any need for it. Sern gave me those abilities in case things took a turn for the worst."

"Well we do have a Bloodbane Wolf tonight, going under his first full moon," Cazian reminded Gavin. "In case things get bad, you may have to help him out."

"Through half a foot of reinforced unbreakable glass, I find that unlikely," Gavin stood up. "But just in case, I will be present to assist."

"I can hardly wait for Sern to come back," Cazian put his hand on Gavin's shoulder.

"Why is that?" Gavin requested, out of a yearning for clarification.

"Then you can talk normal again. This weird formal speech you're using makes you almost a bit robotic." Cazian gently squeezed Gavin's shoulder as they stepped out of the office. "But first, dinner!"

The dining room was much like how it was during breakfast and lunch. The same display of food was already set out, and yet no one saw the catering servers. There were twenty staff servers in Wolf Coven House, all of whom were Patchers, a type of Zombie undead who, despite their outward undead appearance, were still intelligent as human beings. It was odd that they were the ones who did all the services, since many of them required cleaning and cooking; and with the potential for loose body parts falling off during their jobs, it was certainly awkward.

But the Patcher Staff always did get their jobs done very well. Despite the one time threat of unionizing, they were never a bother. Few people even knew them by name; but within the bowels of Wolf Coven House, they had their own little society to themselves.

Considering that most of Wolf Coven House didn't have frequent room service, the Zombie Crew had little to do most of the time. Cooking and cleaning and gardening were their main duties, just like most housekeeping staff. Unlike most staff, they didn't attend to the front door, just in case they would run into someone who was not used to the undead would definitely freak out if they were seen.

Most of the Wolf Coven members were already there. Most of them did give Gavin a few awkward looks. He was wearing the clothing similar to Sern's, the robes and jacket of an Intendant, and even the way he walked was visibly different. Paxton, Jett, Dominic, Coltrane, everyone was there, chattering about the table with various assortments of meals already being eaten.

Gavin could sense that Jett was visibly nervous. He could actually start to feel the full moon coming down on him. It was still only 6:30pm and thus he had about a half hour before the moon would shine on him. Gavin did find it strange that there were no plates by them, perhaps Jett had already eaten, or perhaps he had not eaten anything at all since an earlier meal. Paxton was there by his side, arm around him, always protective of his boyfriend.

Gavin, in many ways, did envy the fact that Jett was facing this difficulty with someone who loved him, there by his side. Everyone who noticed them was always in a state of admiration regarding their relationship, as though this transformation on the two of them had made them even closer.

"How are you both doing?" Gavin asked Jett and Paxton. Cazian went to sit with Coltrane and Trenton.

"I can feel it!" Jett almost growled for a moment. Paxton's arm was around him comforting him.

"The full moon?" Gavin clarified.

"Yeah!" Jett closed his eyes, almost concentrating his thoughts.

"Do you guys want to get into the cell now?" Gavin asked them. The two of them gave each other a look. Jett seemed not to be physically ill, but almost like he was trying to contain some sort of internal rage.

"It's frustrating, I feel like there's a fire inside me," Jett almost slammed his fist down on the table. He was visibly shaking, like a car with its engine starting up. "Sorry," he apologized.

"It's alright," Gavin smiled at the two of them as he got up out of his seat. "I'll get you something first before we go down." he went to the door, connecting the dining room to the kitchen.

"Are you good?" Paxton asked Jett softly.

"Yeah," Jett gritted through his teeth. "It's crazy. I feel like my body just wants to get angry, that I have this incredible urge to scream, and rip things apart," Jett held his hands together, refusing to let his limbs loose, fearing that if he did let himself go, only tragedy would ensue.

"Remember that I'm stronger than you too; I can take you." Paxton kidded with him. It was all that Jett needed to hear to bring a small smile to his face. Just then, Gavin came back into the room, holding a white mug in his hands. There was a heated steaming fluid inside it, and instantly the two of them could smell that it was a rather fruity, pleasant smell. Gavin placed it down on the table in front of the two of them.

"This should help you calm down a bit," Gavin insisted as he slid the mug forwards. Jett picked up the mug. Instantly he could smell something familiar. It was like a mixture of lemon and orange and some other sweet fruit-like scents. The fluid itself was red, but translucent. Jett took a sip, and the instant sweetness was tasted, but not without the trace of something naturally herbal in it.

"A tranquilizer?" Paxton asked Gavin as Jett continued to drink it up.

"Yeah, something to help calm him down. It will take a few minutes to take effect, just a natural herbal cocktail of tranquilizing flowers."

"I hope you don't mean opium," Paxton hoped.

"No, I wouldn't get your boyfriend on drugs before he transforms," Gavin insisted, "but that should help him at least for now. Full moon will rise in about a half hour; best get you both down there." Jett gulped down the rest of the drink, then nodded in agreement.

A few moments later, the entire dining room was empty and the cleanup crowd had already gone in. The more ravenous wolves had gobbled up most of the food, leaving little for midnight snacks; considering the events that were going to take place tonight, it seemed unlikely that anyone would be wanting kitchen food. They proceeded down the main hall and entryway into a side staircase that would lead to the squash courts. Each of the wolves who was vulnerable to the moon was escorted into one of the cells. There were curtains in the cells, some preferring their transformations to take place in private. The reinforced glass alone was more than enough to contain them, as were the reinforced concrete walls and tall ceilings.

There was the presence of a skylight, that in the middle of a full moon would beam the light right into the cells. This was for people to observe and make sure that they could gage the transformations by the moonlight. Jett was led into his.

"I want to go in with him," Paxton told Gavin, quite determined to get compliance from his sire.

"I'm sorry; I can't permit that," Gavin told his childe. Cazian, who stood next to Gavin, nodded in agreement with Gavin.

"You may be stronger, but you don't know how to control your own abilities yet. You also don't know what he'll do. He may end up doing serious damage to you; and though you may heal, he won't realize he's injuring his boyfriend. And when he does realize that, he'll be torn apart, on the inside." Cazian entered the cell to see how Jett was doing. He was examining the room and casually sampling the comfort of the cot in the room. It was something that must have been put in recently. For him it was just something he could rest on if he got tired. But already he could feel the moonlight coming down.

"Time's running short," Dominic warned Gavin as the other wolves got into their cells. As soon as they entered, the doors were sealed behind them. Some of them closed the curtains; it was obvious that they didn't want to showcase what was happening to themselves.

"Agreed," Gavin turned to his companion. "Secure them." Cazian and Dominic and the others who were not affected by the moon, helped lock down the other cells. Paxton stood right outside the cell that Jett was now in. Jett looked almost afraid at the room, standing just beyond the doorway. The skylight was already starting to brighten slightly due to the rising moon.

Jett pulled the curtains in. He left a good two feet open, so Paxton could see inside. Already he could feel the internal anticipation mixed with the rage that he was now feeling, being locked inside the cell. He was pacing about now, beating his fists against his palms, his face, almost snarling at the thought. The light grew brighter, almost seemingly amplified by some unseen force. It hit Jett as he started to groan, then scream. Paxton couldn't hear the sound through the glass, but it was clear that he was feeling the transformation happen.

The moonlight immediately triggered his wolf form to start emerging, first with his hands transforming into sharp claws, each claw morphing from the fingernail that at once it had originated, his face, eyes turned fierce and golden, and his fangs sharpened. Almost instinctively he dropped to all fours, continuing to growl like the beast he was turning into, the subtle fur of the wolf emerging out of his neck, down portions of his face. Paxton wanted to look away, not wanting to see what his boyfriend had now become.

Jett, now fully consumed by the wolf within him, turned his head towards the glass walls, and his eyes locked onto Paxton. Paxton's face was filled with sadness and fear, seeing his boyfriend. Jett's face was full of rage, and it was as though there was a fire in his heart that was burning so hot he needed to lash out. His body was in the position of a prowl, as though he was slowly stalking his prey, slowly moving sideways but keeping his glaring eyes onto Paxton. He let out a roar, so loud that even Paxton could hear it, before leaping at Paxton.

Before Jett hit the glass, Gavin reached out his hand, and an invisible counterforce hit Jett, causing him to fall back to the floor. This invisible pulse of force hit him just enough to temporarily daze him. Jett was not amused by this and while he rolled back on his limbs, he roared again and charged at the glass with his razor sharp claws swiping, but only to hit the reinforced glass. Paxton couldn't help but just stood there helplessly, watching Jett transform into an animal, without any sense of humanity inside him. The way Jett glared at him from inside the cell wasn't the look of a human. Even before, he was able to maintain some sense of his personality, but now with the full moon, he had completely lost control over himself.

"How long will this last?" Paxton pleaded with Gavin, not wanting to take his eyes off of Jett.

"Until sunrise, which won't be for another few hours." Gavin answered. He could feel sympathy for Paxton's predicament despite himself being restrained by Sern's mental presence inside his own mind.

"There has to be a way to help him through this," Paxton turned to the two Werewolf Primes and Dominic and Cazian. They all looked towards each other, hoping someone would say something, but their silence revealed that nothing could be done.

"It's best if you don't watch this," Gavin shut the curtains.

"Here, come with me," Dominic led the distraught young vampire to the lobby of the house. Gavin turned to one of the wolves.

They arrived in one of the large sitting rooms. It was well-lit chamber with comfortable couches around that let people sit in small groups. Paxton just collapsed on one of the couches and leaned back, staring up at the tall ceiling. Dominic sat down on the other side of the couch. Paxton was just desperately seeking anything that would distract him from his current mental state. It was difficult enough knowing that his boyfriend was now a bloodthirsty animal, but that he couldn't do anything to help just made him feel even worse.

Dominic wasn't entirely too sure on this situation. It was definitely unique even for him. He had considered relationships with Werewolves before, but he never had to deal with the first transformations, which were the most painful and difficult ones. Coltrane came into the room as well, and sat down on the carpet in front of them, while leaning against the couch.

"What does it feel like?" Paxton asked Coltrane as he sat up, looking at the towering man who, even though he was sitting on the floor, was still quite imposing.

"Every type of shapeshifter, or wereform, is essentially two people, the beast and the human," Coltrane explained. His voice was deep and almost animal like. "As a Bloodbane wolf, they rely a lot on anger for their strength, the aggression in his blood. He's hungering for violence, and also vampire blood."

"Why did werewolves drink vampire blood?" Paxton asked.

"It's like a drug for them. The reason why Bloodbanes are stronger than Packwalkers is because they have become addicted to vampire blood, which is like a stimulant and drug to them." Dominic added.

"So he's a blood junkie?"

"I wouldn't say it that way, but he will want to drink some, not for nourishment like how you need blood, but to get a fix."

"That's a disturbing thought," Paxton pondered for a moment.

"As for blood, have you had any lately?" Dominic asked.

"Just a cup this afternoon. I haven't really been hungry."

"You need blood. Let's give you some that's fresh." Dominic took out his phone and started to send out a text message.

"How fresh? Didn't you guys say that the stuff we had was already pretty fresh?"

"I mean, this is as fresh as it gets. From the vein, from the neck," Dominic explained.

"You think this is what he really needs right now?" Coltrane asked the older vampire, while he was still sitting on the floor slipping out of his leather jacket.

"These are things that he has to learn, and I see no other time to do it." Dominic's phone vibrated indicating an incoming message. He promptly responded with another text. "Things like this have to be taught. The customs of feeding and privacy have to be taught," Dominic replied to the werewolf. "Come with me," Dominic firmly instructed Paxton.

Instead of the same hall where the residential apartments that the Wolf Coven members were living in, these were in the west wing and featured black doors. One door was quite distinctive, as it was a red door. Dominic opened it, revealing inside a room that was a mixture between a supply room, and a type of display museum exhibit. Inside the room were shelves of what looked like masks. They were domino masks that were like those which superheroes wore, just around the eyes. Dominic went over to the shelves with Paxton and they started examining the various designs. Some were sleeker, cooler more stylish than others. It was a collection of objects that Paxton didn't expect to see. But when he thought about it, Dominic did mention something about privacy, and a mask certainly would help with that.

"Choose one," Dominic offered one of the masks to Paxton to try out. It was a rather simple one, but unlike the typical domino mask this was a figure 8 shape, but sharp corners instead of rounded edges, like two diamonds. It was solid black, though it seemed to be made out of leather and fit quite nicely on his face. The others were of various designs, some more subtle and thinner, this one would pretty much do the job.

"What does yours look like?" Paxton asked. Dominic looked around then reached for one of the masks on an upper shelf. It was thinner than the one that Paxton held in his hand, though similar in design. However the curves were sharper and certainly it was more stylized. Paxton held the one in his hand up to his face and looked into a mirror nearby. He certainly did look like a superhero for a moment. The mask only added to mystify his look, which was enhanced with the single overhead light in the room. He couldn't help but shift his eye colour to that feeding, blood red.

"Sometimes the simple designs are best," Dominic admired the look of the mask on Paxton.

"So what are these for?" Paxton asked, leaving the mask on.

"We can get fresh blood, directly from people who are willing to give it," Dominic explained as he led Paxton out of the room. "It all comes from people who are aware of the Sanctuary Organization and the Supernatural, but they are all physically screened that their blood is safe and that they are healthy. Basically we buy their blood."

"So what's the mask for?"

"To protect your identity when you feed. Sometimes close friendships can come out of feeding. Symbolically, if you take off your mask and offer it to your blood donor, it means you are offering to sire them. Many of these donors are aspiring to become like us so they have to give something to us."

"To help us survive?"

"Yes. We need to feed. Donors are also willing to give us blood, right from the vein."

"Do you mean, they let us bite them?"

"Only if they're okay with it. You're not allowed to use mind manipulation on them."

"What about the bite marks?"

"Lick the wound, doing that will help it heal completely. If that fails, put a bit of your own blood onto the cut."

"I wouldn't ever have guessed to do that. Can our High Order blood heal human injuries?" he asked.

"No, not everything, just minor cuts and gashes. We use our blood to cover up bite marks so our donors don't get awkward questions from people they know."

Paxton's face lit up slightly at the thought of that. "Right from the neck, eh?" Paxton asked. The thought had occurred to him that this was probably the most natural and sensual way to feed, but he thought that with them relying on donated blood, it would have to come in chilled blood packs.

"Yes," Dominic pulled out his phone again. It was vibrating. He turned the screen on and took a quick glance at it before pulling a mask off the shelf and putting it on. "He's here."

"Who?"

"Your meal."

The two of them entered one of the ground level rooms. It was on the west side of the building which, from the outside, also had a parking spot in front of it. It resembled almost a motel, with the rooms each having its own external entrance. The rooms also had another door that connected to the main house, so one could leave and enter without having to go through the main entrance. Dominic and Paxton opened one of the doors, these were steel doors for safety purposes, though Paxton wasn't too sure for what reason. The room certainly looked like a standard motel room.

Casually waiting while sitting on the bed was a young man, probably late 20s. Short strawberry blond hair, and gentle looking blue eyes. He looked fairly unsurprised to see two masked men walking into the room. Since he was a donor, it was likely that he had already done this before. Dominic walked in first, waiting for Paxton to enter.

"I didn't know I'd be feeding two of you." The guy remarked as he stood up to shake their hands.

"Since donors' real names are kept confidential, we go by aliases," Dominic told Paxton. "This is Lucas." Dominic introduced. The young man stood up and shook Paxton's hand. He had a rather warm and friendly grip, matched with an equally warm and friendly smile. There was no sense of hostility from this guy; and from what Paxton sensed, he seemed to be fully aware of what was going on and what to expect.

"This is my first time," Paxton admitted to his donor. "I have to admit, that this situation is a bit strange."

"It's usually the other way around," Lucas replied.

"He's new," Dominic referred to Paxton. "Lucas here signed a confidentiality agreement already with us. He's perfectly safe to talk to."

"As long as he doesn't kill me, I'm alright with this," Lucas joked. It was slightly disturbing to Paxton to have him so calm, considering the circumstances.

"Sorry, it's just a bit strange right now. I'm going to feed off of you and you're just somewhat happy to meet me," Paxton remarked

"Like I said, it's not the first time," Lucas replied with an understanding tone.

"In that case I will leave you two alone," Dominic headed to the doorway, but he turned around. "And Paxton, don't take off the mask," He warned with seriousness in his tone. Paxton instinctively felt his mask, which was sitting on his face without any string attached to the back. For a moment, he hadn't even realized that he was still wearing it. It was a strange feeling, but it didn't seem to have any chance of falling off his face. Perhaps this was to protect his identity and also to prevent the mask from falling off should anything happen to him. As Dominic left the room, the door shut behind him with a metallic clang. The door secured itself with three locks.

Then the room was filled with that awkward silence. Lucas and Paxton just stood there, either expecting the other to make the first move in an awkward, almost sexually tense, moment. Paxton had to ground his mind for a moment, remembering right now his boyfriend was locked in a cell turning into an animal.

"So..." Paxton started, trying to figure out what he was going to say following that word. It was definitely an awkward situation, the air was thick with tension. "How do we do this?"

"Well, I prefer neck as opposed to wrists," Lucas suggested.

"And then what?"

"Most just go at it from there. You're hungry, you bite in," Lucas explained in plain and simple terms. "There really isn't anything else to it. You're hungry, you bite; just remember to heal it after you're done and don't take too much."

"Alright," Paxton thought to himself. He had to mentally trigger his game face, fangs and all. It didn't even take an instant for this to happen. Paxton seemed to get his face on pretty quickly, instinctively without even much intention.

Paxton could feel his eyes changing. There was a visible reddish hue around what he was looking at, almost like he was looking through a pair of red sunglasses. It was enough for him to realize visually what was going on. And of course the fangs were easy enough to detect. He placed his arm around Lucas's head, pulling his head slightly to the left before he brought himself to Lucas's neck.

"Sorry, this is really awkward," Paxton apologized. "The last time I was close to someone like this, it was in a very different context."

"I can imagine," Lucas smirked. For him, this wasn't the first time that this happened. "I do this pretty frequently, two or three times a month."

"Here goes!" Paxton gasped as he sank his teeth in. He could feel Lucas grunting for a moment, wincing briefly at the pain of two sharp teeth piercing his neck. Paxton wanted to apologize for the pain, but then as the hot blood started flowing into his mouth, that became the focus of his attention. It was intoxicating for those first few moments, as Paxton suck in the red life-giving fluid into himself. But for him, since he wasn't that hungry he didn't feel that he was going to take too much. Vague memories of him grimacing at the sight of Gavin's blood only a few days ago was a long memory of an old past that he vaguely remembered, as now he was feeding on another human being, right there, in his arms.

Paxton drank some more, for what to him seemed like a few moments, but Lucas was counting already that he had already spent nearly a minute drinking. Lucas instinctively put his hands on Paxton's shoulders, the two of them were still standing as he was bitten and being drained. Paxton could sense that Lucas wasn't in danger, but he himself had more than quenched his thirst. He wasn't hungry when he started, so he didn't take as much as he would have should he had been hungry. Paxton licked the wounds clean as he released Lucas who gently collapsed onto the bed. He sat up for a moment, his face wasn't even that pale from the draining.

Both knew this was only a partial feeding. Dominic had mentioned earlier that this was more for training than it was for an actual feeding session.

"Are you alright?" Paxton asked as Lucas got up from the bed and looked at his neck in the mirror. Already the two cuts had started to heal; and despite being slightly disorientated, Lucas himself seemed fine.

"Yeah, I'm okay," Lucas said. "You could have taken some more."

"No, it's just, that...."

"You're new to this, newly transformed?"

"Yes," Paxton answered, though he was still visibly distracted. For him, this entire situation was something that seemed a bit out of place.

"I don't know if you know this, but donors also are like bartenders. We also listen to your problems if you want to vent anything to us."

"Well, let me just put it this way," Paxton began to explain. "My boyfriend and I are going through a fairly massive drama tornado right now. And learning how to handle our situation and our new lives right now, is already getting taxing."

"Well I'm not too sure about the specific situations that you are referring to, but I can imagine that your new situation isn't anything that is easily handled, let alone also having to deal with the emotional roller coaster that comes with a boyfriend."

"Yeah, though I'm glad to learn, I really just don't feel this is what I need right now."

"It's alright," Lucas comforted Paxton. It was strange, but though he had just met Lucas, the idea that a perfect stranger seemed to have an understanding and sympathy for what he was going through was oddly comforting. Paxton just collapsed onto the bed; his mind was full of thoughts and ponderings about what was going on, constantly thinking

Chapter 14

The assembled relief force of five hundred Ahri and twenty protectors and ten defenders, with Kito and Sern had climbed over the fifth hill. The Sanctuary Assistants were well on their way. In the distance, they could see the flares that the Ahri Fort was sending upwards, requesting aide. The fort could be seen in the distance, a multi-tiered structure much like the other Ahri fortified towns and cities. This one was large enough to accommodate an entire town of a few thousand Ahri.

A few kilometres away, the front lines were already ablaze with action. The Fire Spawns were charging the trench runs that the Ahri had already carved out with their magic. Entire networks of tunnels stretching from their fortified town were surprisingly narrow, even for them, to prevent easy access. The little Ahri themselves had no problem maneuvering such small passages but the Fire Spawns were another story.

Kito and the others stopped their movement while still behind the peak of the hill. They were able to maintain some distance from the fortified town, but he had to make them aware that help was on the way. Taking his staff, which looked like a bundle of intertwined tree branches encircling a pearl at the top, he pointed it towards the sky. It lit up brightly and suddenly shot upwards into the skies, a flare-like spark. It was so bright that the forces inside the town could see it even from that distance. Behind them, the long row of troops was ready to enter the town. The enormous Crystalline Constructs that the Sanctuary force brought, were lumbering side by side with the rest of the troops.

There seemed to be a protective bubble around the fortified city. Its ramparts and protective defence had numerous Ahri on them, as well as their own constructs, made out of raw elements and held together by what looked like glowing braces and chains. Kito signaled the others behind him with his glowing staff to continue marching forwards towards the town.

"I hope that our relief force will be enough for the defence." Sern reported as he examined the battlefield from their elevated point. There were a few Ahri who were also on the hilltop, building some rudimentary defence. It was likely that this would later be used for a more strategic backup point. They all gave off greetings to the incoming troops, cheering them on. The force marched down towards town.

As they approached the rear gate of the town, there was an entire battalion of Ahri Earth Golems standing guard. Though not as large as the Sanctuary Crystalline Constructs, the Earth Golems were more numerous and could potentially pose a threat to them if the numbers were significant enough. They parted to allow the columns of troops to enter when one of the Ahri Generals, Kiro, Ambassador Kito's brother, was leading them into the city. The few Ahri who were on top of the battlements were shooting up more flares into the sky, signaling the city of the arrival of hope.

As they entered, the hero's welcome was even more vibrant as the Ahri in town threw sparkles of light from their own staves. It seemed that almost every Ahri in town has their own staff. Sern noticed that they were all of various designs and styles, but all incorporated the same type of basic form: the wood almost grew and woven into a central shaft tall enough for them to use as walking staves, and with a handle for them to carry without having to wrap their hands around the entire shaft. Atop every staff was a pearl. Even those Ahri who didn't have staves, were able to create sparks of light from their hands, shooting them from their fingers.

The sunset was starting to fall, and due to the lack of technology, the skies were already starting to show the first twinkles of starlight through the orange horizon of the twin suns that orbited this world. Sern and the other Sanctuary Members were greeted by a delegation of Ahri who hurried to meet General Kiro, who rode his enormous war beast, a Kesek, and Kito who was standing atop his own flying disk. As they rushed, the delegation was bombarding Kiro and Kito with questions and statements. Sern couldn't entirely pick out what they were saying since they were virtually mobbed by the little Ahri. Some of the Sanctuary troops were rather amused by these little folks running around their legs.

As they were chattering about, above them, a vast orange, then red glow appeared, reflecting off the taller buildings at the center of the town. At the heart of the town was a tall tower. Naturally it made an effective method of controlling the local area. The Ahri leaders started to hand out small marble sized pearls to all the Sanctuary Troops.

"What are these for?" Sern asked as Kito handed him.

"These are Thoughtpearls," Kito answered as he pointed to one of Sern's upper shirt pockets. "All you need to do while wearing it, is think of the person who you wish to communicate with, then speak out. Your voice will be transmitted to them."

"And if I need to speak to more than one?" Sern asked again.

"Simply think of all those who you wish to speak to, perhaps a category like Protectors," Kito tapped the pearl that was in Sern's pocket. "It will read your mind so it won't tell the ones you don't want."

"We are going to assume central control in the central tower!" General Kiro commanded to his advisors as the rest of them arrived, and quickly dispatched within minutes by the Ahri dignitaries to separate sections of the town. The main force, however, was concentrated at the front of the town where more Ahri were already starting to build more terraces and fortifications.

The Ahri could manipulate the earth, rock and stone as though it were clay, and on a scale much larger than first assumed. The Protectors and Defenders watched as the little Ahri folks, seemingly with such natural effort, could pull it up and merge it into a wall or something to reinforce a broken layer of defence. Atop the fortifications, more armoured Ahri were hurling bolts of arcane energy at the enemy lines. From the distance, they could not see the Flame Spawns, but the glowing red light indicated that they were out there in small patches throughout the wasteland between the town, its trenches and the front lines.

Kito and Kiro observed a moving image of a map of the area. Similar to the holographic images that Sanctuary Organization agents used to display images, but this was a two-dimensional map with various symbols and icons displaying the forces that they had present. From what Sern could detect, the Ahri were using their spells not to destroy the enemy but to keep the Flame Spawns from getting any closer. From what Sern could observe from the top of the tower, every arcane bolt would explode into a small area of sparks that didn't damage the land, but would erase fire within that area. From the tower, the more powerful battle mages were hurling far larger and more damaging bolts, almost like artillery, at the wastelands in front of the trench systems. These larger bursts took more time to cast and the Ahri would use multiple battle mages to power a single stronger arcane bolt which would go farther and hit with more destructive power.

There were enemy projectiles also being fired back, though not with the same range as the Ahri spells. The Flame Spawns were firing off balls of magma and fiery rock at the Ahri front positions. Some of these fiery rocks were the size of cars, but the Ahri had an enormous success rate of shooting them down or countering them with their own spells. The Ahri Cyromancers, frost mages and Aquamancers, or water mages were raining down on the Flame Spawns heavy shards of ice and summoning geysers of water to burst out from the ground, temporarily halting the Flame Spawns.

The Ahri in front of the town were quickly joined by rows of sanctuary protectors, each assisting in shooting down enemy artillery as best as they could. The occasional fiery boulder would land, but it would smash against some protective barrier that the Ahri had put in place. Many of the injured Ahri were carried away to safe shelters and makeshift hospitals which were heavily shielded in town. The Ahri, though skilled in magic, were more vulnerable to physical harm than the larger more robust races.

"In order to quell this, we will need to summon in a massive torrential flood and ice storm!" Kiro commanded to his fellow Ahri.

"To bring something that large into this area, we will have to use the majority of our people to summon a spell of that magnitude," Kito warned, "which means that our defence will be largely unmanned."

"That's why we have the new Sanctuary Organization reinforcements to help us," Kiro pointed to Sern. "We will need your help in making sure that our defence can hold them while we cast the ice storm spell."

"Reinforce the spell shield you have over the town?" Sern asked the Ambassador.

"We're going to have to pull the other Ahri back from the front. But when we're all in the city, time to summon that storm!"

"Very well," Sern left the main tower as the other Ahri went up to the command room at the top of the tower. He turned to the Thoughtpearls inside his pocket, and instantly started thinking to all of his sanctuary members that were in the city. It was like he was drawing up a roster, inside his head, of all those who he was aware of.

"Everyone. The Ahri, as a collective group, will be summoning a massive ice storm. The Sanctuary Forces will have to hold the defence while they do this!" Of course he also remembered that only those who had Thoughtpearls themselves would be able to hear him. By now they would have been distributed enough throughout the city that even those who didn't have access to one themselves would at least be within contact of someone who did.

He could already see them, from the central tier where the Tower was located that the Ahri were making a withdrawal to the main town itself. They were scurrying throughout the tunnel and trench networks, fleeing from the front lines as the others behind them were covering their retreat. Bolts and entire storms of blasts were shooting from the trenches, even more so than before. The sheer amount of blasts that were blanketing the entire area behind them, every bolt exploding in a small nova of sparkling arcane power. They hurried past the sanctuary shield that the Protectors and Defenders were maintaining. The Constructs that they brought with them were at the front of the shield, making sure no Fire Spawns were getting near their position. The Ahri Artillery that was being fired from the far off distance was doing its job in keeping any Fire Spawns from materializing near the Town's shield.

Volley after volley of piercing arcane bolts blasted the lands behind the Ahri as they evacuated back into town, some helping the Sanctuary troops reinforce the shield, as their more powerful mages sought to help in the central tower. Sern raced through the guarded terraces, dashing past the little Ahri, trying not to trip over so many of them who were fleeing. Some were wearing what looked like normal Ahri clothing, citizen's clothing, simple robes, with simple hoods, nothing too elaborate. Even the Ahri Children, who were huddled around their parents were still around.

Sern watched, as many of them fled to the central more heavily guarded tier of town, up many staircases that were guarded by their Earth and Water Elementals, along with a pair of Ahri Sentries. One group of Ahri Children was following one grown up. The Adult Ahri were only about two feet tall, the children, even smaller. Sern couldn't help but help them by picking four of them up into his arms, and helping them up. As he went back up, he could see a few of the enormous balls of magma getting past their defensive fire, and slamming into the shield! Its impact rocked the entire town, but only for a moment. The shield was still very much intact; the magma that was remaining splashed harmlessly against the shield, as the arcane force vaporized what was remaining.

As they approached the top of the main tier, where the majority of the Ahri had evacuated, Sern put the other four Ahri who were scared, and one even in tears, down to the ground where their guardian was. The little Ahri hugged Sern's leg. Sern looked down on the little folks.

"You have nothing to worry about!" he assured them. They all huddled with each other and around their guardian. "Where are these children's parents?" he asked their guardian.

"They're still fighting at the front and are on their way back. I was charged with evacuating them back to the central tier of the city!" Their guardian answered as she was counting the number of Ahri. As she counted, a desperate expression of fear came across her face. "Where's Rena?" She cried out to the other children. The little ones looked around.

"Where's my sister!" one of the boys called to the others. There was massive confusion as other Ahri were arriving from the evacuating sections of the town.

"Do you have a Thoughtpearl?" Sern picked up the boy, who was Rena's brother.

"Yes! I can track her, but it's too dangerous!" he wailed, trying to wipe the tears from his eyes. Sern's robes instantly started to change. From the back, the hood behind his head enlarged big enough to encompass one of the Ahri.

"Here, little one, get on my back! We're going to find your sister!" Sern turned to their guardian. "Are all the other ones accounted for?"

"Yes, only Rena is missing!"

"I can still hear her! I know where she is!"

"She may be in one of the buildings just outside the shield!" the guardian called. The cloth itself thickened to form safely into belts and straps that kept him secure and safe as Sern leaped down off the terraces as fast as he could, sprinting down the stairs.

More and more Ahri were fleeing but Sern headed into the opposite direction.

"What's your name, little one?" Sern asked as he dodged some falling debris with blazing speed.

"Kolko," the little Ahri answered, holding onto the straps that were almost like those of a backpack which were strapped onto Sern's back, and around his arms. Above his own head was a hood that protected him as well. "I can hear my sister! She's still safe but she's afraid! She's right where our school was, just outside the shield towards that tower!" Kolko pointed towards a round tower, that was just east of their position but still fairly out of the way. There were no more Ahri who were coming in from that direction, but there were some Sanctuary forces nearby who were reinforcing the shield.

One of the little beings down there had a staff like the other Ahri. Staves helped them focus and amplify their magical powers, and this Ahri was using what magic she knew to fend off this giant Flame Spawn. It was breathing fire against a small sphere of protective energy that she had around herself and an even smaller Ahri.

Enraged at what he saw, Sern soared into the air, and like a fire-breathing monster himself, slammed down on the monster, with as much cosmic power as he could summon onto himself, crushing it into bits. Kolko, though he was perfectly secure on Sern's back, was still almost grasping onto him for dear life as Sern went down so fast.

The Flame Spawn was smashed into rubble, the rocks and pebbles bounced against the Ahri's shield. The girl Ahri, who he assumed was Rena was concentrating so hard on the shield she didn't even realize that they had been saved. Sern knelt down to let Kolko out of his back harness.

"Rena!" Kolko yelled through the shield. The Ahri girl, opened her eyes to see her brother. The smaller Ahri, a child, was also holding onto the staff, and helping her boost the shield.

"Who's this?" Rena asked Kolko, as the littlest Ahri hid behind her, seeing Sern standing over the three of them.

"He's one of the Sanctuary's troops."

"My name is Sern," Sern knelt down. "And I'm going to get all three of you back safely." He unstrapped the large harness-pouch from his back as he knelt. The three of them got into it, as Sern put it back on. Instinctively, the pouch closed in, and secured the three little Ahri onto his back as he stood up. "You all okay?"

"Yes!" Kolko called

"Hang on!" Sern looked around the base of the tower. He saw the ground erupting, with Flame Spawns climbing out of the Magma. A lesser man, they would have panicked but Sern could crush a Flame Spawn with just a determined stomp, he felt confident he could repel the others. His eyes, and even his entire form started to glow. The three Ahri watched with wonder as he did, and felt completely safe and confident.

Sern manifested a sword in his right hand, a simple straight blade. The first Flame Spawns noticed immediately the bright light above them, and charged at the tower with their thundering masses. Sern didn't flinch, but instead leaped right over them onto the field between the tower and the town's protective shield. The three Ahri watched as Sern pummeled another of the Spawns to dust, with a single punch, and then sliced another in half with his blade. The Spawn that was sliced in half, unlike the one that he shattered, was reforming with the magma that was now leaking out of the ground, forming two more spawns of equal size to the original!

"So Blades are not as effective as complete obliteration?" Sern muttered to himself as he casually threw the blade at another Spawn, stabbing it into what would be its chest before, then exploding violently, sending another Spawn into oblivion.

Sern didn't bother with the other Spawns, instead he simply raced past them, faster than any human could run, faster than any werewolf or vampire could run, straight up past the defensive fire coming in from the town. The Protectors saw him coming and covered his entrance by heavy concentrated blasts of their own force against the incoming waves of Flame Spawns. These rock-magma beings were still coming out of the ground, climbing out of the cracks in what was a green lush grassland.

After leaping up the final tier, Sern spotted the small group of Ahri and their Guardian. The little Ahri children, swarmed around him, even though he was kneeling down he still towered over them. They were cheering as Sern helped release the three Ahri in his care down to the ground where more Ahri, grown up ones were waiting. The parents, were so gratified someone had rescued their children, they hugged and embraced Sern's legs, the only part of him that they could reach. In the hustle of all the Ahri fleeing and assisting in the casting of this monumental spell, there was so much commotion that Sern didn't have any time to say anything before the Ahri were seeking shelter again. Before running off, the three Ahri who he rescued came back and hugged Sern. This time he knelt down, and embraced all three of them in his arms. Even Sern could feel an emotional attachment to these little Ahri.

"You're quite the hero," a voice came from behind him. He could instantly tell it belonged to Archon Alena. The majority of the Ahri had already gathered around the central tower which was now glowing brilliantly. The clouds were now twisting and swirling around the tower

The vaporous magical cloud shot up towards the sky, breaching the heavy smoke clouds above the town. The Ahri, all were concentrating, eyes closed as the beam of clouds now illuminated by their sheer massive amount of power. Sern and Alena looked up in awe as the white vaporous light spread throughout the sky, forcing the vile smoke clouds away, like ripples in a pond, beaming outwards, forcing the smoke away back into the wastelands. As they did, they left a white layer of clouds above them. They flowed like ink, spreading through water slowly, and as the sky turned light with the bright clouds slowly, rain started to fall.

The Ahri's collective casting was brewing up a powerful chill that everyone started to feel. The winds were also starting to churn around the entire town, in fact, throughout the entire wasteland area. Had it not been for the glowing shield around the city, things would have gotten significantly worse as the winds starting tearing at the rock formations within the wastelands. The Fire Spawns, were starting to struggle against the winds that pushed against them as they attempted to advance towards the town. Without hesitation, the Ahri were more than willing to restart their bombardment, firing volleys of their arcane blasts against the enemy.

The Spawns were facing the incoming volleys, but to make things worse for them, the clouds had now started to pour water on them.

The grounds beneath them was erupted with water, spewing upwards into powerful geysers as the winds started to turn the raindrops into hail. The Fire Spawns, who despite their larger number, were being pounded with a combination of arcane volleys, and hail balls. Relentless, the Ahri Cyromancers, experts in Ice magic, were now summoning entire large shards of ice against the Fire Spawns. Many tried to intensify their own heat in an effort to melt the ice, but still when they did, the flooding of the water put many of them out, flooding the wastelands that were once cracking with fire and magma into a steaming field.

"It's working!" General Kiro called from his command position atop the tower into his Thoughtpearl, to the rest of the Ahri "Continue bombardment!" he commanded. The Sanctuary Troops used their own power, focused into the form of beams, focused with their eyes into the wastelands, carving up as many of the Fire Spawns, ripping apart the fire and magma constructs.

Every single adult Ahri, and some young ones who had staves. They all pointed them towards the wastelands, and projected forwards, more and more powerful winds, enough to blow the ice storm outwards towards the already fleeing Flame Spawns. Sern and Alena watched the vast ice shards dropping down from the sky, hailstorms blasting down on the Flame Spawns. They were being pummeled relentlessly as they fled back farther into the volcanic mountains in the far off distance. It was clear the Ahri had the ability to defeat these Flame Spawns, but with great effort. It was one thing that they could defend their towns and homes, but it was another, to take charge to cleanse and heal their world.

"Well, Ambassador, seems like your Sanctuary Friends have great potential," Kiro commented to his brother, as they both descended down from the tower. Kiro seemed visually impressed as they both approached Archon Alena and Intendant Sern. Sparks of fireworks started to shoot up from the tower's spine, signaling a victory! The Ahri were all cheering, and shooting up more sparks in celebration.

"We're glad we could contribute," Archon Alena bowed to the Ahri leaders, led by their General. One group of Ahri, surrounded by children, and Kolko and his sister and the other Ahri boy approached them. Sern recognized them easily.

"You saved my little ones," said one of them, gratified to the point of tears, came up to Sern. The two Ahri, clutched onto her, until Sern was in front of them, then the two little Ahri rushed forward, hugging Sern's legs. Sern instinctively knelt down again, as they hugged him. Even he had to respond kindly to this affection as they refused to let go.

"The Sanctuary is here to help you," Sern replied as the third little Ahri came up to him. He was the smaller one who was trapped on the tower with Kolko's sister.

"I'm Rena." The little Ahri girl smiled as she hugged Sern's arm.

"Hello, I'm Sern," Sern introduced himself as more of the Ahri surrounded him. They were all inquisitive around this abnormally tall being.

"Seems that you have quite the fan club," Alena smiled at him.

"This is Leeto." Rena pointed to the other smaller Ahri. He was almost hiding behind their mother, in his hand clutching a stuffed animal, resembling something like a bear. He was so timid, almost hiding, shy and slightly afraid to say anything. Kolko went over to the little one and nudged him.

"He's shy." Kolko chuckled, as another Ahri, who Sern assumed was his father, handed him a staff.

"It's okay," Sern smiled at the little Ahri. "Are you alright?" Sern asked Leeto, who was still silent. He just nodded his head at Sern. Sern smiled back at the little guy, as he slowly stepped forwards towards the Intendant. He slowly hugged Sern, barely able to wrap his little arms around Sern's neck. For a brief moment, Sern felt a teardrop rolling down his face. He did save these two little Ahri from danger, something he didn't expect to have done. The Ahri General and Ambassador were watching as the other Ahri surrounded them, cheering Sern for what he did. They were visibly impressed by what Sern did, without even realizing it, showing a demonstration of what their new Sanctuary Allies could help do for them. Even Archon Alena, was thoroughly impressed. She hadn't expected that Sern was going to do this, but now that he did, he had helped solidify the relationship between the Sanctuary Organization and the Ahri.

"As a part of our alliance agreement, are we able to give them crystalweave?" Sern asked Archon Alena, as little Leeto let go of him, then scurried back to his older brother.

"Yes, it's permitted." Alena replied to him. Sern tore three strips of cloth from his robe, which instantly regrew back to fill the damage. The strips were thick and long enough to act as scarves for the Ahri. He placed the three strips over the necks of the three Ahri who he saved. They were wondering what he was doing.

"This is a magical cloth we wear. It also obeys your commands," he explained. "Go on, imagine, a warm cloak to warm you up from all this cold chill," Sern looked up to see that there were now snowflakes starting to descend down from the skies. The three of them looked oddly at each other, wondering what Sern meant.

Kolko closed his eyes and thought of a warm blue cloak, with a warm hood that protected him from the snow, not only that but pants and warm boots too. He wasn't aware of it, but the pale beige cloth had morphed down into exactly what he was thinking. Everyone gasped as he opened his eyes, to feel the warm thick but extremely light fabric. Wondering what people were muttering about, Kolko opened his eyes to see that he was wearing what he was just picturing in his mind. The Ahri started to clap as Rena and Leeto also were now wearing robes, but unique to themselves. Rena's was naturally pink, and Leeto's was a rich emerald green.

"We will be delivering more of this material within the next few days," Archon Alena promised the Ahri.

"It can also turn into metal-like armour which can be greatly helpful," Within moments of Sern saying this, Kolko changed the chest and arm portion of his robes into a thick plate. However when he felt it, it was more like a plastic, ceramic material rather than metal. It was just as light as cloth. Everyone who watched was amazed at what that material could do.

"Could we just take pieces of what they have and grow it from there?" Kito asked the Archon.

"Unfortunately, no. It has to come from a root piece, which is what we wear. If vaporized, the cloth will not regenerate. But it's highly unlikely that it will all be gone," Alena stated. However, that does not stop us from giving what we can for the time being." Alena removed the upper cape of what she was wearing, and stripped off as many scarf-sized cloth pieces as she could, and started handing them out to the Ahri around her. The other nearby Protectors and Defenders did the same thing, since more snow was starting to fall, and was now starting to blanket the ground around them.

"This is greatly appreciated," General Kiro thanked the Archon. "With the snow storm coming, it will be extremely cold here. We will need what we can get," he graciously accepted one of the scarves from Alena, which almost instantaneously changed into an over cloak over what he was already wearing, a richly decorated set of plate armour. The over cloak, which was like a cape, went over his pauldrons and over his head in the form of a large hood. The robe, slipped under his already established armour, and down around his legs. Kiro did appreciate this, since in normal circumstances, wearing robes under armour often made them cumbersome, but with this new material that the Sanctuary had just given them, it made worrying about clothing, even blankets a thing of the past. "We won't have to worry about the cold!" The crowds of Ahri couldn't stop cheering.

"I think it's time you meet with our local leaders," Kito suggested. Archon Alena and Sern wondered what he meant. "We have to go to the capital!"

"I'm afraid Intendant Sern is required back in his original position," Alena apologized to the Ahri representatives. She turned to

Sern, "I'm going to start making arrangements for your return. I think you've done a good job here of setting up a good impression for us."

"Of course. Do you think they will dispatch Ambassadors to us?"

"I'm fairly certain of that," the Archon nodded in agreement. "We will honor the agreements made in the treaty of alliance of course and we will send a diplomatic representative to you."

"I'm sure the Great Enlightened shall appreciate that."

Chapter 15

It was nearing morning when Paxton re-entered the isolation chamber rooms. The light of dawn had already started to spill into the large halls where they were being kept. The curtains had already been withdrawn and he could see that Jett was sound asleep on the floor. Paxton could spend a few hours just watching him, quiet and asleep, making sure that he was well protected.

Throughout the night, it was difficult for Paxton to sleep. With Jett going under his first full moon experience, and himself taking his first meal from a donor, it was already a night of experience that he didn't quite plan on repeating. The mental stress from both situations did strike him, of course seeing his boyfriend turn into an animal was the most dreadful of all. The situation was still something that he had to get used to, and that probably every full moon would be like this. Trenton had told him that over time, the transformation would become easier to deal with, but for him there was no promise that it would be easier for himself to watch his boyfriend turn into an animal. He was just grateful that he wouldn't have to go through this again, at least not for another thirty days.

Paxton sat there on a bench, watching Jett lay there asleep in the isolation chamber. Paxton could see his chest rising, then sinking with every breath. It was a moment of great relief, to see him finally resting and calm.

"He's been out for hours; changing and then relentlessly beating on the glass, then the walls wore him out." a familiar voice came from behind him. Paxton turned around to see Cazian standing behind him. Cazian's slight smile was definitely welcoming.

"It's just good to finally see him sleeping and resting, calmed down." Paxton repeated his thoughts verbally to Cazian. The taller vampire sat down next to him.

"You also have something to go through, a bloodlust," Cazian warned. "And since you're stronger than him, you'll be more dangerous than him once that happens."

"What's that like?" Paxton asked with some dread in his voice.

"I'll tell you later, brother," Cazian patted Paxton on the shoulder. He knew already that Paxton and Jett didn't need any additional stress on their minds. Just then, they both noticed Jett stretched and yawned as he rubbed his eyes. Paxton almost instinctively leaped towards the door, so Cazian entered the key code to let him enter. Paxton raced in and almost leaped on top of Jett who was startled to see him. Jett's eyes focused to see Paxton on top of him, smiling. "Alright boys, if you're going to do what I think you're going to do, may I suggest taking it to the bedroom," he suggested as the two of them realized that Cazian was present. They couldn't help but smirk at the thought before Paxton lifted Jett up in his arms.

"Have you lost weight?" Paxton asked his boyfriend who was now in his arms.

"I don't think so," Jett yawned again.

"You're stronger now," Cazian explained simply to Paxton who seemed to barely flinch having lifted a 180 pound guy in his arms without a problem. There was no problem for him carrying him up the stairway. Jett was more amused by this since he had just woken up and was now being carried up the stairs.

Breakfast was already set in the main dining hall. As usual, the Zombie Crew had managed to assemble a huge feast. Despite having lived there for years, Cazian was always impressed by the sheer speed that they were able to prepare these huge feasts. Then again, that would explain the routine deliveries that Sanctuary received every week. Cazian just passed through the main dining hall while going through to the main entrance. It was delivery day and he knew what to expect.

Just pacing back and forth for a few minutes before taking out his phone to check the time, 8:28am. Cazian just ran through the events of the past few days. After seeing Gavin sire someone, Cazian couldn't help but wonder if he would ever do that too. But his thought was interrupted by the arrival of a large semi truck. Typically holding one of those enormous cargo containers on the back. The drivern a familiar face waved past Cazian. His face was decayed like that of a corpse, and was undoubtedly part of the Zombie Crew.

Cazian followed them to the back road, which connected directly to the kitchen. For him it was just a brisk morning stroll, the morning air was still full of that fresh dew scent. As he reached the back, he saw that they were already starting to unload their supplies. It wasn't anything too fancy, just normal foodstuff, eggs, lots of flour, fruits and vegetables and of course, blood. They came in all sorts of huge crates, storage boxes, and reinforced bags that were being carried into the storage rooms right beneath the kitchen.

"Usual order," one of them approached Cazian with a clipboard. He and the rest of the crew, despite being undead, were wearing typical standard delivery work shirts and matching caps.

"So Kale, standard stuff," Cazian accepted the clipboard and signed his signature at the bottom, then handed it back.

"Nothing too out of the ordinary. Just a small increase in supplies. I guess you've been taking more residents?" Kale asked, casually.

"Yeah, a Bloodbane wolf, of all things," Cazian kept checking the list of items arriving.

"Wow," Kale smirked. "Must be quite a handful."

"Well yeah, and he's hungry. That's why we had to put in bigger orders," Cazian handed the clipboard back to Kale. The zombie read over everything to make sure that things were in order.

The beeping of the forklifts wasn't something easy to miss. But to Cazian, it was just standard stuff. Every week they would come twice, Tuesdays and Fridays. In particular, Cazian could smell the blood deliveries, but that was to be expected. Normally he wouldn't be too interested in grabbing a bag for himself, but today he just felt like a few unorthodox practices.

He marched right into the kitchen, and while Dominic and the other Wolf Primes were bringing the stuff in, he just took one of the many blood packets that were being put in, and started to drink it like a juice box. He was just sipping from the bag as he walked through the kitchen to see the rest of them sitting at the dining hall. The Wolves were having an early breakfast; many were still hungry from last night. They were simply devouring the breakfast, this time, pancakes and oatmeal, more grains than meats.

Within a few minutes of sitting there just content to sip on the blood packet, Jett and Paxton had already come back down. Cazian didn't smell anything out of the ordinary, instead they were just dressed in a new set of clothes, and smelled like they had freshly come out of the shower, soapy. Despite what Cazian thought earlier, it was unlikely that they were going for a morning of passion after what they had gone through.

Jett headed straight for the food. Paxton poured himself a nice warm glass of blood from the buffet table. He sat down in front of Cazian but didn't look up, just sat there, staring at the blood in his cup. He was visibly distracted, somewhat oblivious to everything around him, just staring into that life-giving red fluid.

"You alright?" Cazian asked as he finished up the blood packet. Despite being cold blood, he didn't mind its chilled taste. Paxton didn't even look up, just gave a deep sigh.

"Yeah," he whispered as he rubbed the bridge of his nose with his left hand, then rested his chin on his hand. "Just lots on my mind," he admitted after a long silence. "Just lots to go through," Paxton looked not only visibly tired, but emotionally drained after the night that he had. It had now all started to dawn on him, the massive change in his life, and of course, Jett too. Jett returned from the buffet table with two large plates of food, eggs, sausages, pancakes, fruits, lots of stuff, plenty for him to feast on for the time being. He didn't bother saying anything as he already started chowing the stuff down. No words were exchanged as he was going through the food like an animal. Paxton didn't even bother watching, unlike Cazian who was getting a bit of a kick seeing the young newborn Bloodbane Werewolf eating up his breakfast.

"I know it's tough. It takes weeks, sometimes months, or even years for many of us to come to terms with what we've become," Cazian sympathized. His words were of some comfort to Paxton, despite being brief and simple.

"Funny thing is, I know, but it's still hard to take," Paxton took a sip of his cup.

"It's not just our strengths that are enhanced, and our reflexes, it's also our emotions. When you're depressed, you really feel it as a vampire."

"Everyone has mood swings, but I've never felt like this before," Paxton admitted as he looked up at Cazian. Cazian took out his phone, and showed Paxton the screen. Paxton looked at the image. It was the camera phone's front facing camera that showed his own face looking at him. His eyes, instead of being the chocolate brown that he normally had, were now a deep almost royal blue colour. His own eyes now gazed at his own image in shock. "What's happened?" He stared into his new deep blue eyes in shock.

"Your emotions are reflected in your eye colour," Cazian reminded him. "Remember, blue is when you're scared or sad. Yellow is when you feed; red is when you're angry, silver is when you're going to use your mind manipulation abilities," Cazian explained to him, as he demonstrated himself, by shifting his eyes to yellow, as he tasted the blood.

"It's a bit confusing, because I'm sad right now, but I'm also drinking blood," Paxton wondered. His eyes indeed were very blue at the moment as he looked back into the phone screen.

"Well, that's because your feelings of depression and sadness are right now, stronger than your urge to drink."

"One takes precedent over the other?"

"Exactly, and I guess you're not that hungry? Cazian asked, suspecting that he already knew the answer.

"No, not really," Paxton stared back down into his cup as he handed Cazian his phone back.

"Just make sure that he never tastes your blood," Cazian nodded at Jett, who was too busy eating to hear them.

"Why?" Paxton asked. He had been told before that Bloodbane Wolves were werewolves who were addicted to the blood of vampires, but not sure why.

"Well, your blood is like a drug to them. The more powerful the vampire order, the stronger the effect. You, like me, as a High Order have the strongest type of blood. He can go berserk if he tastes your blood. Even if he smells it, that may be enough for him to go mad."

"Like how mad?"

"Worse than a full moon," Cazian admitted. That alone started flooding him with more worries. "I know that it's not going to be a real issue, but just be careful. If he smells your blood, it will drive him so wild, and mad for a taste you may have to fight back," Cazian warned. Jett had leaped to his feet, then rushed over to the buffet table to get another plate of food. Paxton's mind, as usual, was thinking hard and careful, but as he did, he gulped down the entire cup of blood without thinking much. It was more like he knew he should have some blood even if he didn't feel like it.

In the doorway, Gavin watched as Cazian interacted with Paxton.

"He's taking this rather well," Trenton whispered to Gavin as they both watched the young couple.

"Paxton's mental discipline comes from his new High Order lineage. But it's more evident, that Jett is the key to Paxton's hope," Gavin replied.

"What do you mean?" Trenton wondered. Gavin's words were more enigmatic than before and he had no doubt it was due to Sern's influence.

"You're probably thinking if Jett wasn't a Bloodbane Wolf, that this may be easier? Well I have little doubt that would be true. However, the fact that Jett is vulnerable also makes Paxton vulnerable, but their two vulnerabilities aren't as weak as you may think, because they are relying on each other."

"You mean, the fact that they are relying on each other, makes them stronger?"

"Exactly. Like two side of an arch. Independently they can't stand, but when they rely on each other, they're stronger."

"I didn't think of applying an architectural analogy." Trenton teased at the phrasing of words that Gavin used in his description. "That essence that Sern put in your brain, really has changed you."

"It's only temporary."

"Let's hope." another voice came up behind them. The soldier-like Dominic marched up behind them, also watching the two of the newborns in the dining hall. It just seemed like Cazian was keeping them in casual conversation.

"I showed him how to feed from a donor," Dominic reported to Gavin.

"How did he do?"

"Apparently fine. Lucas didn't lose much blood, seemed that this fiasco has Paxton pretty distracted," Dominic put his arms behind his back, standing perfectly straight. His own clothes were almost military-style. Gavin had always admired Dominic's almost stoic personality.

"So he received his mask?" Trenton wondered.

"Yes."

"Just let them rest today," Gavin suggested to the two of them. "They've gone through enough, time for some relaxation."

After breakfast, Paxton and Jett returned to their room. It was more likely that they went back to sleep. Despite sleeping in his werewolf form, Jett was exhausted after breakfast, mainly due to the fact that he had completely stuffed himself. Paxton was also still exhausted from worry, and after sliding into bed with Jett in his arms, he was finally able to relax. Gavin had returned to Sern's office where he was going through the tomes of books and archives that the Sanctuary had stored there, and through the access terminal on Sern's desk.

While reading through the various sections around the knowledge that the Sanctuary Organization had gathered, under Archivist Saela, a Sanctuary researcher, the records were quite interesting regarding their history:

"Throughout their history, the Packwalkers had branched into two distinctive groups, the Packwalker Proper, and the Bloodbanes. The Packwalkers had learned that vampiric blood's scent, taste and effects were psychotropic, mood altering. The stimulation of the blood would completely block out the fear center of the brain, making the Bloodbane wolf completely fearless. In addition, the potency of the blood would act as a fully enhancing steroid and stimulant, resulting in vastly improved focus, senses and strength. Packwalkers as a society shun this use of vampire blood, believing it to be a detrimental substance that results in the corruption of their race. Bloodbanes embraced this use of vampire blood and thus during the pre-industrial age of mankind, the Bloodbanes became their own distinctive pack of Lycanthrope." Gavin read from the holographic display.

In front of him was an almost medical style diagram of a standard male Bloodbane wolf. Though it hadn't explained it yet in the document, it was fairly clear to him that the term Bloodbane had a double meaning. They were a bane to the Blood Orders, another word for Vampire Orders, and the blood of vampires was a bane on them.

As Gavin read on, he was briefly interrupted by the knocking on Sern's office door. He immediately turned off all the consoles, and put the books which were hovering near him, back on their shelves as he stood up behind the desk.

"Enter" Gavin called to the door. It was Dominic at first who came in. There was clearly someone behind him but they hadn't stepped into the room yet.

"We have a guest, the Lady Elura," Dominic told him, with a hint of warning in his voice. "She says she just wants to chat and visit." A random chat was just unusual, but then again, the Lady Elura was never known to be predictable.

"Alright, welcome her in," Gavin stepped around the desk to the middle of the room. Dominic opened both doors, and a woman stood there between them, elegantly dressed in a long and very skimpy looking black dress that left very little to the imagination. She didn't mind showing her cleavage, and her white skin was complimented with her thick, almost beehive, black hair. Her makeup was quite fittingly seductive, red rich lips, and while the dress was already provocative enough she did wear a rather conservative looking cloak around her shoulders. In her right hand, she held a staff, which was just as tall as her. It was a shimmering black wooden staff, richly decorated with rubies, and at the top, was a statue of a dragon's head, in which in its mouth held a perfectly spherical glass crystal.

Waiting for the doors to stop, Elura entered with a flirtatious walk. She smiled her trademark smile, and winked at Gavin who stood there between her and Sern's desk. She scanned him briefly as Dominic also entered the room. Though he had not received an invitation, it was likely that Gavin may prefer it that he was there too.

"Well, well, well! Look at you!" Elura scanned Gavin, clearly impressed by what he was wearing. "You know, I never figured you to be the bureaucratic type," she placed one hand on her hip as she almost over-obviously scanned him up and downwards with her eyes.

"Sern is currently away on assignment, so he placed me in charge temporarily." Gavin replied firmly.

"Wow, that tone!" Elura playfully mocked. "Too bad he also transferred in his personality," she teased as she sat down in one of the leather armchairs in the room. The staff that she held, now stood by itself beside her as she provocatively crossed her legs, blatantly attempting to over charm Gavin in her typical over the top manner.

"So you decided to pay a spontaneous visit?" Gavin asked her bluntly.

"Well, Hasaan never minded. And it has been a while since I came. I was hoping to meet the new boy in charge, but I guess you'll have to do." Elura winked at Gavin.

"I'm still the same Gavin that you knew before, just with some of Sern's traits while he's gone."

"Well that may be true, but he could at least have left the loving sweet Gavin in charge." Elura replied, almost with a whine in her voice. "But anyways, I'll get right to the point," She leaned back in the chair. "I was on my way to an auction. A mysterious benefactor, is auctioning off a number of very exotic and rare magical artifacts, and I thought I would give you guys the head's up."

"Do you know who this benefactor is?" Dominic inquired.

"No. But from what I heard, just from rumours, he's got some pretty damned rare artifacts." Elura started examining the perfect paint job done on her nails.

"And you thought that we may be interested in checking them out?"

"Well, it's the Sanctuary's job to make sure that none of these types of items go out of control. So I thought you would send someone to come with me, in case some of them are dangerous."

"According to Sern's knowledge and protocol, these events should be monitored but by an Intendant at the very least, with a full enforcement arm," Gavin recalled. His mind was circling through the details and memories that Sern had left him. "Unfortunately, I'm not a full Intendant. I will have to contact Sanctuary first before making that call."

"Well, the Auction isn't for a few days. I thought I would take the chance to come a bit early."

"Feel free to enjoy the place. I'll find you when I have an answer," Gavin initiated a holographic screen over his desk. Elura had no real idea what he was doing. All the Intendant stuff and technologies that they used were not magic but a technology that was well beyond human means. She always wondered to herself what the Intendants were. She hadn't met Sern but she had met Hasaan; and despite looking and talking like a human, she always sensed that they were more than that.

"Alrighty then," she got off the couch to face Dominic. Stoic as always, Dominic stood there with a rather courteous but cautious expression on his face. His mannerisms, as usual, firm and direct. He stepped aside for her as she walked out of the room, taking her time. Her staff simply floated alongside her as she and Dominic left the room, doors quietly shutting behind them. Elura looked back at the closed doors. "A pity," she gazed back reluctantly.

"What is?" Dominic asked.

"That even someone as perfect as Gavin can be brought down by Sanctuary bureaucracy," she sighed with disappointment.

"It's not as bad as you think. I'm fairly confident the old Gavin will return to us soon."

"Hmm, well maybe, but I'm going to take a nice walk in your famous gardens," Elura walked off down the hallway towards the rear exit. Dominic wasn't concerned about her since she had been here before, and wasn't known to be one to cause trouble. "Feel free to come with me if you like," She winked at Dominic suggestively. Dominic tried to ignore the gesture.

"I may join you later," Dominic headed back to the kitchen and storage areas where the unloading was still taking place.

Chapter 16

The Bluestar Bloodbane Pack pulled up their cars to the edge of the forest where they were instructed to meet with their benefactor. However Rake, the Alpha of the Pack stopped the newest of his pack members, a young Bloodbane named Valko. Rake and the other ten wolves were going to enter before he pulled this young one aside.

"This guy, is pretty damned powerful" Rake warned the youngest of his pack, "which is why we all have to back you up." Valko insisted as he tried to get around Rake but was stopped by a powerful hand that blocked his path.

"No, which is why I want insurance," Rake stated bluntly to him. Valko was confused about what was going on. Rake took out his phone, and also took Valko's gently from his hand. They had the same ones, and Rake activated a voice over IP application, then turned on the cameras as though they were going through a video chat. Rake tucked his own phone into his top jacket pocket, where the camera was able to stick out and see directly in front of him. Valko checked his own phone for the image, and it was displaying what Rake's camera phone was seeing, like a remote controlled spycam. "Now you can see and hear what's going on. If you see trouble, don't try to run in and help us. Anything strong enough to take on eleven wolves will kill you easily. I want you to run. I want you not only to run, Valko, but try to find help, if need be, from Sanctuary themselves."

"Alright," Valko reluctantly nodded in compliance. Rake wrapped his arms around Valko, hugging him.

"But things should be fine, just in case though, this is for insurance only," Rake assured him. The young wolf only nodded back, saddened to be left behind. "Remember," Rake reminded him by pointing to the blue four-pointed star tattoo on their forearms, "we're a pack."

The pack was waiting in the midst of the forest a few miles outside Wolf Coven House. They were on edge; the night after a full moon would still leave them very agitated. Rake watched as his pack was around him, some still in chills, shaking from what they wanted as payment for what they did. He himself was keeping an eye out all around him for their benefactor. He looked down to his hands; there were dirt stains all over them, as well as some clotted remaining blood, also stuffed under his fingernails. Not far from here were the rotting remains of a few deer that had the unfortunate chance to have been stalked by a dozen Bloodbane Werewolves in the middle of a full moon night.

Around them, was a fairly warm sunny day, in fact, beams of sunlight were spilling through the canopy of the trees above them as they stood waiting. The air started to get colder around them. The beams of sunlight were starting to get distorted, vanishing, as the air became thicker. A grey mist started to descend around them, first making the clear day abnormally foggy. Almost like tendrils they fog closed off all the areas around them, encircling the eleven of them in their small opening amongst the trees. Within a few seconds, they were completely closed in by the fog.

"We know you're here," Rake called out, yelling to the fog itself. A powerful gust of wind followed through his words, swirling around them until a portion of the fog coalesced into a humanoid form. The figure wore something resembling a long overcoat and simple dress pants. He had no skin that resembled anything human, but he did have the same features as a human form. His face, if you could call it that at all, was made out of small shards of reflective, almost mirror shards. They hovered in place, like he was a three-dimensional mosaic of mirror fragments, but inside him they could see a black void, almost like he was composed of a black smoke-mist like substance, and this was an outer shell used to give him form. "We did what you asked, and we bit two of them. They would have transformed by now," he spoke as the form was materializing right in front of them out of the mist.

"I'm glad to hear it," an almost synthesized voice came from the being. There was something vaguely resembling a smile on the being's face. The voice was deep and extremely artificial, sounding almost digital.

"You have our payment and what we agreed to?" Rake insisted on asking while the others assembled around him, almost like they were backing him up.

"You bit two of them, and infected them with your Bloodbane bite." The being asked again to clarify.

"Yes, during the time that you predicted, they were having some bonfire gathering. We attacked and bit them both." Another one of the wolves growled; he was shaking and almost clutching his own chest from what he wanted as his reward. The being didn't even move. A large chest, what looked like something used to store old fashion luggage, emerged right out of the ground, pushing away the dirt and leaves as it thrust itself out of the earth. The top lid opened itself to reveal the contents inside.

The pack of wolves assembled around the chest; inside was blood bags. They almost lunged for them as fast as they could, and started to devour the contents. The fix was quenched for the moment as their burning skin, their twitching and their focus was now concentrated on drinking this life-giving fluid which was now their addiction. It was ironic that Bloodbanes had just as much a thirst for blood as the vampires whose blood was what they hungered for. But this was a drug with no nutritional value, only stimulation. Rake joined the others as they started to down the stuff.

The being simply watched them for a few moments without even moving. They were completely focused on the blood, which, to their taste was what they wanted. Another figure slowly came through the mist. Unlike their benefactor, this person was clearly human, or at least human-looking. He had the face of a normal young man, but there was clearly something unworldly about him that Rake could tell. The strange upper crest of feathers that he had at the side of his head was an obvious giveaway, and the fact that his suit seemed to gleam despite being made out of cloth was something else to take notice. Rake kept his eye on this one as best as he could without being distracted by the blood- drinking that he and the other five were doing.

As each finished their blood package, they watched as this new figure started eyeing them in a particular way. His gaze was more like that of a scientist examining a specimen, rather than a look of curiosity. Rake was the first to look at this guy. He was handsome, but certainly had a strong ethereal quality to him.

"Who are you?" Rake demanded of the stranger, his wolf fangs already emerged, and his claws had shifted from his hands. The others also were ready to attack. The stranger only kept circling them slowly, each step perfectly timed with the last. "Who are you??!!" Rake roared; his pack now was also shifting to their bestial forms as they surrounded him.

"Such demanding little beings, aren't they?" the stranger mocked. His words seemed to be aimed at the benefactor who stood watching them all, still motionless, frozen like a statue. The benefactor started to move again, in reply to what the stranger said.

"Indeed they are," the benefactor remarked.

Valko watched from the phone screen as he got back into his car, and sat observing what he could from the image that he saw. The sound was a bit muffled, but he could make out the face and features of the figure that was standing. What they called the benefactor was a being with no features he could recognize at all. It was like a mixture of light and shapes.

"And now they have such an abundance of life force inside them," the stranger remarked as Rake was now getting fed up with being spoken over. It was common perception that ignoring someone's presence was rude, but speaking as though they didn't exist was another. With the additional power that the vampiric blood given to them, Rake was already feeling his rage and fury strengthening him and the others. The angrier they got, the more the stranger seemed to enjoy their fury. Rake leaped at the stranger with claws ready to swipe. As he shot through the air towards the stranger, he found himself stopped in mid air, as though being held in place with invisible hands, struggling against what felt like invisible restraints

Held there and unable to move, Rake snarled and growled at the stranger, who only seemed to mock him with a sadistic smile. He was slowly lowered to within arm's reach of the stranger. He felt an unusual warmth forming around his chest. Looking down, he saw the emergence of a glowing green haze around his chest. The other Bloodbane wolves tried to move, but they too were being held in place by some invisible force. The stranger's hand approached the glowing green haze around his midsection. His hand passed right through the now thicker-growing green mist in his chest right into his body. Rake screamed out in searing pain, as though his insides were on fire, as the stranger slowly pulled out his hand, pulling a stream of green energy that the stranger first held in both hands, completely ignoring Rake's agonizing shrills, then almost like a drug addict, gazing at this mysterious metaphysical substance.

The stranger absorbed the vaporous green metaphysical energy, then reached in for more, this time pulling an entire stream of it as the pain that Rake was feeling only intensified, feeling his own life draining out of him. Rake collapsed to the ground, released by the invisible restraints into a pile of lifeless limbs. The others, helpless to assist, were now being pulled in as well. They knew what fate was going to happen to them, but that didn't stop them from struggling, even despite the futility. Around their chests, they too, started to feel the now growing incinerating heat from within them, as the stranger reached out, pulling the same streams of life energies that he had siphoned right out of Rake.

For him, the sweet song of the calming hum of the life stream that he was pulling out of these eleven Bloodbane wolves was all that mattered to him, as he pulled the streams of life right out of them. Their unified screams didn't remotely affect the stranger as he pulled all the glowing life force right into his own body. The benefactor stood casually nearby, observing without any movement. The stranger continued his siphoning until there was nothing left within these ten hovering bodies, which now also joined Rake's corpse in a heap of dead flesh, thumping at first when they hit the ground. There was nothing left within them. If anyone stumbled upon their forms, they would never be able to tell the cause of death.

"That was filling," the stranger closed his eyes, now savouring all of that new life force he had just obtained from these eleven Bloodbane wolves. The surge of power that now ran through his body and his mind was like an infusion of pure raw energy, life and power that all infused every single fiber of his entire physical being. The bodies slowly started to descend down into the ground. The dirt, grass and earth started to move around, opening up as though they were alive, and taking these forms in as payment for what they gave him. The quiet rumbling of the ground, sounded almost like the stretching of flesh, and for a moment it was as though the ground itself was hungry for its own share of food, eating up the eleven corpses, pulling them into the ground.

"Hypnos, you will need to conserve what strength you have until your brother is released," the benefactor instructed firmly.

"You're sure he will be released soon?" Hypnos asked. He already knew what the benefactor was going to say.

"All the pieces are already in place, but we still have to acquire that High Order blood," his benefactor reminded Hypnos.

"I'll take care of that. Thanks to the little wolf that they made, we have our in," Hypnos looked back towards the ground where the five Bloodbanes had landed after he siphoned them. He turned towards the direction of Wolf Coven House.

Valko stared at the screen of his phone. Rake's phone was still active as he collapsed to the ground. The green tendrils, the fog, his entire pack,killed by this being named Hypnos, he saw it all. He shoved his phone back into his pocket then started the engine to his car; and without even releasing the emergency brake, almost crushed the gas pedal under his foot. Then noticing his lack of movement, he released the brake and sped off, getting away as fast as he could.

Chapter 17

Paxton turned on the light to the Mask Room where Dominic had taken him to the night before. Jett gazed at the dozens of various mask designs all over the walls and shelves. It was something that he didn't realize had existed in Wolf Coven House. After all, what use could masks have in a place that protected Supernaturals?

Paxton reached up to grab his own mask, the figure-8 shaped mask with sharp corners that he had put on earlier when he fed on Lucas. It was then that by just briefly remembering, Paxton had to explain to Jett, that feeding from a donor was something that he did. He wasn't too sure on how to reveal this.

"What's the mask for?" Jett asked as Paxton looked at his own mask in his hands. The perfectly sculpted black leather was firm in his hand, but soft enough to fit over the curvature of his face. He slipped it onto his face. "Pretty sexy mask there."

"When we feed on donors, we have to hide our identity." Paxton explained as he looked at Jett's expression, which was now one of confusion.

"Donors?" Jett asked. He knew what the word meant in a normal context, but wasn't entirely too sure what Paxton meant by it.

"Humans who are willing to give blood to us directly," Paxton began, without revealing the more intimate nature.

"Well that's nice of them," Jett said while he was finally concentrating on the words. "Wait. What did you mean by humans who were willing to give blood to you. You mean they do this for free?"

"I'm sure they get paid for it, maybe by any other sort of methods that we have available," Paxton assured him.

"It just seems weird to me, people selling their blood," Jett continued, thinking about the situation. He pictured rows of people with syringes and blood bangs sitting in a hospital, donating blood with calming elevator music playing.

"Well, it's more intimate than that," Paxton suggested. Jett gave him a confused glance. "Oh," Jett whispered as he thought in his mind of what he could have meant. "You mean, fed from the vein?" Paxton nodded.

"The vein on the neck," Paxton admitted, a bit shy about what he had to tell his boyfriend, but considering the intimate nature of feeding from a donor, he should tell him about it.

"You know you can feed from me. You know that, right?" Jett offered, oddly not quite the response that Paxton was expecting.

"Last night while you were roaring like an animal, I had my fangs in some other guy's neck, Jett," Paxton repeated himself almost wanting Jett to get angry at him.

"Did you have sex?" Jett asked rather bluntly.

"No."

"But you were getting food, food you need to live on?"

"Yes."

"Well I'm not going to get angry at you for feeding," Jett took the mask that was in Paxton's hand, then put it over his own face. "Did you kiss him?" He smirked, oddly taking this whole situation very lightly.

"No!" Paxton protested defensively without realizing that Jett was more or less just teasing him. Jett kept his eyes on Paxton, as though expecting another more detailed explanation. "Yeah, he was good-looking. But considering the circumstances that I was in, like you said, you were turning into an animal, and I wasn't interested in anything like that."

"But you still fed."

"Only a little bit. Dominic introduced us, which is why he gave me that mask." Paxton took it back and hung it up on the shelf. "It's to keep my identity secret." Paxton walked over to the back center of the room where the large velvet curtains blocked out the sunlight. In front of the window was a display case. Paxton opened up the curtains to let the light from outside flood into the room, almost blinding them temporarily. The gardens on the east side of the house were just as magnificent as the ones to the back. Paxton guessed that to the west side, were also equally elaborate and pretty gardens.

"What is this?" Jett looked into the display case. Under the dark light earlier, he couldn't see what was inside.

"Dominic, I think, described that as a true silver knife." Paxton examined the blade. It was like a dagger; the gleaming blade was perfectly sharp and shone with so much light. With their newly enhanced vision they couldn't even see a single blemish on the knife blade. The handle and guard were extremely simple, almost deliberately so. The blade was only six or so inches long, and the blade an inch wide at the base where it met the guard. There didn't seem to be any decoration on the blade at all.

"What's true silver?" Jett asked as he opened the case. Oddly there didn't seem to be any lock on the display case. He reached in, but not before Paxton grasped his wrist.

"What are you doing?" Paxton stopped him from grabbing the blade.

"I'm just taking a look," Jett insisted as Paxton gently let go. "What is this true silver stuff?"

"It's supposed to be the only metal that can injure us." Paxton explained nervously to Jett. Jett grasped the handle and removed the blade slowly. The blade was extremely light. Normally a blade like this would have at least some weight, but oddly this was seemingly weightless. Jett turned the blade around, but he accidentally scratched Paxton's upper forearm.

"Ouch!!" Paxton winced for a moment. "Be careful with that thing!" He growled at Jett, his own eyes turning red for a moment, fangs also had extended without him realizing.

"Sorry!" Jett held the blade in his hand, but then his eyes focused on the small cut, which was only an inch long that was on Paxton's arm. A single tiny droplet of blood, crept out of the cut, and instantly he was unable to take his eyes off of the blood. "I didn't mean to...." Jett's voice almost faded as he virtually seemed to lose his attention in completing the sentence.

Something was happening to Jett. His eyes started to shift. Paxton had seen this before; in fact, he had seen this the night before. Jett's eyes changed into their animalistic yellow, a very different look from what Vampires had as yellow eyes. His were feral, where Paxton's eyes would be demonic. Paxton turned to hopefully see his cut heal but it wasn't. He recalled Cazian telling him that his healing would be fast, but he didn't mention how it would react to true silver. Jett's face turned feral as he started to growl at Paxton, while still staring at the wound and the blood that was bleeding out of it.

"Jett, are you okay?" Paxton asked as he bent down and grabbed the dagger that Jett dropped. As he picked it up, he noticed that Jett's hands were morphing into the wolf claws that he had the night before. His eyes, his face, were no longer those of his boyfriend's. "Jett?!" Paxton repeated as he threw the knife into the tall ceiling of the room to keep it out of reach. Jett wasn't remotely interested in the knife anymore as he started to slouch down, bending his spine almost like he was ready to charge at Paxton. "Calm down!" Paxton pleaded as he backed up against the side wall with the masks.

Jett didn't seem interested in any conversation as he lunged at Paxton, sinking his fangs right down on his arm and into the skin around the wound, biting as hard as he could into the wound, sucking out as much blood as he could. The Bloodbane hunger for vampire blood was too powerful, taking complete control of him. Paxton was in pain, but he was full of more confusion than anger. He looked down to realize that Jett was unable to control himself. Instead of being frightened and fighting back, Paxton knew that Jett was unable to control his urges. Paxton, instead, didn't resist; instead, he let Jett sap some of his blood. It certainly didn't feel good with four teeth piercing his skin, but the top of his arm wasn't feeling too much pain at the moment.

It seemed so much longer than a few minutes as Jett kept drinking the blood It wasn't that much that he was taking, since the bites that he gave Paxton were already healing up, and that the single cut wasn't bleeding that much. Paxton collapsed to the floor as Jett huddled near him, continuing to lick what he could get, instinctively grasping onto Paxton's arm like a scared child.

Dominic smelled something familiar as he raced up the stairway towards the residential quarters. Instantly recognized as the scent of blood, but it was vampire blood that he detected. Vampire blood was never spilt or fed at Wolf Coven House, which was enough to make him quicken his steps up the stairs. The scent pulled him to the mask room, where he could already hear the feral growls of some type of animal. As he stepped into the doorway, he saw Paxton sitting on the floor, with a shifted Jett drinking blood from his arm!

"What are you doing!!?" Dominic screamed in shock and anger. He knew the effect that High Order vampire blood could do to a Bloodbane Werewolf. Jett turned to see Dominic, and in response to Dominic's unwelcome presence, Jett sprang to his feet and roared at Dominic. As Jett was drinking, he was getting stronger. Dominic reached over to grab Jett off Paxton, but instead, Jett leaped at the window to the room, smashing the glass with his body as he made an instinctive escape out of the window! Paxton, weakened from the blood drain, struggled to his feet. "I'm going to get him back!"

Dominic called to Paxton as he leaped out the window, trying to maintain sight of Jett, who was speeding through the trees.

Dominic, despite being fast, was losing ground to Jett, who was racing on four limbs instead of two, was easily starting to gain ground on Dominic, who, despite using his wings to glide and push himself faster through the forest, dodging branches and small steps and hills. Dominic tried to follow the loose scent of blood still on the corner of Jett's mouth, but even Dominic couldn't keep up with the speed of a rabid Bloodbane high on High Order vampire blood. He slowed his pace, realizing that Jett was now out of reach. Catching his breath, Dominic had to now find another way of tracking him down.

Jett raced through the forest without even fully realizing what he was doing, his legs moving more on instinct than by any conscious effort. It was as though he wasn't even controlling his body. What mattered to him right now in his mind was the taste and sensations that this vampire blood was making him feel. There was no fear in his mind that his energy level was through the roof as his legs carried him faster than he ever thought possible, and without even remotely getting tired. How he managed to smash right through a window, leap out of the upper floor and land on his feet was already enough to shock him, but he didn't even feel the slightest bit of pain as he sprinted through the forest, now going at it with just feet instead of the four legs.

He stopped for just a second to smell the air; there was a familiar scent in the air, a very desirable scent. He was homing in on it naturally; he sniffed the air, and was visually able to see a stream of red through his vision that would lead him to where he wanted to go. He instinctively followed it through the forest slower, but making sure that he caught the scent.

Dominic climbed back up the twenty feet of wall, up through the window, back to the second floor where Paxton was still waiting. Gavin was with Paxton, holding Paxton in his arms, calming him down. Paxton was still in a blur of wariness mixed with confusion. Dominic recognized what Gavin was doing, and it was more than just Gavin doing his duty as an Intendant replacement, but he was also doing this as Paxton's sire. Paxton leaned over as Gavin put his arms around him. Dominic recognized this. They didn't say anything but he knew that they didn't have to say anything. Dominic looked up towards the ceiling. The true silver dagger was still stuck up there. With a single jump he managed to snatch it back, but not without propelling himself more than five feet off the ground to do it.

"How is he?" Dominic asked Gavin as he held Paxton close to him.

"Distraught. But he's managing. I explained to him about the Bloodbane thirst for vampire blood. Jett was just a victim of his own uncontrollable urges," Gavin explained. "He's just sorting out the information I gave him."

"How did you do that?"

"By memory transfer," Gavin slowly got up off the ground, while helping Paxton do the same.

"I couldn't find him, or keep up," Dominic sighed as he looked at the dagger in his hand. Gavin watched as Dominic's expression changed. He suddenly started to come up with an idea, at least something that would help lure Jett back.

"Wait, what about the tag you had him wear?" Paxton reminded the two of them. Dominic pulled out his phone and reactivated the application. His face was slightly optimistic at first, but then the expression died fast.

"Nothing. I'm not even getting a signal from it," Dominic showed Gavin and Paxton the screen. There was no visible reading on the map display. Dominic was still thinking of something else.

"What was his direction?" Gavin asked, curious as to what Dominic was thinking up.

"Well, I know he headed northwards. Can you sense him?" He asked. In response, Gavin 's eyes started to glow brightly, like how Sern's would when he concentrated on his Intendant abilities. For a few moments, Gavin stood there silently as his eyes continued to fill the room with light, radiating almost like they were portals to some source of vast power. His mind was acting like a radar, scanning mentally the area around them. He could sense Trenton who was in the gym, with Coltrane. He could sense the Zombie crew, cleaning up the breakfast below. His mind tried to spread through the land surrounding Wolf Coven House but somehow it was as though he had hit a cement wall, a barrier. After about twenty seconds of it, the light stopped as Gavin spoke up again.

"He is north, but I can't sense anything specific. It's like there's something there shrouding him," Gavin ran through the mental scan that he just made. It was a strange feeling, almost like how mystics would describe what Astral Projection was like.

"Maybe out of range?" Dominic suggested.

"No, there's something out there, some force that's strong enough to block me. I don't think Sern would have been blocked that easily," Gavin focused his thoughts on the present moment again. "You had a plan?"

"Just a simple suggestion," Dominic raised the dagger, almost as though he was offering it to Paxton. "Jett may be able to track Paxton's blood; so if he bleeds again, he may be able to use it as a way to lure him back." Gavin thought about the suggestion for a moment, but an obvious concern came up.

"Do you think you could do that?" Gavin turned to Paxton.

"Yes," Paxton snatched the dagger from Dominic.

"You don't have to do it now," Gavin cautioned his childe. He put his hand on the true silver knife."Let's get an idea of where he is first. We'll go in a group."

"No," Paxton turned to Gavin with a sense of determination on his face. "We're going now and you're going to track where he is," They were all a bit surprised at his fast determination and directness, and were glad to see him taking this seriously.

Jett could smell the scent as though it was calling to him through the mists. Indeed the area around where he was running through was starting to get very foggy. The smell was now more clear, and wasn't what he expected. Paxton's blood was very rich, but this was far more potent. Even the smell was something unique, had a type of majestic, almost divine, scent to it. There was an obvious trail to it, he could smell the concentration of the blood in drops that were left on the ground. Amongst the odd leaves and rocks, Jett could smell the tiny concentration of the scent coming from the drops that were left.

The blood was still red, barely clotted. Jett ran the tip of his clawed index finger along the droplet, and sure enough, it was very new. Likely whatever was bleeding this, was nearby. Taking a long deep inhale of the blood smell, he was able to lock onto the trailing scent in the forest around him. Paxton's blood was still in him, giving him astounding speed and jumping power, helping him to leap past streams and huge rocks without any effort. His eyes, bestial as they were, were oddly less sensitive than they were as human, and certain colours seemed to be greyed out. Jett remembered that dogs were colour-blind and since dogs, and wolves were related, chances are they would be colour-blind too. The smell of the blood was what attracted him, but he noticed it didn't quite look the same.

He reached an opening in the forest, something that was relatively common in these woods, probably cleared out for the purpose of giving some camping ground for some solitude. Something was here. He couldn't see it, or hear it, but he could smell something. His own werewolf eyes and senses were picking something up despite the lack of colouring. It was strange for him, to see that things that were red, or green were now some strange mixed dark yellow colour. But this wasn't the main focus of his mind for the moment.

The short moment of silence around him was broken by a groan he heard nearby. The sound was coming directly in front of him. It was a male voice, but he couldn't tell too much. After a few more steps in that direction, he could already smell the guy. He had a vampire's scent, definitely true, but it wasn't quite like Paxton's, Dominic's or Gavin's scent. It was strange, but for him, he could smell this person. It was a very strange sensation, being able to smell someone and what they were. It was a scent similar to the three other vampires who he knew, but had a strange difference, almost like the air was less fragrant. The smell was less appealing, though still very alluring.

He followed it into the center of the clearing where the thick grass had grown to obscure whoever was lying there. It was an oddly serene environment for someone to be lying there, especially after Jett got a better look at him. The man was lying there, his neck, clearly bitten by some form of animal. Jett hurried near him, and found that wound was still bleeding. Instinct took over as he didn't even care to ask what his name was or how he was hurt, instead he dug his own teeth right into the young man's neck, drinking in the bleeding blood right away. The taste immediately drove him to frenzied hunger, oddly his vampire healing wasn't curing the wound.

Instead of feeling the rampant ecstasy that was expected from the blood drinking, especially from a vampire, he felt his arms and legs suddenly grow heavy. He gripped his fists to see his claws starting to retract back into human hands, his fangs also retracted back without him having any control. He was now absolutely certain that something was wrong. Slowly he tried to back up but his legs wouldn't move, instead he collapsed backwards.

The young man who was lying there slowly got up off the ground. Jett's eyes were still working, as the flooding of colour returned to him. The face that he didn't even bother to look at earlier was that of one of the Vampires who he had seen in Wolf Coven's dining hall yesterday morning. He didn't get to introduce himself, but he was definitely a vampire. Jett tried to speak, but no voice came out of his mouth. He was able to still stay sitting up but his body wasn't moving, or listening to him. His intense green eyes and light blond hair were particularly radiant. His body may have been that of a vampire but already Jett suspected that there was something more to him than that.

Only now did Jett finally get a look at the guy. It was somewhat difficult to tear his eyes off of this man's intense green eyes. The wound and bite marks on his neck mysteriously healed themselves. The area around him started to slowly vanish as a mysterious fog surrounded them. It was like there was nothing around them anymore. The light was still seen as it diffused through the fog, but aside from that and the ground it was like they were completely cut off from the rest of the world.

"You Bloodbanes should really be careful about what you eat." He mocked as he folded his arms across his chest, his long coat flowing as though it was alive. Jett couldn't do anything but look up at him. His voice, was oddly very enticing, deep but sensitive.

"Is this, what you are going to use to obtain that High Order blood?" The benefactor's voice spoke. He wasn't seen but that same, metallic and artificial sounding resonance came from beyond the mists around him.

"Yes," Hypnos replied as he levitated Jett into the air, reaching his eye level. "One thing you should know about drinking the blood of a god, is that when you do, that blood lets the god control you." He lectured to Jett who was now absorbing every word.

"Give him this," The benefactor's words came at Hypnos again. Out of the mist came a stream of white smoke which swirled around the two of them for a moment, then, almost like they were living snakes made out of smoke, coalesced into a ball in between the two of them. It started to glow brightly, and then after a very vibrant flash, an object was there floating between them. It was a wooden tube of sorts. Hypnos unscrewed the top of it to find something clearly sharp inside. He slowly removed it from the protective tube. It looked like a syringe or needle that was used for medical needs. "This will extract the blood required," The voice ordered Hypnos. The syringe dropped into Hypnos' hand. The material was clearly not ordinary silver.

"True silver," Hypnos grinned. "Interesting that you can find a material that rare." Hypnos commented as he examined the syringe. The metal was so refined and pure that unlike steel or iron, there were no grains or lines in it. It was pure and perfectly made. The syringe had a glass body that let anyone see how much blood it contained. The metal didn't even look forged, it was more like it was molded into shape.

"Have your puppet obtain the blood by this time tomorrow," The benefactor commanded to Hypnos. Hypnos placed his hand onto Jett's head, offering him a temporary moment of comfort. He looked deeply into Jett's eyes, almost like the young Bloodbane werewolf was now just a young animal awaiting instructions.

"Take this, and obtain the blood. You won't reveal anything about me or my benefactor." Hypnos stated clearly, his words were loud, despite him only whispering . Every single word vibrated in Jett's mind, repeating themselves over and over in his head. Jett wasn't going to forget them. "But I feel you will need some help in doing it."

"What help?" Jett asked, now surprised at the fact he was able to speak at all. He was almost still unable to really comprehend what was going on.

"You think stealing blood from a High Order vampire is going to be easy?" Hypnos scoffed at the ignorance that this little being was displaying to him. "This will make it easier." Hypnos placed a ring around Jett's finger. It was silver, and very plain looking. It was still warm from his touch as he slipped it onto Jett's middle finger.

"How will this work?"

"All you need to do is touch a High Order with this ring, and they will fall asleep for a few hours. That will be more than enough time for you to get the blood, then escape back to here." Hypnos started to walk away. "Just be careful who you touch. They may start to suspect something if everyone you shake hands with immediately falls down unconscious." Jett didn't answer but Hypnos knew that the instructions were going to fill his mind over and over again until he completed his duty. "If you manage to complete this task, then I will eliminate all of your blood cravings."

"You can do that?" Jett asked as Hypnos walked away. The god didn't give any answer but simply vanished into the fog.

Jett slipped the ring and the tube holding the syringe into his pocket. His limbs were all starting to feel normal again. He shook his feet and his hands just to get the blood flowing to them again. He dashed right back off, instinctively shifting his hands and feet to their natural wolf speed back towards Wolf Coven House.

Chapter 18

Elura paced around the main foyer of the house. She had noticed much more activities, the shattering of one of the windows upstairs did peak her interest. Despite that, she didn't go investigate since she knew they had the matter handled. Still, when the smashing of glass was heard, anyone with a brain would be concerned at what was going on. She wanted to speak to Gavin about the auction but she felt that there wasn't much of a point to her staying anymore, and headed out the door.

Cazian was up there with Paxton, Gavin, Trenton and Coltrane. Paxton had willingly allowed them to take some of his blood for bait. The scent should carry through, but they weren't too sure how far it would go. It was reasonable to assume that it would all depend on wind and the air to carry his scent. Thanks to Gavin however, the ability to manipulate some wind flow with his quasi-Intendant abilities would let the scent carry further than normal. Even then, the five of them were worried about what could happen.

"You think he will be able to detect my blood?" Paxton asked Gavin. It seemed that Gavin would know more about this than the others.

"He should be able to smell it. Bloodbanes are naturally drawn to the most potent source of vampiric blood, and that's our High Order blood," Gavin assured him.

Elura had exited the house and started walking back to her carriage. The magnificent black stage coach with the four stone horses. As she boarded her coach and sat down on the comfortable black leather seats, she tapped the roof of the coach with her staff. Atop the driver seat materialized the coachman, a faceless, almost invisible being, save for the clothing and hat that he wore.

With a mighty crack of his whip, the four horse statues literally erupted to life as silently roared. The four black horses seemed to shake off their stone appearance, shattering the stone skin in a fury of shards and pebbles as they sprung back to life. The carriage started to move ever so gently, away from the house, trotting away.

Inside, Elura was rather eager to attend this auction. She loved buying new things, and it was certainly possible that she would be able to get something quite worthwhile and precious. But she also suspected that she should keep an eye out for anything suspicious, in case the Sanctuary Organization wanted to keep tab on what was going to be moved around the earth. Powerful arcane artifacts were always up for sale and fetched formidable prices, literally hundreds of thousands to millions of dollars, or for equally rare and precious objects. Of course the most precious of them, the most valuable, were souls.

Elura knew, and everyone knew, that the soul, the eternal life force and living essence of any being, was above all, the most precious of all things that could be traded. If someone offered their own soul, in any bargain or purchase or trade, it was almost always an automatic win. To control the life essence, the eternal being of a living being was above description on how valuable that could be. One could literally be owned for the rest of eternity if they gave up their soul. Of course such a trade was also seen as extremely taboo, and often seen as evil and sinister. Elura never owned or purchased any souls, as most magical practitioners didn't. Such trades were not only seen as selfish, but the resulting trade could also put a bad mark on the buyer.

If a person owned the soul of another, this would mark them as a force for evil, and often be segregated from the rest of the magical community. Elura herself had done a great deal of research into soul trades. She herself wasn't officially a member of the Sanctuary Organization, but many magic users like her preferred to be on the good side of the Intendants. Intendant Hasaan and others have, in the past, had to take firm stances against some of the more ambitious magic users since they were trying to use magic to gain an edge on the Sanctuary Organization's influence.

The Magical World, was one that was extremely difficult to tame since anyone could use magic, and with enough skill and practice anyone could become a powerful user; and to make it more dangerous, Magic was also very difficult to control and highly volatile.

In comparison to becoming a powerful Intendant, becoming a powerful magic user was far easier, meaning that the Sanctuary Organization had to rely on another entire enforcement arm to help them deal with magic users, the Inquisitors.

Elura herself never had a direct run in with the Inquisitors, but she knew that they were around. Whereas the Intendants were more eager and open to dealing with all forms of Supernaturals, the Inquisitors actively dealt with magic-wielding humans. Elura had heard from Hasaan that the power that the Sanctuary Organization held was not magic, but a power that was cosmic in origin, a power that originated from the universe as a whole, and many scales beyond the power of magic. Elura had never seen the Intendants or Inquisitors themselves having to use force, but she heard that their reputation for getting things done was one that had to be taken with respect.

Just then, something caught Elura's eye as she gazed through the forest, someone was running towards Wolf Coven House. He was using hands and legs while running, and Elura immediately realized what it was. Though she wasn't directly involved in the matters at Wolf Coven House, she did hear that one of the werewolves had escaped from Wolf Coven House, and she also heard their plan of using the blood of a High Order to lure him back. Elura thought to herself, should she assist? With only a few seconds to make her decision, she tapped the roof of her carriage with her staff again, issuing an immediate order to the driver to follow the wolf.

The carriage immediately swerved to the left, and re-entered the forest at full speed. Despite maneuvering through the forest, the entire carriage effortlessly glided high in the air, above the shrubbery at first, but then descended low enough to avoid the branches. It soared past the odd birds and squirrels that were probably just as astounded to see a black carriage flying through the forest. Elura looked down to see the werewolf going quite fast, but not fast enough to dodge the carriage that likely he didn't even notice was following him. From the tip of her staff, Elura reached into the glowing crystal ball, and pulled out a materialized single strand of string. She tugged on it, and it thickened into a silk rope. Taking one end in her hand, she aimed it carefully at the wolf that was running and shot at him. The rope surged out of the staff crystal as though endless, and charged right at the werewolf like it was some type of flying snake, immediately wrapping it around the wolf's arms, twirling around them. The wolf, shocked at the surprise, almost tripped over in an effort to unwind the magic rope, but it picked him right off the ground as the carriage itself slowly descended to the ground.

"Slow down, kid!" Elura called from the carriage, assuring him as the rope gently undid itself.

"Who are you?" the young wolf snarled through his fangs.

"Lady Elura," Elura introduced as she stepped out of her carriage, taking generous time to stretch out her long alabaster legs, teasingly flirting with the young werewolf who was now being released from the magic rope.

"What are you? Some kind of witch? " the wolf barked at her as he shrugged out of the rope.

"I prefer sorceress, and I'm a friend of Wolf Coven House," Elura assured him. "And just where do you think you're going?"

"I was heading back there until you got me," Jett stood up on his hind feet, his face was still very much feral, the eyes, facial fur, and fangs fully formed.

"By your look, I would guess, Packwalker, or Bloodbane," Elura assumed for the time being as she walked around him. "And probably with less than 5% body fat too." She smiled, not being able to resist that little remark. "Well, pup, let me give you a ride back. They're worried about you." she offered.

"I'm a Bloodbane," Jett corrected.

"Well, Mr. Bloodbane, I'm not going to bite."

"Alright," Jett thanked, with some caution in his voice.

"And your name is...?" she asked the handsome young Bloodbane werewolf.

"Jett."

"Well Jett, hop in!" The carriage door opened again for Elura to board as she gestured to Jett to follow her. "I'm taking you back there. They're searching for you."

"And how did you find me?" Jett cautiously approached the carriage; the four horses weren't particularly a welcome sight. They were quite ferocious looking, and the invisible man in the coat at the driver seat also made him wary.

"I just happened to be heading home when I caught sight of you. So I decided to stop and get you, and take you back there myself."

"Thanks." The carriage made a gentle touchdown at the entrance without any bump or shaking. The doors to the house swung open as Paxton, Gavin and Cazian came out to meet the carriage that they had seen flying down from a moment ago. It was odd that Elura would return so quickly, but as Jett stepped off the carriage they knew why. Paxton rushed over to him right way and hugged him. Jett thought that Paxton would be angry at him.

"I found a little lost puppy," Elura smiled as she stayed inside her carriage, offering her trademark wink to Gavin. She often did flirt with any handsome supernatural being, especially Gavin.

"How did you find him?" Gavin asked.

"Just saw him outside my carriage as I was leaving. Noticed he was wandering around so I swept down to get him."

"Thanks."

"Oh, and for the auction?" Elura inquired, wanting an answer to the question she asked earlier.

"Yes." Gavin's memory was jogged by Elura. "Yes, do keep an eye out. Keep a list of items, and buyers for us, please."

"You want to send someone with me?"

"No, we have things here to deal with for the time being." Gavin apologized.

"Alright," Elura closed the door to the carriage as it started off again. Paxton and Jett already went back inside the house with the rest of them. Gavin knew that they had a lot to deal with, in terms of Jett's new hunger and abilities. It wasn't a situation that he was looking forwards to investigating.

Chapter 19

Sern waited for the Ahri to finish their preparations. They had already gone back to the Sanctuary outpost, safe within its crystalline walls. There was only just him and a small group of guards at the outpost. Of course Archon Alena was also present, probably wanting to wish them well before they departed. A few of the Ahri had come in and out, mainly attending to various military matters, moving crates of supplies around with the use of their enormous rock golems.

An entourage of Ahri were heading down the road from their capital to the outpost. They were followed by rock golems carrying a few large crates. They were certainly not small and it was quite curious what were contained within as they approached the outpost. The four Ahri who were on their way traveled on the same flying disks that Kito had used earlier. It seemed quite an effective way to travel, considering the shortness of their little feet compared to humans.

"All set to go!" Kito saluted the two of them as he and the others arrived. He turned to introduce the other Ahri who were with him. He pointed to one who wore an elaborate red robe with a hood. The texture of the cloth was likely the same Crystalweave that they were given earlier by the Sanctuary forces. "These are Representatives Kazmo, Kobili and Larita," Kito introduced. Each of the Ahri bowed when their name was announced. Each Ahri wore the same type of red robe, which looked very comfortable, and stretched down to their feet.

Each of the Ahri also carried a staff. Each staff was different. They looked like they were made out of wood, large twigs and branches, that were weaved together to form a tight and long shaft. Every staff coiled upwards around what looked like a pearl, which glowed quietly.

The golems had put down the crates. After placing them down, they simply crumbled back into the ground, into heaps of dirt and rocks which then merged back to the earth.

"Well Sern. You have a diplomatic guest to bring to Wolf Coven House, and I think the situation here has been handled well." Alena praised him.

"Before I do, there will have to be some planning and information given to them first about the world that they will be entering. It's quite different from what they have encountered here." replied the Intendant.

"I have been familiarized with most of them," Kito emphasized. "A realm of humanoids that seem to be abnormally tall, with almost all of them surpassing three feet in height," he began, with the other Ahri nodding their heads in agreement. "which I personally believe to be abnormally tall, and unnecessary." The other Ahri continued to agree with Kito vigorously. Sern slipped Alena a rather odd gaze. Alena herself was rather amused by the statements coming from the little ambassador. "But as long as we can take some of our own supplies there and have the ability to grow our own food, and have access to water, and the ability and freedom to use our own magic, there shouldn't be any issues."

"Absolutely," Alena nodded to Kito. "As with your status as Ambassador, we will provide you with sufficient land to make your own homes which will, by all extent, your own sovereign territory."

"I'm sure that we can find a suitable location for you, within reasonable distance to Wolf Coven House," Sern assured them.

"And I am also aware that most of your members are going to be shape-shifting humanoids." The rest of the Ahri agreed visibly with Kito.

"You seem to know quite a bit about what you are going to be encountering." Sern wondered. The little people seemed very informed.

"We were given a very detailed history of your world, including those you call "Supernatural" people who inhabit your world, who seem to be isolated from the rest of the dominant race, humans, I believe you call them."

"Lots and lots of books! And we can even read your common languages." The only female Ahri chirped cheerfully. Sern remembered that she was named Larita.

"You can read English?"

"And French, Spanish, Chinese, Russian, and Arabic," Kito proudly stated.

"Apparently the Ahri have exceptional memories," Alena explained to Sern. "They seem to be able to recall a great deal of data with little effort, which also explains their vast versatility when it comes to their magical skill." Alena smiled at the little folks. Even an Archon of Alena's long experience was amused by the unique quirks that these little people had to offer.

"Then I feel that their skills will be a great benefit to Sanctuary," Sern turned towards the portal that sat ready and open.

"We've configured this portal to take you directly back to Wolf Coven House without a need to go through the hub. But this is going to be possible only for the next hour. After that, you will have to venture through the hub again, then to Aurastar to take a portal back to here," the Archon instructed as the portal guards marched aside, allowing for their departure.

Sern stepped towards the enormous sphere of distorted space as the Ahri tapped the ground around the ten enormous crates of supplies. Whereas they were using rock golems to move their goods before, now they simply used a spell for levitation. The four Ahri and Sern stepped through the portal and were followed by the floating crates, all ten of them, rippling through the vast portal sphere as they vanished back to Earth.

Paxton, Jett and Gavin were in the lobby of Wolf Coven House. Dominic and Cazian had gone upstairs, and the wolves had gone for a run. The temporary tranquility of the moment was interrupted as the fountain in the center of the atrium, just in the room next door, stopped flowing with water. The flowing water was interrupted by silence as the fountain itself started to activate, its central pillar opening up, and lowering to reveal the inner portal that was protected normally by the structure around it.

Gavin went to investigate the portal, followed by Paxton and Jett who had never seen anything like this before. The odd rippling sound was almost like that of water as the portal showed the destination that was inside it. It looked strange to the two of them.

"What in the world is that?" Jett asked Gavin who seemed calm at the situation.

"It's a portal," Gavin answered.

"Like, magic?" Paxton asked as they peered at the portal from different angles. The viewpoint from within the portal also shifted. It looked like a beautiful grassy plain surrounded by large glowing white crystals. "Weird!" Paxton ran around the portal for a second, amazed that the perspective shifted with every different angle, as though it was a miniature world itself. Suddenly something leaped out of it.

The three of them stood there, as what leaped out stood there, staring at the three of them. It was a small little being. It was no more than two feet tall, and looked like a small toddler, but with a larger head. Its cherubic-like features were accented by a large pair of innocent looking brown eyes and large pointed ears, and an almost chipmunk like nose. Despite the very infantile appearance, it wore a very well embroidered red robe, and carried a wooden staff that looked like it was weaved from branches, and at the top of the staff was a glowing pearl. Its head tilted to the side, perplexed by what it saw as well.

"Um... and what is that?" Jett asked Gavin, who he expected to know the answer.

"I think it is an Ahri," Gavin whispered back as Paxton joined the two of them.

"It's kind of cute!" Paxton almost giggled. The little being looked like it understood what they were saying, as one of its eyebrows crooked downwards. Paxton knelt down to eye level of the little being as he held out his hand. "Hi there!" he charmed the little being as though he was talking to a puppy or a child.

"It's not polite to stare!" It said, in perfect English. Its voice was high, like that of a cheerful child. Then from the portal stepped another being, this one of a very familiar face, shape and demeanor. "Hello," Sern greeted to the three of them, as behind him were three more small little beings. They were similarly dressed, and also each carried a staff. "Gavin, we're going to have to have a general meeting. Please assemble everyone in the dining hall."

"Of course, Sern." Gavin agreed. "Should we say within the next thirty minutes?"

"Yes, that's sufficient. I have to set-up the hospitality for our friends here," Sern looked at the four Ahri around him. "This is Ambassador Kito, the leader of the Ahri delegation," Sern pointed to the Ahri with brown hair who held the most ornate staff. "And these are representatives, Kazmo, Kobili and Larita." Each of the Ahri bowed when their name was mentioned. "I'll explain more during the meeting," Sern introduced as he led the Ahri and their floating luggage out of the atrium.

Paxton and Jett followed Gavin as he walked away, but not able to restrain themselves from looking back at the little beings who were guests. Sern and the Ahri passed down to the hallway, with the row of ten enormous floating crates following them. Then they noticed that the little folks weren't walking, but instead were hovering disks.

"As though I didn't think things were getting any stranger here," Paxton told Gavin as they headed towards the dining hall.

"In my experience, I mean Sern's experience..." Gavin corrected himself for a moment, "little beings are never to be underestimated. More than often, they possess powers and skills that we should never prejudge," Gavin warned. "They may be cute, but they're probably extremely powerful."

"How could you tell?" Jett asked. "They look like pudgy little kids."

"I could sense it, and I also sensed that Sern knew that they were powerful."

"Powerful in what way?" Jett asked again.

"I'm sure Sern will explain everything. In the meantime, head to the dining hall, and I'll get everyone else." Gavin headed up the stairs to the resident apartments.

Thirty of the Wolf Coven Members gathered in the dining hall. Aside from the High Order Vampires who were Cazian, Dominic, Gavin and Paxton, there were Coltrane and Trenton the Prime Wolves, and many others of various supernatural origins. Jett and Paxton did get a few interesting glances from the others whom they hadn't been introduced to yet, but they weren't really judged. There was clearly discussion and some gossip going on, wondering why Sern was away. Of course the sight of these little people at Wolf Coven House, despite only being around for fifteen or so minutes, was enough to spur plenty of speculation.

The room was configured like that of a hemicycle with the chairs set-up in a semicircle to let everyone be seen and see what was going on. There wasn't much going on until people noticed Sern entering the room, behind him were the four little creatures who floated on their disks behind him. Sern levitated five chairs from the back of the room up to the front where he sat down. The four little ones climbed up onto their own chairs and sat, waiting for Sern to make his announcements.

"Alright, everyone." Sern announced. "It's good to see you now that I'm back. I was on a diplomatic mission. And as many of you knew, Gavin was put in charge while I was gone." Paxton was listening to Sern speak but Jett seemed a bit distracted, obviously amused by the four little beings who were sitting beside Sern. "As you can already tell, we have a few guests here." Sern pointed to the two who sat to his left, then to his right. "They are the Ahri, a race of beings from another location where Sanctuary is active. These four are here, to set-up a small diplomatic mission and to basically examine this world and the Supernaturals such as yourselves," Sern then pointed to the lead Ahri. "This is Ambassador Kito. He is the leader of the delegation." Then he pointed to the others. "These are Representatives Kobili, Kazmo and Larita," and again like before, they all nodded as their names were called. But this time they added a gentle tap with their staves to the ground. Each time they did, the pearl atop their staves glowed, to show the ones being indicated by name.

Kito seemed to take center stage; he drew a circle on the floor with the base of his own staff. Each line that he made glowed with a yellow light outlining a circle that was large enough for him to stand in. Then from the ground, raised a silver glowing disk, the same type that they were using before. Kito stood atop the hovering disk as it levitated him up to eye level with Sern. His staff stood by itself on the edge of the platform, and was still glowing gently with a white glow from the pearl.

"The Ahri are practitioners of magic arts, particularly those that center around the elements," Kito explained to the crowd of Supernaturals who were watching him just floating there atop his disk. "We are also here to help in the creation of magical portals, to help you go from place to place without the need of your traveling machines."

"Why did you have to go to their world?" Cazian asked Sern, asking a question that everyone seemed to be curious to find the answer.

"I was summoned by my superiors. They wanted me to first meet Kito and his delegation before they came to our world. The agreement was that the Ahri will help us with the creation of portals and we help them with their own world."

"So are they going to show some of their magic power?"

"The Ahri are a part of a diplomatic mission. They are not here for our amusement or for…"

"Yes!" Larita chirped as she hopped up on her own magical disk, interrupting Sern. With a wave of her staff, the upper portions of the dining hall started to sparkle and shine in mid air, as though there were tiny stars twinkling above them. Everyone's attention shifted to the light display above their heads. As the twinkles became brighter and brighter, they erupted in a display of sparks and fireworks above their heads. They streamed downwards and fizzled harmlessly as more and more started to appear above them.

"Pardon Larita, but she has a fondness for pretty light shows," Kito mockingly scolded the female Ahri. The array of hovering sparks and lights soon vanished on their own, ending the spontaneous pyrotechnic display that took place over their heads. It was certainly something unexpected and came out of the blue. To Jett, Paxton and the others, they already suspected that these little creatures were going to be full of surprises. "We are a diplomatic ensemble looking forwards to meeting and learning about you. We don't want to conduct interviews but want to learn as you are willing to tell us."

"This is just an informal orientation to just give you the basic information on what is going to be happening throughout the next few months. We hope to start construction on their mission soon. And until then, they will be using our storage space to stockpile their own goods. I'm sure that the Ahri will be pleased to talk with you all on your own time." Sern symbolically ended the meeting by turning up the lights in the room. As the chattering of voices started to get slightly louder, with Jett and Paxton being the first to walk up and start talking to the Ahri, Sern gestured to Gavin to follow him. The taller High Order vampire approached his Intendant Superior. "I need to speak to you in private, please." Sern asked Gavin.

"Your office then?" Gavin asked

"Yes, now please." Though it had only been a few days since Sern departed and made Gavin his temporary replacement, it was somewhat strange for Gavin to be speaking to Sern on almost equal levels, at least equal, psychologically. Gavin also felt that Sern had double-secured the room with a shield, something that only he now would be able to sense due to the infusion he was given. "How have things been?" Sern asked as he sat down back at his old desk. Gavin took his seat across from him on an equally comfortable seat that had moved into place.

"Interesting, to say the least," Gavin started. His own facial expression was a sign of relief to know that Sern had returned. He didn't say anything else beyond those few words, which gave the room a very awkward silence.

"Something wrong?" Sern inquired to his Deputy Intendant. He asked the question but he had a somewhat fair approximation in his mind of what was bothering Gavin.

"When you said that you had given me some of your thoughts, I had no idea that you were going to literally give me your mind." Gavin stated. His mind was already starting to flow through the vast assembly of thoughts, almost like an entire archive and library of knowledge and experience that were being re-flooded into his mind.

"In order to give you the experience needed, I had to literally give you my history, in the form of memories. In essence, Gavin, you know me better than anyone else."

"Yes, and that's what troubled me." Gavin looked up from his original focus, which was his hands, into Sern's eyes. "I know a lot about you, Sern." The final words echoed in both their minds. Quite literally they resonated and echoed as though the were being repeated over and over again.

"I see," Sern responded. He didn't seem to respond, as he already knew what Gavin was closing in on. His mind, his concentrated thoughts, and experience were all transferred into Gavin's mind when he left, and now Gavin knew what he knew about certain experience. "And since you have my memories, you also know the context to which those thoughts were based."

"Yes, I do," Gavin stared back. He and Sern were thinking of the same things, and certain thoughts were better meant to be kept secret. It was very strange, since before Sern departed, Gavin knew that he had these memories, but it simply had never occurred to him to dig into them before. Now that he was facing Sern right here, face to face, things were very different. It was as though Sern was summoning the memories that were in his mind and dredging them to the surface without even realizing it.

"I think that you know that these memories can be blocked off easily. Though I would prefer not to have to do this," Sern said to Gavin, with his trademark stern expression.

"The strange thing is that I would completely understand why you would do that. If they knew what I knew about you, then they would be terrified of you."

"But you also know that I am not here for those purposes. I was appointed as an Intendant and I am here to serve that purpose only."

"Well, that I can believe."

"Of course you believe it. You have my thoughts in your mind. Which brings me to the next issue," Sern continued. His words were not lost at all upon Gavin; in fact, the way their situation was going, it was clear that Gavin knew almost exactly what Sern was going to say before he said it.

"You want to reverse the infusion."

"Yes. As I said before I left, and I am sure that you knew that this was going to be the case, that you have to be ready to surrender the infused properties when I return."

"Yes. I completely understand." Gavin stood up. "However, there is one request that I have to make."

"And that is?" Sern asked curiously.

"May I keep the memories? The knowledge that came with your memories could greatly assist me in helping you here at Wolf Coven House."

"Actually I did not intend to block them at all. I fully intended to give you full access to them."

"Very well. Let us proceed." Sern got up from behind the desk. He walked around to stand in front of Gavin while the High Order stood prepared. Sern slowly reached out with his hand, which faced Gavin's chest as it started to glow white again. His eyes also responded with the same illuminated glow, slowly increasing its intensity as from the center of Gavin's chest a corresponding glow also appeared. It was the same white colour as what was coming from glows in Sern's eyes. The same stream of light that from his chest streamed towards Sern's hand. Gavin and Sern's eyes were both glowing, and flickering as though they were like two computers, exchanging information. As the surging beam penetrated Gavin's chest, he could feel the enormous power that was once within his body starting to slowly drain out of him. It felt like his senses and physical sensations, were being taken out of him, piece by piece, first centering in his chest, then radiated through his upper and lower bodies, to his limbs, toes, ears, head and fingers. His own eye glow faded quickly, and Sern's grew stronger as he retrieved the power that he had given Gavin. Slowly with every passing moment, Gavin slowly reverted to his normal High Order form as he slowly sank into one of the seats.

Sern stood there for a moment, which soon passed as minutes, as Gavin sought to regain his mental bearings, again attempting to anchor himself back into reality after this strange draining of his own internal power. Sern's eyes continued to glow as he stared blankly into the air. Gavin also started to filter through his mind, wondering, thinking of what he was going through, realizing that all of his thoughts and memories were still intact despite not having Sern's memories in his mind.

Sern, on the other hand was still processing the information that he just received. He now was flooded with over a hundred years of experience that Gavin's mind had also possessed. He suspected that the infusion that he had just performed on Gavin would bring back some memories, but he had no idea that it would bring them all! Every memorized thought, every memorized experience that Gavin had gone through in his entire life that he openly remembered, or could recall with his mind, was now immediately flooding Sern's mind. Smells, tastes, touches, thoughts, feelings, emotions experience, all came as strong as a boulder crashing through what he had prepared as mental barriers.

No such preparation could have prepared even an Intendant for this additional lifetime of experience that were all coming into his mind as he physically was struggling to organize them. Sern started to stumble from what was, at one time, his trademark pose, perfectly composed and dignified, standing perfectly straight. His face was also showing a clear sign of struggle as he almost collapsed, had Gavin not caught him.

"Sern? You alright?" the High Order asked as the Intendant regained his bearings.

"I'm attempting to process your information," Sern groaned, as he gritted his teeth. Gavin had never seen this type of behavior in an Intendant before, but then again, he had never known about a memory transfer like this before. "I knew that I was going to receive all the information, but I wasn't aware of the sensations!" Sern cried out, almost like his entire body was now going through some sort of strange reorganization. His own mind was struggling to maintain some composure as his brain was attempting to make sense of all the additional memories that were still flooding in. "It's, going to take some time," he gasped as he couldn't stop his eyes from glowing, a clear sign of him using his Intendant abilities. They were flaring brightly as he sat there, Gavin helped move him to the seat behind his desk, as he quickly activated some form of display on the desk.

"You didn't take all your power back!" Gavin attempted to tell Sern. The interface on the desk still responded to Gavin, even though it was not supposed to do this.

"I made sure to keep a tiny residual portion of it in your body, to help you protect those memories that came from me. It's to safeguard you," Sern spoke, his voice was transforming, into a strangely robotic sound, almost like it was a digital sound. "It will also offer resistance to other forms of interference."

Gavin knew that Sern had to be left alone for a while to arrange these thoughts for himself. Thanks to his own knowledge of Sern's memories, he could fulfill the function of leading Wolf Coven for the time being. He cautiously left the room to allow Sern to do what he needed to do to maintain his mental stability. Gavin also noticed his clothes had reverted to what he was wearing at the exact moment where he was changed before.

Jett and Paxton were with the crowd of Supernaturals in the gardens watching the Ahri perform many of their magical tricks. Unlike a stage magician who had props and perhaps a set of giant metal rings to do their show, the Ahri showed off what they called elemental magic. Kito had described this art as "taming natural forces" for their own use and benefits. The two of them had almost no experience in seeing the magical arts; but from what they heard from other people in Wolf Coven House, it was definitely not anything that was easy to understand. For Jett, it was seeing Elura's flying carriage; that was certainly magical, but she didn't offer him any explanation on how it worked.

The Ahri were launching out fireworks as a symbol of them celebrating their warm welcome to Wolf Coven House, and also the fact that they were the first diplomatic mission sent to the Earth world. And considering there were only four Ahri who were putting on the show, it was still spectacular.

Paxton and Jett sat in a more isolated corner of the gardens, on two lawn chairs that were side by side. Jett was curled up against Paxton's chest as they looked upwards at the sky, without the need to strain their necks. They were just glad to be together, and enjoying a moment of relaxation. Jett did find it interesting that Paxton still had a heartbeat and wasn't cold to the touch, despite what Hollywood would have told them about vampires. It was not like he had to worry about the sunrise, which wasn't going to be for another few hours. The fireworks just kept going, never the same patterns. First were bursts of red then blue then green then yellow, then rainbows of all sorts. It was truly spectacular for them to see this.

"Having fun?" Paxton asked Jett as he looked down at his boyfriend for a reply.

"Yeah," Jett hugged him slightly tighter. "Just to lie here without worry for a few minutes is worth it," he smiled back at him. There was a definitely a sense of relief in Jett's eyes.

"How's the wolf?" Paxton asked, hoping to get a comforting answer out of Jett.

"Still wanting to take a nibble out of his vampire," Jett grinned.

"Oh really?" Paxton leaned down to Jett.

"Definitely. And how's the vampire?" Jett whispered back, anticipating an equally suggestive answer from his boyfriend.

"Oddly, not hungry," Paxton admitted, knowing that it wasn't quite what Jett was hoping to hear. And sure enough, Jett's face displayed some disappointment. "But there's always room for dessert." That was enough to bring a smile back to Jett's face.

"You want to go inside?" Jett asked Paxton with some more devious expression on his face. He was already slowly thinking of the ring that was in his pocket, the one that Hypnos gave him that had the sleeping enchantment. He knew very well he couldn't use it here in the garden since everyone would see him taking blood from Paxton, and also Paxton would be asleep for hours.

"Back to the room?" Paxton grinned. Jett almost jumped to his feet, as he scooped Paxton into his arms. A few others around them also caught the sight of the two of them. A few smirks and whispers came around but they were all obviously of the same topic as Jett effortlessly carried Paxton up the stone stairs back to the house.

Paxton was amazed how fast Jett could move as he carried him to their apartment. Paxton noticed already that Jett's face was starting to morph. His eyes had started to turn into that same feral, animal yellow, and his fangs had subtly started to change. He never got an entirely clear look at him, but now with the normal lighting of the house around them, and in their room, he did.

"What's wrong?" Jett asked, only just now noticing that he had a double pair of fangs in his mouth. "Wow, that's weird," he moved his tongue around the sharp teeth. "It's tough to talk like this." He struggled. His words were very odd-sounding, considering he had to mouth the words around these sharp canines.

"Yeah." Paxton smirked at him as he was gently let down out of Jett's arms when they entered their apartment. The lights to the ultra modern apartment came on right away after detecting their presence.

"Let's see how you talk with your fangs on." Jett mocked as he went into the bedroom, teasing Paxton to follow him as he stripped off his shirt. Paxton was only all the more eager to follow him. As he did, Jett stood there waiting. Paxton came up close for a fast kiss, but as he did, Jett slipped into his pocket, and retrieved the ring. He quickly pressed it into Paxton's hands. Without any warning, Paxton instantly fell onto the bed silently into a deep sleep. He slumped over completely, almost lifeless in expression, but Jett could still hear his heart beating, and his breathing. Jett gently nudged Paxton to see if he was awake at all. Sure enough, Paxton didn't move at all; but every moment Jett was paying close attention to his heartbeats and breathing, and all things seemed to be just fine. Slowly he pulled the ring out of Paxton's hand and then slipped it back into his pocket, while at the same time removing the wooden tube from his other. He went back into the main living area and locked the door, before slipping the syringe out of the tube.

He slipped back into the bedroom where Paxton was lying, still sleeping soundly, just as Hypnos told him the ring would succeed in doing. Jett slowly inserted the point of the syringe into Paxton's left arm. The syringe injected itself before he even put the tip of the needle under the skin, slowly stretched itself as the internal tube of the syringe slowly started to fill with blood. The glass container within the syringe was about the size of a cigar and was slowly filling with that precious High Order blood.

It took so much concentration for him to maintain his control as the scent of the blood started to fill the air around him. Normally a human wouldn't be able to smell this blood, but he certainly could. His own Bloodbane hunger was starting to surface, and he could see it in the sharpening of his claws and his canine fur emerging out of the sides of his face. But he had to take this blood to his master who was going to wait for him. Hypnos had promised a method to help him control his own blood hunger if he succeeded, and he hoped it would be something definite.

The blood was almost to the end of the glass as the tip of the syringe slowly pulled itself out. The point of the syringe had melted and formed around the glass, in a protective shell that he slipped back into the wooden tube. He slipped it back into his pocket, but noticed that there was a tiny bit of bleeding on Paxton's arm. He bent down and slowly licked it off Paxton's arm. He almost lost control as he tasted that blood, its potent life force had already nearly pushed him beyond his control, as he literally had to push himself away from Paxton, stumbling backwards against the wall as he watched Paxton, oblivious to what was happening, maintain his quiet slumber.

Jett crawled out of the rooms, having to use all fours to keep himself from biting into Paxton even more. That single taste of blood was enough to make himself revert almost to his full Bloodbane form. He had the High Order blood in his pocket, now was the trickier task to get out of Wolf Coven House. He completely ignored the fact that he was shirtless but he did notice that the fur that had lined his hands, had now grown up on his arms, but hadn't reached his upper arms. His own face had slightly changed, a much more feral animal-like fur was there as well along the side of his face and down his neck.

Slowly he heard that there was no footsteps outside his door, peeking out for a few more seconds before he opened the door, he wanted to make sure that there were no noise. Sure enough, still none was heard as he unlocked the door and prowled out.

"What are you?!?" A startled little voice cried out as Jett looked around to see where it was coming from. It was one of the Ahri, who wasn't walking but stood on a flying disk. His staff was held out defensively as the faint form of a protective bubble hovered around him. The startled little being seemed to be prepared to defend himself.

Knowing that he was already discovered, there was no other choice but to make a fast escape. He sprinted into the Mask Room which was just around the corner, and leaped out of the smashed open window with as much speed as he could gain, and dashed into the forest as fast as his four legs could carry him, but not before the little Ahri also followed in pursuit. "Halt immediately!" the little Ahri called back, but Jett dashed away as fast as he could.

Jett cursed himself as he was sprinting on all fours through every hill and branch in the forest. He didn't think about it much more, just knew that there was a calling to him, a voice which he now heard was luring him back to where he encountered Hypnos earlier. He could see within his wolf eyes as he sprinted through the forest, a grey mist that was always slightly out of his reach, leading like a trail of breadcrumbs back to a familiar location.

He could sense the familiarity of the area, every array of trees, branches, leaves and wind was similar to what he encountered earlier. That same mist also had a very unique, yet unworldly scent as he caught that, and locked onto it like a missile, speeding through the forest, partially empowered by that blood he tasted from Paxton, who he hoped was still safe and asleep in the house. For many more minutes he dashed through the woods, ignoring the fact that he was also leaving tracks, but he didn't even care if the Ahri could track him through the disturbed dirt or prints he left in the ground.

The grey mists had now started to surround him as he reached that same familiar opening, which was now only lit by moonlight. It was enough for him to see around him, and sure enough as he had expected, the mist had closed in to envelope him and his surroundings in what was almost like an infinite wall of grey haze. He could smell, and hear, and feel something approaching, as the mists started to gather in front of him into a spire of grey clouds.

Emerging out of the mist stood the same handsome figure that had appeared before. Hypnos stood there with a rather double meaning smile that he had on his face. His same coat was almost alive as he slowly stepped towards the Bloodbane wolf that was panting through the mist, standing there, slowly retrieving that wooden tube from his pocket.

"Quite the specimen." He mocked, as he concentrated his sights on the wooden tube that he already knew contained what he wanted. "And I see that you brought me what I asked for."

"Yes," Jett snarled at him, fangs and claws seemed ready to defend himself.

"Watch who you growl at, dog," Hypnos glared at the young wolf. His eyes were dead serious, and immediately Jett had a feeling that Hypnos was not someone to whom he should be testing, but he also knew that he wanted to get what Hypnos had offered. "And the ring," he reminded Jett.

"What about our deal, that you would help me eliminate my bloodlust?" Jett asked as he took the ring out of his pocket.

"One step at a time," Hypnos brought out his hand as the tube and ring slowly floated from Jett's grip and floated into his hand. He twisted open the tube and sure enough the syringe revealed itself while he slipped the ring into his own pocket. He carefully examined the prize. Almost taking more time that he needed, Hypnos grinned with satisfaction. His expression was clearly one of a remote sense of agreement with the young wolf. "Very good."

Jett folded his arms across his bare chest, almost slightly annoyed with having to wait. Hypnos slipped the blood vial into his coat as another figure now came out of the mist. This one looked very strange. His face was completely hidden by the shadows. Despite his enhanced wolf senses, this figure was only seen by his outline. There was no word heard form him but Hypnos was clearly communicating with him in some manner. Hypnos handed the vial of blood over to the figure who then vanished after receiving the vial.

This perplexed Jett but he didn't care what was going to be done with the blood, all that mattered was an end to this bloodlust that he was constantly feeling. Even now he still felt it, the aggression within him was boiling up, not only from the waiting but out of fear that he would be discovered again, after running away from Wolf Coven House now for the second time, and then there was the stealing of blood, but if he could manage to hold back his blood hunger it would all be worth it.

"You're fortunate. My benefactor is pleased with what he got," Hypnos smiled as he approached the wolf. "A god like myself wouldn't have to normally resort to using others to get what he needs, but times have changed."

"Hmmm." Jett only growled, quietly this time but with a clear sign of disapproval of his waiting.

"Impatient, aren't we?" Hypnos again mocked. Despite being a supposed god, Jett could smell something very strange, almost vampiric in him. He certainly did have vampiric scent to him but Jett didn't know that certain vampires had powers like this one. "But you did complete your task, and I did make an agreement to eliminate that blood hunger," Hypnos held in his hand something. It was so small that it could fit into his fist completely. He slowly brought up his right fist, which inside, Jett was certain, was what the mysterious figure had given him.

Slowly Hypnos opened his hand, and inside was a small black marble. Jett couldn't quite see what it was with all the darkness around them, and the object certainly didn't emit any light. Hypnos picked it up with his left hand and held it in his fingers. It left a trail of black vapor behind it. While holding it in his left hand, his right raised up again, and with almost a pulling gesture, he pulled out more of the black vapor, like it was a string, pulling more and more strands of it out into his hands as though he was undoing a ball of knotted string.

As he did, the small marble sized ball shrank and shrank until what was left in his hands was this black thick cloud of some mysterious substance. With a push of his hands, a stream of black smoke shot right into Jett's body, impaling him in a force that felt like he was being stabbed by a thousand sharp needles.

The werewolf screamed out with a howl of pain as it surged from his chest, throughout his body, up through his neck to his head, through his arms, through his legs to his feet and toes, every single cell in his body seemed to scream out in pain, his own voice crying out, mixed with the wolf roar. Hypnos, not remotely caring what happened to the wolf, threw another volley of this black shadow vapor shards at him, this time even more of it, and throughout more of his body! This time the pain was just as serious but oddly Jett was slightly getting used to it as slow volleys of the material shot out at him even more.

A bright light busted out of the mist and fog towards them, brightly illuminating the area. Hypnos looked around to see what was going on; even his own vision was blinded for a moment as his protective fog was blasted away by the light. Then another one came at him, this one was faster and more direct. The god almost fell over as he dodged the ball of light when he saw some figures approaching. Two small beings, seemingly hovering in mid- air with a human-size figure were seen.

Hypnos shrouded himself in a protective barrier, but the ball of light flew towards him so fast that he didn't even notice it until it smashed violently like a boulder of glass shattering against his shield. The shield held in place but it startled him to the point where he lost his own balance.

The human, or what he believed was human, was glowing with power that he never knew a human could possess. Hypnos felt some worry for the time being as he got up to his feet again. The two smaller beings were standing on what looked like plates or disks, and the central human figure was now glowing even brighter, his eyes were almost like they were in flames, but instead of red or orange flames flickering against the surface of his skin, they were pure white and the haze of a white smoke was seeping out of his eye sockets with an intense fury. Hypnos immediately knew just by the pure power that he sensed that this was no human.

"Protect Jett!" Sern commanded to one of the Ahri.

"Immediately!" one of them, a female complied as she rushed over to the werewolf, lying there on the ground, strangely in some strange phase of transformation beyond even what a Bloodbane was capable of doing. Her staff in her hand glowed bright white, in an attempt to offer comfort.

Sern glared at Hypnos before he charged forwards, slamming his fist at the god. Hypnos caught the fist in his hand, thinking he could simply just catch it and then twist it around without effort, but Sern's pure physical strength was considerably stronger than he thought. His own eyes widened with shock as Sern's fist was indeed stopped but only barely. Sern's own facial expression was betrayed by a dead serious expression that intended on doing damage to Hypnos. Hypnos fired off his own power in the form of a blast of black and grey beams from his own eyes towards Sern who leaped backwards, almost in a back flip out of the way, as the cascading wave of black and grey ripples missed him, but only just.

The little beings, the female had already surrounded herself and Jett with a glowing blue light. The other stood guard over Jett carefully observing the battle between Sern and Hypnos. Seeing Sern now safely out of the way, Kobili took his chance, and began to conjure up his own attack.

As Sern landed near Larita and Jett, Kobili himself started to glow fiery red. The glow was coming from his staff, as he was mentally concentrating deeply on something in his mind that manifested physically into a powerful red aura around him. It blazed brightly as he grasped his staff with both his hands, and almost like a baseball bat he swung the staff around in a circle. Out of the staff flew a rapid succession of brilliantly hot fireballs at Hypnos. The God of Sleep's shield managed to hold, but only barely, as the first ten of them splashed at first harmlessly against it, but as more and more started to hit, this time from Kobili focusing on the attack, even Hypnos had to start dodging them, retreating backwards.

Hypnos, for the first time in a long time, knew that he didn't have enough strength to fully use his power, and was fearful that he would lose this battle. But he had already gotten what was required, the High Order Blood, and tried to pull in as much of the mist that surrounded them to try to cover his retreat, as he slowly rose into the air. But the fiery attack from Kobili condensed the fog and mist, stopping them from forming around Hypnos. More and more of the fireballs landed on the ground, bursting into small explosions that soon left moving trails of fire that were clearly trying to encircle Hypnos.

Sern took his own chance and summoned to his hand, a straight sword. Sern wielded it with incredible speed, almost lightning fast, as he made slash and swipe against Hypnos. It was apparent that he couldn't get through Hypnos's own magical protection but with every direct slash that could have hit the god, hit the god's protective barrier. Every strike and thrust and slash hit the shield. Hypnos at first wondered what he was doing until he realized that Sern was only doing this to wear down his defenses.

The little Ahri, Kobili also flew up to join Sern, but not in hitting the barrier instead this time, pulling up rocks from the ground that flew towards himself at first like a chain of flying stones, then directing them all at Hypnos. Seeing the rocks coming, Sern slowly backed off, allowing the flying avalanche to collide with Hypnos, knocking him to the ground, falling almost fifty meters from the air.

Hypnos floated back up to his feet as he glared at Sern. Throwing all of his own power and magical skill into a powerful beam of shadow power at Sern, he did what he could in an all out attack to try to defeat the Intendant. The beam came at him so fast that Sern was knocked back a good dozen feet until he regained his balance, his hands blocking the burning and incinerating impact of the shadow attack. Sern's own cosmic power focused on his own shield as it held back the crackling bolts of shadow energy that Hypnos was throwing at him.

Sern focused his mind, his effort, and his energy entirely on Hypnos's attack. Concentrating his mind, he threw his own mental focus onto his shield which was now effectively blocking any of the shadow bolts from pushing against him. Slowly Sern's own power was growing as he tapped into his Va'Nai Essences which now were more than aware they were being attacked. His own eyes, and hands were glowing brilliantly as his light was slowly pushing away Hypnos' shadow.

The ground under Sern was starting to shake; bolts of his own energy were sparkling and starting to crack through the air around him. Forcing Hypnos' own energy out from him, Sern's gathering tidal wave of his own cosmic power was pulsating forwards towards Hypnos, blasting away with enough force to send him smashing into one of the boulders bordering the field.

Coughing up what his body could only eject as blood, Hypnos was fearful he was outmatched. The spewing of this bloody liquid was something he had never done before, and something a God would never be fearful of doing, but these two were more than what he thought he could handle. The impact slammed him like a brick wall until, with his last ditch concentration, the mist finally managed to reach him as he barely managed to get to his feet. He made a mad dash for the fog, which cost him the last of his energy as the two were descending down on him.

Not for a moment did Sern flinch. Intendant training in combat was limited but it was clear that it was more than sufficient for driving some rogue magic user away. He turned to Jett who was lying there; his body was changing, not like any Bloodbane.

His claws were far more wolf-like, his face also had become far more bestial. His limbs were also partially changed. It was as though he was now some cross between a Bloodbane or Packwalker, and a Wolf Prime! Sern didn't have much time to think about it before he picked up Jett and prepared to return to Wolf Coven house with Kobili and Larita who had joined him. It was definitely fortunate that Larita had notified them of the situation.

Chapter 20

Jett's eyes slowly crept open. He could feel his entire body aching as he realized that he was in the warmth of the bed, tucked under the covers. The grogginess of the sleep was still upon him. Beside him he could feel Paxton's warmth. He slowly turned over to see Paxton staring down. There was a smile on his vampire boyfriend's face.

"How long was I out?" he croaked, barely able to get the sound out of his throat

"Just a few hours," Paxton held him. "Sern explained to me what happened, your bloodlust took over again and you went wild in the forest and someone tried to kidnap you. Luckily Larita was on your tail and she alerted everyone else."

"I don't remember anything. I remember coming up to the bedroom, then I blacked out!" Jett recalled as he rubbed the bridge of his nose then his eyes.

"You don't remember the disappearance? You leaving the house?" Paxton asked again, sounding more concerned about what was happening. "You were found in the forest, and you were in the middle of a wolf transformation!"

"Maybe that was it; maybe I had just gone feral again." Jett reluctantly looked up at Paxton again, deeply ashamed that he couldn't control his wolf nature. The urge to run wild in the forest was one that was always difficult to control, but then the blood hunger on top of that was even more difficult.

"I got them to bring in some breakfast. Eat up and clean up," Paxton got out of the bed, he was wearing just a pair of casual sweat pants and a t-shirt before he wheeled in the room service cart.

"Thanks," Jett started helping himself to the bacon. The plate was stuffed to the top with various breakfast foods.

"I'm going to go talk to Sern."

"Ok!" Jett looked slightly happy again as he started to chomp down more food as Paxton quietly exited the room. In the living area, Dominic sat there like a security guard. His stalwart appearance, which normally gave some people a sense of intimidation, was a welcome sign of security.

"They're in Sern's office." Dominic stated to Paxton, who was already on his way out of the apartment. He was relieved that Jett was feeling all right and was now awake and kicking again. It was strange that Jett could get over the wolf rages but be consumed by them while they were happening. And it was strange that Jett didn't remember anything from the night before.

Paxton made his way to Sern's office where he expected to see Gavin and Sern. As usual the doors were closed when he arrived, suggesting that there may have already been something going on inside, but he wasn't entirely too sure. When the doors opened, it turned out that there was more than just Sern and Gavin inside. Paxton stepped in to see that the four Ahri, as well as Trenton and Cazian were sitting in the room. The four Ahri sat in pairs, each on the opposite side of Sern's desk. They sat on their floating disks as though they were almost like flying carpets, just floating up about at waist level.

"Are you alright?" Gavin asked. "And I'm sorry because I've been saying that a lot to you," he apologized again. It seemed that indeed lately many things have been happening to the two of them.

"I'm fine." Paxton started, but clearly he had more to say. "But we've been going through this cycle quite a bit. Jett running wild, then something happening to him," he turned to look at everyone else around him. Two of the Ahri were visibly sympathetic to what he was saying. "It has to stop. Is there anything that you can do for him?" He was almost pleading to Sern for some form of assistance. "It's clear the recent events were really starting to take a toll on him." Everyone looked at Sern for a possible answer.

"When Jett escaped last night, he went to find someone who was capable of using a very advanced form of magic. He was literally turning Jett into another wolf breed."

"What breed was that?" Paxton instinctively turned to Trenton, almost expecting him to know.

"From what we can tell, he was being transformed into a Prime Wolf," Sern also instinctively looked at Trenton, who was the only Prime Wolf in the room.

"I didn't know that it was possible, to transform into another breed of wolf." Paxton reiterated as he sat down on one of the comfortable leather seats.

"You can't. Cross transformations are impossible. Once you're one wolf form, you're that wolf breed, nothing can change that," Trenton added, to some disappointment.

"Apparently not," Kito said to himself, audible enough for everyone to hear him.

"From what I could see, Paxton, the spell that was being used, was a form of what's called transmogrification, basically a transformation spell." Sern could tell that Paxton was slightly confused with what he was hearing. "A permanent transformation. Magic." Paxton simply just rubbed his temples in frustration.

"Magic?" he groaned with frustration in his voice. "You know, over the past few days, I've started to learn that magic, though fun and useful, can also be pretty annoying to control." He let out without even thinking that the Ambassador for a magically attuned race was sitting with them.

"Magic is not an easy power to control," Sern replied, well aware of the awkwardness that Paxton's statement may have caused the Ahri. But it seemed that they were aware of his stress and didn't seem to take offence. "And yes, it takes a great deal of skill to control. Our Ahri friends have used it for thousands of years, for them it's second nature. But apparently this transmogrification spell was working. Unfortunately we weren't aware of what this sorcerer was doing to Jett, so we interrupted the spell and drove the sorcerer away."

"Can Jett be left the way he is right now? As a hybrid wolf?" Paxton asked again, as Cazian handed him a cup of tea that was just poured.

"No," Sern shook his head. "Right now there are quite literally two wolves fighting for dominance in him. When he's in his human form, Jett is oblivious to the damage that they will do if he shifts. They will tear his body apart for dominance," Sern stated with some remorse in his voice. "Unfortunately we have to act quickly before he shifts, or he could end up seriously injured. We have never seen anything like this before, Paxton, so we have to act now, to save him."

"Who can perform this magical ritual thing?" Paxton looked around the room. "As far as I know none of you are sorcerers, right?"

"No, we are Ahri." Kito interjected. "Though I am only an Ambassador, the Great Enlightened has also given us permission to help you." Kito had a great deal of pride and confidence in his voice.

"We have a great deal of experience with spells of this skill level. They may normally be beyond your abilities, but not ours." There was definitely confidence in Kito's voice but it was honest confidence, and not mindless arrogance. From what Sern had told them, the Ahri were an ancient race and had been using magic since before humans were even living in huts. "We will need one of your Prime Wolves to be there for us to use as a template, while we do the transformation spell."

"I'll do it," Trenton stood up before the Ahri had even finished explaining anything.

"You won't be harmed, we will just need you present to act as a template," Kobili hovered towards the tall Prime Wolf, "but we should begin preparations for this immediately," he suggested to Kito.

"We will need a large open room for this to take place," Kito asked the Wolf Coven members. He seemed eager to begin the process. "I will get Jett. You prepare the chamber." He ordered the other Ahri who immediately headed to the door.

Paxton was clearly nervous, even as they entered the apartment to see Jett and Dominic engaged in a casual game of chess in the living room.

"Perhaps I should explain to him…" Paxton whispered to Kito. "No, we cannot risk him shifting," Kito pointed his staff towards Jett, and sent out a small bolt of energy towards him. The bolt was silent, as it struck Jett in the back. Jett fell limp and collapsed onto the couch without warning, surprising Dominic in the process and made him jump to his feet only to see Kito hovering into the room with Paxton behind him. "You need not worry. He's only asleep and will remain so until we wake him up," Kito again triggered his staff's pearl to glow brightly as Jett was levitated up into the air by an unseen force.

"You doing that?" Paxton asked the Ahri, clearly worried about his boyfriend's well being.

"You have no need to worry, It's a simple levitation enchantment." Kito assured him, as he left the room with a hovering Jett being towed alongside them.

Sern, with Trenton, and the other three Ahri entered one of the large unused ballrooms in Wolf Coven House. As soon as they entered, Kobili and Kazmo darted ahead of them, immediately drawing a glowing circle on the floor. The light came from the base of their staves, which they simply dragged along the carpet, leaving behind a glowing gold residual substance of sorts that outlined the circle. They proceeded to continue drawing more and more strange designs onto the circle as Larita flew towards the center where she immediately started to cast another spell. From what started to emerge, it was some form of magical bubble that expanded to the borders of the circle that was outlined, which began to glow more brightly.

"Will you need my assistance?" Sern offered to the three Ahri. Kobili approached him.

"Yes, if you could please keep the subject unconscious and immune to pain, then we can proceed quickly," Kobili requested to the Intendant. Unlike Kito's bluntness, Kobili seemed to have a much more friendly demeanor.

The three of them started to pull in a pair of wooden tables on the other side of the room set aside in case anyone needed them. Much to the amazement of Trenton and even Sern, the Ahri staves began to glow green as wood from the tables started to grow, almost like the wood was alive again. They took root on the floor, acting as additional legs, while the tabletops spread out to accommodate two people who would be required to lie down on them. The manipulation of the table was something that showed Sern and Trenton that the Ahri magic could be very powerful.

Kito entered with Paxton, and Dominic with Jett. He was hovering on his back asleep as Kito levitated him into the room, and then slowly approached the center wooden altar that they had just grown out of the wooden furniture. With his intendant abilities, Sern placed his hand onto Jett's body, encasing him with a tiny portion of his power that he knew would dull all of his senses.

"Remember, everyone, this is going to be a magical ritual, not a surgery," Kito assured everyone who was in the room. "Please, Big Wolf, lie down next to him," he requested of Trenton who slowly put himself on the wooden altar next to Jett. Larita started first with her staff glowing white around the two of them. Kito placed his staff onto Jett's chest. Kobili did the same to Trenton, who remained still completely conscious. The colour of the orbs on their staves flashing from yellow, to red, to blue, as they seemed to be trying to match the colours. The colour settled to a brown before they continued. Kazmo, the only one who was not directly a part of the casting stood by prepared to intervene.

"Please stay outside the circle," Kazmo asked the observers. Everyone did what they were told and shuffled behind the gold glowing lines.

"Proceed to transform into your full wolf form," Kobili requested of Trenton who looked up at them slightly puzzled.

"My highest form?" Trenton asked, wanting them to clarify. He didn't know that he would have to do this but soon realized it was something that he had to do in order to save Jett's life. He sat up and quickly stripped off his own shirt and threw it away. Immediately

Paxton watched as Trenton started to transform. It was something that he had never seen before. Trenton's face and jaws were all stretching, then reforming, into a wolf form; his body was also getting larger as his bones began to stretch as the muscles thickened. Out of his skin, thick, fine animal fur started to grow over the expanse of his already huge form, which lay atop the table. Paxton stared uncontrollably as Trenton was able to change into this form without any sort of visible pain. In fact, he could have sworn that when Trenton began to change, his eyes rolled back into his head almost like it was pleasurable. Trenton's enormous hands were now tipped with razor-sharp claws, far more formidable than the ones that Jett had. His entire form was now the mix between that of a four-legged wolf and a two-legged man.

"That didn't hurt him at all?" Paxton whispered to Sern. Before Sern could give an answer, another voice interrupted his thoughts.

"For us to change is hardly painful at all," the voice growled. Coltrane's voice was deep and savage, and far from human. Paxton turned around to see a similar looking wolf man behind him. Its own fur wasn't like Trenton's, which was a rich, almost chocolate brown, with a few wisps of grey. His fur was entirely black but with a brown stripe down his back, and some grey. Instead of being afraid, Paxton's vampire fangs emerged in defensive response as he snarled back at the creature. He accidentally bumped into Sern who watched as out of Paxton's own back two huge, almost dragon-like wings, had sprouted from his back, trademark of a High Order.

Sern tapped Paxton on his back, temporarily bringing him out of his defensive gesture. Paxton's red eyes looked back at Sern, who simply just stared at his new wings, before Paxton realized that he was looking at something behind him. Paxton turned his head to see the two wings, then reached back over his shoulder to touch them.

"Congratulations," Cazian smiled at Paxton, who instinctively knew how to flap the enormous wings on his back. They had ripped right through his t-shirt. He almost scratched Sern's face when he expanded his wings. "You're an angel who just got his wings." He patted Paxton's back.

"I have no idea how I did that," Paxton questioned to himself as he stood there in confusion, almost completely forgetting that his boyfriend was undergoing a ritual on the altar in front of them.

"It was through a defensive reflex. When Coltrane here appeared to you in full wolf form, you were scared so you instinctively call up what strength you have as a defensive measure to intimidate your opponent," Sern explained to him.

Kito and Kobili had managed to have their pearls match colour, which was almost a rich royal blue colour, a very healing colour. They tapped the staff pearls together. As they did, two energy beams projected from the staves and connected Trenton to Jett, who was still sound asleep on the alter, not feeling what was going on at all, as Paxton continued to watch. Kito and Kobili maintained the touching of the pearls atop their staves as they took up positions opposite each other. Kito moved towards Jett's head while Kobili moved to his feet, the two of them casting the blue aura over Jett. Jett's own body started to change as well, mimicking the same transformation that Trenton had gone through. His own claws first starting, then his face, and body. His new-grown muscle mass ripped right through his shirt. His pants, though starting to rip, did keep themselves intact, preserving some sense of dignity. His entire body was morphed into the full wolf form; the two of them, Trenton and Jett, lay next to each other. Despite being in this form, Jett's form was clearly smaller than Trenton's, but no less impressive. The Ahri dimmed their staves as the bubble around them also vanished. The glowing light of the spells stopped as the Ahri backed up, indicating that their spell was finished.

Paxton rushed forwards towards Jett. Seeing him lying there as a full werewolf was not what he had expected. He slowly picked up Jett's hand, examining the size of his claws and the talon-like nails that tipped the edge of every finger. They were vast and powerful. He then gazed at the entire form. Jett was slightly shorter than Paxton in human form, now he was a good foot taller. His face bestial, but oddly, had some of his human features. His fur along his head was light brown, almost golden, not unlike Jett's naturally blond hair, which often flowed over his forehead like bangs.

Jett slowly awoke, at first almost without thinking, instinctively stretching his arms and then yawning, showing off a mouth full of vast sharp teeth that gave Paxton a moment to think. He slowly sat up as his vision cleared, and focused on a red eyed, fanged and now winged Paxton standing in front of him, in a large dark room.

"Dude, what happened to you?" Jett's new deep, monster- like voice growled at him. "You look like a freak!" Paxton couldn't help but smirk, then almost giggle with the sound of what Jett was saying. Jett wasn't even aware of what he looked like, and Larita and the other Ahri certainly noticed the irony of the moment. Paxton gently held onto Jett's enormous new monster hand, which made him look down. Jett's enormous wolf eyes, still blue like his human eyes, looked down, and widened fast as he stared at the beast hands that were now moving to his command. "What the hell?!?" he roared as he leaped right to his feet, his new lupine form, towered over Paxton. "What did you do to me?!!?" he growled at them, demanding an answer. His talons and claws were expanded, ready to rip off anyone's head.

Before he could do anything, another pair of arms, even larger, wrapped around him, quickly immobilizing him. Though Jett could feel that his strength was much greater, but whoever was behind him was easily able to overpower him.

"Calm down, pup!" an even more intimidating beast voice came from behind him. It was Trenton, also still in his full wolf form. Jett wasn't furious, just confused, as he stopped struggling against Trenton's clearly superior strength.

"Alright," Jett growled back, trying to get used to talking with these enormous fangs in his mouth. He stood there calmly for a moment, as Trenton slowly let go. Coltrane walked up to the two of them, himself also in wolf form. The three towering werewolves stood there in the middle of the room with four Ahri, three vampires and Sern watching them. Paxton still had his own wings out, and he didn't know how he could pull them back in.

"How do I put these away?" Paxton pointed to his wings while looking up at Gavin. Cazian smirked at him, mockingly rolling his eyes at the inexperienced young High Order who first experienced his wings. Gavin simply just gave Cazian a visual confirmation, as Cazian aggressively tapped the center of Paxton's spine. The two powerful pushes against him instinctively pulled the wings right back into his body almost as fast as they emerged. "How did you do that?" Paxton looked back at Cazian.

"It's just a natural reflex that triggers when you get poked in the back hard enough. It has to be roughly around the bottom of the neck, top of the spine," Cazian patted him on the shoulder. "I'll train ya."

"And what about me?" the small werewolf looked up at the two bigger wolves. "You can't tell me that I'm going to be stuck like this."

"Just think of something very, very calming. Something that will relax you." Trenton instructed the young wolf. Before he did it, Jett couldn't help but notice that everyone else in the room was staring at him, expecting something like a visual demonstration. "Uh..." he grumbled. Sern understood the cue and nodded at the others to leave the room discreetly. Paxton, on the other hand, didn't want to go and stayed with the other three wolves, as the rest of the Ahri, Cazian and Gavin left the chamber.

Jett's mind drifted to the vacation to Mexico that he and Paxton took a few years back. He recalls the warmth of the sun on his skin, the perfect sounds of the ocean waves, lapping against the shore, not a single cloud in sight, not a worry in his mind, not a single bird above. He could remember the perfect peace around him, lying there enjoying the warmth, sounds and smell, and most importantly Paxton by his side. As he felt these thoughts wash over him like warm beach water, Jett didn't even realize that he had completely transformed back into human again, his claws and fangs retracting, the fur pulling back into his skin as he stood there. The only physical sign was that his skin felt slightly cooler, due to the fur vanishing. He looked at what used to be the huge claws, now returning to his fingers. He almost shuddered as he blinked his eyes almost rapidly to anchor himself back to the current moment.

"How do you feel?" Paxton asked as he grasped Jett in his arms in a tight hug. Jett returned the favor by squeezing Paxton tightly.

"Amazing!" He kissed Paxton. "The bloodlust, it's completely gone! And that transformation, it actually felt pretty amazing!" he smiled. It was a smile of genuine joy that, for a long time, Paxton hadn't seen in any of them. "And what about those badass wings?" He gently patted Paxton's back where they had once been present.

"I'm going to have to get Cazian and Gavin to teach me more about those," Paxton hugged him again. "But I do admit, having a pair of wings is pretty cool. I wonder if I can fly with them." Paxton looked up at the two wolves that were still in their wolf forms.

"I'm pretty sure you can. Dominic is almost a master at that." Trenton answered. He was still standing there in that form as Coltrane started walking to the exit. "We're going to start teaching you how to control your change soon. You're a Prime now!" Trenton congratulated the new young wolf as they all left the room.

"I'm an uber-wolf?"

"Yeah I guess you can put it that way." Trenton slowly started to morph back into his human form. Without a shirt, he was even more buff than they thought.

"Gym much?" Jett smirked as he poked Trenton's almost boulder sized shoulders.

"It's a natural trait of natural Wolf Primes. Coltrane and I were born this way, so we naturally had the genes to make us physically strong. Most Wolf Primes who were bitten, and not born, would be normal human-size, like you."

"Ah," Jett turned to Paxton. Then he looked almost inquisitively at his boyfriend with a thought in his mind. "I wonder who's stronger, you or him?" he asked Paxton. The thought hadn't even occurred to him before to compare this trait.

"I wouldn't know." Paxton admitted. He turned to see Coltrane and Trenton both looking at each other also slightly curious. "Though it would be interesting to find out."

"Maybe later. I think I should get used to some of these new cool abilities I got!" Jett tugged Paxton's hand. He flashed Paxton a quick wink, which already suggested plenty on what he was thinking in his mind.

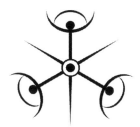

Chapter 21

The Ahri were helping with some of the landscaping outside Wolf Coven House. One of Intendant Hasaan's original intentions before being reassigned, was to expand the gardens to give more outside space for them to practice or use their abilities in a wide open space without the need to damage any property. The Ahri could actually move and replant trees as easily as it was to pick up a pebble from the ground and place it elsewhere. It was quite a sight for Paxton, Jett and the others to see the little people demonstrating such power.

It was like they were conducting music, but it was nature that was following their commands. Waving their staves and weaving water and grass, and trees and rocks around, bending the earth and the terrain seemed to be so simple for them. The trees that had once occupied a rather close position at the end of the garden were being moved farther away, clearing up more land in the garden for a large field.

"I had no idea they were able to do these things," Jett watched as the Ahri continued their epic scale landscaping.

"They are an extremely knowledgeable race," Sern replied. Even he was amazed at what the Ahri were doing. "Though it is perplexing," he continued with his thoughts verbally to Jett. "Their magical power seems to be far greater than I observed before."

"You saw them fighting in their world?" Paxton asked as he joined them on the balcony.

"It was actually a colony world. The Ahri home world was not the one that we visited. But it does seem like their magical powers here, somehow are much stronger."

"And useful," Jett smiled, referring to the transmogrification spell that they used on him. "So that spell that they used on me, can be used on anyone to be turned into a Wolf Prime?"

"No, that spell can't be used by humans because humans simply aren't powerful enough to be able to use it. Ahri are capable but even they would be extremely reluctant to do it. The use of the spell on you was to save you from a circumstance that should never even have happened." Sern turned to Gavin who was with them on the balcony, watching the landscaping. "I need to talk to you in private, Gavin." He whispered. The tall High Order followed him once again to his office.

As always almost out of habit, Sern sealed the room, and with a visual barrier that prevented anyone from entering, overhearing or seeing what was going on inside the room, even if they were spying through the windows. Gavin found it unusual that Sern would put in such precautions within the room. Sern did have a rather concerned expression on his face, one that he didn't see too often.

"What's on your mind?" Gavin asked as Sern took up his usual position behind his desk. The Intendant was certainly thinking of something extremely deep in his mind.

"I failed to realize the consequences of my actions," He confessed to Gavin but only doing more to confuse the High Order of his intentions.

"What are you talking about?" Gavin almost smiled at him, thinking that if there was something on Sern's mind, he was maybe blowing it out of proportion.

"The transmogrification spell, Gavin. If news leaks out that all one needs to do is kidnap or force a magic user of enough power to cast this spell, then that means magic users in this world are under serious threat. Ambitious Supernaturals will want to use this to...upgrade themselves." Sern thought about the word that he had just used. Upgrade, was likely the most effective method to describe what was in his mind. Gavin had to think for a moment using the context of some of Sern's own memories that were in his mind. Being one who did a memory transfer with Sern, only he could fully understand what Sern was thinking.

"I'm starting to understand why you're worried," Gavin thought out loud. The words could have easily been meant for Sern to hear as they were for himself. "If you are going to protect this secret, you're going to have to do a wide scale memory block for everyone who is aware of it, basically everyone here."

"That was what I was afraid of doing."

"I know, tampering with people's memories, though it's within your ability, is something you prefer not to do."

"It's not something that we can find morally acceptable." Sern admitted. It was rather fortunate that Gavin was here, and with his own mental experience, something that could help Sern. In a way, Gavin was helping Sern understand his own decisions.

"Well, I know from personal experience that Intendants have to always think of the greater good. The ends justify the means."

"Sounds so logical when you say it," Sern almost laughed at the bluntness and awkwardness of the situation. They both gave each other a glance, which was something that revealed an entire tidal wave of emotional awareness. "Seems you're talking like me more than I am," Sern remarked to Gavin who realized that he could easily say the same right back.

"Memory transferring is the best way to understand someone. And it gives you literally an entirely new perspective to work on. You're seeing now, that despite the effectiveness of Intendant-level decisions and actions, there are some things to worry about afterwards."

"Something I never had to worry about when I was just a deputy in Aurastar. But now here, with you and knowing how you care about everyone around you, all your experience after being downloaded into my mind, makes my decisions harder."

"And possibly easier, if you know that in the long run, you can protect them." Gavin comforted.

"The only one who I can trust to maintain these memories without manipulation is you," Sern looked up at Gavin before he sat down at his desk again.

"Why would you keep mine intact?"

"Because you know the reasons why I'm doing this. You literally have a portion of me in your mind, and you understand the situation."

"If you want me to keep them, I will. But I also understand if you want to block them from my access," Gavin sat down also, in front of the desk. "Remember Sern, we now know each other better than either of us realizes. I can perfectly understand why you would need to block my own memories too."

"But I won't," Sern agreed with him in principle but a part of him had to keep the truth present at least in someone's mind.

"So what are you going to do?"

"Erase the presence of the Bloodbane memories from everyone. Even the Ahri will have to have their memories blocked of the entire ritual. Everyone has to now believe that Jett was bitten by a Wolf Prime and that his transformation had nothing to do with the transmogrifying spell."

"You're going to need help with this."

"Yes. I'm going to have to bring someone in for assistance."

"More intendants?"

"Adjustors, who specialize in memory blocks. It's going to take place tonight, and by morning everyone won't recall any of the escapes that he made, or anything related to his Bloodbane past."

"I'm sure it will work. It'seasier to do that than to let things go wild."

"The entire balance of order will be thrown out if I don't do this. Imagine legions of Wolf Primes running around would be chaotic, to say the least."

"I understand."

Sern activated the console on his desk once again. Gavin decided to make himself scarce and promptly left the room. Sern allowed him to leave and then re-sealed the room afterwards, locking the doors from a distance as he started to contact the Sanctuary Organization. For him, it was just a matter of measuring the logical outcomes of what he was going to do. If he allowed the spell to be known as well as the effects, the trouble that could come out of that would be potentially world shattering. For Sanctuary members, it wasn't difficult to make the decision, but now that he had some moral grounding, thanks to Gavin's own memories and experience in him, he had to justify it not just by logic, but to justify it morally.

"All finished!" Kito declared as the four Ahri gathered at the balcony. They had completely physically reworked the entire outer part of the gardens, not into anything fancy, but open grass fields. "The difficult part was finding out where to put all the stuff that we moved." He looked back to see people starting to walk over the re-landscaped terrain. Marking the new boundary between the forest and the new grass field was an earthen wall that the Ahri had made, by repeatedly pounding on dirt and earth layers with enormous stones. Tapped Earth, was what it was called.

The field was fairly vast, about twice the size of an average soccer field. There was a strategically placed fire pit built into the center of the field, with a gravel circle around it, all made from the removed rocks and stones that they had crushed into small enough sizes to make the area rather accommodating.

Cazian and the others were clearly impressed. It would have taken a team of landscapers perhaps a few weeks to do what the Ahri did in just a few hours. The trees of course, were the most difficult part, but the Ahri did manage to push them far out of the way to allow for this open space. The trees also had another purpose, which was to provide cover and privacy for those who were going to use the field.

"Impressive work," Dominic agreed with the Ahri Ambassador. "This field could prove extremely useful to us, especially when teaching our young fledglings."

"Well, we are glad to be of service; after all, the Sanctuary and us Ahri are allies," Kito bowed. His demeanor was interestingly quirky, like most of the other Ahri. They seemed playfully mischievous when wanted to be, but also serious and intellectual when the situation called for it.

"I wasn't aware of the full extent of the situation," Dominic excused.

"Well, it's true. Though the Ahri are not members of the Sanctuary, we are certainly your allies and friends. You help us; we help you."

"You scratch our back?" Dominic referred.

"Scratching?" Kito asked, bewildered for a moment at the human phrase.

"A metaphor." Dominic explained. "It means basically you help us, we help you. You scratch our back; we scratch yours."

"Ah yessums," Kito nodded. "Then we shall scratch indeed!" Dominic himself couldn't resist a slight smirk of amusement at the Ahri Ambassador's fairly vague understanding of the term. Though he could learn the language, learning the vocabulary was another issue.

"Are you going to be setting up your mission soon?"

"Not until Sern has shown us the location. We are actually in no real rush to do so. The accommodations that he has setup for us in the house are quite comfortable, and there is a generous amount of storage space for our supplies."

"Well, I would recommend you enjoy it. Wolf Coven House is quite a fascinating place."

"I also noticed some enchantments within the house. Certain spells, rather rudimentary I must say, for defense and stealth?" Kito commented. It was obvious that he was referring to the protective spells that Elura and some other Wolf Coven affiliated magicians had used to protect Wolf Coven House from the human public.

"Yes, we put those in to hide our location from the rest of the humans. For our safety and theirs."

"Well, they're quite simplistic, but I guess they'll be sufficient."

"Are you going to enhance them?" Dominic wondered. Though he wasn't entirely too interested, it would nonetheless be somewhat interesting to see what the Ahri could do.

"Not unless asked," Kito smiled, almost for a moment being stingy with his magical abilities. "But if we were to help, we could significantly enhance them."

"Such as?"

"Well if Sern wished it, we could make this entire area an island, or even a flying island!" he chirped in a jovial tone.

"I don't think that's entirely necessary, though it would be interesting. However, the decision is Sern's, not mine."

"It would be fun though!" Kito called back as he flew away on his disk to join the other Ahri who headed back into the house. The Ahri, despite their enormous magical powers that they were easily able to demonstrate, had childish and playful personalities. It was an amusing juxtaposition that was interesting, to say the least, to Dominic. Many times he had encountered magic users who were deadly serious with their talents, but the Ahri, who could easily outmatch any of those who he met before, used their abilities as simple tools, without coveting their use at all.

Trenton and Jett joined Dominic on the field. It was much larger at ground level when they came down from the outer balcony where they watched the fireworks display that the Ahri were giving the night before. The fire pit was certainly a nice touch. Trenton stretched, then slipped off his shirt and put it down on one of the benches around the fire pit. Jett looked at him slightly bashfully. The sight of a tall and very muscular guy like Trenton was something that he found somewhat difficult to avoid staring at.

"So, time for the first lesson," Trenton smiled as he pointed to Jett's hoodie. It was a simple grey one, no logos or designs but still, it would potentially obstruct his transformation.

"Alright," Jett sighed as he saw Paxton and Cazian coming down and making their way to the fire pit, also taking their seats on the bench as they watched. Jett knew that they were going to be observing. He reluctantly took it off and gently tossed it to Paxton. Paxton never quite understood Jett's personal insecurities about being shirtless since he was in amazing shape, at least to Paxton. "The pants are staying on!" He declared without any exception to Trenton, who couldn't help but smirk.

"Yes, I told you to wear loose fitting or stretchable pants, that way you'll be fine."

"And shoes?" Jett asked. "Just for the record, I hate cold, wet ground and I really hate going barefoot." He couldn't help but insist. Before he never really had to worry about his feet, oddly his feet didn't change when the rest of his body did, but then again he was only Bloodbane before, which was half of what he saw out of Trenton and Coltrane's forms.

"Take them off for now," Trenton instructed. With great reluctance, Jett slipped out of his runners, and his socks. Trenton also slipped out of his own shoes.

"So how do we trigger this?" Jett asked, wanting to immediately find out how to enter his wolf form. He seemed oddly eager to do it.

"Depends which form you want," Trenton folded his arms across his chest.

"What do you mean?" Jett asked, assuming that he would be the entire man-wolf like form that he saw earlier, and the form that he actually had taken.

"We're Primes. There are two full forms we can take, and we can also shift slightly between them. For example," Trenton's eyes shifted to gold, and his fangs, and claws emerged but his form was still mainly human looking. There was a slight growth of fur on his chest and upper arms that had begun to appear. His face also became more bestial, but still recognizable as human. His feral eyes focused on Jett. "Your ability to change relies on your need. You have to want to change and transform. Concentrate on it, the eyes, the teeth, the claws, the fur," Trenton explained in rather simplistic terms. "Think of it like flexing a muscle or making a gesture. You have to have the intention, need, and mental concentration."

"Can't be that simple," Jett questioned. To transform into another physical form, growing muscles, fur and claws, fangs and eye colours wasn't something that could just be willed to him.

"It is. Takes practice but everyone learns how to control it," Trenton shifted his teeth and claws and fur away back to his normal look. Even Paxton and Cazian were impressed on how he could just switch on and off with these features without even the slightest sign of effort.

"It's the same with your wings too." Cazian whispered to Paxton. "The only time for us that the transformation can't be helped, meaning your fangs and eyes, is if you're too hungry and you're going through a bloodlust," He explained.

"What's the bloodlust again?" Paxton asked. He already somewhat feared the answer.

"Not that different from what Jett went through before during a full moon. It happens to us all, every one hundred days, so you don't have to worry about it for another three months, but it basically turns you into your primal blood hungry form, sort of a primal vampire. Dominic will be going through his probably in the next few weeks, so you can observe his."

"Lovely," Paxton sneered sarcastically. Jett focused his mind on his body, but instead of just the claws and fangs forming, his entire form started to change. Beyond what Trenton did, Jett's muscles were growing in size, as was his height, and his shape, and form. His ears even shifted, they grew longer, very wolf-like, as his form was now bestial.

"And remember, if you want to sire someone, meaning turn them into a vampire like you, you can only do it once during each Bloodlust phase, meaning one turning at most every one hundred days," Cazian sounded almost like he was lecturing Paxton.

"I don't think I will be making any vampires soon," Paxton assured Cazian. "But what happens if you make more than one?"

"Your aggression spikes up. You become a lot meaner and cruel. Because every time you turn someone, a portion of your soul is sort of "loaned" out to them. You basically are linked to them for that hundred days until your next bloodlust phase, and then you recover enough to do it again. Some High Orders who transform more than one child become more aggressive and just plain nasty. Its best if you never do it."

"Have you ever met any High Orders who did turn more than one childe during their bloodlust cycles?" Cazian gave Trenton a wary look. Trenton nodded his head almost like he was giving Cazian some form of permission to say what was on his mind.

"There's a faction of High Orders, they call themselves the Blood Royal. They basically believe that they should be ruling over not just other High Orders but all vampire orders, and even some other Supernatural factions. Real jerks, basically, and they tried to increase their numbers fast, and before we realized it, they basically became corrupted and sadistic. So if you don't want to turn evil, don't make more than one other vampire every one hundred days." Cazian commanded to Paxton.

"Got it," Paxton agreed. They turned to see Jett fully morphed into a man-wolf form right in front of them.

"Impressive," Said Cazian as they both turned to look at Jett standing there in full man-wolf form.

"How's that? Ah, weird!" Jett asked but then realizing his mouth was full of sharp teeth. "Always with the freaking fangs!" he whined. He stood over six feet tall, gaining half a foot in just height, never mind the muscle mass difference. Paxton got up and walked up to his boyfriend. The shimmering brown fur that covered his body was topped by the same gold almost blond fur on his head, the same colour that Jett has as his hair. Jett saw Paxton walking up to him and turned to face him. His face wasn't angry or anything. It was very much a wolf's face, but a humanoid like body, standing up on his hind legs. "So what do you think?" Wolf Jett asked Paxton who looked deep into his eyes. He focused carefully for a few moments without answering while still staring into the wolf's eyes. They were the same gentle ones that were always there, despite being a wolf. A smile crept onto Paxton's face.

"That is pretty damned cool." Paxton smiled as he put his hand onto Jett's shoulder. It was a strange feeling, the fine wolf fur over coated powerful muscles underneath. He seemed particularly fascinated by his gold and black speckled eyes.

"Still see the real me?" Jett asked Paxton, his voice now bestial but still with the same kindness.

"Yeah," Paxton answered as he backed up.

"You know I only asked you to change partially." Trenton lightly scolded Jett.

"Sorry, I just took all of the wolf's abilities. I wasn't sure how else to do it."

"Think of the amount of wolf transformation to be something like that, a wide range of abilities and powers. Now just concentrate your mind only on a select few that would make you only partially changed. You don't need the vast muscle mass, or the fur, so think of that," Trenton instructed. Jett had to close his eyes to concentrate, but already he started to shrink slightly. The fur was pulled back into his skin, and sure enough his limbs and bones and muscle mass started to decrease. Slowly and steadily it took a few seconds to start but he began shifting to a more human appearance. Despite that his ears, fangs and claws were still slightly lupine but his face was now almost completely human again, save for a few mean ridges near the center of his forehead. His gold wolf eyes opened slightly to ask without words if he was doing it right. "Better!" Trenton congratulated him.

"Much better." Paxton agreed. He noticed that the shrinkage in height made him taller than Jett again, but only by that single inch that separated their heights.

"Could you do the same with your wings?" Cazian asked Paxton.

"If it's the same method," Paxton mentally concentrated. He didn't have to focus too much on what he was doing since their own High Order forms were more simplistic. But in his mind, he thought of the wings carefully, the location on his back, behind the shoulder blades. He instinctively stretched his back, as the two fast spans of flesh sprouted right out of him. It was unnaturally large for the wings to fit inside his body; but before he knew it, the two dragon-like wings came out of him. Cazian also had his out, which he seemed to do without even thinking whereas Paxton had to concentrate more.

"Alright, it seems our boys are learning their forms," Cazian walked over beside Trenton. "Now spread them!" The words made Paxton feel a bit awkward. Cazian only gave him the look of additional expectations as he himself spread the wings outwards, flapping them once. Trenton had to step forward a step to avoid getting scratched by the two vast leathery wings that came out of Cazian. His total wingspan was over 12 feet wide.

"Alright. How's that?" Paxton asked as he also mentally told his new limbs to reach outwards. They were almost just as large as Cazian's own wingspan, and almost identical as well in appearance. Jett was also visually impressed by what he saw.

"Again, you're both quite adept at this. Just give yourselves a few tries with your full forms," Trenton sounded impressed and so did Cazian. "Eventually you'll have no problems."

"What about flying?" Paxton asked with eagerness in his voice. "That will have to definitely wait. And Dominic is probably the one who will teach you. I can't do it yet myself and I've been a Vampire for not nearly as long," Cazian smirked. "Then again, I love driving."

"Most impressive!" A chirpy little voice came from nearby. The four of them noticed one of the Ahri was coming towards them on their hovering disks. It was Ambassador Kito. In a heartbeat, Cazian and Paxton's wings hid themselves again, almost like they were surprised and instinctively sought to hide. "I wasn't aware that you had such shape-shifting powers. Again I am very impressed." He also congratulated the four of them. "I was wondering what you thought of our work?" He pointed with his staff to the various land features around them.

"It's very nice! A good place and wide open space for us to use," Trenton thanked the little Ahri ambassador. Kito seemed very flattered at the compliment and proud of himself.

"Well that is good to know! We have plans for our mission once the spot has been selected, and if you think this place is nice, you should see what we have in store!" he boasted without any sense of humility. Kito then pointed his staff towards the fire pit. The white pearl started slowly turning red and within a second a funnel of flames shot out towards the fire pit igniting it, and the wood that was sitting inside that was at first too deep for anyone to see.

"We do have matches you know," Cazian giggled slightly at the Ahri's almost overuse of magic.

"True, but I prefer to use our own skills."

"We could use this as a barbecue," Jett suggested to Trenton, whose face lit up at the idea.

"Maybe another time," Trenton smiled at him, though the idea certainly did warm him up. It wasn't like he wasn't interested in having a barbecue but it just wasn't really the right time.

Sern patiently waited in his office while he viewed the activities outside. The clearing of this landscape was beneficial to Wolf Coven House, and seemed to be quite popular with everyone. But despite this he knew that he had a task to perform which was something that he didn't expect to do. For him, the act of sealing off memories was something that he didn't expect to do, but he also knew that it was required for maintaining secrecy.

He had already dispatched a message back to Aurastar for an immediate memory restructuring team to come. And with a fast reply they were already en route, and with the use of a portal, it would only take a few minutes for them to arrive. Nonetheless he was slightly nervous that he would have to undertake such a decision to prevent this information from leaking out.

Just as Sern's mind was wandering, his console informed him that the portal in the center of Wolf Coven House had activated, with an immediate transport from Aurastar itself. He rushed right to the atrium where the portal was located. Four officials had already stepped out, waiting for him. He recognized a few of them with the ranks of Adjustors, a rank that was somewhat benign-sounding, another way of putting memory manipulation into a title. Unlike Sern's rather elegant robe-like uniform, theirs looked almost like technicians, suited up in a jumpsuit and even with military-styled caps. Despite this they were made out of the same material, the same geometric type of glowing designs along the edges. It was a style that the Sanctuary Organization adopted from their study of human organizations and their own uniforms, which made sense.

"Intendant Sern!" The Head Adjustor greeted.

"That's me." Sern introduced himself.

"Yes. I'm Head Adjustor Shamaran and we're going to be doing this as soon as you're ready." Shamaran declared rather simplistically. Though Sern was aware that he could easily do it from here, he preferred some discursion.

"To my office first," Sern insisted.

"Alright, Team," Shamaran turned to the other three Adjustors who came with him. Sern's office awaited them, and as usual to Sern's recent behavior, it sealed itself as soon as they were all inside.

Sern started the procedure by placing his hand on his own desk while the others joined in doing the same thing. The desk console itself was a living piece of techno-organic machinery that the Sanctuary made to respond to any infused being's needs. It also acted as an efficient method for them to link their minds and intentions. Sern didn't have to explain his intentions as they were automatically downloaded into the other Adjustors who immediately recognized what he wanted: to lock out the memories of Jett ever being attacked by a Bloodbane, and also all the immediate consequences of what happened afterwards, from his bloodlust rage to him accidentally biting Paxton and all other situations related. Instead, he wanted to replace it with a more streamlined memory of Jett being bitten and transformed by a Prime Wolf. This also meant altering the memories of everyone else who was involved, so the memory manipulation would have to take place immediately.

"This entire situation will have to take place when they're all unconscious," Shamaran warned Sern.

"I am aware, and this includes the Ahri."

"Very well. We will proceed immediately." The five of them started to glow brightly, with the same type of infused light that they had demonstrated in the past when using their internal power. The light became so bright that it began to spill out of the room, and in an ever-expanding bubble, engulfed them all in the room, then the wing of the house, past the walls and out of the building, engulfing everything in its pathway until it reached its limit, which was just beyond the magical barrier that shrouded Wolf Coven House from the rest of the world. Everyone immediately halted their movements, mentally stunned and placed in a strange limbo state while the Adjustors did their duty.

Sern was only there to provide additional power to them. With an Intendant assisting the Adjustors, it was going to be a faster job than without him. Sern himself didn't have any direct action, but the Adjustors used his intentions and his wishes to fulfill what they were doing. It was almost like mental surgery. Sern's main usefulness was keeping everyone else unconscious and unaware.

Sern could feel the Adjustors sewing and stitching memories and scenarios in their minds, shoving other memories into areas that they were blocking off. It was like mental renovations going on that Sern was quite content to not know the finer details. Though he had no direct action in actually doing the tasks that the Adjustors were performing, it was his will and his decision to do this, and ultimately he knew it was also his responsibility.

He could sense that even Gavin was placed in this temporary freeze, as were the Ahri. Gifted as the Ahri were in magic, even magic couldn't compare to the cosmic-level power that the Sanctuary Organization used for its own measures, and that went down all the way to the Intendants who were field operatives.

Sern could feel that his mental instructions were being copied and implanted into the minds of all thirty people who were members of Wolf Coven House. The Adjustors themselves were able to already seal off memories of anything Bloodbane-related within the recent weeks. The thoughts that he wanted to preserve, was that a Prime Wolf bit Jett and that he had to be turned fully by another Prime Wolf, being Trenton, in order to survive. The fact that he had to remain at Wolf Coven House to learn how to control his abilities was why he was here.

It only took a moment for the five of them to finish their task. It was important that even the Ahri forgot about what they had done. Sern realized that by doing this, he had violated the principle of diplomatic immunity, but he had to consider the bigger picture. Even allowing the Ahri to know what they were capable of doing was an enormous threat he could not ignore. Sern knew that the responsibility was his and that he had no other choice in the matter.

Within the next moment, their collective light slowly dimmed and eventually ceased after a few more seconds. Sern could feel them removing their presence from the minds of the Wolf Coven members.

"Was everyone affected?" Sern asked to make sure.

"Absolutely. Everyone within a fifteen-kilometer radius was sought out just to make sure. We didn't want any loose ends," Adjustor Shamaran replied confidently. There was a certain amount of pride in his voice, which suggested that he was quite sure of what he did.

"I want no loose ends, Shamaran," Sern warned. "The potential danger of anyone leaking this information could be disastrous."

"No one can undo our mind blocks except us. Even you can't do anything to change them. You can block more but you can never undo what we did."

"Good, then I won't have to worry about accidentally releasing memories."

"They'll come to like nothing has happened in a few minutes after we depart," Shamaran affirmed. "I think it's time we make ourselves scarce." He signaled to the others who started to follow him and Sern out of the office, but he stopped after just a few steps and turned to the Intendant. "I think I am particularly proud of the memory we created for your new Prime Wolf, Jett."

"You had a memory created that Coltrane was his wolf creator?"

"Yes, and we altered Coltrane, as well as everyone's memories to match that story."

"What was the motive for Coltrane turning him into a Prime Wolf?" Sern asked.

"It was accidental. Trenton went to transform in the forest. Jett followed him through the night, and Trenton attacked him by accident and infected him."

"I take it that you infused Trenton's memories and personality with a sense of guilt."

"There was no need. We noticed that Jett actually enjoys being a werewolf. The abilities are something he enjoys, and he told Trenton that he isn't afraid of being what he is."

"Very convenient," Sern commented as he led them to the portal.

"It is good that Jett enjoys it. There was little else to modify in terms of motives after we discovered that."

"You have done a good job. I hope I won't have to contact you again."

"I agree ... " Adjustor Shamaran shook the Intendant's hand.

Sern watched as the group re-entered their portal, then vanished from sight. Then he made his way to the kitchen balcony where most of the members were still outside, frozen in place without any realization that they were having their memories altered. Still it was what he wanted and needed, and hopefully things would turn out for the better.

Chapter 22

For Sern, a good few days had passed without incident. He had mentally scanned through all Wolf Coven member's minds to make sure that everything was in order. Every memory that was created was believable and nothing was out of the ordinary. Gavin and Cazian were doing an excellent job teaching Paxton his new abilities as a High Order, and Trenton and Coltrane were doing the same excellent job with Jett.

The Ahri were also becoming accustomed to their surroundings, learning about human culture through the use of the Internet and television which to Sern may have seemed like a questionable method. But he had enough trust in the Ahri that they would make sound judgment when it came to a verdict on human culture. He knew that they were only doing this out of curiosity.

It was just then while he was going through sending another report back to Aurastar that he heard a knock on the door to his office. Opening the door from the other side of the room, Sern saw Gavin coming into the room. He was holding his phone in his hand as though he had just received a phone call.

"They're pushing up the schedule for the next season," He sighed as he slumped down in one of the seats in the office.

"Is that a bad thing?" Sern asked curiously in response to Gavin's rather obvious reluctance.

"Yes. It means instead of a six week break, we get two. And to make things extra fun, they want to plan a promotional photo shoot, tomorrow," He slipped his phone back into his pocket.

"So why are you telling me this? I have no say over what you do with Eternal Knights," Sern pondered, still curious to why Gavin was a bit disgruntled.

"It's because they want to have the photo shoot here." Gavin looked up at the Intendant, expecting a clear visual sign of some concern from Sern's face.

"Ah, I see the problem."

"What are we going to do with our little guests?" Gavin asked, referring to the Ahri.

"The benefit to Eternal Knights and RedCo is that they are all Sanctuary-funded. I'm sure things will be fine. I mean, the entire crew and cast are almost all Supernaturals, so I don't see any problem." Sern comforted Gavin's concerns.

"So I can give them the okay? On the photo shoot?" Gavin asked as he prepared to text a reply on his phone.

"Certainly. I think it should be fine."

"Alright then," Gavin texted a few words into his phone and sent it off. "I hope you don't mind all these new visitors coming to Wolf Coven House."

"They're all Sanctuary members; it's perfectly fine. Of course, as long as they keep things in order without any chaos, I'm sure things will go smoothly."

"Or you could do another memory block," Gavin hinted suggestively at Sern.

"I doubt that will be necessary," the Intendant assured the High Order. "Have you thought of including Paxton and Jett in the show as well?" he suggested at the spur of a moment.

"Not really, but it could be interesting. That's more for the writers to decide."

"Well considering you now have another High Order and a Prime Wolf, you could see if you could do something. Paxton was on the show before, wasn't he?"

"Yes. That was a few years back. I think something can be done about it."

"Consider it." Sern suggested as Gavin got up off the couch again, and headed for the door before turning around.

"It's not going to be that many people, just about a dozen or so. It's just a photo shoot."

"I trust your judgment."

Jett and Paxton were in their room, watching one of the episodes of Eternal Knights on DVD while they were just relaxing through the day. Paxton had gotten used to the fact that his boyfriend could transform into a massive wolf-man creature with bulging muscles and fur all over his body, and Jett had gotten used to the fact that his boyfriend was a blood-drinking vampire. Still the two of them got over this, and in some ways they rather liked it.

Being just a normal gay couple for Paxton and Jett was unique enough, but now that they both had supernatural power and were no longer human gave their relationship a very unique taste. For Paxton, he had now grown accustomed to his new power, especially his liquid diet, low in carbs, low in fat, organic and gluten-free. For Jett, his metabolism pretty much made him ignore any barrier for junk food, and still maintain a fitness model body. It was also beneficial for their relationship that the supernatural element to them also made their more intimidate activities much more exciting.

"They look amazing," Jett whispered into Paxton's ear as they watched Cazian and Gavin exchange dialogues in a scene. They were standing on a rooftop in the scene wearing their trademark black silk dress shirts, conveniently unbuttoned, revealing no shortage of their muscular physique that was clearly fan service.

"Gavin hates doing those scenes," Paxton smirked, as he was amazed that Gavin could keep a straight face on screen. "Still, they both do look amazing."

"Glistening almost," Jett nudged. The scene was at night, but clearly it was shot indoor, with the light conveniently lighting them up from beneath, which only did more to show off their bodies. Eternal Knights was a series that didn't hesitate about showing off the natural beauty of its cast, which was predominantly male. It was no surprise that it had a huge gay male and straight women following. Paxton turned his view towards Jett. It didn't take long before Jett realized his boyfriend was staring at him, while running his fingers through Jett's hair.

"What is it?" Jett asked as he turned to face Paxton. Paxton only replied with a deep sigh at first.

"I was just thinking of how things have changed for us," Paxton slowly sat up a bit, "I mean, I'm a vampire now, and you're a werewolf."

"I'll be honest." Jett looked away for a moment. "I love being what I am." he revealed, much to Paxton's surprise.

"Really?"

"Yeah, this really is a wolf gift. My senses are enhanced, I'm much stronger and faster." Paxton slowly smiled at the response his boyfriend was giving. "Everything is improved for me. In a way I'm glad Trenton bit me by accident, otherwise I wouldn't have this new experience."

"I didn't know it was that amazing."

"It is!" Jett almost growled in satisfaction of thinking about it. "When I transform, my muscles and body feel infused with this vast supernatural strength. I feel invincible when it happens."

"I'm glad you're not one of those stereotypical self-loathing monsters."

"Why would I be? I can practically be a superhero," Jett smiled back at Paxton.

"Well, for me, it's pretty good too. I'm glad I don't sparkle," Paxton admitted, provoking a good chuckle from Jett.

"Trust me. I'm happy you don't either."

"And I'm also pretty strong too."

"And toned up. Actually we're both fitter than before." Jett couldn't help but pull his shirt up a tad, revealing a very chiseled washboard stomach that he didn't have before.

"I'm not complaining," Paxton grinned at Jett, as he pulled him down. Just then, they were interrupted by a knock on the door.

"Come in," Paxton called. They could tell by the footsteps that it was Gavin.

"Hey, boys." Gavin looked down at the couch to see the two of them cuddling while staring at the enormous flat screen television. The screen showed him and Cazian doing a scene from Eternal Knights, and sure enough, like almost fifty percent of the time, he was shirtless, and perfectly done up in makeup that it almost made it difficult to breathe. "Oh jeez," he caught a glimpse of the TV screen. His eyes rolled as he had to face some of his own work, something he was never fond of doing.

"You look amazing," Jett grinned playfully at Gavin as he tugged at Gavin's silk red dress shirt, which only made his skin seem a bit paler, and his black hair only made him look more vampiric. "Good thing Vampires don't need to use the gym."

"Ya ya ya." Gavin took the jab.

"Did I mention my boyfriend is a fanboy?" Paxton continued to watch the TV, seeing an equally well-built Cazian take the screen.

"Yeah I got the feeling when we first met, by how giddy he was." Gavin smiled down at the two of them, almost sarcastically at their response, and the fact that they were also watching his show and gawking at him didn't quite make the situation a happy one. "Anyways, I just want to tell you guys, that tomorrow there is a photo crew coming for a photo shoot for Eternal Knights," he gently pat the couch, signaling an end to his sentence as though it was some form of physical punctuation.

"Wait, they're doing it here? I thought you were on hiatus right now," Paxton sat up from leaning up against Jett's warm chest.

"Well they decided to move the shoot from six weeks to two weeks. So we're going to be back on set early," Gavin sighed with reluctance.

"Four weeks removed from vacation. That must suck," Jett sympathized with Gavin. He had some reasonable understanding of film industry terms from Paxton's own experience.

"And I'll talk to the writers about getting you boys on the show." Those few words were enough to make Jett's face light up like a puppy dog about to get treats, or in his case, a puppy wolf. "Shouldn't be hard, Paxton, since your character wasn't killed off and can always make a return."

"That would be nice," Paxton smiled.

"And there is something else that we have to talk about," Gavin sat down with them. His face turned rather serious, which brought the mood down a bit. The two of them turned off the television set and casually tossed the remote control aside. "I didn't mention before, but we have to talk about what you want to do for the rest of your life."

"That's a loaded question," Jett smirked.

"It's a big one, and a serious one too," Gavin looked up, somewhat regretting putting such a serious note on their mood. "But if you guys want, Sanctuary can help smooth things over by basically erasing your records and everyone's memories of you, so you can live new lives, or you can return to your old lives, at least for the next ten years or so. And then afterwards, you can do the record erasing."

"Why ten years?" Paxton asked.

"For you especially since you won't be aging anymore, people may take notice that you're not aging. So before people become suspicious, you have to pretty much disappear."

"This is a huge decision, and I can't really make it right now on the spot," Paxton answered with Jett agreeing with him. "We're going to need some time to think about this."

"I know. I just wanted to tell you that."

"Well, chances are, we're going to stay here, no rent, no need to worry about food." Jett smirked, happy with many of the perks that came with living at Wolf Coven House.

"There are benefits definitely, and likely you'll stay in a bigger place than this, assuming you're going to be living together."

"Well, again, we'll need some time to think about this."

"Take your time. There's still some things that Jett still has to learn from Coltrane."

"Ya, there's one thing that has been on my mind," Jett sat up a bit more, making his seating posture more formal.

"What is it?"

"Age," Jett looked up into Gavin's gentle eyes. He always seemed to put on that face of gentility whenever they had questions to ask about the supernatural. "I'm pretty sure that Paxton and you aren't going to get any older, forever young and all that, but what about me?" Jett asked. It was a rather serious question that had serious consequences.

"Prime Wolves do age, but very very slowly. The oldest Prime, I've met a few who were over two hundred years old, and were still in great shape."

"So will that mean I will be a long living old man?"

"Well, you will age, and eventually you will get old, but trust me when you have more than a century to worry about that. After about age 30 or so, Prime Wolves barely age for the next few decades. I've met Prime Wolves who were 55 and looked 30."

"How often do I have to change into my werewolf form?"

"Never actually. Since a Prime Wolf can change at will, there's nothing that can force you to change at all. You can stay human forever if you want."

"Never thought about it that way before," Jett pondered the thought. It was something that didn't even occur to him.

"So he can go through life without ever changing?" Paxton asked. Gavin nodded his head in agreement.

"Yes. Though I don't know why he would."

"Changing form feels amazing," Jett thought out loud. "It's the ultimate high. Strength, everything." His mind was flowing back to when he first changed form, and it was nothing at all like what Hollywood made it. It was not at all painful or agonizing.

"Oh, believe me, I know. I've seen you transform before and it was more like you were enjoying it more than suffering." Paxton put his head on Jett's shoulders in a rare display of opposite side affection. Usually it was Jett who was the cuddlier one.

"Alright," Gavin stood back up straight. "They're coming tomorrow early in the morning to set things up. They may want photos of you, not sure, but so far it's mainly just myself and Cazian."

"Photo shoot!" Jett cheered. "We get to see Cazian and Gavin get it on!" He teased, well aware that Gavin still was in the room.

"Sounds hot," Paxton gloated.

"Our characters aren't dating," Gavin protested casually. He was well aware thatthis was all at his own expense.

"Suuuure they're not," Jett continued.

"Ya ya…." Gavin surrendered as he left the room.

"Photo shoot!" Jett giggled to Paxton.

"So the Fanboy's back?" Paxton feigned non-enthusiasm, clearly unable to hide his own satisfaction at seeing Jett happy again.

"Well I like their characters. Don't get me wrong, Cazian and Gavin are amazingly hot, but I love the characters a bit more. I knew that I wouldn't be getting the roles, but it's still nice to see them even dressed up as those character would be, really cool."

"So you want to see them in those silk black shirts, with the buttons barely done up?"

"Yes," Jett smiled, almost unaware that his fangs were starting to get primal on him.

"So that's what it takes?" Paxton observed the gleaming sharp teeth.

"Huh?" Jett then felt the fangs in his mouth.

"Sexual arousal," Paxton smirked.

"Ah, yeah, I guess it's the same for us all."

"I guess when you're just thinking of using your teeth, or being aggressive, they naturally show."

The next morning, bright and early, sure enough the suits had arrived with the crew to do the photo shoot, with a convoy one vehicle short of the D-Day invasion, to setup multiple locations throughout Wolf Coven House. They had wanted to use the studios but they were still doing set construction and had to use what Wolf Coven House had offered, which was convenient considering many of the studio locations were reproductions of Wolf Coven House.

Sern had spent the night in meditation. Deliberately sealing off the rest of his senses to concentrate on his thoughts, Sern didn't know what was going on outside of his office. All that he expected was that there would be some people arriving to set up a photo shoot for Gavin and Cazian.

Sern did what protocol stated during these occasions, which was to act as host. It was unique for him since he was not experienced in these matters, but thankfully with the input from Hasaan's reports and of course Gavin's input of memories, things were going to be fine for him. They added catering from the Zombie Crew, and the greatest benefit of all, that the entire crew and RedCo were Supernaturals themselves so he felt that there was little to worry about. Most Intendants, understandingly, would be concerned with the influx of so many people coming into the house, but it seemed maybe he was worrying about more than he needed to.

As Sern wandered through the setups, there were cables and wires going everywhere for the lighting fixtures, and they were generous enough to bring in large sheets of cardboard that they put against the walls to stop equipment and moving objects from scratching the delicate furnishings around. Sern did notice a larger abundance of equipment than before, and then when they brought in enormous high definition cameras with their trolleys and tracks, he was slightly wondering if this was going to be more than just a photo shoot. Sern was concerned that there would be more than a dozen people; in fact, there seemed to be more and more people flowing in, all with specific functions. One of them was standing watch at the doorway, wearing a construction vest. With the partially decaying facial features, he was definitely a zombie as well.

"Excuse me. Where is the man in charge?" Sern asked him with as much courtesy as he could muster out of the frustration he was feeling.

"Uh..." The young undead man took out a few folded sheets of paper that resembled that of a call sheet for TV productions. This pretty much already confirmed to Sern that they were doing film shoots, and not just a photo shoot. With all these people around, it seemed somewhat difficult to find where anyone is. "Ya, Director is Sir Hugo, I think he's in the main banquet hall right now." The guy reached for his radio.

"No need. I shall find him myself." Sern left the front entrance, as more and more people were coming in, some carrying ramps and rails that were for the camera's "dolly" mechanism. There was even a crane outside for what would only be guessed was for the film cameras. Sern was growing more and more frustrated with all this commotion. He had no idea that they were going to bring this much equipment into the house, but with every step he got closer to the dining hall, the more he saw the people were setting up for various scenes.

In front of what was known as video village, as though this was some fort of a central command area where they would be doing all of the coordination, it looked more like a military operation than anything else. Sitting in one of those cloth and wood-type folding chairs that the film industry always seemed to carry around was probably the director, sitting reviewing some forms and things with two others who were sitting next to him. Thanks to Sern's excellent hearing he could pickup their conversation despite the noise from the entrance.

The three of them, sitting around the monitors did notice Sern walking towards them, and also that no one made any effort to stop the rather determined intendant. Sern simply brushed past them without incident as he approached with an unimpressed expression on his face.

"Ah, you must be Intendant Sern!" the director reached out with his hand, his voice was tinted with the presence of an English accent.

"And you're Sir Hugo." Sern declared as he scanned their surroundings to see some trolleys of video equipment, cables, many types of various machines and accessories for their equipment.

"Yes, I heard you were in meditation upstairs and didn't want to disturb you when we arrived." The director said as he stepped off his chair. He was noticeably shorter than Sern, almost by a head in height.

"That was most courteous of you," Sern responded with a tad hint of sarcasm in his voice.

"I guess you're not particularly pleased with the masses of equipment we brought?" The young director asked with obvious expectation to a rather obvious question.

"No. I was assured that they were simply doing a photo shoot, I was expecting only a small group of people with some photo cameras; that's it!" Sern reiterated his irritation to them.

"Unfortunately our schedule has moved up. The network commissioned another six episodes, so we have to bump our schedule up more," he explained.

"It was only yesterday that I was made aware that you needed a photo shoot. Are you telling me that within the time period of twenty-four hours, that the studio ordered another six additional weeks of filming?" Sern found that though the situation could be handled, he would have appreciated that they would be filming ahead of schedule. "Furthermore, I wasn't aware that Wolf Coven House itself would become a location!"

"I'm sorry these things were arranged all at the last minute. The entire crew had to be virtually conscripted in the past day, and trust me, that wasn't easy either. The Suits want them to start some filming here for the first episode. We're only going to be here for today and tomorrow, maximum!"

"I'm glad to hear that. Since the Suits should show at least the courtesy of sending a request ahead of time before they decided to do this again." Sern insisted to the director as he was gently guided out of the dining hall. "Furthermore," Sern stopped in his tracks, "I expect as little inconvenience as possible, for those who are living here."

"Of course, the crew have already been told to avoid the upper levels past the second floor. No one will be disturbed up there." Sir Hugo assured Sern. Sern had little reason to not trust this director. In all honesty, Sern knew that in a production, the director did have lots of say but as for the budget and all that, it was not his authority that mattered. More likely it was the producers or anyone else in the studio hierarchy that made these decisions.

"Forty-eifrom hours," Sern reasserted. "And then you're all out, whether finished or not."

"Yes, absolutely." Sir Hugo nodded attempting to be accommodating. "We brought plenty of catering and craft service, please do help yourself. I know you intendants don't need to eat but you may find something you like."

"Thank you for the offer," Sern replied as he headed out of the dining hall to the upstairs level where, luckily, no one was awake yet. First he was going to investigate the second floor where there were people moving about, setting up what looked like smaller makeup and dressing rooms. There was a great deal of activities, especially with these makeup and wardrobe ladies coming up the stairs with kits of makeup and racks of clothing.

Sern stepped aside for the human convoy to pass by as he slowly went up the stairway. He casually slipped past a few of the open empty rooms, which were used as reserve guest rooms on the central wing of the building. It was only the side wings that were used as residence and so these were naturally empty. Despite this, he wanted to go check up on the others in the upper rooms in case they were disturbed by the arrival of the crew and equipment.

Luckily, from what he could tell from most of the rooms, they were all asleep. However, as he approached Gavin's room, he heard someone inside already as he knocked on the door.

"Come in!" Gavin called from inside. He sounded slightly distracted as the door opened and Sern came in. He was drying off his hair. Apparently he had just come out of the shower, and while wearing a pair of comfortable sweat pants, he was still shirtless.

"Apparently we have a few people here already." Sern stated, clearly underestimating the overall numbers of the people who were coming in.

"Has the photographer arrived yet?" Gavin asked as he took off the towel from off his neck.

"Oh yes. The photographer has arrived," Sern stated bluntly as he took a scan of the room, "so has the lighting, the directors, at least twenty production assistants, the camera operators, sound operators, grips, you name it."

"Wait, grips? Sound? Cameras? Why would they be here?" Gavin asked from his bedroom,.

"Yes, apparently they have decided to move ahead with the filming schedule to today," Sern folded his arms across his chest, annoyed by the fact this was done without his permission.

"Wait, filming? Today?" Gavin came back out of the bedroom, slipping on a black t-shirt.

"Yes, the 'Suits', as they were referred to by Sir Hugo, your director, said that they wanted to move the schedule up even more, so literally they are going to be filming scenes today while the photo shoot is going on. Apparently you and Cazian are the only ones that are going to be used but still, they want to do some filming in this house." Sern explained. It was unusual to see an intendant, who was visibly annoyed.

"Well if that's what they want, it's not like we can stop them."

"I guess I better wake Cazian," Sern turned to leave the room.

"Yeah, again I'm sorry they did this."

"Well I did give them ample warning, that they were only going to be allowed to film here until the end of tomorrow, otherwise I will move their equipment out myself," Sern warned clearly though not to threaten Gavin but just as a method of verbally venting what he is thinking.

"Well if we get things fast, then they won't be in our faces for much longer." Gavin assured the intendant.

"If that's what it takes."

As Sern approached Cazian's apartment, he also heard noise inside' again it sounded just like he too was showering. It already seemed like Cazian was aware of the situation, likely Gavin texted him already about what was going on before Sern got to the door. Instead of intruding, Sern decided to head back down to the foyer and lobby when he saw a familiar person coming through the front door.

"Trey! Where have you been for the past few days?" Sern greeted the Prime Wolf who came through, just as amazed as Sern was at first to see all the commotion going on.

"Well, after we went looking for the Bloodbanes, I told Trenton and Coltrane that I was going to head back to my own place, had stuff to do. I haven't gone running in the forest for a while, so I took a few days off."

"Ah, so you remember all that stuff about the Bloodbanes?" Sern reiterated to Trey, wanting to know for sure that he was still aware of memories that he had to modify.

"Yeah, poor Jett, I hope he was fine during his first full moon." Trey whispered to Sern, knowing that such a topic was preferably one that was best kept quiet.

"Yes it was, please come with me right away," Sern pulled Trey's arm as the tall Prime Wolf followed the Intendant to his office. There wasn't anyone in this section of the house fortunately, since this was a more administrative area and nothing here was particularly special enough to warrant filming.

Sern led Trey into the office, and moments after he closed the door, he tapped Trey's forehead with his right index finger, immediately triggering his inteindant mind manipulation abilities with his eyes, which now glowed brightly.

"I need you to return to town. You are not going to mention any of this Bloodbane situation or anything referring to Jett's transformation," Sern instructed, as his voice infused the commands into Trey's mind. "You are going to find out where this last Bloodbane is, using your contacts, and when you do, notify us. I will send Dominic to assist you when you alert us." Sern gave a few moments to Trey's mind to process the instructions. "Repeat what I said." He ordered.

"I'm to return to town. I'm not going to mention any of this Bloodbane situation or Jett's transformation," Trey repeated without being aware of what he was saying.

It seemed very awkward for a moment for Sern to see Trey return, then to send him back on his way to town so quickly, but it was more useful that Trey's memories for the time being were not blocked. After a few minutes of this, Sern released the mindlink and Trey slowly came back to consciousness. He hadn't even noticed that any time at all had passed by

"So they're filming already? I thought they had at least a couple of weeks before it was going to happen."

"Oh no, apparently the studio executives thought it would be a wise decision to move ahead with filming despite the lack of rest time that the actors and crew had." Sern sneered with slight hints of sarcasm in his voice, in a mocking praise of the executive decisions.

"Well I'm sure things will work out fine." Trey assured the Intendant. "They filmed here before, and they were always on schedule." He recalled the other events of filming at the House. It was rare but occasionally they did happen under Hasaan's watch.

"Well I gave them a stern warning. They said they only needed two days, so I am going to just give them two days to do it." Sern restated his terms to Trey. "And I told them, once the deadline passes, their equipment will be moved whether they like it or not."

"That's taking a firm stance." Trey couldn't help but admire the directness of Sern's words. "Hasaan would have been gentler."

"I have little patience for these changes in schedules, and in addition we have other guests too." Sern thought of the Ahri, and what they would be thinking of this film crew.

"We have other guests?" Trey asked, curious to what Sern was referring to. He hadn't encountered the Ahri before; in fact, he didn't even know that they had guests.

"Yes, we have a delegation of small little beings, they're magic users who have teamed up with the Sanctuary Organization. Right now they're living in the far side of the east wing until we give some land for them to use as a diplomatic mission," Sern repeated the orders that he gave to everyone else. "They're a diplomatic mission, so please treat them with respect. I heard that to human eyes, they can seem rather "cute", but please remember that these are diplomats and very powerful users of magic and also foremost; they are Sanctuary Allies. Best to keep a distance or maintain absolute politeness to them." Sern instructed Trey. Again he didn't mince words; he was direct in what he wanted.

"Shouldn't be a problem. I've dealt with magic users before and I never had issues." Trey assured the Intendant.

"Well I wasn't going to suggest that you were going to cause a diplomatic incident, but I have to say these things."
"Completely understandable," Trey reassured Sern. "Well, I'm going to take a long nap back in my room. I hate mornings." Trey turned around as the doors opened up by Sern's mental command. "But I came to get some stuff and I'm going to find more on these Bloodbanes."

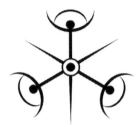

Chapter 23

Trey sat at the Red Moon Bar, one of the werewolf hangouts in the city. Vancouver was one of those more quiet urban landscapes, and this one bar, located in one of the suburbs near the railroad junctions on the coast, was a perfect place for wolves to meet up and sometimes even disappear. Being near the railroad tracks was a great place for wolves to cross country too without being caught in the wild.

Trey was a familiar sight here. Though a Prime Wolf, he kept a low profile and it was more often his ears that he used to listen.

"So, usual?" Lucas the bartender asked Trey, who was visibly fixed just on his phone for the time being. He was just gazing at a screensaver application that showed him random nice scenic spots around the world while letting his ears do the listening around him.

"Hmm?" Trey looked up at Lucas for a moment, shifting his hearing back to the local spot where he was sitting. "Uh, yeah." Trey quickly gave his back a stretch. Sitting on a bar stool wasn't always the most comfortable thing to do.

"So how are things up at the House?" Lucas asked, as he filled Trey's glass up again with that same frothy gold-colour liquid.

"Well, as good as they can be, I guess." Trey took down a gulp. "You get called up?" the wolf asked back as he gently put his glass back down on the cardboard coaster.

"I did get called up a few days ago. Blood donation."

"Oh?" Trey was intrigued. He had spent the entire few weeks down in the city since Paxton and Jett were reunited, so he didn't hear anything about what was going on up at the house.

"Yeah, apparently a new High Order. Pretty handsome guy I have to admit." Lucas leaned against the counter.

"Oh? What did he look like?" Trey probed a bit.

"About my height, well built guy, also about my age, mid-twenties. Had thick black hair, pretty chiseled handsome look to him."

"Really..." Trey's mind drifted right to Paxton's profile in his head. That young new vampire certainly had lots of bonus points in the looks department, he thought to himself.

"Yeah but he wasn't really into feeding. It was on the night of the full moon and apparently his boyfriend is a werewolf." Alarms started going off in Trey's head.

"A werewolf, he didn't say what kind did he?" Trey took another gulp of the rather generic tasting beer.

"Um ... let me think," Lucas pondered visibly as Trey watched intently. "Bloodbane?" he asked himself out loud. "Yeah, definitely Bloodbane. He had a blue star tattooed on his forearm."

"Bloodbanes." Trey repeated. "Not really a common sight around these parts."

"No. I have to admit, I was rather surprised to hear it myself." Lucas waved to a few folks who were coming into the bar. At this hour in the evening, it was more just a casual place. Trey instinctively started to sniff the air. He definitely did pick up a trace of Bloodbane scent, recent too.

"Did any of them come into here?" he asked only to validate the scent that still lingered in the air.

"Yeah, last night actually. He may be back tonight; he's been here every night, waiting for something or someone."

"What time?"

"Usually past sunset. Once that twilight hits, he's here. Young kid too, maybe not much older than early twenties."

Trey downed the entire contents of his enormous beer mug. Then, standing up to his full height over six feet, he towered over Lucas as he reached for his wallet.

"Here, text me at this number when he shows up," Trey requested as he slipped Lucas a fifty-dollar bill.

"Sure thing. Expect a text around sunset."

Trey headed back to his apartment, which was only a few blocks away. It was one of those nice evenings where the lingering of the summer was still around despite being in early November. It was unusually warm in the late afternoon. There were a few people out of their jackets who were enjoying this unusual warm atmosphere of the city. New West as it was called, was much more scenic.

When he got back to his apartment Trey slipped out his phone and dialed right away back to Gavin. The phone rang for a moment before a voice picked up.

"Yeah?" Gavin's voice answered from the other side."

"I think I may have caught one of the Bloodbanes. One of the bartenders at Red Moon thinks that he will show up this evening there. I'm going to see if it's him."

"Remember they have a tattoo of a blue star on their forearm. If you can spot that, it's positive."

"Alright."

"I can't come down, but I think Sern will send Dominic to help you out," Gavin offered. He sounded relieved to hear the news.

"Fine. I think I can handle one Bloodbane but if you think Dominic should be here too, I'm good with that."

"Alright, again, if you need anymore backup tell us!" Gavin offered again.

"I will," Trey ended the phone conversation and put his phone back onto the charging dock next to his computer. From Wolf Coven House, it would take Dominic probably an hour to get to his place from Wolf Coven House into the city. There really wasn't much else to do but to wait.

A firm knock on the door came almost exactly an hour from when they hung up the conversation. It was likely to be Dominic, no one was as punctual and by the book as this guy. Sure enough as the door opened, the battle-hardened and tough-looking Dominic stood there. His very chiseled facial features made him look serious, as did the intensity of his eyes.

"Well, right on the dot, one hour," Trey looked at his phone.

"As expected," Dominic stepped into the apartment. It was decorated rather in a rather minimalist manner. "I could have been here sooner, but Sern was still working out the magical portal spells." He knew that this apartment wasn't exactly Trey's personal property but just one of the many places that Wolf Coven members or Sanctuary members could use temporarily as shelter. It also made a good place for observation. "So when will we be heading out to find this Bloodbane one of your sources found?" he asked directly.

"Well the source, as you put it, was actually just one of our blood donors," Trey leaned against the closed apartment door. He was somewhat amused by the sheer height difference between him and Dominic. Though stern-looking and certainly no pushover, Dominic stood maybe only 5'10 inches at most. Trey, much like Trenton was over 6 foot 5 inches in height, towering easily over Dominic. That said though, Dominic was a High Order vampire, and he was easily two to three times stronger than a Prime Wolf, which, if things got ugly at the Red Moon, would be very useful.

"Calvin?" Dominic recalled one of the donors that he fed on many months ago. He didn't use donors that often.

"No young bloke, around late 20s strawberry blond, really nice guy. I think you introduced Paxton to him," Trey recalled in his mind.

"Oh, Lucas. I didn't know he worked at the Red Moon."

"Bartender. And, well, he spotted a Bloodbane. Not many wolves order drinks garnished with some Vampire blood I guess. And supposedly Lucas spotted the tattoo."

"Makes sense that he would. Bloodbanes don't exactly hide their pack tattoos. It shows others they have backup."

"I don't think we will have problems, but if we do, have your eyes ready."

"For hypnotism?"

"Exactly. It better to be safe than sorry, I think." Dominic was fairly sure that he wanted to keep things under control without incident, and this was going to be the way to do it. Dominic seemed rather distracted for a few moments, which didn't escape Trey's notice.

"What's wrong?" He asked the Vampire.

"Before I came, Gavin and Sern met with me." He started as he sat down at one of the kitchen chairs. He was slightly distraught, as much as the stern Dominic could ever look when it came to being distraught. "They told me that I am to help you in looking for a Bloodbane Wolf."

"Yeah, because his pack bit Jett and turned him into one." Trey finished the thought for Dominic, believing that it was what he would have said.

"If that were true, why is Jett a Prime Wolf?" Dominic asked, slowly revealing the end to the sentence like he was luring Trey into some plot twist.

"What?" Trey almost struggled for a moment to make sure he heard what he thought he heard correctly.

"Jett, is a Prime Wolf, like you." Dominic repeated.

"That's impossible. The wolves that bit him were Bloodbanes; I know becauseI saw the wound. I could smell the Bloodbanes on him, and he also had their scent. No way possible."

"And yet he is." Dominic asserted again.

"Its impossible to become a Prime Wolf without being bitten by one and on a full moon too, and there was none there that bit him."

"Apparently there was," Dominic slowly nudged out one of the chairs for Trey, suggesting he sit down for a longer story. Trey did just that, sitting next to the much shorter man. "Sern used a memory block on us," Dominic revealed to Trey. "You see, you were away from the house at the time so you weren't affected. I guess Sern may have forgotten that you still knew that Jett was originally a Bloodbane."

"Or maybe he knew all along, and wanted me to find that lone wolf, so then I would bring him back to have his and my memories both altered." Trey surmised. He wasn't entirely too sure on the situation, but he did suspect that Sern was up to more than he was going to reveal.

"Which I guess, in context to what Sern has to do, what he's capable of doing, and most importantly what he has to do, isn't entirely that surprising."

"Still, a memory block is somewhat drastic, don't you think? Trey asked. "I sometimes wonder about his ability to do that. I mean, how much memories has he blocked before, or changed?"

"I once spoke to Hasaan about this very topic," Dominic recalled. "If an intendant has to resort to this, memory blocking, it must be extremely important." Dominic surrendered his suspicions with a certain level of reluctance. "I think intendants were aware of a far larger picture of what was going on, but they can't reveal it all to us. He said they can never erase memories, only block your mind from accessing some of them. Still yes, memory alterations are somewhat drastic, I do have to agree."

"Which is exactly what he would tell us if he wanted us to stop remembering."

"Actually I do know the full reason. Sern unlocked the original memories in my mind before I left, to give me just reason to understand why he did it."

"And that is?" Trey was eager to hear it.

"Jett was captured by some sorcerer, some powerful user of magic, and was in the middle of what Sern calls a transmogrification spell when Sern and some new allies of ours saved him and interrupted the spell. But the spell was irreversible and only partially effective. He was being changed into a Prime Wolf, like you."

"Ugh, magic." Trey snarled. "I never trusted that stuff."

"Well in this case the spell wasn't effective, but basically put Jett into a state between two different wolf breeds, meaning if he transformed, the two wolf forms would tear him apart. So Sern had to complete the ritual with our new allies," Dominic explained.

"And that's all it takes? A simple magic spell?" Trey laughed at the simplicity of it all.

"Apparently, Sern said that the sheer power of such a spell was so draining that a human magic-user wouldn't survive its casting. The spell would drain a human magician so much that he would die before even half the spell was completed."

"So how did we, I mean, Sern get it done?"

"Our new friends, they're called the Ahri,"

"Ahri eh? Sern told me a bit about them. New allies," Trey repeated the name for a second, thinking in his mind of what kind of creatures would have this name.

"You'll love them." Dominic smirked for a second.

"Why?"

"They're tiny little almost midget-dwarf gnome size little beings. Jett and Paxton always call them cute. They're spunky, chirpy little folks and they're supremely powerful at magic."

"You've seen them use the stuff?" Trey tried to imagine the image of these little folks in his head.

"They helped complete the spell, three of them, and Sern combined power to finish the transformation spell on Jett. They used Trenton as some sort of template, and after that, Jett became a Prime Wolf."

"I still don't see why Sern had to wipe your memories."

"I'm guessing it's because the idea of Supernaturals just being able to simply "upgrade" what they are, is potentially dangerous. And if they find out that magic practitioners are the key, then anyone with magical potential could become a target. So in a large way, I can understand why he had to keep it secret."

"I guess. I still don't trust magic as a whole."

"And Sern is probably going to have our memories altered again once this situation is dealt with."

"Well, I'm sure he knows best," Trey surrendered the moment slightly with a bit of sarcasm in his voice."

"At least if he alters your memory, you won't remember any reason not to trust him," Dominic replied. The double meaning of his words had to be processed for a moment in Trey's mind.

"Alright, whatever, just as long as my brain is still intact in the morning, I don't care," he stood up from his seat. "Something that complicated is best forgotten."

The Red Moon Bar was only a few blocks away, easy for them to get there. It wasn't long before the text message came with a vibrating alarm on Trey's phone. The text showed exactly what Trey expected. "The Bloodbane kid is here. He just arrived." the text read. It was simple and to the point.

"Alright, let's head out," Trey stood up from his massage chair. Dominic was already prepared. He was wearing a rather nice looking leather jacket, and comfortable jeans that didn't show off too much. Trey was in a rather bland-looking grey t-shirt and jeans as well, but his were somewhat more suggestive. Considering Trey's huge size, he didn't really bother to care if the clothes were tight on him or not.

When they reached the bar, its occupancy was only about half full. The place certainly smelled like werewolves to Trey. That distinctive canine scent wasn't unlike that which pet owners would smell when their dog came in from the wet rain. Humans wouldn't be able to detect it that easily, but certainly other werewolves and even vampires had no problem.

The bar was a renovated warehouse. It was fairly large and had even a modest dance floor. Of course the biker-style decorations made it more of a bar than a club. The bar itself was rather large and had a number of seats. Most of the space was taken up by the various seats and tables in various arrangements. There were clusters of guests and patrons just sitting around, mostly talking.

Trey was aware of the clear difference between the social groupings that vampires had in comparison to wolves. Certainly the wolves had their own cliques, but they were happier when away from humans. Vampires loved to linger and mingle with humans, probably more out of necessity than anything else since they were a food source. Vampires owned clubs and had huge raves where they would feed, Wolves tried best to avoid these situations. Though a few did mingle with their fanged friends, they were often just there for the atmosphere than anything else.

He didn't have to worry about being there with Dominic. There were no hostilities between the two races despite what comic books and Hollywood would make humans believe. The two had no conflicts since they didn't have the same needs. Wolves didn't feed on blood and were no threat to Vampiric food supplies. For him and the others, there was little reason to fear the Vampiric presence. For Trey and Dominic, most of the Supernaturals had little issues with each other since the Sanctuary Presence world help diffuse any types of tension, and that it was better that they left each other alone rather than starting turf wars.

When the two of them entered the bar, it was filled with an awkward silence. It was like the scene from some Western movies where the sheriff entered the saloon through the two swinging doors, and suddenly everyone went silent, even the piano player in his bowler hat. Dominic's presence didn't go unnoticed at all. Despite the wolves instantly noticing that Dominic wasn't one of them, there was no scent of hostility. Dominic himself sensed that they found his presence unusual but not threatening.

"Over there," Trey pointed to the bar where Lucas was. He was keeping eye contact with Trey, signaling that he wanted them to head over to him.

There were a few gazes at Dominic. He did seem somewhat out of place in this area. His scent was certainly not something that everyone was used to. Some gazes were out of confusion, some out of hostility. Many wolves were territorial, and for a foreign intruder like him to be there, he did get a few subtle growls. But it only took a single glare from Dominic towards the direction of the glare that helped quiet the atmosphere for a brief moment. It was almost comical for Trey when he did see it. Dominic was certainly no novice at that infamous glare that he could give that could freeze anyone's spine. And the scary thing was that Dominic was probably the most powerful one , physically, in the bar, and antagonizing him would be a very unwise decision.

"He's over there in the corner," Lucas whispered to Trey when they got to the bar. Lighting from the bar itself made him look more clandestine than normal. "Over there, in the navy blue hoodie," Lucas pointed. Sure enough, here was a young guy, probably no older than his early 20s, apparently sitting with another wolf. Despite being in a hoodie, his sleeves were rolled up just enough for a blue four-point star to be seen.

Dominic seemed to be listening in on their conversation. His vampiric ears were better at picking up noise than Trey's currently non-wolf ears. In his Prime Wolf form, his hearing was far more sensitive. The word "pack" came up very frequently, as well as "joining" which suggested to Dominic that this lone Bloodbane was thinking of changing wolf packs, something that was highly irregular.

Trey and Dominic approached the two at the table slowly and calmly, making sure that they were undetected. Subtlety was required in their line of work. Gavin and Cazian wouldn't be able to do these types of tasks since they were also TV stars and celebrities, not only in the human world but also in the Supernatural world. Dominic made sure that he moved particularly carefully, not wanting to alarm any of the nearby wolves. It was like he was walking on eggshells to make sure that though he was being noticed, those who were watching him weren't going to be alarmed.

When they got to the table, the two wolves only just casually looked up for a casual moment to see who was coming nearby. Trey approached the target wolf from behind while Dominic took the other one. They had to make sure that these two were not going to panic when confronted. What was as simple as taking a walk across the bar had to be strategic, and carefully carried out. Luckily they were too engrossed in conversation to notice even Trey approaching, and before they knew it, each of them was looking at a stranger behind the other.

"Can we help you?" The other wolf asked, with a hint of courtesy in his voice like he was genuinely surprised to see Dominic and Trey.

To him, of course they were just having a casual conversation. Valko tried to get up from his seat, but Trey put his enormous hand on his shoulder and flashed him a yellow eye gaze, a warning to the young Bloodbane.

"We would like to have a talk with the two of you," Trey whispered as he bent downwards a bit to make sure they were still subtle.

"What's this about?" Valko asked, his voice slightly trembling.

"I think you know," Dominic glared at the young Bloodbane. Valko saw Dominic's eyes turn red, something no wolf could ever do. It was clear to him, in that instant, that Dominic wasn't even a wolf like him or the others.

"Look, we don't want any trouble," the other wolf said calmly as though he was honestly trying to make some diplomatic effort. Valko, on the other hand, was visibly shaken, nervous, and even afraid. He was visibly trying to avoid any eye contact at all.

The other wolf rolled up the sleeve to his black leather jacket, revealing a Packwalker tattoo, in his case, the symbol of three crescent shaped moons. Valko's pack tattoo was also visible, the Blue Star, which Paxton, Gavin and Cazian remembered to tell them. The tattoo itself confirmed that this wolf was indeed one of the ones that attacked Jett, or at least was a part of the same pack.

"There won't be, if you two follow us," Trey gripped his hand around Valko's arm, firmly though not tight enough to cause him pain.

"Both of you," Dominic assured the two of them. His own hands sat on the other wolf's shoulders. Dominic locked his gaze onto Valko who couldn't help but also stared back. The brief moment of eye contact was all Dominic needed to calm down this Wolf enough to make him obedient. "You're going to come with us."

"Alright, but I just don't want any trouble," Valko asked, almost begged.

"Come on, let's go." Dominic then faced the other wolf and also locked his gaze. For him to implant the mental suggestion of obedience was just a gaze and it would last as long as he was around for the time being.

"Looks like it was a good thing Gavin sent you after all," Trey smirked at the Vampire. The four of them casually left, and stepped out, but not before Trey left a $100 bill on the table, then signaled for Lucas to collect it as they stepped out of the bar.

The walked back to the apartment went without incident. Trey secured the place with the reinforced locks. The door closed quietly despite being made out of reinforced steel, and they felt safe enough to talk since the walls were also soundproof. The magical enhancement put in by Elura made sure that isolation and protection were paramount.

Dominic made sure to keep them constantly aware of his presence, so his mental suggestion was still active as they sat down on the couch. Trey stood over the two of them. He almost felt like pacing but he refrained from doing so.

"So you're the one who was part of the pack that attacked our guests," he stated sternly at Valko. The young wolf only nodded gently, almost unwilling to admit it for a moment. "What's your name?"

"V ...Valko," he answered. Dominic had allowed his mental influence to wear down by now, so Valko was more of sound mind. The Vampire sat down across from the two of them, with a serious glare on his face. It was a silent reminder to the two of them that he was very much present and listening carefully to what they were saying.

"And where is your pack, Valko?" Trey also sat down next to Dominic, slightly intimidating them, now that the 6'5 tall Werewolf was at their eye level.

"I don't have a pack anymore," Valko confessed to them.

"He was meeting with me to see if he could join ours," the other answered. This other wolf wasn't as scared as Valko.

"And your name?" Trey turned to the other wolf.

"Connor," he said.

"That's Irish I believe, for Wolf Lover," Dominic smirked. "How appropriate," Dominic took out his phone almost like he didn't care about what was going on for a moment. It looked like he was sending a text out to someone. Trey could only assume that he was sending news back to Wolf Coven House.

"So then, Connor, why would you let a Bloodbane into your pack?" Trey folded his arms across his massive chest, almost in a display of intimidation to the other two young wolves.

"I haven't even made up my mind to introduce him to our Alpha yet. It was hardly a done deal," Connor asserted.

"So no one knew about Valko here, aside from you?" Dominic asked, listening carefully to his heart rate, his words, his inflections, everything about his body language being taken note.

"No. Not a single one."

"And what happened to your pack, Valko?" Trey continued with the questions.

"Why should we tell you anything?" Connor blurted out defiantly. "I have my own pack. You deal with all of us if you're going to give us any trouble." Connor stood up almost ready to leave, but not before his two opponents did the same, ready to stop him.

"Because it's in your interest to tell us the truth," a stern voice came from the back of the room. It wasn't Dominic's voice or Trey's.

"That was fast, Sern," Dominic looked at his phone. Gavin had sent a reply to him telling him that he was going to tell Sern, which was less than a minute ago.

"The Ahri and myself succeeded in creating a portal. So they were generous enough to open up a portal in that room." Sern pointed towards the den, which was beyond the living room. "Leads straight back to Wolf Coven House as long as it's active." The Intendant looked towards the two young wolves.

"There's no point in trying to lie to us," Trey lectured to Valko. "This guy can literally read every thought in your head," he sounded like he was warning the two of them.

"This one is innocent," Sern pointed to Connor. "But for the time being, I cannot allow him to divulge any news of this situation to his pack. He has to come with us too."

"Fuck that!" Connor growled, his hands already starting to shift into claws, and his fangs emerging. As though Dominic's own eyes and fangs weren't fierce enough combined with Trey's face starting to go bestial, Sern's own eyes flashed brightly, bright enough to fill the room with light, if only for a moment.

"This is for the safety of your pack, and it's best if we keep this situation quiet. I promise that you won't be hurt." Sern slowly walked up to Connor as his eyes faded back to normal. He almost looked like he was comforting the agitated wolf. "You won't be hurt. Sanctuary isn't in the business of taking hostages."

Connor looked extremely reluctant to cooperate. Valko was almost surrendering. "Besides, he's a Prime Wolf, and he's a High Order vampire." Sern pointed to Dominic and Trey. "Don't give them any excuse to flex those muscles." It was almost like Sern was playing good cop bad cop. Connor turned to Valko, almost expecting him to give him instructions. Sern could sense a certain form of loyalty between the two of them. Valko just nodded his head in compliance to what Sern was saying.

"Alright," Valko agreed. The five of them slowly walked towards the den, Dominic and Trey behind the two wolf boys. Inside the den, was a large, almost swirling, light blue vortex of light. It filled up the room almost to the height of the ceiling. It made no sounds, and looked like it was just a gathering of light. There was a slight breeze in the room, but nothing to suggest that it was, in any way, affecting anything in the room aside from its light.

"Step through, please," Sern instructed the two of them. They stood there, not quite sure what to do, seeing this magical portal for the first time was something no one was quite prepared for. "Just step through like it wasn't there," he assured them. Valko and Connor looked at each other, bewildered and unsure of quite what to do. Valko just shook his head and walked into it like it wasn't there as he vanished into it. Sern followed him, and soon everyone went through the portal.

Chapter 24

"As promised," the Benefactor said. "You fulfilled the agreement adequately." He produced a large clay Pithos Jar in his hands, which materialized out of thin air. It was a very plain- looking vase, almost completely void of any decorative properties aside from being grey and dull looking. It was sealed at the top with the same material that made up the body.

"Are you sure that this is him?" Hypnos asked as he stepped up to the vase. He couldn't help but examine the exterior before being handed it by the Benefactor.

"Without question, your brother Thanatos is resting within this."

"Then I'll free him soon enough."

"You know that the seal to this cannot be broken by anyone who knows what is inside, or anyone who is manipulated by anyone with knowledge of what is inside it."

"I suspected that the safeguards would prevent me from opening it directly, but still, I have it and now just have to find the method." Hypnos grasped the vase in his hand and put it on the table in the middle of the penthouse living room.

"And now we have two High Order bodies to use." Hypnos grinned. He was eager to continue with his plans.

"Have you considered what you can do with him?" the Benefactor pointed to the Pithos Jar that Hypnos was now embedding with various runes and enchantments.

"I have to find a way to open it," Hypnos almost gave up. "Against my power, that simple clay jar is indestructible. I can't even hypnotize someone to destroy it," Almost with a casual attitude of submissiveness, he hurled one of his energy bolts at the Pithos that the Benefactor held, only to have the energy that normally would blast a hole in a wall, completely fizzing uselessly against clay surface. "See? Useless," He groaned. "And to think that my brother is inside there, completely unaware that I'm trying to break him out of his prison."

"There is always another opportunity," the Benefactor started to suggest.

"I completely see no way. That Pithos was made to specifically prevent any intervention from any god. I can't tell someone, I can't manipulate anyone to break that thing. I cannot have any part in its destruction to free my brother."

"Your host is the key, God of Sleep." the Benefactor almost grinned as he revealed some hints. Hypnos knew that the Benefactor always had information that Hypnos had no idea how he knew it.

"If I control his mind, it won't work," Hypnos already protested. "And you know, no god can survive for very long on Earth with or without a host body, without our power diminishing."

"No, but he can bring it somewhere, under your influence, where then the custody of the Pithos shifts, and then they will proceed to destroy it for you."

"Like how?"

"First, one step at a time," the Benefactor assured Hypnos as he gestured for Hypnos to follow him into one of the many rooms in the penthouse.

They entered one of the guest rooms where a simple pair of twin beds lay, with their occupants lying there in a peaceful and uninterrupted sleep. The twins who owned the apartment were obviously placed there under a sleeping spell by Hypnos himself.

"Are you prepared to turn them?" the Benefactor asked as he also produced the syringe of High Order blood that Jett had managed to acquire. The large vial of blood seemed to materialize out of thin air to the Benefactor when, before, it too was kept under lock and key by Hypnos.

"I was going to, but waiting for you to come and assist me," Hypnos admitted as he stepped up to look at the twin bodies. Identical males, just as how he and Thanatos were in Elysium and in their true God forms. "But you know that I can't just jump into a new body, especially a freshly turned High Order vessel. It has to be ready."

239

"And is that why you were waiting for me to give these bodies some form of early preparation?"

"Only that once I inject these bodies, you help them go through the Turning as fast as possible. You probably have some sort of trick that you can do with our power to make the transition faster and smoother, so then I can use one of these as a host."

"You want to avoid being a non-corporeal."

"Our power diminishes without a host form in this human world," Hypnos almost sounded like he was complaining to the Benefactor. "Without a host, what power I have now will fade away fast, and then I'll just be as weak as Thanatos is, and that's without even the safety of a magical cage to keep me intact."

"Very well, once you have injected the blood, I will proceed to hasten their change," the Benefactor assured Hypnos.

"But what about my brother?" Hypnos returned to the point at hand. "I can't free him, and if you know of a solution, I want to hear it!"

"One step at a time," the Benefactor almost sounded comforting to Hypnos. The vial of High Order blood floated between the two brothers, levitated by the unseen will of the Benefactor. Almost like every molecule was moldable, it simply melted in half, splitting the blood equally into two smaller vials, then moved towards the necks of the twins who lay there, peacefully asleep. The syringes floated quietly and slowly towards them as the ends stretched out into thin pointed needles, and slowly slipped into the veins of the target victims. By an unseen force the blood flowed into the bodies of the twins as Hypnos watched.

"Is the blood in?" He asked.

"Yes." The syringes pulled out, and vanished as though they were of no more use. "The blood is injected, and now it's going to spread throughout their bodies." Hypnos couldn't sense or see anything, but he trusted his Benefactor enough to accept what he was told.

"Now what?" Hypnos asked. "Are you going to speed up their transformation?"

"You can assist in that. You know, for them to turn, they have to first die. An effective method of killing them is to simply just drain out the life-force," the Benefactor stepped aside for Hypnos to approach within physical reach.

"They're only humans, not quite enough life force to take for anything worth while."

"This siphoning is not about your nourishment, it's about killing them and making efficient use of what life force they have left. But if you want me to take their lives faster..." the Benefactor raised his hands towards the twins before Hypnos intervened.

240

"No!" Hypnos interrupted. "I will do it," he stood between the two beds. Hypnos placed his hands on the chests of the twins. As before, when he drained the pack of wolves that were far richer in life force than these two humans, he could trigger his own power to open up access to them.

His hands reached right through the skin, muscle and bone of the bodies, as though they were nothing more than a vapor, and touched right into their souls for a moment, then to pull his hands out, with streams of their own glowing life force being pulled out. Like a gaseous substance, it was absorbed by Hypnos in the manner that his Benefactor had taught him. Though they were human, they provided him with enough of a boost that he was slightly stronger, but only just. Humans simply didn't have enough life force for him to make much use unless he committed mass slaughter.

As the streams of life energy flowed into him, they were abruptly ended. Hypnos didn't cut if off, it simply wasn't much in them left. His own host's vampiric hearing, though only that of a Drake Order of Vampire ,could hear the heartbeats slowing, getting slower and slower. He mentally reached into them again, and pulled out the last remaining life essences as their hearts simply halted.

"Well done," the Benefactor congratulated without much expression in his very digital sounding voice. He almost pushed Hypnos out of the way with an unseen psychokinetic force. The god was caught off balance for a moment, but then regained his footing as he was pulled back to the room entrance. The Benefactor's internal light was shifting from a mysterious looking grey light into dark purple. His own physical form was still the same though; because his skin plates were translucent, the dark purple also glowed through him. The two twins were also being shrouded by this same energy that he was creating, which acted and looked very different from the siphoning that Hypnos had done. It was rather quick as the shrouding purple cloud dissipated within a minute. The purple energy seemed to saturate every part of their bodies.

"You can't be done that quickly," Hypnos was in a state of some disbelief.

"The blood was doing all the work already. High Orders instinctively are prepared for their results when they change from being human. The only thing I eliminated was their primary bloodlust which happens after they change," the Benefactor turned around to face Hypnos. "Choose your new body," he commanded the god.

"Well since they're identical," Hypnos didn't seem to care which one he chose. From the eyes of his host, he exited his previous physical body in the form of a gold and silver cloud of mist, which was the form that he and Thanatos would have to use. Swirling out of the Drake Vampire body, he immediately entered the twin to the left, also through the eyes which were now open at his command. As he did, he felt the sheer internal strength and power of the new High Order body, far more powerful and stronger, and more durable than the Drake, even though Drakes were not pushovers in the slightest.

As he stretched in his new physical shell, he couldn't help but grin at the new enhanced sensations that this body gave him, as his previous one just slumped over and collapsed almost lifelessly to the ground.

"And what are we going to do with him?" Hypnos pointed to the Drake body which was now more asleep than fainted on the ground.

"You never even mentioned his name before," the Benefactor stated again with the typical emotional level of a vegetable.

"Arthur. He's also a Wolf Coven Member," Hypnos was getting used to the voice of his new body. He was a few years younger than his previous body, and in some regards, more physically fit.

"Wolf Coven. Perfect opportunity," the Benefactor almost smiled at the thought, clearly pondering a new set of circumstance that he could use to his advantage. "A simple small transformation spell on the Pithos can make it look like anything else. Simply have him bring the Pithos to Wolf Coven House, and let someone there destroy it. Make it into something breakable," He instructed Hypnos.

"That sounds too easy."

"It has to be broken by free will. If it is changed into something naturally breakable, then there will be no interference. You are not making them break it; they choose to."

"I can take control of Arthur easily. In fact, plant the thought right into his mind without him realizing it."

"And you can also change the form of the Pithos to something smaller, easier to carry, and more fragile to break," the Benefactor slowly started to walk away.

"And if Thanatos is freed?"

"You said your brother is cunning enough to seize control of a body strong enough, likely another High Order who is there."

"How can I bring him here once he's freed? In fact, how will I know?" Hypnos asked, wanting more instructions from his Benefactor who seemed more interested in only letting Hypnos know what he wanted him to know.

"We will deal with that when the time comes. I will inform you," the Benefactor answered.

Hypnos didn't bother wasting time as he got off the bed, getting used to his new feet, walking for a moment before heading back into the living room where the Pithos still stood. He grasped it with his hands, oddly it was very light despite being made out of thick clay. Sealed completely, it was sturdy enough to take a few hits but although he knew that as a God, he was powerless against it. But he also knew that though the Pithos could not be opened, it could however be changed in form.

He also felt his new body had significant improvements. He felt that he could use more of his power and more of his magical strength than the previous body. Already he could levitate Arthur's body into the room and place it on the couch for him to rest on, as he molded and melted the physical Pithos form into something smaller. He wanted something small, that could fit into Arthur's hand and pocket without being detected, and also the ability for it to also change into something else.

The other problem was that though he could easily take control of Arthur as a puppet, the more magical influence he used over him, the more the magically inclined members of Wolf Coven could sense and detect something. The more subtle, the better. A powerful mental suggestive link would be better hidden than a mental control link, he thought to himself as he molded the Pithos into a small glass ball, no larger than a golf ball to fit into his hand.

It only just hit him, the odd feeling he had, holding a small glass orb in his hand that contained his brother. He placed it into Arthur's hands, then slowly triggered his former host to awaken, but not before entrancing him with his own magic.

"What...." Arthur groaned, his green eyes blinked a few times as he struggled to get a grasp on where he was and what he was doing here. Memories of the moment before being taken as a body were slowly starting to flood back into his mind, but not until he met the hypnotic gaze of Hypnos' own eyes, enhanced by an entrapment spell.

"You only need to hear my instructions, and they will repeat in your mind." Hypnos started, before he would explain his commands to his new pawn. "First however, you're rather thirsty." Hypnos materialized a wine glass in his hand. With a quick slash of his razor sharp nails against his left wrist, he bled a steady stream of his new mixed High Order and Divine blood into the glass. He let it bleed for only until the small glass was halfway full then handed it to Arthur who was still under his magical control. "Have a drink of this." Hypnos suggested. Arthur slowly took the glass and immediately drank all of its contents.

"A very wise precaution," the Benefactor complimented the god, "using your own blood as a method of effective control without even them knowing you're in command of their body and thoughts."

"It worked on the werewolves, no reason why it wouldn't work on these blood drinkers. Divine Blood is always an effective way of controlling mortals." Hypnos gazed into Arthur's eyes, mentally commanding him to do what he was told.

As Arthur drove up the Sea To Sky Highway towards Wolf Coven House, he was gently feeling the glass orb in his pocket. It was a lovely little trinket that he got, though oddly for him, there didn't seem to be any purpose for him to have it with him. However, he felt some strange connection to it, and the need to keep it with him.

He took the left turn that would take him down into the concealed areas of the Wolf Coven Lands and forests. He had an odd feeling that something wasn't quite right. As his car continued down the roads, he could see large trucks parked up by the sides of the road outside the house. These were supply trucks, and some of them massive sized trailers, some with even dual floors. He instantly recognized this as a convoy of movie industry trailers and trucks. Normally in this arrangement, it was like a caravan that was nicknamed the "circus", like how a circus would be set up with its own trailers and cargo trucks. He drove past them casually up to the main entryway to Wolf Coven House.

His usual parking spot was situated just off the side to the house where they would have the donor rooms. This side almost looked slightly like a motel, with the separate entry doors for the donor rooms. He had fed here and it was always enjoyable getting blood fresh from the vein.

There were a few people around with reflector-lined jackets. Arthur recognized them as production assistants, basically people who helped look after the area and the location. One of them ran towards his car, on all fours. Clearly a Were-form of some sort from the distant view of his rear view mirror. As Arthur got out of his car, he got a much clearer view. This fellow was definitely a Were-form, but not a wolf, instead it was a cat, or rather mountain-lion animal-humanoid.

"Um, are you crew or cast?" The guy asked as he stood up on his hind legs. He was shorter than Arthur, and his feline facial features merged almost perfectly with his human face. He even had hair, and oddly, a tail. Arthur could see his claws were out, not really out of any aggressive gesture but just that he shifted.

"Neither, resident," Arthur smiled gently at the cat-boy as he did up his vest and suit jacket.

"Oh, sorry. We're just doing some filming here," the cat-boy replied to him, clearly pointing to the enormous crane outside the west wing of the house that held a huge spotlight aiming at the windows on the second and third floors of the house.

"I can see," Arthur replied somewhat with a hint of sarcasm at the blatantly obvious sign of trucks.

"Ya, we're filming until end of tomorrow."

"Good to know, I take it Sern only allowed you guys to use just one side of the building?" Arthur asked, hoping that his room was not going to be in the filming zone.

"Yeah, so far." the cat-boy pulled out a rolled up bundle of stapled papers. On the front was some sort of chart. He checked it and took a look at the listings of the location spots. "Um....yes, just this side of the building. Everywhere else is off limits to the crew." he checked.

"Can I see that?" Arthur asked him, pointing to the sheets.

"The call sheet?" The PA asked him.

"Yes, just want to check it out."

"Ok, I have another copy here," he flipped through the bundles to reveal that it was actually two copies of the sheets which included the dialogue and script parts that they were filming for the current and next days.

"Thanks," Arthur started to walk away. The cat-boy got back to patrolling the area just to make sure that people were able to find their way around.

Arthur started scanning through the two charts, one that showed the production for the two days. There was the listing of the cast, Cazian and Gavin of course were listed, as were a few of their co-stars from the Eternal Knights show, but none that Arthur himself recognized. Arthur never watched the show and had no interest in an active deception of the Supernatural to human kind. He and the other Drakes, were interested in aristocratic lifestyles. After returning from a quiet few nights alone at his own apartment downtown, he was ready to make himself more comfortable back at his apartment at Wolf Coven House.

He stepped through the front door that was already open with some of the cables from one of the trucks. As he stepped in he could see huge sheets of cardboard lining the side of the walls, probably to protect the wood panels and paint from scratches from equipment that were being brought in throughout the day. How courteous, he thought to himself as he continued to scan down the call sheet.

As looked through the scenes, there was one where Cazian would have to destroy a "Sacred Box". For some unknown reason to Arthur, that was of particular interest, almost like alarms went off in his mind for some unknown reason. As he walked through the house, following the equipment and cables, he suddenly became increasingly intrigued in the behind the scenes action. It was a very strange feeling because normally he wouldn't give a second thought to this type of activity.

In particular, the mysterious description of this object, the Sacred Box, was running through his head. He wanted to see the Sacred Box for some reason. Naturally he looked around for anymore production assistants in construction vest. Just then, another one came around the corner; this was a Zombie for sure. His very pale almost greenish skin was a dead giveaway.

"Hey, where's the props department?" He asked the Zombie. The undead fellow had to slightly adjust his jaw for a moment before answering.

"Um, down this hall, at the green ballroom to the right." The zombie pointed downwards.

"Thanks." Arthur answered as he continued down. He wondered what the box would look like, what it would be made out of, and the design. His mind was consumed now on the box. He imagined it was perhaps black metal, or maybe a rich rosewood. How big? Maybe the size of a music box, or something that would carry a piece of jewelry? The box was all he could focus on.

Arthur turned down the hallway where the Zombie told him to turn, and sure enough there was the collection with various strange artifacts, most of which though looking like they were ancient were made out of things like resin and plaster. Arthur wasn't entirely sure, but with the sheer almost museum scale variety of things such as swords that were made out of rubber, plastic cell phones, fake name tags, pretty much anything an actor would be holding or using.

"You lost?" a crew member came from behind a stack of foam guns. He looked human enough.

"Oh I was just looking around. I live here." Arthur greeted.

"Ah, sorry we're taking up all this space.'"

"Oh well you can make it up for me." Arthur offered. It was an unusual thing to say but he really wanted to see this Sacred Box.

"Oh? Ok." The prop guy answered back.

"I want to see the Sacred Box prop that is going to be featured," Arthur requested. The prop guy turned around and pulled out a tray that sat on shelf. On top were four black boxes appeared to be made out of obsidian. Arthur gazed at them, almost unable to take his eyes off of them. They were quite small, no larger than perhaps a typical smart phone, though they were about three times as thick, large enough to contain something. "Beautiful!" Arthur remarked as the Prop guy put it onto a large table to make it easier to see.

"This is the original," he pointed at the one on the far left. They were all lined up in a straight line. "Carved out of wood, painted with lacquer." Arthur slowly ran his finger along the edges, jagged-edged though not enough to cut skin. The others were perfectly identical in appearance.

"And the others?" Arthur asked before touching them.

"The next one, is a rubber one for stunts," he pressed on the second box to see that it was indeed soft enough for his finger to go right into it.

"And these two?"

"Breakable. Since Cazian's going to smash one, we'll be using one for his general action, the other for a close up. Either way both are going to get smashed by him."

"Interesting," Arthur smiled in slight amusement as he felt in his pocket the glass orb that he had somehow acquired. He had no idea why he was holding it in his hand. "Such a pity to destroy such a nice piece of work," Arthur admired the quality even on the breakable duplicates. "Such nice craftsmanship."

"All part of the job. We can make more out of resin that would be ready in half an hour but that's if they need more," the prop guy explained. "Some things always get destroyed. But I got to set up some stuff," the prop guy said as he wandered off. "Just don't disturb the stuff, please," he said as he walked away.

"No problem," Arthur called back. In his hand, he pulled out the glass orb which started to melt and change its form into one of the black obsidian boxes. He picked up the two breakable ones to notice that they were marked A and B on the bottom. He slipped Box A into his pocket, the former glass orb that morphed into one of the one he hid. He looked at the bottom of the newly formed box, and sure enough there was the letter A on the bottom. He slipped the original decoy breakable box into his pocket, leaving the orb transformed box in its place.

Arthur exited the ballroom, only remembering seeing the boxes and then returning to the main hallway where he proceeded to his apartment. Now he wasn't even sure why he was in the prop room, and simply just thought for a moment that he got lost. The walls were still covered with those long lines of cardboard. He knew very well which part of the house he was in and now just thought that he got lost from all the equipment disguising everything around him. He never liked these productions, especially when they came to Wolf Coven House.

Chapter 25

Sern and the others exited the magical portal that was in the center of a large room in the basement of Wolf Coven House. There were a few lights, and in front of them stood two of the Ahri. Larita and Kazmo were the ones who seemed to be controlling the portal with what looked like little effort. They didn't seem to be straining much as they simply kept the spell active within what looked like strange arch made out of woven tree branches. It looked like it had grown right out of the floor.

Instantly, Trey got a view of the two little Ahri who stood there in front of him, stopping the channeling process which looked more like they were praying than actually using any visible form of magical power. The towering wolf who was easily taller than anyone else there was endlessly amused by the little beings so much that his face was almost in a perpetual state of a smile. The other two, Valko and Connor also came through the portal as fast as they stepped into it without the slightest clue of where they were now.

All of them looked around to wonder where they were, but only Trey and Sern knew it. Wolf Coven House had many basement levels that housed a large number of rooms for many purposes. Apparently this was also due to the House's past during the years of the Cold War when there was a bomb shelter built and excavated into the basement of the building. Over the years the basement and the shelter were enlarged. It was clear that this room was one of the many that was originally planned to be just a standard storage room. Thanks to the plain white walls with grey carpeting, it was a rather bland looking room. The single exception to its dull appearance was the Ahri tree arch that was sitting in the centre.

"Welcome back!" Kazmo greeted with that typical Ahri chirpiness. Again that brought another comforting smirk from Trey.

"Thank you. The spell was highly successful," Sern thanked the two little Ahri. The five of them looked back at the door frame to see the spell portal vanish as the last exited it.

"Do you want the portal to stay active?" Larita asked the Intendant.

"No, I prefer not. Such a powerful spell shouldn't be left unguarded," he suggested to them.

"Well, if you need another one opened, we're ready," the two Ahri tapped their staves against the ground. Their circular disks rose out of the ground and floated them up to face level height. The two Ahri proceeded to exit the room without introducing themselves to the rest of them. Apparently they were aware that this situation wasn't a friendly introduction. They knew that Sern, Dominic and Trey were off getting someone that was likely to be trouble. Normally they thought that they, as Ahri, should be present, but it was probably better that they leave Sern to his duties.

"I've arranged for a room for you both," The phones that they kept in their pockets floated out of their jackets towards Sern's hands. "And I'm afraid I cannot allow you to contact anyone yet," he confiscated the two smart phones, much to the visual protest of their owners. Sadly with Trey and Dominic around, they knew they couldn't do much to stop Sern as he took the phones into his hand from mid air. "I have a room in the east wing ready for these two." He instructed Dominic and Trey. "I will take them there, but both you and I want to stay at Wolf Coven house in the meantime. I don't want you to leave yet," Sern instructed the towering Prime Wolf.

"Alright ,whatever you want," Trey agreed without hesitation. Dominic already suspected why he wanted them to stay, Likely it was to make sure that they were not going to leave, and have him track them down to block out more memories.

"Afterwards Sern, can I have a talk with you?" Dominic asked the Intendant.

"Yes, just wait for me in my office."

Sern, Connor and Valko went upstairs with the other two. The sheer size of the bottom floors rivals the upstairs levels. There were so many unused rooms, many of which looked like they were fitted for living, they had bunks and washrooms, and it seemed that Wolf Coven

House had a much larger capacity than expected. But as they went upwards, they realized that there was yet another floor of the same design above them, and then another as well. Three full floors of additional living quarters with some large storage room and other multipurpose recreation rooms as well. It seemed to be unnecessarily large, but Dominic and Trey knew that the House was, at one time, designed as a resort rather than a glorified dormitory.

When they reached the main floor, the two wolves proceeded up the stairs to the residential areas, escorted closely by Sern. The place was still full of film equipment but the main entrance was now locked and secured. Sern's words to make sure that the front entrance was not disturbed kept the crew going through side entrances.

"Alright, I'm going to get a bite to eat," Trey said to them as his stomach only started now to growl, but at a volume that they all could hear it.

"I'll join you." Dominic stated, then slowly turned back to look at the two wolves, as he licked his fangs, "unless I can feed on one of these two." Dominic glared at the two wolves, clearly attempting to scare them.

"That won't be necessary, Dominic," Sern put his hand out to stop Dominic, though he suspected that this was done more in jest. "After you're done just meet me at my office."

"Too bad, I don't get to feed on wolf blood that often." Dominic slowly walked away, but not before morphing his eye color to that same blood frenzy red that struck fear into anyone who saw his gaze.

The two left, as Sern turned to Connor and Valko. "You two, follow me," he instructed. After seeing Sern's display of sheer power back in Trey's apartment, the two realized they had little choice but to follow his instructions. To the two of them, they guessed that they would probably be locked in some police station style cell. Instead the door that Sern led them to was that of a rather elegant looking oak door. The door opened automatically, even the door handle turned by itself as he led the two into what looked like an extremely nice looking apartment that was decorated in the standard style to the others like the one that Jett and Paxton were staying at in another wing of the house.

Like all the others, it was rather nicely decorated in the more modern fashion despite the classical style hallways. They grey carpets complemented the steel and white furniture. The kitchen was a few steps higher than the living room, and from what they could see, there were two bedrooms, simple looking but more than what they thought they would be getting in a cell.

"I want you both to stay here while I investigate this little incident. In the mean time, the door and windows are all sealed. I wouldn't bother trying to escape," Sern warned them. Though Connor was clearly still resisting the realism of the moment, Sern could sense that Valko had surrendered already. He could feel that the young Bloodbane was not really afraid, but resigned to do what he was told for the time being.

"Wait, how long are we going to be here for?" Connor called to Sern who approached the door.

"As long as it takes to get the information from you both on why his pack attacked my members," Sern pointed to Valko. Connor was shocked to hear what Sern had just said.

"He what?" Connor stammered to ask, wanting Sern to repeat his words.

"Perhaps he should explain it to you," Sern reiterated as he stepped through the door. When it closed behind him, he made sure that the door was not only solid but also indestructible by infusing the door and the surrounding walls and windows to the apartment with a slight extension of his own intendant power. It would not be possible for them to break through anything.

The two wolves stood there in silence as Connor glared at Valko. Connor's normally friendly and cheerful face was now infused with hatred as his eyes started to shift. Valko sat down on one of the couches, trying to avoid eye contact with Connor. He put his face in his hands as he curled up almost into a ball.

"Spit it out," Connor growled at Valko through the slight emergence of his fangs. Valko was still unwilling to look up There was a sense of true dread that Connor could smell from Valko. As he prowled towards Valko, standing over him, his already clawed hands reached down, and slowly pushed Valko's chin upwards forcing him to look up.

"My pack leader made some deal with this insanely powerful sorcerer or something. I wasn't too sure what he was but he was pretty damned powerful," Valko started as Connor still kept his glare on him. "He said that he would give us as much vampiric blood as we wanted to stop our bloodlust, and we could sell the rest for so much money."

"So what happened?" Connor started to calm down as he sat down next to Valko, listening carefully to what he was saying.

"We were just supposed to ambush and bite two of them, humans apparently, and infect them with the wolf bite. That was it. Just bite them." Valko looked intensely into Connor's eyes. "I only did this because it was what our pack wanted. We don't sell our bite and we don't just give it away, but we were paid this time to bite these two. What happened afterwards we weren't told, and we didn't care. We just wanted the blood."

"Whatever the reason, they now have the two of us. They think I'm in on this with you," Connor sounded like he was complaining more out of inconvenience than anything else.

"I didn't know they would come after me, or you," Valko admitted. He felt that there was nothing else that he could do. "And these Wolf Coven people aren't pushovers. These Wolf Coven people aren't like anything I've ever seen before," Valko warned Connor.

"So where's your pack?"

"Well we returned to the forest where this happened. I was told to stay behind and not enter," Valko reached for his phone, only to remember that Sern had taken them. "And damnit, there was camera footage of what happened on my phone."

"You caught it on camera?"

"No, well, Rake, my alpha connected his camera with my phone and so what his phone recorded, I saw. I saw our Benefactor, which was what he wanted us to call him, do some magic spell that sucked the life right out of the pack, all eleven of them," Valko's brown eyes looked over to Connor. "My pack was killed and I ran away," Connor calmed down enough for his claws to change back into hands.

"So that's why you wanted to join our pack? Because your own was killed?

"Ya," Valko coughed up, his voice trembling slightly from the overwhelming grief of his pack being killed. They were the only family that he had.

"I don't know what I'm going to do with you," Connor leaned back against the sofa. "We, well I can't do anything to help you right now. I just happened to be with you when you were caught by them, so I'm the innocent bystander here who was dragged into this."

"You can't leave me packless. You know what happens to a wolf without a pack?" Valko almost sounded like he was begging for a moment.

"He makes his own! Or he gets killed by hunters," Connor replied. His voice was pretty frustrated with this whole situation, that he was dragged into this by sheer bad luck.

"I don't have what it takes to be an alpha," Valko admitted.

"And you think that my pack will take you in, after you get me kidnapped by these Wolf Coven people?"

"Look, I'm sorry," Valko stood up and looked down at Connor. "I didn't know how to explain to you that my pack had their life drained out of them by some magical monster." he confessed. "It was easier just to lie. I didn't know the two guys we bit were a part of this group. And if you don't take me into your pack, I'll either get killed by hunters or be left alone."

"Maybe you're better off alone," Connor retorted, for a moment seriously hurting Valko. Valko could hear the harsh words almost stabbing his heart like a knife.

Dominic sat and sipped his blood as he watched Trey go through the second half of an entire chicken. He had grabbed it from off the rotisserie spit in the kitchen that the Zombie Crew were working on, with his bare hands no less. He was simply chewing and devouring the thing with his hands, skin and all. Even if Trey was just an ordinary human, his sheer size demanded a huge diet. But since he wasn't human but a Prime Wolf, that hunger would only increase. It wasn't strange to find hunted deer and animals in the forests when werewolves were around since they would feed on those creatures whenever they could.

"Hungry, I see," a familiar form sat down next to Trey with another full chicken on his plate. Trey swallowed the bite that he had just taken and looked up to see Trenton sitting down next to him.

"Well well!" Trey wiped his hands and face with a napkin. "If it isn't my little wolfling."

"Ya, little wolf," Trenton agreed sarcastically.

"Who is bigger anyways?" Dominic asked. The size difference between the two wolves was not that different since they were both Prime Wolves. Trey was certainly older by a few years. He was almost thirty years old whereas Trenton was probably just in his early twenties. That said he could tell that they were Wolf Primes from birth, which accounted for their sheer size. Both were over six feet tall, and easily over 250 pounds of solid muscle each; and with their bodies in such huge proportion, their meals matched them easily.

"Him," Trenton pointed to Trey, as he started to dig into his dinner.

"Wolf Primes don't really get weaker as they age until we pass the century mark," Trey answered as he finished the rest of his meal.

"Must be great for a career in film or modeling," Dominic remarked.

"Look who's talking," Trey smiled at the vampire. "You'll never get old at all, always going to be that chiseled handsome blood drinker," Trey almost sounded like he was flirting for a moment. "Ya know, sometimes I have to admit, I do wonder what it would be like to be you guys." Trey wiped off the grease from his hands as he reached for one of the sanitary hand wipes at the middle of the table. "Using that beautiful excuse, to feed, to bite someone's neck." He smirked at Trenton who nodded in agreement.

"We don't have to do it that way," Dominic sounded almost like he was denying an accusation of excessive lust.

"But I'm sure you don't mind it. Breathing your hot breath against their neck, then sinking your fangs into the flesh of their neck," Trey tempted Dominic.

"Not a bad thing at all," Dominic took a long sip from his own cup, realizing that the very images that they were planting into his head were meant specifically to trigger his vamp face.

"I've never seen you in your full vampiric form before," Trey mentioned almost casually, with a slight hint in his voice that he was actually interested in seeing it.

"If you're talking about our complete and truly demonic form, I don't even think Gavin has changed into that before."

"What's it like?" two more sat down next to them. It was the young lovers, Jett and Paxton. They also had gotten their own dinners, Paxton a nice warm mug of blood, Jett also with a full chicken on his plate. It seemed to be the werewolf meal of choice for the day.

"What are we talking about?" Jett asked as he took a bite out of his chicken.

"Dominic is going to show us his true, and absolutely the most powerful form, the Demon Vampire!" Trey boasted, making Dominic not particularly joyous at the moment of being put on the spot.

"We have a demon form?" Paxton asked as another two joined them at the table.

"Oh yeah, we do." Gavin sat down on Dominic's other side with Cazian also joining them.

"Aren't you guys still filming?" Dominic asked Gavin.

"Break time, one hour," Cazian answered as he sat down next to Trenton, across from Gavin. "So what's this about a demon?" He curiously asked as he crossed his arms casually across his chest.

"Apparently we have some type of demon form!" Paxton repeated, curious to know. After he said that, all eye seemed to turn to Dominic and Cazian, but in particular to Gavin. There was an awkward silence for a moment as they sat waiting for him to speak.

"Well?" Paxton asked. "I think if this kind of demon thing is real, I should know!"

"Yeah, me too!" Jett agreed. "I don't want him to be fucking me, then suddenly turning into a monster and devour me alive," he blurted out without even thinking of what he was saying. This warranted a very awkward look from everyone else, plus a few snickers and giggles. "I mean, devour me alive, in a bad way," he continued to chomp down his food.

"Gavin, I think you should answer this since you actually saw it before," Dominic asked him.

"Alright," Gavin leaned back. "From what I know from my own Sire, Lance, he showed me the form only once, but I would never forget it," he began to explain much to the anticipation of everyone else at the table. They all hushed up, listening carefully to what he was saying. "Our wings, arc actually the first form, second is our skin, then third is everything else. After we get our wings, our skin turns darker, dirtier, almost matted, like it was something between skin and scales. Then, our faces and limbs change to a more demonic form."

"Faces? Like how?" Paxton asked curiously.

"Here," Gavin pointed to his cheek bones right beneath his eyes. "And here," he pointed to his jaw line. "It gets more prominent, ridged and almost jagged. It looks pretty scary actually."

"Yeah what is that about us? Sern mentioned that we were related to demons or something?" Paxton asked.

"Well, again from what my sire taught me, yes, we have a lineage with Demons. Apparently not necessarily all demons are bad; some are just more interested in mingling with humans. Apparently one did, and our entire vampire heritage and bloodline was born. At least that's what I know so far. Sern is the one who really knows more."

"Why would he know?" Paxton asked. "He's not a vampire, at least I don't think he is."

"Honestly, none of us knows what Sern really is, just that he is also an Intendant." Cazian said. "But when our ancestors, the demons and the humans "mingled", the result was us High Orders. Apparently also, they were cursed to never breed, so that's why there are no women High Orders."

"But that didn't stop anyone from siring."

"No. There are also half-breeds, High Order men who had kids with human women."

"Really? So like Blade?" Jett asked curiously.

"Sort of." Gavin answered, with Cazian rolling his eyes at the reference. "They do exist, but they're pretty rare. Most of them want to be fully turned when they get older."

"What about this demon form? Can you transform into it?" Jett pushed.

"Well, when my sire transformed, it was when one of his own childes was killed, meaning you have to be so angry, literally in a state of psychotic rage, so powerful that it triggers our primal form. I have never been that angry before to do that, and let's hope you never do either."

"Why not?" Jett asked again, while taking another bite out of his chicken.

"Because by then, we're not even vampires or part human anymore, we're demons. And good luck reasoning with an enraged demon. It's one of the reasons we have so much mental control, to avoid ever having to go that far."

"I've noticed that," Paxton replied, "I'm much calmer than before. It's like I'm more able to cope with emotional pain."

"That's to enable us to live without the urges and violence that other Orders go through. The trade off is, of course, our bloodlust."

"Every one hundred days?" Paxton clarified in question.

"Yes. And mine will be happening probably next week." Dominic revealed, much to Paxton's surprise. "It's not really a pleasant situation. but it's something that we have to all go through."

"Fascinating," Cazian almost sounded bored out of his mind. He heard all of this before, and that they were all sitting talking about it seemed like a very repetitive situation. But then again he also knew that his brother, Paxton, at least blood brother, had to know this stuff.

"A necessary evil," Dominic continued much to the ignoring of Cazian's statements. "It's something that we cannot avoid, and we have to endure. Over time it gets easier."

It was then, that Sern entered the room to find them sitting there. He approached with almost what seemed like a form of anticipation, but they weren't entirely that sure. Sern wasn't easy to read at the best of times, unlike Intendant Hasaan. He approached their table as Trey pulled up a chair for him. There was an unusual sense of quietness that came over them as Sern sat down.

"On your lunch time, I take it?" He asked Cazian and Gavin.

"Yeah, we already had something to eat, so then they're going to spend another half an hour after that setting up the next scene." Gavin explained to him.

"And how are the two wolves?" Dominic asked Sern.

"They're calming down right now in their own quarters. I've made sure they're going to stay there quietly," Sern answered.

"Which two wolves?" Jett asked as he finished off his chicken dinner.

"We're just settling a dispute between two packs. A Bloodbane wolf and a Packwalker wolf."

"Ah. Could we meet them later?" Jett asked curiously wondering about the other werewolves.

"It could be possible," Sern suggested to him, "though I prefer to settle this dispute before things go any further. There's a chance they may decide to stay here."

"And what of, certain records?" Dominic suggested to Sern, with especial emphasis on the word "records" in the tone of his voice.

"Everything will be cleared up later," Sern answered firmly giving notice to Dominic that another full memory block would have to take place. "And as for the film crew, I told the director he has forty-eight hours to complete all the shooting around here, after that everything has to go."

"Why so soon?" Paxton asked.

"This is a coven house, not a movie studio," Sern asserted simply. "We have situations here which are best kept out of camera view, so I am only allowing them to stay for a short time. Also that they just decided to show up without telling us that they were coming didn't fit well with me."

Paxton and Jett were going up the stairs to their room where they were going to get changed before heading to the gym. As the did, they noticed another man coming down the hallway. He was taller than both of them, but only just. Very average height for a man who looked maybe early 30s at most. His blond, almost strawberry blond hair was perfectly combed and he wore a red dress shirt underneath a stylish vest and black dress pants. Paxton didn't even ask Jett what his scent was, and already assumed he was a vampire, just by the fashionable clothes he was wearing.

"Hey!" Jett greeted, as they approached their apartment door as the guy was approaching.

"Hello," he returned with the same level of kindness that Jett greeted him with.

"I'm Jett, and this is Paxton. We're new here." Paxton held out his hand.

"I'm Arthur," he gently shook their hands in greeting. "So how long have you both been here?" he asked. Paxton and Jett noticed he had a very kind and gentle smile.

"About a few weeks. The week before Halloween was when we arrived." Paxton looked to Jett for some confirmation on the information he was giving out.

"Sounds about right." Jett agreed.

"So I'm going to guess..." Arthur gently started to rub his chin, observing the two of them carefully. "Don't tell me what you are." He smiled as he started eyeing Paxton. The thick dark hair, the chiseled sculpted smile and face, the elegant demeanor. "You're a vampire too?" He pointed at Paxton with one eyebrow raised, wondering if he was right, in the form of a question and statement. Paxton nodded in agreement. "A Drake?" Arthur guessed again. This time Paxton had to shake his head at the wrong answer. "Wait, no, a High Order?" Arthur guessed, this time surprised at Paxton nodding for a yes. "Wow, don't get to see many new High Orders."

"Gavin said that not many new ones are made these days."

"I guess he could make dozens if he wanted to, but they just don't do it that often."

"What are you?" Jett asked.

"If you're what I think you are, you should be able to guess that." Arthur suggested to the two of them.

"Vampire! Drake too!" Jett guessed. A smile came across Arthur's face.

"Very good. That werewolf nose works for you, smell any blood on me?"

"No, it's just your style of clothing, very slick and cool." Jett held onto Paxton's arm.

"I wouldn't have guessed you for a werewolf." Arthur admitted. "You're much smaller than the other wolves here, which means that you're not a Prime, and you're at least so far, gentle, not aggressive." Paxton and Jett looked towards each other.

"Actually I am a prime wolf." Jett smiled.

"A transformed prime? Wouldn't have been my first guess, I would have thought a Packwalker or Bloodbane first," Arthur admitted.

"We're going to get a workout. Care to join us?" Paxton offered.

"No, I was going to go speak to Sern," Arthur declined politely.

"Alright. See you around," Jett said as he entered their apartment.

"See you!" Paxton also saluted as he went into their rooms.

Sern approached the room where he secured Valko and Connor. As he did, around the corner came Arthur. Sern hadn't seen Arthur since the last full moon. The handsome, very stylishly dressed Drake Vampire was certainly not someone that you would miss seeing if he passed by.

"Ah, Sern," Arthur greeted. "We haven't been formally introduced."

"Well, I'm aware of your record, Arthur Randolph, Drac, or Drake Vampire, closing on 200 years of age and resident here." Sern recalled from his memory of the files he had memorized.

"Well, I think I look good for two centuries."

"Yes," Sern opened the door. Arthur couldn't help but curiously take a peek inside the apartment to see a young man sitting at the kitchen table. He had dark hair similar to Paxton, but he was definitely a werewolf; and from the sight of him, he couldn't have been much older than just fresh out of high school. The young man looked up, only to catch a glimpse, at first, of Arthur. His wolf eyes focused more and so did his ears, onto his face and voice, and right there his memories were triggered. That face and that voice were the same as what was on his camera phone, of that Sorcerer or wizard or demon that killed his pack!

"I'll leave you to your business," Arthur smiled as he walked away, and Sern stepped into the apartment, then sealed the door behind him.

"Who was that?!" Valko demanded, his fangs and claws starting to emerge. Sern was puzzled at his reaction to his presence until he realized he was referring to Arthur. He instinctively charged towards the doorway, claws and fangs and fur already fully raised, ready for battle, but Sern stopped him with only one hand that held him back just below the neck. Sern wasn't trying to squeeze the air out of him, but just to hold him back. Sern's grip was like steel and he was completely unmovable as he gently pushed him back, his eyes flared with the same light, instantly calming down the wolf.

"Calm yourself," Sern's eyes glowed with intense light. It was enough to infuse Valko with a sense of calm. "That was just one of our wolf coven members," Sern dismissively stated as he walked up and sat down at the same table as the now-almost-fully- morphed Valko. Despite his earlier shyness and fear, he was now standing over Sern, with his claws and facial ridges, fangs and all fully ready. Sern didn't even seem to react in the slightest as Valko gave a deep growl at him. "Sit down, please," Sern stated firmly.

"What's going on?" Connor asked as he came out of his room, stretching slightly from what could only have been a nap.

"Do you have our phones on you?" Valko snarled at Sern.

"Yes, but I want some questions answered first," The Intendant started.

"Look, I have video footage on my phone that can tell you everything!" Valko roared impatiently at the Intendant who looked up, slightly firmly at him for a moment, more like he wanted Valko to calm down.

"You had video footage of your pack getting killed?" Sern asked again.

"Yes! The reason I survived was for insurance. My Alpha, Rake, wanted me to make sure if anything happened to them, others would find out." Valko pointed to Sern, almost like he was assuming that Sern had the phones on him.

Sern cooperated with the young wolf's demand and reached into the pocket of his robe, and pulled out the two smart phones that were inside. Valko snatched his and started to press a few buttons and scroll through the touch screens, finding the video player and the file.

"Here!" He put the phone on the table, and started the video, which was more than five minutes long.

The video footage was surprisingly clear, a testament to camera quality on phones these days. Sern watched as the pack traced their trail back to the opening in the forest, the same one that he would later find Jett. The being that he battled there had his face concealed, and he couldn't fully see the identity, but this time he saw it. Arthur's face was unmistakably obvious, as were his clothes, but his eyes were not the same. As he spoke, his voice was also slightly different, to the point where only an Intendant would notice. There was something else speaking within him. Sern watched as the words came out; the voice spoke but it wasn't truly him. The intention and inflections weren't Arthur's. Then the being that was Arthur, used some sort of spell, that was ripping out and stealing the life force from the pack after he immobilized all eleven of them. Sern could tell that this was more than just sorcery, and that they were not dealing with any normal magic user.

Then the camera got a glimpse of another being behind Arthur, something very enigmatic and immediately unworldly. A being who resembled the shape of a human but had skin that was almost made out of metal and glass plates that hovered around a human-like shape, but inside his body featured a glowing core of purple, almost dark shadowy like energy and gas that was contained by these hovering shards and plates. Even in Sern's own experience and knowledge, he hadn't ever seen something like this before.

"We were promised a lot of vampire blood for what we were hired to do, just attack a few campers; we didn't know they were Wolf Coven members. And for the amount of blood they were offering to us, we would have done anything." Valko admitted, as his face and fangs slowly receded back to normal. He sat down again, after standing over the phone screen with the others, as he sank again into depression. "He called that guy the Benefactor." Valko admitted with great reluctance in his voice, reluctant to admit it to himself that such an obvious question he didn't even think of at the time.

"So this is how your pack was killed?" Connor folded his arms across his chest, still looking disappointedly at Valko.

"It was his pack leader's decision." Sern defended Valko. "And that life siphoning technique, I've never seen it used to that extent. That was more than just a spell."

"So what are you going to do with us?" Valko asked almost afraid of the answer.

"If this video evidence is true, I will have to investigate more on the matter. But I cannot allow you both to leave this place, otherwise you will put yourselves and in your case, Connor, your pack, in danger."

"I had nothing to do with this!" Connor growled as he clenched his fists.

"But you're involved in it now," Sern stated firmly. Connor's eyes focused on Valko as they started to shift, as he grabbed Valko up by his shirt, then shoved him against a wall. Valko, also enraged by this shifted forms too, the two wolves pitched against each other.

"I didn't know what that thing was, and I didn't know what it was going to do to us." Valko snarled back. The two of them looked equally matched in size and strength so Sern wasn't going to guess who would win in a fight.

"Calm yourselves," Sern stated bluntly to the two of them, as he simply separated them by slamming them against the opposite sides of the room and held them there by an unseen force."Unfortunately I can't let you both get out of control for the time being," Sern grabbed Valko and put him onto the couch, then pulled Connor onto the other. They were still transformed, but found that they couldn't move their hands or feet, but they could still turn their heads and look around and talk.

"What are you going to do?" Valko almost croaked as he strained to look up. The invisible restraints around him were keeping him completely still.

"Going to make sure you don't cause anymore trouble for the time being. You'll just go to sleep until I can figure out this situation." Sern tapped Connor on his forehead. Instantly the wolf fell completely limp and unconscious without hesitation. His werewolf features were slowly transforming back to human.

"Wait. You can't just trap us here like this!" Valko begged.

"It's only a temporary measure, and I can't let either of you leave or spread this information around." Sern slowly walked over. "I sympathize. But you can't join his pack either. You're a Bloodbane wolf and they are Packwalkers; they won't accept you."

"I have nowhere else to go," Valko sounded like he was on the edge of tears.

"You can stay here, at Wolf Coven House. That's our purpose," Sern offered. "But I have to clear up this situation first. And if that being that killed your pack is out there, we will find it," Sern assured him as he brought his hand to Valko's head.

"Wait!" Valko almost yelled out. Sern's hand stopped for a moment, waiting for him to finish his thoughts. "When you find that thing, I want to be there when you kill it," he asked, his almost puppy dog eyes were begging for a yes answer from Sern. Sern thought deeply for a moment.

"Assuming that we do, then yes, I will allow that," Sern answered. Valko relax for a moment, almost like he was preparing for being locked in sleep. Sern's finger touched his forehead and instantly Valko fell asleep. Sern got up and left the room, but again not before he again sealed the entire room just as an added precaution against escape or intrusion. He now realized he had more to deal with as he shoved the two phones into his pocket again.

He knew that first and foremost, he had to backup the data that was on the phone; this video evidence was vital and had to be stored and backed up. He couldn't and wouldn't trust such valuable evidence to anyone else. Sern headed directly to his office. He wanted to re-examine the video footage as well, to make sure that what he saw was real, that it was Arthur's face.

Sealing the room once again as he entered his office, Sern secured it. His console atop his desk activated on his mental command and started to scan the phone's storage data. Every single 0 and 1 in binary code was scanned and recorded into the console as he placed it atop the table. The glowing holographic display was very clear to him what it showed, that it was not tampered or edited footage, simply just the raw recording. He replayed the footage again, this time from a much larger display. The clarity of the footage was quite admirable even for human technology.

The face was, without question, Arthur's face. However, the odd thing about this was that it also recorded some audio, and from what Sern could tell of the voice, it was similar to Arthur's but not quite his voice. Earlier when he had seen Arthur outside the door of Valko and Connor's rooms, he didn't sense or notice anything out of the ordinary. He didn't sense or detect any deception or nervousness. In fact, he seemed perfectly normal despite what Sern would have expected if he was trying to conceal anything.

As he went frame by frame on the display, watching the abilities that this being, who was apparently Arthur, possessed. It was some type of siphoning ability, far more potent than just a simple spell. In his own experience through the reading of many thousands of archives and tomes and records of Sanctuary operatives and their experience, he had only heard of vague references to this type of ability, all of which were forms of magic. Sucking the life force out of others in order to gain strength was something not unlike that of a vampire's hunger for blood. But this was usually to take more than just blood, but life force itself. It was only slightly effective and wouldn't be considered reliable if used on humans, with unknown effects if used on werewolves.

Sern immediately uploaded this data to Sanctuary, back at Aurastar and to specifically to Superintendent Lya and Archon Alena. He also sent it to Intendant Hasaan as an extra precaution just to get their input on whatever they had to offer in terms of information. Sern suspected that if this was indeed a magical form of life-draining, it was well beyond those of a human magic practitioner. He knew it was possible for an Intendant or someone infused with Va'Nai strength to do this, but with their near- immortal status and their sheer vast amount of power, it seemed to be completely unnecessary.

Sern wasn't entirely sure on what to do, as he slumped down into his seat. First and foremost, he had to summon Arthur into the office to perform a full mind-check on him to make sure that he was who he said he was.

Sern turned to the digital display on the side of his desk which was that of a human style computer, highly primitive but still able to do what he needed. He looked up Arthur's phone number and entered a text message. "Report to my office immediately, please. - Sern" Simple and straight forward.

About twenty seconds later three letters appeared on the reply display, "OMW" it read. It took Sern a moment to realize what this meant - on my way. Human use of wording and shortcuts in speech were very puzzling, but Sern only figured that with time he would learn what they meant.

A moment later, there was a knock on the door. Sern instinctively opened the doors with a mere telekinetic thought from his mind. The two huge oak doors slowly opened by an unseen force. Arthur stood waiting.

"Please, come sit," Sern welcomed him as he stepped in. Arthur was somewhat curious to why he was summoned. The look was obvious on his face.

"So, what's new Sern? I didn't have much time to talk to you since you replaced Hasaan." Arthur sat down across from Sern at his desk.

"That is true. I have had some interesting business to attend to. But I have also some questions for you to answer, please," Sern got right to business.

"Alright," Arthur replied casually.

"Where were you and what were you doing on October 30th?" Sern asked directly.

"Oh" Arthur tilted his head back for a moment as he tried to recall. The question wasn't quite something he was prepared for. "Day before Halloween?" Arthur asked openly, not really expecting an answer. "That morning I was here, stayed overnight from the night before, and in the morning I had breakfast and simply went back to bed. For some reason, I remember, I was really tired so I went back to bed."

"Do you remember what time you woke up and went back to bed?" Sern asked carefully.

"I think it was around 9:30 or so in the morning that I went back to my room. I didn't even wake up until almost 3 in the afternoon. I'm fairly certain since I wanted to get back to town before the evening." Arthur replied, fairly confident in his words.

"And you don't recall anything else significant happening?" Sern asked as he kept a watch on every expression that Arthur had. Sern's eyes, and ears, and even nose were focused on Arthur's reactions, but nothing at all was remotely out of the ordinary.

"No, I just remembered that I went back to bed, I didn't get undressed or anything, I just collapsed onto the bed and I think I fell asleep until mid afternoon," Arthur thought carefully to his memory. "No, that was pretty much it, just a nap, then later I went back to my apartment in town."

"What did you do for the rest of the day?" Sern inquired. He recalled that the video file was made at 1:20pm, after lunch and easily during the time that Arthur was asleep. Sern was reading through

Arthur's thoughts every time he spoke, through a subtle and weaker mindlink but he couldn't find anything deceptive. Arthur was telling the truth, or at least the truth to the best of his knowledge. He couldn't hear any symptoms of deception or anything visually, or even his scent. Even vampires would give off signals if they were lying. Sern couldn't pick up a single hint. It wasn't even as though Arthur was lying, it's that Arthur was completely unaware. His hands were folded on his lap, his breathing normal, everything was normal. Even the best liar couldn't fool a mindlink.

"Well, it was going to be Halloween so I figured I would avoid the crowds and just stay home. I love watching the festivities from my apartment, but not participating in them you know. Halloween is just one of those holidays where I prefer solitude."

"Wouldn't you have had more solitude here?" Sern wondered why someone would go to a city to be left alone.

"Yes and no, my apartment in town is mine; my apartment here is still not really a home for me," Arthur explained. Sern never quite understood this concept of a home quite yet. "So Sern, what's this about?" Arthur asked. Sern wasn't too sure if he was going to reveal the information that he had yet. He knew that he had to sort things out with not just Valko and Connor, but also with Trey and Dominic, since they also now knew about the Transmogrification spell that they used.

"I can't explain right now, but I have to insist that you stay at Wolf Coven House for the time being." Sern sounded quite regretful in giving this request.

"Can't leave?" Arthur asked.

"I'm afraid not, until further notice. I have some important issues to clear up that sadly do involve you."

"What did I do?" Arthur asked, sounding quite worried.

"Again I can't say for the time being, but I will tell you." Arthur gave out a deep sigh. His face was justifiably frustrated at the thought of being restrained.

"Alright, but I want to know before day's end," Arthur demanded firmly to the Intendant.

"That I can't fully promise you," Sern excused. "But I can try."

"Fine," Arthur stood up.

"Unfortunately to make sure, I have to place you on lockdown, but you can still go about the property."

"Yeah, whatever," Arthur turned around and headed to the doors.

"Arthur, believe me when I say, when I explain this all to you, you'll understand," Sern stated as Arthur opened the doors, which Sern made no effort to restrain. He knew from what he could read inside Arthur's mind that he wouldn't make any effort to escape or leave. He was disappointed and frustrated at the lack of information that he got but Arthur wasn't one to cause trouble.

Sern looked at the display to his console which he now searched for the potential hazards of additional mind blocks, especially ones that were so soon after the previous ones. He thought carefully through his mind first before initiating contact with Adjustor Shamaran. He wasn't entirely sure about the consequences of another mind block so soon but he knew that he had to consider something. The last one he was foolish enough not to have expanded the range, and as a result lives could be completely ruined, and then there was the issue of Arthur to add on top of this.

Sern had to think carefully since he could not detect anything wrong in Arthur's memory. Perhaps the Adjustors could find something he couldn't. Either way it was important for him to contact them immediately.

As Sern's weighing of the pros and cons of the situation were teetering like a scale in his mind he knew what he had to do.

"Adjustor Shamaran here," the visual display showed the Adjustor's face; in the background was that glowing crystalline background of Aurastar that was a familiar sight to Sern.

"I'm sorry to interrupt you, Adjustor," Sern began with an apology. "But I am inquiring as to how effective or dangerous an additional memory block would be if performed so soon after the previous one."

"What types of memory would you want altered?" the Adjustor asked from his side of the screen.

"Short term mainly, like the last ones."

"Well, if they were human I would be highly against it. To alter memories in a human mind, with their limited healing abilities, would be dangerous if they didn't have a minimum of three months to recover. Are these Supernaturals we are talking about?" The Adjustor asked.

"Yes, one Bloodbane wolf, one Packwalker, one Prime and a High Order vampire."

"Are you sure this is all?" Adjustor Shamaran asked seemingly wanting Sern to recall in detail and considering the consequences of his actions.

"Actually I would prefer a massive wide-scale memory block to eliminate any chance of someone slipping through."

"How massive are we talking about?"

"I would estimate at least within a 250 kilometer radius of the main city." Sern estimated.

"With millions of minds, that would take a team of a hundred Adjustors of my skill. Simply put, Sern, for the time being it can't be done."

"It would cover all loose ends," Sern stated.

"No, to cover all loose ends you'd have to do a planetary memory block of more than 7 billion minds, and to that we would need something the size of a Va'Nai city ship to amplify our efforts enough. Again Sern, can't be done. What I can do is come and do the memory block within a few kilometres or so of Wolf Coven House again."

"I'm guessing that the enhanced healing abilities of our residents make this more possible to do more frequently?"

"Yes, of course. It's like minor brain surgery. All of them are easily able to heal and not notice a thing."

"Another thing that I have to ask you, how good are you at detecting foreign memory blocks?"

"Foreign? I would have to take a look first if you don't mind."

"Of course."

"My team and I will be there within the hour, Sern." The Adjustor declared.

"Thank you for your prompt timing," Sern thanked his compatriot.

"For convenience, we will have to do this within an enhanced time dilation field."

"Slowing down the time flow in our local area?" Sern asked to clarify what the Adjustor wanted to do. "Isn't that rather, drastic?" Sern was slightly concerned about the suggestion.

"Just a suggestion, but I don't think there is a need for that," the Adjustor recanted his previous statement. "Maybe just temporarily freezing them would be better, to leave no suspicion of anything. We can find the details when I arrive."

"Very well, the portal will signal me when you arrive." Sern thanked the Adjustor as the display closed down. He was fairly sure that the Adjustors would clear up the situation as well as help him investigate what Arthur's memory had that he wasn't aware of.

Sern had gathered Trey, Dominic, Arthur and the sleeping Valko and Connor in one of the isolation rooms that normally was used by wolves during full moon. The two wolves were still unconscious, quietly sleeping. He remembered that Dominic and Trey wanted to talk to him. He knew it was about the memory blocks, but considering the delicate matter of the situation, Sern didn't want to waste time with repetitive discussions.

Sern wanted to make sure that they were in an area that was not going to be commonly disturbed. The Adjustor, and his team of five had arrived just as they did a few days earlier. Trey, Dominic and Arthur couldn't recall ever having met these other Sanctuary officials, but that was by design. Adjustors were not meant to be remembered, and their presence was always erased from the minds of those who they encountered, just to make sure that there was no suspicion of any memory modification.

The other three who were awake were none too pleased to see more Sanctuary officials arriving, especially in this abundance.

"So what's this about?" Trey asked impatiently. Valko and Connor were asleep on the bed that was used in the room for normal resting time for lunar cycle werewolves, not moving, just gently breathing.

"It won't make much of a point to explain since you won't remember," Sern created some orbs of light in his hand, which were about the size of golf balls. They shot out towards Dominic, Trey and Arthur, gently entering their bodies in silent motion, then knocking them unconscious. The other Adjustors caught them and gently lay them on the ground.

"Standard memory containment?" One of them asked Shamaran. Adjustor Shamaran turned to Sern for an answer.

"My mind has the instructions and details." Sern answered for him, as his own eyes started to glow in that typical mindlink trademark form that many had now gotten used to seeing. All of the others also connected with each other in a group mindlink. The instructions were being related mentally, in all forms and details, sights and sounds, specific instructions all done in an instant without the need to explain verbally. Sern wanted all knowledge of this being's attack on the Bloodbane pack blocked, Valko's survival was also to be blocked, Valko and Connor's entire friendship, memories of each other, all thoughts to be blocked. To add to that Dominic and Trey's own encounters and experiences in the past few days, were to be blocked.

Arthur wasn't aware of any transmogrification spell or any Bloodbane Wolves. He himself was only just aware of Paxton and Jett, and Jett was already a prime wolf so it seemed rather unusual that he was present.

The team proceeded with the alterations, almost like they were filing information, mentally. Selecting and slicing up thoughts, categorizing them and then putting them in a corner of the mind, blocking it off with a barrier. It was quite literally a mental renovation and re-categorization. They could not eliminate memories or remove them but blocking them was just as effective and without the traceable hints of anything left in their minds and with only five people here, four of which were to have their memories changed; this was a rather fast task.

From what Sern could tell earlier from his searching through Connor's mind, he told the truth when he said he didn't tell his pack he was meeting with Valko; in fact, they didn't even know he was gone or had any encounters with this Bloodbane. From Valko's own mind they could tell that his pack had made no encounters with anyone when they were in this area but then one name and thought popped into the Adjustor's mind who wasn't present.

"Lucas!" Sern blurted out as he monitored their progress. "Trey used him as a source as they were finding Valko, he's aware that Lucas is a Bloodbane."

"We'll find him. Red Moon Bar is where he works." Adjustor Shamaran recalled out of Trey's mind. "My team will block his memories too after we're done here."

"And him?" Sern asked as Adjustor Shamaran was concentrating on Arthur. He seemed to find something interesting in Arthur.

"This is very interesting." The Adjustor turned to Sern.

"What is?" Sern probed.

"His memory is indeed blocked by the use of a divine force." The Adjustor gazed into Arthur's mind which was projected to them in a form of various swirls and colors that hovered above Arthur's head.

"Elaborate please." Sern requested of the Adjustor.

"Well, as I said before, and you know, memories can't be erased, but they can be blocked. So his were also blocked. But it wasn't Va'Nai power that did this, it was that of a divine and another power.."

"Divine power?" Sern grew increasingly concerned with this new evidence.

"Yes, and the only sources of divine power are deities, or gods." the Adjustor declared.

"So a god did this to him?"

"Yes. And at least another power, even higher than a deity" The Adjustor "But I can't access those memories."

"Even you can't access the blocked memories?" Sern was growing more concerned at this fact.

"No, the memories were blocked by two forms of power, divine and another unknown. I already broke through the divine barrier, but this other memory block I can't break through."

"You're one of our Adjustors, how can there be a form of memory block that you can't access?" Sern almost demanded from the Adjustor.

"I don't know, I have to take him back with us to Aurastar to do more investigating on this. I have never encountered any form of memory block I couldn't break," Shamaran stated with as much frustration in his voice as Sern.

"Then what did you find in the deity blocked areas?"

"Apparently he was taken control by a deity. Hypnos, the god of sleep. But after that, there was nothing else that I could find."

"How did you find the name? His identity?"

"It's a remnant, like an echo. The god's own presence was there and I could sense some of the remaining thoughts that were in Arthur's mind."

"Explain," Sern demanded.

"It's strange. If you do a link now, you will see some remaining memories that somehow weren't fully blocked. Naturally when Arthur was possessed, the being that did it was self-aware. Some of that "first person" perspective is still there, and that includes what he called himself, his name."

"So he was possessed and then everything was out of his control?" Sern asked.

"It would appear so," the Adjustor answered back, trying to organize what he found.

"Do what you have to. It's best that perhaps Arthur isn't here for the time being. Take him with you then," Sern admitted. despite the fear that if there was something even the Adjustors couldn't find out, then it was truly something that would warrant his concern.

"I will get to the bottom of this, Sern," the Adjustor turned to his team that was already finishing up with the others present.

"We will go and find this Lucas," one of them reported to Adjustor Shamaran and Sern. "And we will return Connor to his home."

"Do what you must," Sern turned around and headed out of the room. He knew that the Adjustors would be able to handle the rest of the situation fine; but this mental block which was unbreakable to Adjustor Shamaran, was something of great concern to him. To an intendant, or for that matter, any Sanctuary field operative, the unknown was never a welcome guest.

To compound this frustration, he now knew that there was a divine entity, the god of sleep no less, present that was causing some sort of disturbance, and then it made sense to him. The transmogrification spell wouldn't be possible for a human, but a god certainly could do it. Sern's interruption may have endangered Jett's life, but at least he remedied the situation.

At least for the time being, the memories of everyone were now safe and secure, that life could return to normal at Wolf Coven House. But until the film crew were done with their project at the house, nothing was going to be quite normal.

Chapter 26

The production had taken two of the ballrooms as studios. In fact, most of the members of Wolf Coven House called these two ballrooms the "studio" rooms. They were fitted to be filmed in, despite the rarity of them being used as such. Sern wasn't exactly fond of the idea of a large film crew present at Wolf Coven House. Despite his personal opinion, he did allow for some exceptions, especially since the crew rudely moved right in without notifying Sern. His own personal civility allowed him to permit this, as a single exception.

Sern takes a slow sip of the bitter smelling brown brew within the mug that one the assistants handed him. It was hot and gave a slight sting to his fingers, then his palm, as he grasped it. Always interested in trying new things, it was a little strange for him to taste it. Coffee, he thought to himself, was such an unusual substance, especially to drink. Its caffeine levels were far too high for regular consumption, though that didn't seem to worry those around him who always had a cup of it. He sat behind Sir Hugo, who was staring with a dedicated focus towards the two large monitors in front of him.

The concept of acting, for Sern, was an unusual one, people actually deliberately pretending to be something they are not. In this case he could understand a more practical reason; the deliberate deception was double-sided. He had to admire some of the cunning and economics of the situation; what better way to portray accurate supernatural beings on a television show than to use real supernatural beings? It seemed rather cunning since the birth of this media empire that RedCo had founded based on the Eternal Knight's franchise of novels, then turned into a television series with three spin off series all with top ratings, and billions of dollars now in merchandise and fan materials, RedCo and the Eternal Knights business were flourishing. That huge profit was funneled back into the Sanctuary Organization to be used to maintain their network of safe houses and Coven Houses.

Sern watched as they rehearsed the scene. Cazian and Gavin looked quite good on the screen, the lighting was made especially to make them look far paler than normal. He noticed this came from a special covering on the lens of the camera. He never appreciated the details of such a scene that would take hours to do, despite having only taking up a few seconds to minutes on screen. He had little concern over the dialogue; in fact, it was what he preferred deliberately to ignore.

Sern watched as Gavin and Cazian did their lines, then according to the script, Gavin was supposed to bite his friend, and that was something even Sern found awkward to see, let alone have them rehearse it over the past few hours, and then wait for additional close up shots. This was the seventh time they had to do the scene, and even by now, Sern himself had almost memorized the entire dialogue, something he preferred not to have to think about. It was also somewhat difficult for Gavin to keep his "vampire" face and wings active for such a long time, something he didn't show that often. Of course for makeup and wardrobe, these were slightly more nightmarish than they had hoped.

Gavin stood there, in all his mighty "undead" glory, the black leather trench coat was something he seriously had preferred not to wear if he had anything to do with it. It was thick, hot and didn't breathe well, making him sweat. The makeup and hair ladies were pampering him up, making sure that every curl in his black hair was perfect, every possible blemish was covered up and despite the coloration of the lenses, his skin was almost as white as alabaster.

"You know, this stuff will take me almost an hour to get off my face," he whimpered as Sern walked up to him, with a smirk on his face. Seeing his friend like this was certainly something he had never quite expected. The bleached blond girl who was doing his makeup was almost relentlessly scanning every part of his face looking for anything to cover up.

"Yeah, well part of the job right?" She giggled, betraying a slightly smitten attitude towards the six foot four figure in front of her. Her tattooed eyebrows furrowed slightly as she finally gave a wink of confirmation. "Perfect!" She smiled.

"The makeup or me?" Cazian called over from a few feet away, he too, going under the same type of scrutiny, this time with the fake bite marks on his neck that looked surprisingly real. This time he had an entire crew of special effects artists around him, strategically pouring and painting blood into his entire left side of his neck. The dyed corn syrup was sticky, and Sern could tell just from Cazian's facial expressions as the goo started to go down his neck and onto his shirt. The grimace and discomfort was something he certainly didn't like, but he knew he had to suck it in since this was what he was getting five digits a week for. "Geez, this stuff is nasty." He complained, though with a professional smile on his face.

"You know if I had really bitten you, that would look a lot worse," Gavin commented as the crew finished with him.

"Yeah, I know, remember?" Cazian gave Gavin a slightly dirty look reminding him that, yes, that situation had indeed happened before since Gavin was Cazian's maker. That type of expression that only signaled a far deeper, almost epic storyline that only time could reveal. "Nearly bit my neck off," Cazian groaned. Cazian was always one to have a self-depreciating self of humour that helped him deal with certain issues. It was a standard giveaway that he would always mock what made him uncomfortable, especially if it was a topic about him.

"All right, guys, be ready in five!" the pushy butch first assistant director came around the corner, always firmly established in the world of business as a no-nonsense caretaker of the set. Cazian always wondered why almost every single first AD on every set he was on, was always a lesbian if it was a woman. It was a very strange cultural stereotype with film. On that note, he always wondered why every male in wardrobe, hair or makeup was definitely gay. "Alright, everyone, first team in five!" She called back into her radio, rushing back to the set as fast as she marched to the area.

"You liking this dialogue?" Cazian asked Sern, who was still holding his mug of coffee while at the same time showing absolutely no interest in it.

"It's fascinating. I have to be honest; I never anticipated that you would feel that way about your situation," Sern answered with a mode of emotion that was about equal to that of a stalk of celery.

"You do know I didn't write this stuff," Cazian reiterated to the young Intendant.

"I'm aware of that. It just seems that the dialogue seems to be meant to evoke a certain emotional appeal from those who seem to lack emotional development of their own."

"That's a fairly accurate way of putting it," Gavin snickered, amused by Sern's extensive and wordy vocabulary.

The makeup crew finished putting the last touches on Gavin's wings. The enormous dragon-like wings spread out as Gavin stretched them showing a wingspan more than twelve feet across. Their size was amazing in concert with the fact that the clothes that Gavin was given to wear made him look like some sort of dark angel. Cazian also expanded his just to stretch them for a moment. It was quite a satisfying stretch considering he didn't expand his wings that often.

As the makeup procedure kept going, adding some tonal highlights to the skin colour and blending them in, a pair of prop guys came up to Cazian. They were dressed in the typical style of crew members, in a style that lacked any style whatsoever. They looked like they just got out of bed, which again, was not uncommon considering the fourteen-hour days that they worked. One carried with him an obsidian looking box, which was going to be used in the upcoming scene. Cazian got a good look at it from a distance with his enhanced vision. It was a box about the size of a package of cigarettes, which fit into the palm of one's hand, being made out of a black almost obsidian coating. It had ridges like it was made of obsidian, and unusually realistic in its texture, not like the usual props that were rubber or plastic.

"Alright, with this we have a special effect put into it." The taller prop man introduced. "It's rigged to be smashed so when you throw it on the ground it will shatter; so be careful," He handed the small box over to Cazian. "Once you do, the smoke will automatically release," Cazian took a good look at it.

"Wow, you guys really went out of your way with the quality on this thing," he started looking at it from other angles and really did admire the almost authentic looking craftsmanship. "It looks almost real."

"We go for the best, since it's going to be featured up close in the scene, we have to make this one extra special. The others are made out of black resin and rubber for stunts, if we need to go that far."

"Doubt it." Gavin replied as the makeup artists finished with him. "Considering the scenes for those have already been shot with the doubles." Gavin remembers doing a few previous scenes with the double cubes; they were made out of black rubber and weren't nearly as detailed as this one. They were also bouncy something that was relatively amusing in the stunt scenes since the box was supposed to be made out of obsidian and should shatter if dropped.

"Alright, people. Second team out, first team in!" The AD called through the radio. The two of them were rushed off to the set. Sern took his position again behind the director and script supervisor, behind the twin high definition monitors that were now showing the stand-ins being replaced by Sern and Cazian.

Sern shut off his hearing to the script and lines that Sern and Cazian were rehearsing. He was so glad that he had that ability, considering that the dialogue was meant clearly for an age group and gender group who made a latest "tween vampire" sensation and a New York Times Best Seller. It was something that Sern preferred not to have to endure since this Eternal Knight's franchise was riding entirely on the coat tails of the "tween sparkly vampire" craze.

The scene is that of an intensive confrontation between Cazian and Gavin; Gavin tries to take the wooden box from Cazian in the scene. Cazian smashes open the box, and the smoke, representing a demon, escapes into Cazian's body, putting him into a coma, and thus starting the season on a cliffhanger. The summary in Sern's mind sufficiently described the situation of what was going on.

Sern could tell from the dialogue that they were preparing for the action and special effects shot. He watched the monitors as Gavin tried to reach for the box that was in Cazian's hand. Cazian blocked Gavin's hand and threw the box to the ground and it shattered. Thanks to the art of multiple cameras for these types of shots, they managed to catch all sorts of angles. The sacred box fell to the ground and shattered like glass, and just as expected on queue, the smoke effect came on. The black vapor was almost alive the way it swirled out of the ground and up towards Cazian's face. There wasn't much in terms of detail, but later in post production they would enhance, but he did notice a natural glare of silver in Cazian's eyes, as it was depicted within the script that he was to show some sign that an entity of sorts entered Cazian's body through his eyes.

"Cut!" Sir Hugo yelled as the bells rang through the studio signaling a "cut" command.

Cazian gasped for a few moments, then coughed a bit from the smoke. It was amazing he didn't cough at all during that dead space between the smoke entering him and the "cut" command being called. He struggled to his feet for a second, but then brushed off the discomfort and headed back to his seat as the stand-ins came and took their last positions.

"So how did you like your first tour of our day jobs?" Gavin asked as he sat down on chair, specially made for comfort.

"Interesting, a great deal more tedious than I thought. I never knew it took roughly a week to film just forty-three minutes for a television show," Sern stated with a humbling sense of little interest in his voice. Gavin and Cazian could tell he was simply being polite. They knew very well that this was not his particular cup of tea, or coffee, in today's case.

"Maybe you'll let them film here more often?" Gavin suggested. "I mean it's easy for me to get to work this way." He smiled at the Intendant.

"We will see," Sern remarked back.

"Well Sern? What do you think?" Sir Hugo asked the Intendant as he slipped off his headphones.

"Interesting," Sern stated with the tiniest hint of enthusiasm.

"Oh, come now, certainly you can appreciate this art form?" the young director insisted as they replayed the scene.

"I can certainly appreciate the art, yes, memorizing so many lines so quickly, the financial benefits to RedCo, and Eternal Knights being entirely Sanctuary-owned and run, and many other factors, but I can't swallow this dialogue," Sern almost lectured to the director who, in some ways, could agree with what the Intendant was saying.

"Well, if you put it that way, I do agree. Bills are bills, and paycheques are paycheques. We all have jobs to do as well," Sir Hugo lamented. "But that said, the viewership to this last season was high, and let's hope we keep it that way. Ratings are ratings after all," he smiled as he went back to the video village, what apparently was the term for the little video command post that he was putting on.

"Checking the gate, moving on to the next scene!" His first assistant director called as Cazian and Gavin stepped aside.

Cazian was a bit bothered by that black mist. He almost looked like he had some headache as he sat back in his seat.

"Are you alright?" Sern asked Cazian as the makeup ladies came back again. "One moment," Sern halted them as he attended to Cazian first.

"Yeah, I'll be fine. They just put something in that smoke, smelled rank!" Cazian rubbed his eyes for a moment.

"Rank? Oh, yes the smell wasn't pleasant."

"Had this weird ancient smell to it, hard to put it but I'll be fine," Cazian insisted as he took a sip of the blood cup that he had left there earlier. Sern visibly scanned Cazian. From what he could tell, there wasn't anything wrong with Cazian but still, Sern felt a need to keep an eye on him.

"Well, if anything causes you trouble, let me know," Sern comforted his ward as he nodded again to the makeup team that was waiting impatiently to continue their work. As soon as Sern stepped out of the way, they almost swarmed around him like a swarm of locusts, wiping, patting down, cleaning up, anything they had to do to make their jobs seem worth the money they were getting paid.

Then off by the side of the studio, Sern could see two familiar shapes. One was a tall fierce looking wolf-man creature with that trademark blond-gold stripe of fur along his head, and a young handsome dark haired man. They slowly approached Sern, carefully taking in the scene of what they were seeing. The wolf seemed almost predatory, being in awe, of what he was seeing.

"Sorry, Jett really wanted to take a look," Paxton groaned as the huge wolf also stepped in. "We just finished our photo shoot." He assured the Intendant.

"They just finished one scene, but they still have a few more to go."

"This is so awesome!" The wolf sounded almost giddy. It was a very unusual juxtaposition. This fierce beast creature was almost laughing, and his voice was deep and ferocious despite the words and expression.

"Yes, most amusing," Sern almost dismissed.

"I still find it weird; you've been hanging out with Gavin and Cazian for the past week.

"Yeah, just them as normal guys, but now they're the characters again!" Jett explained. "It's not the same! They're the Eternal Knights!" his voice almost jumped back to human tone for a moment.

"My boyfriend, the fan boy," Paxton casually mocked as Gavin approached the three of them.

"So how did the shoot go?" Sern asked, looking up at the huge wolf-beast that was at one time a timid young man.

"Pretty good. They loved his look," Paxton referred to Jett who was still in his wolf form. He wondered if Jett was even aware of this, or was too distracted to change back. "That gold-blond he has really stands out."

"Yeah it does. I've never known a wolf to have that. Certainly is unique," Gavin flattered as he pat Jett's shoulder, who was still oddly mesmerized by the very fact that he was actually on the Eternal Knight's set, seeing them film.

"You're not going to ask me for my autograph are you?" Gavin joked to the tall wolf, briefly snapping him back to reality.

"Huh?" Sorry, just, this is so cool!" he yipped again. It was odd seeing him behave like this, especially in wolf form.

"You going to change back?" Paxton reminded him. "People are starting to stare!" A few people had looked to see him there, standing in his wolf-man form, but it was more like a passing amusement more than anything.

"Yeah yea…" Jett reluctantly gave in. Right there and then he started to shift back, fur disappearing, his physical form starting to shrink a bit as his height went back to normal, the muscles condensing back to his human scale. It was quite an achievement for him to be able to handle his transforming at this skill level, despite him being rather new at it.

"Need a shirt?" Paxton asked his boyfriend, noticing that he was still only wearing a pair of loose shorts.

"I'm good," Jett insisted, not wanting to leave the set as he looked to Paxton, almost seeking permission to look around.

"He can stay with me," Sern said.

"Can I?" Jett asked Paxton, like an excited little child.

"Alright, alright." Paxton gently wrapped his arm around Jett. Gavin couldn't help but smile at the sight of Jett who was giggling like a child.

"Just behave!" Paxton teasingly warned him before heading towards the exit.

"I'm not needed for the next two scenes, so I'll be back in my room." Cazian stumbled out of his chair. He was still slightly groggy from that smoke effect.

"Want me to come with you?" Paxton suggested.

"Nah, I'll be fine. Just that damn smoke. Stank like hell," Cazian groaned as he headed walked out of the studio.

Cazian managed to drag himself up the long staircases of Wolf Coven House; even the perfectly waxed cedar handrails to the grand staircase somehow seemed even stickier and more rubbery than usual. He felt like there were weights tied to his brain and all over his body, and somehow his head felt like it was made of cement. Despite his ability to bench press the weight of a car he still felt especially sluggish. Running through his mind were all the potential causes that he may have encountered for this strange abnormality in his well being. Then of course the most obvious event was the black smoke that came out of the special effects Sacred Box during the film scene. Though he never knew it would cause a sense of nausea like this.

Despite the effort he dragged himself up the stairs to his room. Throwing his coat on his leather lounge chair was the last thing he did before he collapsed onto his bed in a heap. He felt the need to summon sleep faster than normal, anything to get this over with. Being a vampire of the highest order has its unique advantages.

Cazian's mind wandered through the same garden that he always seemed to take comfort in when he was in his sleep. It was one of their traits, to remember and control their dreams. Cazian recalled when he was turned from human to vampire, it was as though his mind had been opened to a vast new world of possibilities and thoughts. It seemed natural when he was turned that he would naturally look at things in a very different manner. But in his dream garden, things were always peaceful.

He could smell the fresh dew on the grass that stood at the edge of the light gravel road that gave that soft crunch whenever his feet stepped onto it. The edge of the gravel road was lit by candles that didn't flicker, and remained quite calm despite the obvious fact that all the trees around were slowly swaying amongst the breeze, remarkably not affecting the flicker of the candles, when they flickered at all. The path would always curve naturally into an s-shape that he could walk always within a few minutes of his dream time. It was always the same dream for him if he wanted something peaceful and quiet, him walking through this serene night time garden with the moonlight beaming down on the open fields that surrounded the garden.

For Cazian, the garden itself was this unusual place that he never recalled ever seeing in his real life as a human. It was a well- manicured garden, with virtually endless varieties of flowers and trees. It seemed to be a garden that nature would have created, the only path through it was this single three-foot wide gravel pathway, with natural linings of candles and flowers, some that seemed almost fantasy-like, that glowed with their own bulb lights that pulsed like they had heartbeats. It was something he enjoyed while he dreamed, entering this perfect garden.

He approached the center of the garden where there would always be a small lake and an island at the center, with some flowers on it. It was always the same little winding of the road for Cazian as he walked through, but this time he noticed something different. At the center island Cazian noticed there was someone there, but he was simply lyinig there, facing upwards towards the sky.

Cazian could tell that there was something very familiar with this person, clearly a male lying on the island. There seems to be no way to tell if that man was asleep or dead. As Cazian got closer, he got a better view to tell if a man was definitely asleep. Cazian could tell from the slow rising and falling of the man's chest that he was breathing. It didn't occur at all to him that it was strange that he could have such senses, in the middle of a dream, though Cazian did recall this was the first time he saw someone sleeping there. Normally there were very few people he would encounter in his dreams, but this was the first that occurred in this type of situation. It didn't seem to be someone who was unfamiliar to Cazian.

As he approached the person, he immediately recognized the face. It was his own face and body. Literally standing beside himself, he took a careful look at his double who was lying asleep on the ground. There was something, unworldly about his twin, but Cazian couldn't quite put his metaphysical finger on it. As he stood towards the edge of the water, the water froze by itself the moment his bare feet touched the cool and now solid surface

Cazian walked without any problems on the ice towards the island at the center of the pond. The ice felt more like cool marble than ice. Each step he took the ice melted into water as he passed it, the crystals dissolving back into a liquid as easy as they turned to ice. Cazian saw his twin up close, completely identical to him, even the clothing he wore. The eyes opened with a quick flash, to reveal a pair of silver eyes staring back at Cazian, sending a shock through him powerful enough to wake him up from his slumber.

He stood there, staring right at a double of himself, who was gazing back at him. His face that he looked at was expressionless, and was completely unresponsive to his own presence. The only thing his double did, was with those silver eyes gazing right into him, as though he could see right into his soul.

Cazian opened his mouth to say something, but found that no words would come out; in fact, his voice didn't even react at all to his commands. He wanted to say something but something was preventing him from talking. He tried to step back, but his feet wouldn't move, his legs wouldn't move, nothing responded to him. His double slowly got off the ground and just stood there staring at him, but Cazian could now tell that it was more than a stare, it was turning into something far more sinister.

His own body wasn't responding anymore as he kept struggling to move, but it wasn't like he was being restrained. It was that his entire body had lost all control, in that the commands from his brain simply weren't reaching his limbs. His double sneered with a menacing glare in his eyes as he slowly walked towards Cazian.

Using his only weapon he had left, his mind, he started to try to move the ground, anything around him. His control of his own dream world was not even in his own hands anymore. He felt completely helpless; his own willpower was weakening as though it was being drained right out of him. He felt that every time he tried to resist, his own willpower and concentration grew weaker as though this doppelganger of his was draining it out of him.

"You will do nicely," his double spoke. His voice was identical to Cazian's in every way. From his eyes erupted a silver mist, like tendrils of living fog. Cazian recognized it as the same type of gas that came from the box that he opened on the set! But it was the last thing he thought of as the gas entered his eyes, draining now his consciousness into nothing but a pit of darkness.

"Caz?" Gavin knocked on the door. It was curious why Cazian didn't answer any of his texts. They had heard that he had gone up to his room. "Caz? You there?" Gavin slowly turned the doorknob, finding it unlocked. He entered Cazian's room, peering first into the apartment, nothing out of the ordinary. Cazian wasn't much of a neat freak like Gavin, but things were orderly enough to not seem out of the ordinary. He could see into the bedroom, to have Cazian just lying there on his back, just in his t-shirt and jeans, what he was wearing when he came off the set just a few hours earlier. Cazian was just lying there, apparently asleep. Gavin knew that he was required down on the set for a quick pickup shot. "Hey!" Gavin gently patted Cazian on the shoulder, regretting the act instantly because he didn't want him to be stirred up.

Cazian didn't move. Gavin could tell he was still asleep, but something was very strange. His heartbeat was quite fast as though something was happening. More than likely it was just a bad dream, but his body itself wasn't responding to stirring or shaking.

"Hey!" Gavin loudly called into Cazian's ears. Gavin knew that Sern was going to kick the film crew out the next day, so these late shots had to be done. Gavin shook Cazian a bit more this time, and suddenly, without warning, Cazian's eyes shot open.

But they weren't Cazian's normal grey eyes; instead, they were entirely silver, and were almost shimmering in the darkness. Gavin instantly got the close view of the eyes. They were shimmering, but now were changing to a strange silvery glow that was clearly not within the abilities of a High Order.

"Cazian, what's wrong?" Gavin asked as he tried to shake Cazian out of what was a trance-like state. Something was seriously wrong.

At first Cazian was limp like his eyes were open but he was still unconscious. Then his joints and neck started to stiffen up again, as it seemed like he was regaining some form of control. His pupils, and irises were gone, and all that were inside his eyes were these two shimmering silver glows. His face changed slightly as he now seemed to glare right at Gavin, his face turned much more sinister.

Suddenly Gavin felt a pair of invisible hands pulling him right off of his feet, and back towards the wall, smashing the High Order against it, then collapsing to the ground.

"Don't you dare touch me," Cazian growled at him. His face was ferocious, his fangs fully emerged, his hands revealed their sharp talon-like nails that High Order's only used when they were ready to kill. He walked past Gavin who was still on the ground for a moment, getting his breath back as Cazian walked out of the apartment. But as he reached the hallway, he felt an enormous weight of mass behind him. Gavin rushed at him and tackled him, pushing him towards the ground trying to temporarily stun him. Cazian lay there for a moment, but almost floated back up to his feet as he turned towards Gavin again.

Cazian's wings now unfolded behind him. His face was full of fury. Gavin watched him, his own wings also now spread out, in a defensive display of battle-readiness. Gavin knew he was stronger than Cazian, but this unearthly strength that Cazian was showing was something far beyond either of their abilities. Gavin waited for Cazian to make the first move. But there was no move made, at least none that he could see before he felt a pair of cold metallic grip around his neck. He felt it clasping around his jugular with such powerful strength that it lifted him off his feet. Gavin tried to grasp for this invisible hand but he couldn't feel anything there. It hurled him backwards, this time almost halfway down the hall.

Jett and Paxton were coming up when the noise drew them to see what was going on. Cazian turned around to see them standing there, in shock to what they were seeing. He reached for one of the solid oak tables along the hallway walls with his hands, and threw it at the pair who stood at their own doorway. Paxton pushed Jett out of the way, but the huge table smashed right into him with stunning force. Paxton wasn't knocked though, as he seemed mentally prepared to take this hit. Jett, seeing his boyfriend under the shattered remains of the table, roared a feral, bestial roar, that was so loud it was sure that everyone else in the house could hear it. Almost faster than before, Jett transformed into his wolf form, muscles almost bursting out of his body as he charged at Cazian, but not to grab him, instinctively instead biting his fangs deep into Cazian's left upper arm.

The High Order wasn't even phased as he simply grabbed the wolf and casually also threw him off of him. His shoulder only bled slightly, instantly starting to repair itself as he just marched past them. Like a fast animal, Jett got right back to his feet and pounced at him, this time from behind. Paxton also came up from under the oak table's planks and shattered table legs and surged at Cazian, grabbing his right arm from behind. Another huge mass of strength came from behind them, both as Gavin wrapped his super strong arms from behind, around Cazian's torso, attempting to restrain him the best he could.

Like before, Cazian's supernatural strength was more than even the three of them could handle. This time, he rammed Jett and Paxton together, stunning them enough for him. Cazian was starting to radiate some sort of silver color mist from his body that pushed Gavin off him before they turned into almost tentacles, and slashed at Gavin who jumped out of the way. The mist tendrils vanished fairly quickly as Cazian made a dash for the exit of the house, the closest one, the main entrance.

He reached the balcony and leaped down the central atrium into the main foyer where there were a pair of crew men starting to load things into their trucks. They were simply smashed aside as Cazian raced past them, but not before Larita caught sight of them as she followed the noise. Behind her, Kazmo was also with her on their flying disks heading toward the commotion.

They spotted Cazian standing outside the main entrance, almost like he was looking for directions on where to go, scanning the sights around him, clearly not familiar with where he was.

"Stop him!" Gavin's voice roared at the two Ahri as they caught sight of him, Jett and Paxton raced towards the entrance. Larita only flashed Kazmo a confirming nod as they two Ahri dashed towards Cazian, not with force but with their staves glowing brightly with the preparation of a magical incantation.

The two Ahri shot out white glowing beams of energy at Cazian, also this time at his arms, but they weren't a real form of attack it seemed. The beams solidified into almost glowing ropes, wrapping them around his arms, restraining him from moving. Then between them, a third brighter rope came and lashed around Cazian's chest. It was Kito who had now come to help them. Cazian tried to resist these magical bindings but they were too strong, and the Ahri were keeping him still for the time being as he struggled, his wings flapping almost manically, throwing out gusts of wind around them.

Though the bindings didn't give way, the little Ahri were not physically strong enough to prevent Cazian from moving much longer. He grabbed the magical rope bindings from them, and tried to pull himself free with some success. The Ahri simply weren't able to hold back enough. The energy rope was unbreakable but that didn't prevent them from being pulled away. The mist that came from his body started to grow thicker and stronger this time. Kito noticed this, and shot out a powerful bolt of arcane power at Cazian, sending the demented High Order flying forward, and slamming into one of the film trucks with so much strength and force that the huge moving van sized vehicle fell over onto its side. The mist, however stayed around, and started to gather in small, almost fist-sized clumps, as they shot themselves towards the six of them, now with Trenton, Trey and Coltrane coming outside to see what was going on. The silver clumps turned into blades before their eyes only microseconds before hitting them. The three Ahri summoned a powerful glass-looking wall between them and the projectiles.

They couldn't quite see Cazian, but he was slowly getting to his feet again. His face and skin were turning almost grayish blue; his face was more bestial than anything everyone else had ever seen, and his wings seemed more dragon-looking. He reached under the moving truck and with the creaking of the metal sound being heard, picked up the entire vehicle with his two bare arms.

Kazmo and Larita reinforced the power of their defensive wall as Cazian, with unknown levels of strength, threw the entire vehicle at them. But as it came towards them, the truck was sent flying back at Cazian once again, this time by another huge powerful arcane bolt from Kito that knocked the truck back enough to send it back to Cazian.

Suddenly a blazing white light came from behind them and smashed Cazian into the ground. It was Sern. His eyes blazing with the same pure white light that he showed before when using his Va'Nai gifted power. Cazian, stunned at what could possibly hit him with such force, saw Sern's radiating eyes, blazing with energy and power, flapped his enormous dragon-like wings, shooting himself up into the air and headed towards the direction of the forest.

"Gavin! Contact Sanctuary and tell them we are going to need help. Everyone else stay here," Sern commanded as he rushed off, also through the air following Cazian.

"Why does he want us to stay here? We can help!" Paxton almost sounded hopeless, but not before another winged being landed in front of them as Sern vanished out of sight. It was Dominic with his own wings ready.

"Kito, can you open a portal by yourself back to here?" He asked the Ahri Ambassador.

"Yes!" The Ambassador answered.

"Alright," Dominic reached down and picked up Kito almost like he was a child. He was incredibly light as Dominic placed him on his back. The little Ahri grasped on between his wings as Dominic flew up into the air.

"I'll give you a little boost!" Kito yelled to Dominic through the gusts of wind and air. Kito's own robes had shifted into a longer and warmer protective form as his staff glowed with a red light, wrapping him and Dominic in a protective barrier that Dominic used to fly even faster without worrying about the air resistance.

"What are we going to do?" Jett turned to the other four wolves. "I don't even think we can help, really."

"We can try!" Larita answered back. The last Ahri, Kobili dashed out of the house as well, curious as to the commotion.

"What is going on?" the last Ahri almost demanded to know, seeing the demolished moving truck in the driveway, a crater in the cement.

"Long story. Check your pearls! Link with Kito's!" Kazmo ordered. The Ahri gazed into the pearls that ordained the top of their stsaves, seeing the images that Kito's was also seeing, but no one else seemed to see what they were viewing.

Chapter 27

Sern dashed atop the trees to see Cazian had landed near a clearing of trees. He leaped with blazing speed from tree branch to tree branch. He could sense that there was a powerful presence, not mortal, and clearly something beyond this world. It was like a smell that he was able to catch with his own sixth sense. He was careful enough to make as little noise as possible, but he was able to tell that there was that same presence that he felt in Cazian's body. It was nearby and he had to be on the lookout. He could sense that it was in front of him but he wasn't entirely sure. There was something else nearby that seemed to distract his concentration.

A blast of bright red light came at Sern. Instinctively he smacked his arm backwards, like he was warding off a fly, hitting the red blast right back towards the direction it had come. It didn't harm him but the alarms of an attack were sounding in his head. They knew where he was and were now lying in wait just beyond the opening where the trees were. Another three more red blasts came towards him; these were stronger as they smashed into his shield with enough force to knock him a few steps backwards. He could tell that these three weren't shot out from one but two different directions.

Instantly Sern realized, that this magical power that was used against him was not just normal magic, it was something far more powerful. Not even a Sorceress like Elura was capable of this level of magical strength. As his mind started to eliminate the chances of anyone mortal being able to do this, Sern feared this was something far more dangerous and powerful.

He could also sense that one was from the entity that possessed Cazian, but the other was different. It was similar enough to be from a related source but distinctively different. Sern could recall in his mind that Arthur was also possessed by a divine power. Could these two be working together, he thought.

Sern stabilized his feet as he returned the attack with a counter of his own, firing off a beam of pure Va'Nai energy at his attacker from his hand. The beam followed the path of his attackers who were still unseen. They were hiding out of view, using some sort of invisible magical spell. Sern could smell that type of magic. He was not going to waste anyone's time; he could sense Kito and another from Wolf Coven were on their way. He raised his right arm upwards, pointing to the sky. He fired upwards a blindingly bright beam of light into the sky above him. Like a signal flare, it lit up the area around them almost to the brightness of daylight.

"That's Sern down there!" Kito yelled into Dominic's ear, trying to get through the loud air and wind that were flapping around them. Dominic didn't bother replying as he headed right towards the pillar of light, which was high enough to be seen from above the tree line. They landed gently on the ground and Kito hopped off Dominic's back, back onto his disk, which had followed them from Wolf Coven House.

"There he is," Dominic saw Sern outside the tree line in the middle of a field opening in the woods. The light was a dead giveaway as Sern continued the flare for a few more seconds.

"Wait!" Kito tugged on Dominic's pants for a second. "You really think you can do anything to help? Whatever took over Cazian was strong enough to beat Gavin, and he's stronger than you." Kito asserted before pointing his staff towards Dominic. "I am going to put a protection enchantment on you and myself, but I don't know how well it will work against them!" The two of them were enveloped by a warm green glow for a moment. There was only a slight tingling sensation throughout his skin all over his body, but then it faded quickly as Kito's staff light also faded.

"We should keep our distance!" Dominic started to prowl closer to the battle.

"I'm bringing backup!" Kito turned again to face the trees, where he started gathering branches, twigs, rocks and dirt with his staff, levitating them into the air, and twisting, bending, merging them into some form of archway, almost perfectly circular but merging into the ground as though it was a tree, grown into that form. Dominic watched as the space within the archway also started to glow, and form into a swirling blue light thick like a liquid that hovered in the space.

Kito was doing some form of spell that Dominic had seen them use before, and by now he was familiar with it. The vortex rippled and fluctuated in size, expanding then shrinking slightly before Kito managed to get it within the archway.

"It's stable!" Kito spoke into the pearl at the top of his staff. Moments later, the other Ahri and Wolf Coven members came through, joining them. The other Ahri instinctively started to secure where they were with powerful wards and spells that they were putting all throughout the ground and the trees, marking off where they were in a protective bubble-like field.

Sern kept blocking the various bolts and blasts that were coming in at all directions, but none were able to get through his protective field. A few times he simply reflected them back at where they were coming from. He knew as long as they were doing this, they were still in the area. It should have been obvious by now that despite the fact they were able to beat Gavin and the others, Sern was far more powerful than the others. Dashing to one side, Sern conjured up a similar binding spell to what the Ahri used. Like a whip, he lashed out with the binding rope from his hand as the length of the rope whipped into the forest, latching onto what he concentrated his sights on, which was Cazian's body.

Sern pulled with his strength as Cazian tried to resist. His own vampire form was augmented into something like its demon form, which he had only speculated about in the past. He was far stronger than normal, far more enraged, his size was larger but with the rope that Sern used, wrapped around him and with Sern using his own force and power against him, even Cazian couldn't stop himself from being pulled in.

Then another figure appeared. Sern only barely caught a glimpse of him as a large blade slashed near Sern's head, but not before the Intendant dodged it and turned to see another High Order pointing the blade at him.

Sern didn't bother with any speech or statement but turned his hand at this new unknown High Order, who was also in the same form as Cazian was, demonic and boosted with some dark form of magic. Sern's other hand was still holding tightly to the rope he conjured that ensnared Cazian. Another fast slash came around Sern, but he managed to dodge it again. This was followed by a stab, which almost hit Sern had his left hand had not grabbed the blade itself. The material of the blade shocked Sern. It was made out of pure true silver, the only metal capable of doing serious damage to a High Order.

Instantly Sern knew this blade had to be confiscated as he pulled the blade back with all his strength, ripping it out of the hand of this other Vampire. Sern shoved it down his belt where, from his other hand, he threw out the other end of a rope which wrapped itself around the other vampire, ensnaring him down as well. Sern materialized yet another rope into his hands, this time smaller, and had them tied around these two prisoner's hands and legs. He also had them gagged before he looked around to see what else there was to deal with, as from behind him he saw the familiar faces of the Wolf Coven members coming through the forest. They resisted but the constraints only got tighter every time they tried to pull away.

"I thought I told you all to stay at the house!" Sern commanded them, his eyes were still glowing from the fight he just had to do.

"We couldn't let you handle this on your own." Kito replied, somewhat defiantly at the Intendant. "Besides, my Ahri and I are not under your authority."

"But they are," Sern pointed to everyone else.

"They did this at my request to maintain good relations." Kito answered again, quite able to stand up to the Intendant.

"Well I am going to give this order again for your own safety. Return to the house." The others were keeping their distance, especially from the demonic Cazian who was unable to speak but was still as ferocious as before. His wings, arms, legs were all struggling against the glowing bindings.

There were whispers and gossip already spreading throughout the crowd as they saw what Cazian and the other vampire had become. They weren't sure if it was a result of some tampered magic or something beyond, but they didn't get too close. Paxton and Jett, in particular, looked worried, mainly from Jett seeing what Paxton could become.

Before Sern could stop them from getting closer, another blast came out from the forest, a shadowy purple hue glowed from that direction. It hit Sern in the back, knocking him to the ground for a moment as the Ahri rushed to his aid. Sern's back was almost sizzling from the heat of whatever energy that was. He seemed to be alright, but stunned for a moment. The two imprisoned vampire and everyone else saw a strange looking being, almost radiating that same color of shadowy energy, coming from another portal that also opened up, this one from an unknown origin.

"Those two I could handle. I know now they're not mortal or even supernatural." He thought to himself. "But this, is something even beyond them. It's beyond me!" He kept himself concentrated on whatever he could do to try to stop this new being.

Sern retaliated with a series of blasts of his own, throwing them out of his hands with as much force and power that they were enough to shake the ground as everyone backed unto what they thought was a safer distance, some hiding behind whatever cover they could as the wind grew more and more fierce.

Sern's bolts hit this figure but to no avail. The Ahri joined the Intendant in hurling whatever magical spells they could at him, only temporarily pushing him back with their combined effort. Cazian and the other vampire, while still ensnared, were pulled towards this figure. Sern tried to pull them back with his own power, but they were being dragged into the enemy portal. They weren't making any effort resisting, it seemed more like they were trying to go into the portal deliberately. Sern struggled with more power than he had used before, but guarding against the onslaught of shattering blasts and bolts, and waves of dark energy coming at him from this new assailant, he was powerless to stop the two vampires from escaping into the portal. He reinforced the protection of the shield that he had around himself, and threw it outwards, to expand around himself and the Ahri and everyone else. With every meter it stretched, it weakened against the peppering of the countless attacks this new figure was making against him.

The Ahri, attempted with all their own magical might to reinforce his protection field, but their magic wasn't much better than it was on them than before. Kito pulled out one of the huge trees with his own magic, and hurled it right at this powerful enemy, who sliced the tree's huge trunk in half, but just enough to distract him as the others made a run for the portal which this enemy wasn't stopping them from doing.

Sern, believing he had the moment of distraction, fired off with as much power and energy that his infusion granted him at this opponent, blasting him to the ground as Cazian and the other fled into the enemy portal. The enemy combatant dropped to the ground, hit by Sern's all out attack, but Sern himself was weakened. With what was left of his own strength, Sern pushed the other Ahri towards the portal back to Wolf Coven House, as he himself stumbled to get to the portal as well, completely drained from his last attack.

Then, he felt a huge wave of energy coming at him as it smashed into his body, then all sight, sound, and vision and senses shut off, and everything turned silent and dark.

Gavin paced impatiently at the atrium as the portal from Aurastar lowered and formed. He was almost biting his nails to the flesh had they not grown back instantly. Out of the portal stepped Archon Alena, Superintendent Lya and Intendant Hasaan, as well as four other operatives, from what he recognized as Protectors.

"We received your message. What is going on?" Alena requested as she caught Gavin as he ran out of the door, waving for them to follow him. He wasn't aware but the magical portal that the Ahri had summoned was still active and they were all coming through, back to the house.

"Where's Sern?" he yelled out to everyone.

"He was the last one left, I think he was protecting us as we came back through," Trenton called from the magical portal as the Ahri were the last ones, turning around to reinforce the portal and stand ready for whatever came through it.

It was almost like he was viewing the evacuation of a building, going through the portal looking to see familiar faces. He could see the seven sanctuary officials coming out from the house, feeling slightly secure.

The portal stayed active for as long as the Ahri wanted. It didn't look like they needed to keep anything running but they stood at it ready in case something did come through.

What came through was a huge wolf, glowing with an ethereal glow, partially translucent. It had to almost bend its head downwards to fit through the portal as it stepped through, towering over everyone else who was there.

"The Spirit Wolf!" Paxton brushed his way past the crowd up to the huge wolf. Sern lay on its back as it reached the middle of the parking lot before the Ahri ceased their portal spell, closing it off, and the dirt and branch structure melted back into the ground where it had come from.

"Quick, get him down," Trenton and Trey reached up over the huge wolf creature and gently pulled Sern down as the huge Spirit Wolf also lay down to make it easier for them to get him. Everyone else, in particular the film crew, were being escorted in by the Protectors, as Sern lay there on the ground for the time being, his uniform tattered and ripped but still mostly intact. Most shocking was his skin was ripped and torn in some places, but not bleeding. Instead the wounds were leaking out some glowing white fluid. The other cuts that were not bleeding that liquid were radiating light out of them as though his skin was just a shell.

"We will take him with us," Alena pointed to the main doorway where a slab, looking like the same materials that composed Sern's desk, hovered past the crowd and floated towards them. Trenton picked up Sern and placed him on the slab, still unconscious, as it hovered slowly back into the house, with everyone by its side. The Spirit Wolf, turned around and faced the roadway that led out of the house, almost in a protective stance, watching and wary of anything that would come in.

"Is he alive?" Gavin asked as he caught up to Alena.

"Yes," Alena calmed him down, with a gentle hand on his own. "Your Intendant will be fine but he will need to come with us to recover," she spoke to the rest of them. Her voice was quite deep and resonant, despite herself being a very short and elderly woman. "For the time being, Intendant Hasaan will re-assume his duty here until Sern is alright. I'm also assigning Superintendent Lya here, and the four Protectors to guard the house for the time being," she declared to the rest of them as the portal to Aurastar was still active before they stepped inside.

Hasaan approached Gavin, with a friendly handshake.

"I'm sorry that we had to meet again like this," he apologized to Gavin.

"Same, I would have hoped for better circumstances," Gavin accepted the handshake. "I was also afraid that the console in Sern's office wouldn't respond to me, if I had to take charge again."

"But he gave you a temporary infusion right? That's all it needs to recognize you." Hasaan looked around at a few of the new faces that gathered around him, in particular a new Prime Wolf and a new High Order. "These are two new ones who joined you?" he shook their hands as he walked up to them.

"Yeah, I'm Paxton, and this is Jett," Paxton pointed to his boyfriend. Jett shook his hand but was still visibly stunned and nervous at the situation.

"We're going to need information from you all, but for the time being, that can wait." Hasaan turned to the other Protectors. "For the time being, I have to order a complete lockdown. That includes the film crew as well. No one will be permitted to leave or enter." The protectors nodded in compliance as they dispersed. It seemed they were going to patrol the hallways. "I'm going to ask the Superintendent to make our protection here a bit more sturdy just in case," Hasaan told Gavin.

"Precaution is all," Lya remarked. "Hasaan, don't get too comfortable, I'm sure after Sern makes a fully recovery, he'll be returned to this post." Lya headed upstairs towards Sern's office where there was probably some central place where she could observe what was happening throughout the house.

Gavin wasn't entirely sure what was happening but after Cazian's monstrous escape, and Sern getting injured, it was like they were all under some unknown threat that he or anyone else had never encountered before. For the time being though, he trusted as well as everyone else trusted that Hasaan and the Sanctuary were going to do what they could to protect them.

"What do you think is going on?" Gavin asked Hasaan as they were both going up to the office.

"I have no idea yet until I complete some investigations around here. But I can tell you this, if something is able to beat an Intendant like that, you can bet that Sanctuary isn't going to take anything lightly from this matter," Hasaan reported back as they entered the office. Lya was already standing there behind Sern's desk activating more consoles than Hasaan or Sern had ever used. It was almost like a room-wide computer system, projecting dozens of holographic screens from the desk that rotated around them.

"This house was originally protected by a cloaking spell that my sister put in place?" Lya asked Gavin and Hasaan.

"Yes, Elura put in the enchantments," Hasaan answered as he recalled the events from his tenure.

"My sister's good, but I'm better. Whatever that being was that you claimed took over Cazian's body wasn't some mere spirit or possession," Lya viewed some of the strange symbols and graphic displays that were being shown. Gavin was surprised he could understand them, they were magical symbols that were emblazoned all over the house. "I'm going to have to enhance them, good thing we brought four protectors around for this.

"What should I do?" Gavin asked.

"Let us do our work to secure this place. You don't have to worry about supplies. I'm having them rerouted from your typical truck routes, to go through the hub and right into the portal in the center of the building." Lya was relaying orders and sending out commands on the holographic displays at a dizzying rate. Gavin didn't know how to make heads or tails of it, so he just trusted that they knew what they were doing. "Keep everyone calm. We'll inform you all on what's going to happen later."

"I'll keep you appraised," Hasaan assured Gavin as he escorted him out of the office. "For the time being, you're safe with all of us here."

"Wait, what about Cazian?" Gavin urged Hasaan.

"We will bring in people to help find him. I have no idea what his state is, but as a High Order, he should be pretty resilient."

"I hope so." Gavin replied as he slowly walked out of the office. He trusted Hasaan and he knew Sanctuary wasn't taking this situation lightly if Archon Alena herself had to make an appearance. He already got the sense that there was something far more serious at work than a mere possession. Maybe it was a result of his own infusion with Sern that seemed to give him some instinctive sixth sense that they weren't fully telling him what was dangerous at first. He felt they were hiding something but he also trusted that they weren't ready to reveal it yet. Nonetheless Gavin did know that he had to make sure everyone was calm, and that everyone wasn't going to panic despite the fact that their Intendant was out of commission for the time being.

EPILOGUE

Sern's eyelids slowly opened. He hadn't felt or heard anything for an unknown amount of time. Inside his mind he had shut himself off like a machine that was out of power, as his body was protecting and healing itself. He had completely lost all track of time, the last thing that he remembered was being hit by that powerful blast from behind which was enough to overload his system. He rubbed his head, then his eyes, for a moment, just to adjust himself to wherever he was.

He was lying on top of a glowing light green colored stone slab. The color was almost like a light green jade and was very translucent. It hummed gently with a comforting sound. He recognized it as one of the regeneration beds that was in the Va'Nai healing room .

He was definitely in a healing room. He was enclosed within a rather serene chamber. There was a vast window behind him that gave him a clear and stunning view of the Earth. Just then, it hit him that he was in orbit of Earth. Sern wasn't aware that there was anything that was this close to the planet. As he stood up, he could feel his body was still aching. Clearly it had been more than just a few minutes or hours since he was knocked out.

"Up on your feet already?" Hasaan asked as he stood there by the doorway.

"Hasaan?" Sern asked as he turned around wanting to verify who was there. Sure enough Hasaan was standing, or rather leaning against the door frame, arms crossed but with a pleased expression to see Sern back on his feet.

"The system alerted us when you were conscious," Hasaan walked up to Sern who was holding the edge of the window for balance as he looked outward towards the planet. "Your outer form was pretty damaged. Some of your skin was even blasted right off you."

"Apparently you all repaired me," Sern felt his face, "and in the process, revealed to the Wolf Coven members that I'm not entirely human."

"I'm pretty sure they know none of us are entirely human, Sern." Hasaan went up to him. "But we did fix you up. All the damage is gone and fixed up nicely." Sern seemed a bit distracted as he looked out the window.

"I had no idea that the Archons were planning to send a larger presence to Earth," he looked outward towards the reaching branches of the City Ship. Its vast size was clearly obvious when he saw the rest of the City Ship below him, the towering crystalline pinnacles and glowing blue and white lights shimmering around them. Even for the normal stern Sern, it was an impressive sight, to say the least.

"Considering that there was something on Earth that was able to take out an Intendant, even if it was temporary, was something that the Va'Nai didn't want to take lightly." Hasaan walked up to Sern, joining him for the amazing view. "We simply were not going to take any chances. Alena herself dispatched this City Ship to Earth, specifically to act as an orbital operations HQ. They're also sending more Ahri our way."

"What about the Ahri colony world?" Sern asked, remembering his diplomatic mission in which he managed to save two Ahri children.

"With our help, the Ahri managed to secure their settlements. They've also started to go on the offensive, and are managing to cleanse the fire from their world."

"Powerful little fellows, aren't they?" Sern admired.

"Extremely. I saw the full use of their magic against the Flame Autarchs. The Ahri were able to summon an entire tsunami and flood vast portions of land, basically dousing out entire armies of elementals."

"Impressive," Sern kept watching the view, but noticed that the range of the City Ship seemed to be well within detection of Earth satellites. "Aren't we a bit close to the humans?" He asked.

"We're cloaked, of course, and we'll be pulling back to a Lunar orbit. You know we wouldn't have come this close without the protection of a cloaking field." Hasaan smiled. "I hope they didn't knock too much out of you," he almost laughed at Sern's expense.

"No laughing matter," a stern deep sounding voice came from the doorway. Sern could feel the powerful and respected presence of Archon Alena from the voice alone.

"How are you?" she asked the Intendant.

"Recovering nicely," Sern answered, as he turned around and sat back down on the platform.

"While you were unconscious, Sern, we had to do a mindlink to get the information out of you and everyone else at Wolf Coven House." she reported to Sern.

"Wait, how long was I out for?" he asked, looking up to the two of them for an answer.

"A week," Alena answered. "One week, Sern. One week," Alena almost lectured, sounding slightly matriarchal but in a kind way. She gently patted Sern's knee. Sern and many of the Intendants have always looked upon Alena as a mother-like figure. "We found something about that entity that possessed Cazian."

"Yes?" Sern urged her to continue.

"It was magic, as you suspected, but it was more than that. Divine Magic."

"A deity," Sern confirmed.

"Yes, and as you identified, it was Hypnos, God of Sleep. We had no idea he was freed and no idea why he is doing what he did, but a renegade god is definitely a source of concern."

"How accurate was I?" Sern made sure that they knew exactly what they were talking about.

"Very accurate," Alena assured him.

"But there's more than that," Hasaan added as he nodded to Alena.

"The Adjustors tried to break through the final mental block in Arthur's mind. They couldn't because it utilized a form of energy even greater than Divine power. It was cosmic, much like us, meaning something with that power manipulated Arthur's mind to block out memories." Alena continued. Sern looked even more wary of the incoming answer. "Say that again?" Sern almost wondered if he heard them wrong.

"It's a cosmic level power, like the Va'Nai that was helping the two gods," Hasaan stated.

"So what will that mean for the Supernaturals? And humans? What about my members at Wolf Coven House?"

"When Sanctuary put a full-out deployment to the Ahri Colony World, they succeeded in pushing the Flame Autarchs back and the Ahri themselves have decided that they can do this without our needed assistance. That has allowed us to pull forces from other parts of our domain to help here. Suffice to say, Sern, if this single cosmic entity is helping two gods, then we are going to have some serious trouble on our hands." Alena stood up and gazed out at the same window to Earth.

"There's something about the Ahri Colony world we found most interesting, and it relates to Earth," she spoke. There was a brief silence as Alena brought up a projection of what were the maps that the Ahri made of their colony world settlements.

The projection of the settlements were scattered all over a rather familiar looking continent. Then the image zoomed out until the display in front of Sern was something quite surprising.

"Earth?" Sern spoke in dismay of what he saw.

"Yes, the Ahri apparently have colonies on what would be North America on another version of Earth," Alena looked over at Hasaan who was just as surprised at what he saw.

"How did you get these images?" Hasaan asked.

"We were permitted to send a few Observers and Scouts. They scouted the entire planet that the Ahri called a Colony World, and it turns out that this may very well be an alternate dimension of Earth; and also from what the Ahri know of this new colony world, they have explored very little. The Observers ascended into orbit to scan the planet, and we did discover many other civilizations that were present, of which the Ahri currently are not aware."

"What will the Ahri have to deal with once they make contact with these other races?"

"We don't know yet. That is a domestic issue for them to figure out. We're only supporting them until these Flame Autarchs are defeated, then we can shift our forces elsewhere. I've yet to meet with the Va'Nai to discuss anything else regarding this parallel Earth situation."

"More forces to send here, perhaps?" Sern questioned as he stretched his legs.

"Potentially. The Va'Nai didn't take the attack on one of their Intendants lightly. So we dispatched Terrastar here, to Earth."

"Again, the Va'Nai aren't taking any chances." Hasaan pointed towards the groups of Sanctuary forces that were gathering below them on the main streets of the cityscape. "And your wards back at Wolf Coven House are fine right now. Superintendent Lya is there for the time being, overseeing it."

"Am I to resume my tenure there?"

"Yes," Alena answered, "with a stronger Sanctuary presence to help you as well. We have no intention of letting that god snatch away Cazian from you. We're going to help you find him and the others, and stop those rogue gods and their benefactor from causing more trouble." She comforted him.

"What did you get from the others? Mindlinks I mean." Sern asked.

"Nothing entirely that useful. Except for Arthur. As I said, his mind was still blocked but we managed to find scattered bits of information. The power of Siphoning Lifeforce is one that these gods are using to increase their power and strength, for what reason we don't know; but out of what we gathered, they get far more energy and power from siphoning than they ever did from worship and prayer; so we are going to be watching for this."

"But we can't expect to recruit all Supernaturals into helping us do this. They have their own lives to lead," Sern almost sounded like he was protesting their decision to become more active.

"We understand that. We're not doing conscription here; we're just sending more Sanctuary forces to the Coven Houses and creating other observation areas, like in more remote places such as the Sahara, the Gobi, the Canadian Shield, the Outback and Siberia. Sanctuary is now going to keep more of an eye out, rather than just have a handful of Intendants on Earth to do everything at once."

"Alright." Sern stood up. "I'm prepared to return to Wolf Coven House right now," he declared assertively.

"Apparently you are," Alena smiled as she guided him to the doorway.

Sern was led to the main portal to Wolf Coven House, which lined the outer ring of the circular terminal building. There were other portals that led to various other locations throughout Earth, through other Coven Houses. The central portal was guarded by four enormous crystalline golems.

"Sern, you and the other Intendants on Earth don't have to worry about facing anything there, alone anymore," Alena assured him. "We're here in the heavens above, waiting on your words. If you need help, it will come," she reached out with her hand. Sern smiled as he accepted the friendly handshake.

"Take care of the guys for me, Sern," Hasaan also shook his hand. "I'll return to help you out too, if you need it."

"Of course," Sern answered with a consideration to accept the offer." The two of them turned and departed back upwards towards the central spire.

Sern took a look around, and his mind was filled with a strange thought. He said nothing but his eyes scanned the surrounding area. The glowing blue and green walls, the light and brilliant beauty of Va'Nai construction around him while above him, the Cosmic Eye, brightly burning above his head.

Before, he was a deputy waiting to receive his promotion, now he was waiting to proceed onto the next phase of his duties, and more importantly, his own journey. Though his time at Wolf Coven House was relatively short, Sern did feel he had made significant progress. He had helped with the protection and training of Jett and Paxton who were a definite surprise to the entire House, and Sern felt that by his self-sacrificing acts, now twice, he had earned Sanctuary more trust, both from the Ahri and from Wolf Coven members.

It was then, that a familiar shape drew Sern's attention as he neared the portal. Standing there with a smile on his face, was Gavin. It was like seeing an old friend as his High Order friend walked up to him. There were no words, only a friendly hug.

"So, Sern. I see you're fully recovered now." Gavin smiled down at him.

"Yes, they were able to heal me adequately, and I have been released to return to Wolf Coven House again to resume my intendantship." Sern smiled back at Gavin, almost sending him into shock.

"Well, I hope we see that more often." Gavin remarked.

"What?" asked the confused Intendant.

"A smile. It's not hard to do, you know," Gavin put his hand on Sern's shoulder.

"I will endeavor to make more frequent attempts," Sern answered with his trademark analytical accent.

"Well, Jett and Paxton are waiting to see you again, and we just have an interesting visit from an interesting family."

"Oh?" He asked back.

"Yes, the mother is a Packwalker wolf, and the father is a Drake Vampire." Gavin summarized.

"And by mother and father, you imply the existence of a child?"

"By child, you mean a 23 year old son, yes. Who is now showing signs that he's a hybrid."

"A most complex situation. But I think I can help resolve the issues at hand," Sern spoke confidently.

"I wouldn't doubt it." Gavin turned towards the portal. "Shall we?" as he held his arm out, allowing Sern to enter first.

Before Sern stepped through the portal, he took a longing gaze at all around him. At the shimmering towering pinnacles of Terrastar's buildings, to the bright Cosmic Eye that watched over not just them, but also now Earth, to Gavin who stood beside him, then to the large assemblies of incoming Ahri and Sanctuary forces that were ready for battle should the call be sounded. It hadn't been that long since he was just a newcomer. It seemed almost like everything was going full circle. He was ready to return, to begin the next phase of journey. Sern looked deeply at the portal in front of him, and walked forward with Gavin following him through the portal and back to his new life and his new home, at Wolf Coven House.

ABOUT THE AUTHOR

Having been a fan for years of the supernatural, paranormal, mythology and history, C.X. Cheng has always wanted to give his unique twist on what he liked. Originally planned as a screenplay for a web series to be produced with the help of friends, it soon dawned upon C.X. that his strength was not in scripts but in prose. The Wolf Coven Universe was born out of a love for the mysterious and the supernatural, but a viewpoint that focused more on character interactions. Taking a year to create the outline, then another year to write the novel, Blood Moon is the first of a planned series of Wolf Coven novels that will take you into the Wolf Coven Universe and the vast mythos that it contains.

About the Editor

Caroline Y.M. Ng's writing career started early when she began ghostwriting and editing her classmates' homework in French and English in high school in super natural Vancouver, Canada, the same city as Wolf Coven House. Her academic background in French linguistics and second-language teaching (French, English, and Mandarin), coupled with her MBA in international management, brought her to work in places such as China, Myanmar, and Hong Kong for over fifteen years. She also worked as an English editor at Time Life Asia and Oxford University Press, and later with VTech writing instructional manuals.

Decades of teaching French and English to senior secondary and university students in and out of institutional settings made Caroline acutely meticulous about grammar, spelling, and writing style.

Over the years, Caroline's editorial repertoire covers a wide spectrum including scientific research, Ph.D. theses, corporate documents and annual reports, text books, scripts for stage plays, covering various genres of subject areas.

carolineymng@gmail.com

<u>Cover designed by</u>

S. A. Hunt

http://www.Theusualmadman.net

And

http://www.Facebook.com/authorSamHunt

Please follow us on:

http://www.Twitter.com/WolfCovenBooks

and

http://www.Facebook.com/WolfCovenBookSeries

Made in the USA
Charleston, SC
25 October 2013